LINDA CHAIKIN
is an award-winning writer
of more than 18 books.
Thursday's Child is the fourth book in
the popular A Day to Remember
series. Linda and her husband, Steve,
make their home in California.

❧

PART ONE

London, England

1

Paulette marveled at how her life could have turned so quickly, so devastatingly. Within a three-month period she had met and married a man who had seemed everything she had ever wanted—tender, yet masculine; understanding, yet showing strong leadership; passionate, yet disciplined. Then, within a few weeks after becoming Mrs. Garret Brandt, she began fearing that she had married a sinister stranger. How could she have allowed herself to marry so swiftly, and to have made such a life-altering blunder? How she wished she had never found that matchbook.

Paulette picked up a framed photograph, recognizing the things that had first attracted her to Garret Brandt. Her husband had what she described as Teutonic appeal: hair the color of warm, harvest-ready wheat and gray-blue eyes that were clear and vitally alive. Garret also possessed the ability to make a woman feel that she was the most important person in his universe. She had first met him on a September afternoon in 1940 when joining her best friend Rhoda and her husband Fergus Nickerson at a mountain lodge near Neuchâtel, Switzerland. A fair-haired man with a rugged outdoor tan had entered wearing a mountain climbing habit. Paulette had noticed his strong, square jawline and the easy self-confidence he displayed, which harmonized with an appearance of superb physical fitness. It was no wonder she had mistaken him for an Olympic gold medal ski champion. Their eyes had met from across the room as though he were unaware of the small crowd, and her lonely heart had believed the moment a wonderful accident in time, a fairy-tale beginning undesigned by human hand.

For all the drama of the moment, she felt she had miserably blundered the opportunity to show herself a princess-in-waiting. He had walked to where she stood to introduce himself when she had spoken too quickly: "Congratulations on your medal."

He had looked at her with puzzlement in his eyes, and possibly a glint of amusement.

She had become even more encumbered by reverting to what she had read about him in the newspaper, that he was returning to Germany to offer his services to his "fatherland."

"You're a pilot in the Luftwaffe?"

She detected nothing in his glance now except caution.

"Are you expecting one?" he had asked.

She felt her cheeks grow warm as she realized how foolish she must sound. It only just then began to dawn on her that she had mistaken him for Hans Strasser, the skier. But by this time she was withdrawing into her shell and was afraid to say anything more for fear of adding to the ungraceful beginning.

Rhoda, who was standing just behind her, must have heard the bungled exchange, for she nearly choked on her hot cider. "Paulette darling, this is Garret Brandt. Garret, this is Paulette Harrington, my best friend and most astute feature writer for the news magazine *Horizon*."

Garret Brandt. Not Hans Strasser. Paulette wanted to sink into the floor.

Rhoda smiled at her. "Fergus met him in London last month. Garret's in England on business from New York. He's an American." Rhoda had lightly emphasized the word "American" so Paulette wouldn't miss it.

"Oh," Paulette had said in a small, tight voice.

He looked at her, measuringly, and something must have convinced him that her questions were innocently posed, because the tension she sensed in him melted away.

"I admit this *is* a plausible spot for the Luftwaffe to drop a few paratroopers to spy out the countryside." He nodded, almost idly, toward the window that directly faced the mountains covered with fir trees. "But it's not likely at present. You see, since the French government has capitulated to the Third Reich the front door has been opened, so there's no need for spying through a back window."

"Yes, I see...I'm so sorry. I'm afraid I mistakenly took you for the Olympic skier from Bavaria."

"So I gathered. Hans Strasser, isn't it?"

"Yes. The newspaper said he was returning to Germany to become a member of Goering's air force."

There came an infinitesimal pause. "Yes, he's making an unfortunate mistake."

"I'm sorry about *my* mistake. It's quite embarrassing really—"

"Don't apologize, Miss Harrington." Garret smiled unexpectedly, and a romantic spark reignited a flame in her heart.

"Perhaps you weren't all that wrong in your judgment. I do speak German," he said with a smile in his voice. "I hope that doesn't make me look like the enemy?"

She laughed. "No, of course not."

"Do you understand any German?"

She sensed his watchfulness, but was unable to judge his motive.

"Not very well. Enough to make a wild guess at what's being said if—"

"If?"

"If words are spoken slowly in a conversation. Very slowly."

He accepted a glass of something cool from a waiter's tray and looked at her questioningly. She shook her head no.

"I have cousins somewhere in Germany, but I've lost track of them," he said. "I'm not one to keep in touch. It's one of my weaknesses."

She was surprised that he had any.

"Relatives living in Berlin aren't a commodity one eagerly announces to Britishers on holiday," he concluded.

Rhoda, who had left a few moments earlier to find her husband, was now leading him across the lodge toward Paulette and Garret.

Paulette had grown up with Rhoda after Rhoda's maiden aunt, Opal Harrington, had adopted Paulette from an orphanage after the Great War. Naturally the two of them, with just a few years difference in their ages, were as close as sisters. Paulette was pleased that Rhoda's marriage to Fergus had brought her so much satisfaction. The Nickersons made a perfect couple. While Rhoda could lay no particular claim to beauty with auburn hair that was stubbornly unruly above a freckled face with amber eyes, she possessed remarkably good humor in the most difficult of outdoor circumstances, which in Fergus' line of work as a devoted archaeologist—always in dusty, hot locations—proved very uplifting. Rhoda and Fergus had been married for two years and she was impatiently hoping to start a family. "If I keep waiting, hoping for some tranquil spot in the countryside of England, we shall never have a baby," she had told Paulette. "Fergus' work usually brings us to exotic places with natives running about with spears and feathers. So I'll just need to risk having children in another culture." This time, however, civilization actually beckoned. "What better place to live than the cradle of democracy, Greece?" Rhoda had sighed in ecstasy. "Of course the position isn't Fergus' yet. We're praying about it every night. Imagine, working with a scholar like Dr. Bristow."

Fergus, on the other hand, was a tall, lanky American with reddish hair, Scotch-blue eyes, and a bold nose. Paulette had been with Rhoda when she'd met him on his summer walking tour through England four years earlier. She had even assisted in the blossoming of their romance.

Fergus grinned as he came up, extending his hand. "Hullo there, Garret, what are you doing up here? I didn't know you also enjoyed mountain climbing. Thought you were on your way back to New York by now."

"There's been a delay." Garret asked Fergus if he had received a response yet to his letter of inquiry to the renowned Dr. Bristow about joining his research team in Athens.

"We're expecting an answer anytime. That is, if the blasted Nazis don't ruin our travel plans. It's getting pretty risky, voyaging the Atlantic."

Garret looked thoughtful for a moment. Then he explained that, as his travels were quite frequent, he knew of civilian pilots from America who were making money with their skills in avoiding German and Italian aircraft. "We'll see if we can arrange something when the letter comes from Bristow."

"If it comes," Fergus lamented.

"Darling, it will come. It must," Rhoda encouraged.

Paulette suddenly remembered something and turned with a smile. "How beastly of me to forget. Uncle Gilly sent that letter of recommendation to Dr. Bristow over a month ago. I'm sure it will help your chances of hearing from him."

"Ah! We're forever in your debt," Fergus said happily, and Rhoda grinned her confidence and looked up at him. "See, darling? What did I tell you? I knew we could depend on Paulette."

"How did you manage?" Fergus asked her. "I couldn't get near him. I thought he was some old hermit guarding his gold mine with a shotgun when I entered the yard."

"It wasn't easy," Paulette said with a laugh. "It helps being a niece, and even with that I've only been invited to his estate a few times in my entire life, as Rhoda can tell you."

"Don't be too hard on Gilly Simington," Rhoda told Fergus. "You did break through his security system. And trampled his Michaelmas daisies."

Fergus winced. "Who could forget? I climbed over his wall beside the gate," he admitted wryly. "It was a mistake. That was his flower plot."

"You're just lucky he doesn't have dogs," Rhoda cautioned.

Paulette smiled until she glanced at Garret Brandt and noticed a look of masked indifference, and was sure it wasn't genuine. Just why she would think this, she couldn't explain even to herself. His eyes met hers and, as she caught the flicker, she guessed she must have shown what she was thinking, for he asked: "Gilbert Simington, the collector?"

"You've heard of him?" she asked with a hint of surprise.

"I've heard of his collection. Very masterful, I understand."

"Uncle Gilly hasn't opened his collection for public viewing in several years, but yes, you're right," she said proudly. "It's fabulous."

Again, that very attractive smile. "So I've heard. Word gets around to those profoundly interested in Egyptology."

"I can see why it would." Did this mean Mr. Brandt was one of them?

"His collection of Egyptian artifacts is very large, I understand," he went on. "Accumulated through the years he lived in Cairo."

"Yes. He's retired now, though. You might think that gives him time to permit showings, but he rarely opens the display to the public."

"He lives in England?"

"Yes, just outside London. Uncle Gilly is, well, rather odd at times," she apologized. "You see, he was badly injured in the last war and has turned into somewhat of a recluse."

"Oh? I'm disappointed. I work for Kimball, Baylor, and Lammiter, international dealers in museum pieces, Egyptian and otherwise. I understand his collection is tremendous. I'd enjoy meeting him. Since I've recently moved to London, maybe that isn't out of the question."

There was a moment of awkward silence, but it did not appear to trouble Mr. Brandt. Finally, Rhoda spoke up. "That shouldn't be too difficult, should it, Paulette? Maybe you could arrange it?"

As Paulette watched him, she could almost believe that he had expected and counted on Rhoda's response. Rhoda was the type who couldn't resist coming to someone's aid. Then, had he already known she was Gilbert Simington's niece when he entered the lodge? That thought disappointed. The dramatic moment earlier, when their eyes met, had it not been an out-of-the-ordinary emotion for him as well? She had thought so. She had even *felt* it. Now she wondered if perhaps what he had wanted all along was merely her influence for arranging to see her uncle's collection. It was depressing and troubling that he could have such a strong effect upon her feelings after having just met him—a sure sign that she must be prudent.

Annoyed with herself and determined he had already fooled her as much as she was going to allow, she said rather coolly: "I'm sorry, but my uncle isn't easily swayed, Mr. Brandt, not even by me."

"I quite understand," he said soberly, but his rather amused gaze said that he had guessed why she refused to involve herself. "Perhaps another time."

"Perhaps," she said simply.

Fergus and Rhoda had noticed friends in the hiking club enter the lodge and went to speak with them. Paulette also wished to get away, but Garret seemed to be in no hurry.

"Do you have other relatives living in Egypt?"

"No. My parents died at sea during the last war, so I was never able to ask them about family."

His eyes showed sympathy, and she found herself enjoying the strength he offered. His questions continued so casually that she hardly noticed she was giving away her biography.

"I believe Rhoda once mentioned that you were raised by your aunt, Opal Harrington," he said. "Is she related to Mr. Simington? I notice their last names aren't the same."

"No relation at all. Opal wasn't a blood aunt. She was related to Rhoda, actually. Opal worked in the orphanage after the war and she arranged with the authorities to take me home. Until her death I considered her and Rhoda my closest relatives."

"Yes, of course you would. And you grew up with Rhoda."

"Mostly. We went to school together, even college. She's like a sister."

"When will you be returning to London?" he asked.

She delayed, wondering how much more she cared to reveal about herself. "Tomorrow."

"What a coincidence. So am I."

She was now leery of coincidences. He stood, and watched her as if he knew.

"Perhaps you'll permit me to call on you some evening. I'm a stranger in London."

"I'm quite busy at *Horizon*, Mr. Brandt."

"Garret. May I call you Paulette?"

When she made no response he smiled at her reticence. "I hope we'll meet again in London."

≈≈≈

Returning to London, though Paulette almost hoped she wouldn't see him again, she found she couldn't dismiss him from her mind. The fact was, he did call. He located her number at *Horizon* and invited her to dinner and the theater, and when she politely put him off, he obliged by accepting the rebuff, only to call again, and again. Flowers arrived at her desk with a note apologizing for anything he might have done to offend her, and perhaps she would explain what it was. That left her almost obligated to respond. He certainly knew how to keep the door open and showed no offense over her haughtiness. She began to feel ashamed. After all, she could have been wrong about him wishing only to reach her uncle through her. She mentioned her concern to Rhoda.

"I hardly think he could have known who you were. He didn't learn it from me, but I'll ask Fergus."

Rhoda called her at the flat that evening. "Fergus says he was totally surprised when he saw Garret at the lodge. He doesn't recall ever discussing you with him. Look, Paulette, never mind all that. I've wonderful news!"

Paulette smiled to herself. "You're going to Athens to join Dr. Bristow's team?"

"Yes! Isn't it exciting? We received the letter of notification this morning. Fergus is elated. And we have you to thank as well. Your uncle's endorsement helped to convince Dr. Bristow to take a chance on Fergus."

"When are you leaving?"

"In just a few days. We have all the papers we need to enter Greece. Come over for dinner after work tomorrow and help us celebrate."

Paulette was pleased about their opportunity for archaeology, but she was also a little depressed. She would miss Rhoda terribly. She and Fergus were now the only family she had. Uncle Gilly, who was more of a stranger than an uncle, didn't count. She actually knew her landlord, Mr. Hoadley, better than she did the mysterious Gilbert Simington of Cairo.

After work the next evening, Paulette walked to Rhoda's. She looked up at the blue shutters on the top floor of the apartment building in downtown London, not more than two blocks from her own tiny flat in another brownstone building, and entered Rhoda's doorway. Her finger pushed the button beside the little white card that read "Nickerson."

Paulette, determined to hide her feelings of emotional loss, was wearing a smile when Fergus opened the door— except that it wasn't Fergus—it was Garret Brandt.

2

"Oh!" Paulette said. "I didn't expect—" she stopped. Had Rhoda arranged this?

But if she were surprised, so was he. She saw the faint flicker of masculine victory in his gray-blue eyes turning to one of surprise as his glance swept over her. It suddenly dawned on her why. She was still wearing her tortoiseshell eyeglasses, a rather drab brown business suit under her dark raincoat, and flat-heeled oxfords for walking. There was nothing out of the ordinary in her wearing an efficient suit to work, especially when she had expected rain and knew she'd be walking home. Perhaps it was her overall demeanor of efficiency that made the encounter all wrong. He had expected the girl at the lodge: pretty, demure, and maybe just a bit too naive? Her present fashion dictated a no-nonsense businesswoman. And when looking back through brown-rimmed glasses with a level gaze, she had been told she was deadly challenging. Compared with the frilly, feminine clothes that Rhoda always wore, her suit undoubtedly looked dull.

Paulette touched the thick hair smoothed back into a chignon at the back of her neck. She often wore it this way as she walked the eight blocks to and from *Horizon* each day. The wind tended to play havoc with the new hairstyle of long, loose waves behind the ears and down the back. She had seen her reflection too many times in the store windows not to know that she had shocked Garret Brandt with an impression of a brisk professional.

Paulette was as embarrassed as he now appeared, and equally amused. *Well, well. Perhaps now I won't need to expect any more phone calls from the clever Garret Brandt. He might even find a sudden excuse to leave the party!* She ought to be pleased by how well this encounter was turning out. It served him right. If all he had been looking for was an introduction to Gilbert Simington and a pretty face and figure to go with it, he had gotten his just dessert.

But she found she really wasn't all that pleased after all.

"Hello," he said, and stepped back, allowing her to enter the cluttered living room piled with half-packed boxes, books, and stacks of research papers that would soon be on their way to Athens. Garret closed the door. There followed a moment of penetrating silence. She turned to look at him, and he was leaning there, hand on the doorknob, a thoughtful smile in his eyes. Paulette removed her glasses. *Well?* she appeared to challenge. *Are you disappointed?*

He smiled, as if he knew what she was thinking and held her gaze, a challenge of his own in that steady look. *You're trying to put me off*, it seemed to say, *and it won't work.*

Her cheeks colored and she looked about the room quickly to gather her composure. "Where are our missing host and hostess?" she asked nonchalantly.

"Rhoda's in the kitchen making sandwiches, and she asked me to get the door." He, too, glanced about the small living room. "Maybe they asked us over to help them pack."

His light amused remark broke the tension and she laughed. "That would be just like Rhoda. But I don't think Fergus would trust me handling his archaeological books and papers."

"Let's hope the plane can get off the runway," he said, sizing up the crates.

She smiled. At the lodge Garret had mentioned helping them get safely to Athens. She gave him a side glance, wondering how he could arrange it.

"Fergus is somewhere around. I was a little early, I'm afraid," he said. "That's what happens when you're a stranger in this part of the world. I was too anxious to get out of my lonely hotel room."

Was he telling the truth, or was he trying to convince her of his guilelessness? She could hardly conceive of this handsome, capable man being lonely in London or anywhere else. He offered the impression of being very self-sufficient.

"How do you like living in London, Mr. Brandt?"

"I was thinking I needed a companion to show me around the city, the historical places, you know," he said with a glimmer in his eyes. "Naturally, just anyone wouldn't do. I'm pretty particular about history. I like accuracy and detail. So my companion would need to be of the intelligent sort."

She avoided his eyes. "I'm sure any of the tourist businesses would be delighted to arrange for such a guide."

"I wasn't thinking of hiring a tour guide. No, what I need is a no-nonsense person who could help me avoid tourist traps."

"Are you easily trapped?"

"I've a soft heart for such things. I always end up paying too much for postcards and souvenirs. What do you think, Miss Harrington? What are my chances of finding such a jewel?"

"Rather difficult." She tried not to smile. She didn't think getting around London was all that new to him, not if he had traveled as he claimed.

He smiled. "Your honesty is disappointing, but I appreciate that quality in a woman. A man soon gets bored with fluttering lashes."

"I don't know of any woman who actually flutters her lashes, Mr. Brandt, but I accept your compliment at face value."

"Good. Because you are a rare breath of fresh air, Miss Harrington, and I'd hate you to think I was being anything less than completely truthful with you."

Paulette smiled. "Now why would I ever think otherwise?"

He let her comment slip by. "I'm sure I'll find exactly what I'm looking for. Patience has its rewards, as they say."

She glanced at him and caught an unexpected smile. He had been looking her over again, including the flat walking shoes she wore. He must think she knew her way around London like a whiz. He'd be surprised if he knew how easily she could get lost in the city in which she'd grown up.

"Speaking of finding one's way around," she said, "if I recall, you suggested helping Fergus and Rhoda with safe passage to Greece." She hadn't meant to sound worried, but tension tightened her voice. "Is it really possible?"

She marveled at the quick change in his personality. He was suddenly the perceptive, vigorous stranger. "There's always risk," he said, turning pensive. "Especially around the Gibraltar straits. Both Italian and German air forces are active in the area." His eyes reflected sympathy. "I hope I haven't upset you."

"No—I'm aware of our uncertain times."

"Yes, danger is part of it, I'm afraid, and it is likely to get a whole lot worse before it's over. But why did you ask? Were you thinking of going with them to Athens?"

She looked at him, curiously wondering what caused him to think she might. "Well, I do intend to visit Athens one day. I would like to write a feature article on Dr. Bristow and his work, but I've no immediate plans. My present work keeps me here in London."

"Bristow is an interesting man. You'd enjoy him, I think."

Evidently she'd convinced him of her serious and studious nature. She covered her smile. If he knew just how silly and immature she could be sometimes when she and Rhoda got together for an evening, he would raise his brows.

"What made you think I was planning on going to Athens with the Nickersons?"

"It was something Rhoda said about you and *Horizon* winning an award for coverage of international affairs. She said you were mulling over the idea of doing a feature on the politics surrounding the king of Greece."

She smiled, the mention of *Horizon* bringing her to life. "The award was given over a year ago, and wasn't mine, I'm sorry to admit. But it did go to a very good friend who was working at *Horizon* at the time."

"Quinn O'Brien?"

"You know him?" she asked, surprised.

"I've heard about him."

"Again, from Rhoda?"

He smiled. "She brags on your talents. A true friend. Not a spark of jealousy."

He sounded casual enough. What did he know about her past relationship with Quinn?

"*London Times*, right?" he said. "O'Brien has a reputation for being relentless when it comes to getting to the bones of the story. Why did he leave *Horizon*?"

She paused, uncertain whether to say anything about the trouble between Mort Collier, who ran the magazine, and Quinn. "Quinn told everyone the opportunities were better for travel, for writing the kinds of news stories he believed were keenly important for the times."

"He didn't have that luxury at *Horizon*?"

She fiddled with her eyeglasses, twirling them in hand. "Well, he did, but *Horizon* is a monthly magazine. It's true we go in depth on certain subjects—like Nazi Germany—but we can't be on top of hourly events the way a daily can."

"Maybe it's just as well you're not going to Athens now. Tensions are running high over there. There's no love for Germany, but the Communists are a strong and vocal group that have penetrated the regular army under General Papagos."

"You appear to know a great deal about Greece."

"I was there recently to see Dr. Bristow. He arranged a meeting with a collector from Corinth willing to sell a classical bronze Venus."

She changed the subject. "And so you're able to assist Fergus and Rhoda's travel plans?"

"A flight from Crete into the Peloponnese looks possible," he said. "Then from Sparta it's possible to reach Corinth over land."

"Arranged by your American friends, the pilots?" she inquired, interested in how Garret knew them.

"The 'Lucky Seven' they call themselves." He smiled. "They've formed a private organization of high-risk flyers with the approval of President Roosevelt."

"Very brave and praiseworthy of them. Are you one of them, by any chance?"

"I'm strictly a dealer in antiquities."

"I see." But she wondered.

Rhoda appeared from the kitchen, smiling, wearing a neat little white apron tied about her waist. As Paulette had expected, she wore a pretty gray organdy dress gathered at the waistline and cinched with a neat black patent leather belt.

"Hi, Paulette. Give me a hand with the sandwiches will you?" She called toward the bedroom: "Fergus? You haven't fallen asleep, have you, dear?" and she winked in Paulette and Garret's direction.

Fergus appeared at the bedroom doorway carrying the telephone as far as the cord would allow. He was just saying goodbye to someone on the other end, and hung up. "That was Larry. He and Peggy can't make it tonight. Bobby's got colic. So Peggy's upset and wanting to call her mother to come over."

"Oh, poor baby, and Peggy, too. She's worried to death over that child. Bobby's sick so much of the time. Well, then, I won't need to send out for more ice."

Fergus was smiling and holding a hand out to Garret. "How's it going in London, Brandt? Hello, Paulette. Enjoy your jaunt over from *Horizon*?"

"I won't enjoy the walk home. It looks like a downpour."

Rhoda said, "Paulette, take this, will you?" as she handed her the ice bucket. "Set it on the buffet table. Oh— look at the time. The others will be here soon." She hurried back to the kitchen.

Paulette arranged the bucket of ice on the long cherry wood table by the window overlooking the street. The traffic was buzzing by and pedestrians crossed to and fro on their way home from work. Men carried newspapers, some pausing to glance at the headlines. Women carried bags of groceries, their anxious thoughts on the dinner that awaited fixing. Paulette was thinking how much would soon be changing, and yet how much would never change. Men would always be glancing at the evening headlines, and women would always be concerned with the need to feed their husbands and children. *And what of me?* she wondered unemotionally. *What will I be doing five years from now? Ten? Even twenty?*

She heard Fergus and Garret discussing the plane flight to Athens. "Wednesday will do us fine," Fergus was saying.

Paulette went into the kitchenette, and Rhoda cast her a smile. "I should have had all this done this morning, but you know how things go. Then Fergus' brother telephoned from Los Angeles to see if we'd received news yet about getting the post with Dr. Bristow. When I told him we just heard the good news yesterday, he must have talked for ten minutes hoping Fergus would get home. Carl's in for a beastly telephone bill." She handed Paulette an apron, glancing at her brown suit. "I should have warned you Garret was here."

"That might have been nice. If you weren't married and madly in love with Fergus, I'd think you wanted me to look like a dowager."

Rhoda laughed as Paulette made a face at her pretty dress. "I didn't know Garret was coming tonight, honestly," she said when Paulette gave her a doubtful glance. "Here, you slice the cheese. I'll mash the sardines."

"Are you going to add a good dash of lemon?" Paulette asked, eying the sardines with less than excitement.

Rhoda picked up a bright waxy lemon to assuage her fears, then handed her the buttered crackers. Paulette began slicing the cheese. "You didn't know he was coming?" Paulette asked in a low voice.

"Garret Brandt?"

"Mr. Dreamboat himself."

"You think he's good looking?"

Paulette stopped slicing cheese and looked at her. Rhoda smiled and began chopping eggs. "Yes, you're right. Anyway, I didn't plan this as some cozy foursome, if that's what you're thinking." She glanced over her shoulder at the kitchen swing door, keeping her voice low. "I hope you're not upset."

"You told me at the lodge he's a friend of Fergus'. I've no right to be bothered about your guests. Actually, he's a little more congenial than I first imagined." She thought of the new blue silky dress she had bought at Rainier's department store last Saturday. It would have been perfect for tonight.

"That makes me feel better." Rhoda shot her a worried glance. "Fergus ran into him when leaving the university today," she went on, as though needing to explain. "Garret was coming by anyway to discuss the flight into Athens. Fergus says it would have been rude not to ask him to stay. He's been a tremendous help to us." She picked up the salt shaker, then frowned. "Did I already add salt?"

Paulette laughed at her fluster. "To sardines?"

"Oh. I was thinking of the deviled eggs."

"You needn't keep apologizing about Garret being here." Paulette arranged the cheese cubes and slices on the platter beside the black and green pimento-stuffed olives. "Maybe I got the wrong impression at the lodge." She frowned, then took off several pieces of cheese, adding sprigs of parsley for a final touch. She began spreading the egg mixture on the bread slices while Rhoda mashed the sardines to spread on water crackers.

"You mean about his interest in your uncle?" Rhoda looked at her.

"He hasn't mentioned Uncle Gilly. He *has* called several times to ask me to dinner."

Rhoda stopped. "You lucky thing. And you mean to say you didn't accept?"

Paulette made no reply and Rhoda shrugged. "It doesn't sound as if his only interest was in using you to meet your uncle."

"Unless he's playing it coy."

"You're too suspicious. It's perfectly reasonable he would be interested in your uncle. The Egyptian collection is fabulous, and Garret buys antiquities for Kimball, Baylor, and someone-or-other."

"Kimball, Baylor, and Lammiter. Yes, he told me. He's also been in Greece recently. He seems to know Dr. Bristow rather well."

"You see? There was nothing to it after all. Why not relax, darling, and enjoy the evening. There's even one of your dresses in my closet," she said as she paused to smile into Paulette's rather flushed face. "The one I borrowed for the dinner at the college and haven't returned."

"If I rush to change now it will look too obvious, as though I'm trying to please him after all. I'll suffer through, but I will redo my hair, if you don't mind."

"Do. And those shoes—"

"No." And she grinned at Rhoda. "He tried to convince me he's looking for a companion to walk him around historical places in town. A woman with stuffy, businesslike manners—who feels comfortable wearing oxfords." *I may just take him up on that offer if he asks again.*

"Did he really? How sweet of him. He's trying so hard to win you over."

Paulette wasn't at all convinced that Garret Brandt was as nice and cooperative as Rhoda seemed to think. She had gotten the feeling he found her stuffy behavior amusing and wanted to see if he could break down her resistance. And once Rhoda and Fergus went away, Paulette's lonely mood might respond to his phone calls. That is, if he did telephone after tonight. Realizing she would be disappointed if he did not was depressing, because it showed that he was already successfully wearing her down.

A few minutes later, with the sandwiches all done, Rhoda turned to her with unexpected shining eyes and a touch of bright pink to her own cheeks. "I've some other news. I've saved it. I haven't told Fergus yet, either."

Paulette noted the excitement and at first thought it had to do with Fergus getting the job on Dr. Bristow's team. But because she already knew about it, she could see there was something else bringing joy and excitement to Rhoda's life. Paulette drew in a quick breath as she guessed. "Don't tell me—" she said as she was untying her apron.

"Yes. I'm definitely expecting. The baby will be born in Athens."

"Oh, Rhoda! That's wonderful news." She hugged her. Rhoda had been hoping to have a baby for more than a year. Paulette drew away with sudden concern. "You'll be safe and healthy in Athens?"

Rhoda laughed. "There you go, just like Fergus. You'll both worry your heads off. I'll be fine. Athens, my dear girl, is quite civilized, remember? It's the birthplace of Western democracy. My doctor already knows someone there to take over my case, a Dr. Kozani. They went to medical school together in America. So, no need to worry." She picked up one of the platters and started toward the door. "I'm waiting until everyone leaves tonight to tell Fergus."

Paulette followed with the other large platter. "He'll wonder why you didn't tell him sooner, won't he?"

"Well I couldn't. When I got home this afternoon he and Garret were already in the living room discussing politics."

"Fergus will be pleasantly shocked. He'll have a hard time getting to sleep tonight."

"What will really shock him will be all the baby things I'll need to buy once we're in Greece. My word! I'd better save my shillings. I hope we can find housing close to Dr. Bristow's camp." As if on second thought, she stopped before going through the swinging door.

"You'll come to Athens, won't you, Paulette? Perhaps on assignment for *Horizon*?"

"I wouldn't miss it. I'm planning on next summer if I can save enough money." Her smile faded. "That is, if Hitler hasn't decided to interrupt everyone's life by then."

Rhoda stood without moving. "Yes, that's what I meant."

Paulette, seeing the sudden seriousness in Rhoda's eyes, waited. "Is there something else bothering you?"

Rhoda explained: "I told you how Fergus and Garret were already talking when I returned from my doctor's appointment. They didn't hear me come through the front door. They were here in the kitchen, having coffee. I overheard a few things they wouldn't likely have said in front of me."

Paulette looked at her. She was still uneasy about Garret Brandt, though she couldn't say just why. Except for her persistent suspicion that he'd sought her out at the lodge with ulterior motives in mind, there really wasn't anything, and that suspicion was fast fading.

"What kinds of things?" Paulette asked uneasily.

"Oh, you know. The kind of talk Londoners are good at in private."

Paulette knew very well. The bombing of England. The ordeal had first begun last summer after France had surrendered. It had become second nature to drop what she was doing and take cover when she heard the air raid sirens and the subsequent scream of bombs. There was also talk of a massive invasion of paratroopers landing like locusts intent on covering the land. German soldiers breaking into houses. Rape, pillage, murder, concentration camps. Paulette's appetite died.

"When men like Fergus and Garrett say the same things, it takes on a darker tone. We're so accustomed to attributing these things to the hysterical thinking of the typical bridge club dowagers passing smelling salts around the table."

Paulette stood there trying to think of something encouraging to say to her until she realized that Rhoda wasn't worried about herself, but her friend, alone in London. Alone, without family, living in a two-room flat by herself. A stark, haunting sensation of desolation swept over Paulette's heart like a passing cloud.

"I wish you were coming with us," Rhoda said suddenly.

Paulette resisted the need to cling to her friends. She had always been alone since her parents drowned at sea. Alone at the orphanage until Aunt Opal took her. Alone after Quinn left *Horizon* and traveled with the wind. Alone, now that Rhoda was leaving London. Alone, but not without God watching over her.

"Look," she said firmly, "if things get as bad as they say, even Greece won't escape for long. There's nothing any of us can do except what we must. Endure and pray and hope for the best."

"Yes, Garret said as much." Rhoda was frowning down at her platter of crackers and sardines. "He spoke of Communists in Greece who were just as violent and murderous as Nazis."

Paulette tried to divert her. "Let's not ruin tonight by worrying. Let's say goodbye with a smile, as though it's only for a little while. And indeed it is, because I will come, somehow."

"Yes, let's. You mentioned redoing your hair. I'll bring these in, you go ahead."

Paulette escaped thankfully in the direction of Rhoda's little bedroom, but the challenge to smile showed on her reflection in the mirror above the vanity table. She located the hairbrush in her handbag and arranged her hair, using a pair of Rhoda's side combs to hold the thick golden-brown waves behind her ears. She was going to miss Fergus and Rhoda. Miss them badly. She added lipstick, and on second thought removed her suit jacket. The white blouse didn't look bad with the plain brown skirt. She looked at her shoes. She went slowly to Rhoda's closet and found a pair of heeled sandals that fit well enough. On the way out she glanced at her image in the mirror and made a face at herself. *You're all talk, Paulette. This mysterious man has already won. And once you go out with your hair down and heels on, he'll know it, too. You're asking for trouble and you'll probably find it.*

3

Other guests were arriving. Paulette heard the introductions, the light remarks, the laughter. She left Rhoda's bedroom and entered the small living room, still cluttered with things to be packed, given away, or trashed. *There's one benefit to moving,* she thought. *It forces you to get rid of clutter. I keep so many mementos, perhaps I'm too sentimental.*

It seemed as though there was now a crowd in the Nickersons' living room, though it had gained only two other couples, both from the college where Fergus had been substitute teaching for the past school year. There was an older history professor and another younger man from the English department. Their wives had brought bon voyage presents for Rhoda, who was having the time of her life laughing over the "gifts": airsick pills and a toy shovel—"so you can help Fergus at the digs. It may provide your only chance to see him."

Garret was discussing a business trip to Greece regarding classical pottery with the history professor when another lone guest arrived. Since Rhoda was making over her airsick pills, Paulette motioned to Fergus that she would answer the door. She opened it to a tall, dark-haired, dark-eyed man with strong shoulders and a ready grin. He held his beat-up hat in one hand and a bouquet of spring flowers in the other. His overcoat was damp with a sprinkling of rain.

"Quinn!" Paulette said warmly, welcoming him into the flat and closing the door. The others turned to see who had arrived when they heard the enthusiasm in her voice.

"Of all the surprises," she was saying, taking his arm. "When did you arrive in London?"

"Hello, beautiful. Two days ago. I've been reporting to Osgood," he said of his boss at the *Times*, "otherwise I'd have called you at *Horizon*. Here, these are for you." He handed her the flowers.

She laughed. "They are not."

"They are now," he whispered close to her ear, and made use of his opportunity to land a brief kiss on her cheek.

"Same old Quinn," she said, but there was laughter in her eyes. "I'll put these in water so we can all enjoy them."

Rhoda came to welcome him and take his hat and coat. "I'm glad you could drop by, Quinn. Welcome home to merry old England."

"Not so merry, it seems. Just got word of a closed-door meeting between Churchill and members of Parliament. Some hot controversy over a peace overture to Adolf. Churchill won't hear of it."

"I should hope not," Rhoda said indignantly, going to the bedroom door to place Quinn's hat and coat on a chair.

Fergus put out his hand. "Come in, old fellow. You know my colleagues, don't you? And this is Garret Brandt from Philadelphia. He's helping arrange our flight to Athens. We don't know what we'd do without him."

Quinn walked up boldly. They were nearly the same height, and though Quinn was quite slim, he was known to be able to handle himself in most situations. They stood there, dark and light, and Paulette imagined that Quinn forced direct eye contact to see Garret's response. Quinn smiled and shoved out his hand.

"Hello there, Brandt, didn't expect to see you in London. What brings you here from Egypt? More meetings with Ambassador Hastings?"

A pause of expectant silence held the room.

Garret smiled. "Wrong man, Quinn. Never met Ambassador Hastings."

"Is that right?" Quinn reached in his pocket for a cigarette. "I was so sure. Alexandria, wasn't it? A couple of weeks ago. At Ambassador Hasting's place. I was there covering the Italian invasion for the *Times*."

A couple of weeks ago I was mountain climbing in Switzerland.

Fergus tossed Quinn a book of matches. "Here you go, O'Brien."

Garret intercepted them in midair and handed them to Quinn. He took a long time lighting his cigarette.

"My mistake then. Sorry. An Egyptologist, aren't you?"

"You could say that."

"Have you met Paulette's uncle, Gilbert Simington? He has an amazing collection of artifacts."

Garret looked at her, and she saw a shade of amusement in his eyes. "No," he said, "I've not yet had the opportunity." He turned back to Quinn. "Did you just return from Egypt?"

"Yeah. Covering General Wavell's bungle with the Italians." He shook his head sadly. "The guy has cold feet. He had opportunity to do Mussolini some real damage but pulled his tanks back. Looks like the Italians will soon occupy the Suez."

Garret raised his glass, making no comment. Quinn, lacking a response, turned toward Fergus. "What's this about you and Rhoda going to Athens? Doc Bristow must have finally realized he needed you on his team."

"Isn't it grand?" Rhoda called, entering the room with a big bowl of nuts. "We leave on Wednesday. Fergus will be charting some of the ancient history on first century Corinth."

"Apostolic times," Fergus explained.

"Bristow was working at Delphi, wasn't he?"

"He still is. I could end up there as well. We won't know exactly until I meet with Dr. Bristow in Athens and he explains what stage the team is at in their findings."

"Is the American School involved in Corinth?" Quinn asked of the archaeology school in Athens.

"Yes, and others."

"The German School was there and did most of the work until 1938," Garret said. "That's when Bristow arrived, wasn't it, Fergus? I thought he worked for a time with the Berlin group."

"He did," Fergus agreed. "Most of the members of the school went home when Hitler invaded Poland, but there are some Germans still working there."

"Probably agents," Quinn said with distaste, crushing out his cigarette and loading up his plate with several egg sandwiches.

Paulette placed the vase of flowers on the telephone table, watching Quinn.

"I try to keep up with your articles in the *Times*," Fergus was saying to Quinn. "Is Wavell really so bad off that there's a chance we'll be driven out of Cairo?"

"If he can't hold Tobruk, it's straight desert all the way to the Suez. The Brits would likely hold them off for a time, but if Rommel arrives from Libya, it's all over. They'll be raising the swastika over King Farouk's palace by the end of the year."

"Farouk's loyalties are so misplaced he would likely celebrate," Professor Wainwright remarked acidly.

Paulette remembered that King Farouk, the "boy king" as he was sometimes called, favored Italy, and some said Germany, although he did not openly admit it. Though he wanted independence from England, he didn't have the military might to oust British rule, and out of necessity often complied with their demands. Some insisted Farouk wouldn't be sorry at all to welcome either Field Marshal Graziani or Rommel to Cairo in place of British General Wavell.

Fergus was scowling into his cup. "So you think it's that bad for the desert army, Quinn?"

"Getting tougher by the day," Quinn acknowledged. "I've interviewed officers close to Wavell and some soldiers in the desert. I can tell you their fighting spirit is getting pretty low."

Garret looked over at him. For a mere second Paulette thought she saw a flicker of amusement in his eyes. The instant passed so rapidly that she couldn't be certain, but it startled her. It was almost as if he were *glad!* She must have imagined that momentary response—

The others began to dispute Quinn's conclusions. Paulette expected Garret would make some remark. He was standing by the telephone table listening, but offered no opinion. He glanced at the flowers, then at her. She looked away.

It was raining heavier since Quinn had arrived, and the wind ruffled the flimsy white curtain through the partially opened window. Paulette felt cold and walked over to close it. Garret came up and closed the window for her. For a moment they stood beside each other, but too aware of him, she walked away and sat down on the edge of the sofa, reaching for her teacup.

"I hope you're not going to write these things in your next article, Quinn," Rhoda was saying. "It breeds low morale here at home."

"Come on, Rhoda, you're too smart to fall for that old line from the government. It's just a way to squelch criticism. But criticism strengthens, unless the rotting process has already begun. Then it won't matter anyway."

"I'm not so sure of that," Fergus said slowly, thoughtfully. They all looked at him. "The morale of the people must be kept high if we expect them to endure suffering. Remember, we've taking a pounding from the Luftwaffe. The men and women who read your words have their sons in the Egyptian desert. And if Hitler's threat is genuine, we may undergo an invasion."

Paulette set her cup down. "He's right, Quinn. The desert soldiers are mostly our colonials, aren't they? Australians?"

Garret glanced at her with approval. "You're quite right, Miss Harrington. Add to the Aussies the New Zealanders and South Africans, and you practically have the entire desert army. They're great fighting men. But they will need tanks that will take on Rommel's Panzer division if they're to win in the future."

Quinn's gaze sharpened at the mention of tanks. "Is that your take on it, Brandt? More tanks for Wavell?"

Garret was inscrutable as he looked across the little room at him.

"What's wrong with British tanks? Don't think they can beat back the Italians?" Quinn persisted.

Garret hadn't left the window. He smiled. "I'm an American. We're not at war with Germany or Italy. And it's hardly fitting for a guest in your country to criticize the British war effort. Or their tanks. After all, it was the British who first developed the idea of the tank."

"I haven't met an American yet who didn't have an opinion on the subject," Quinn scoffed with a grin. "There's a lot of talk about whether we'll get American tanks. It could make a big difference in the desert."

"You won't hear the British generals concluding that," Garret suggested.

"No, but the ordinary Brit does. I've talked to them over there. What's your take on whether Roosevelt will sell the newest American tanks to Churchill?"

"He'll need to get around stiff opposition in Congress. That won't be easy to pull off, even for Roosevelt. Not with an election year coming up. Polls show the Americans don't want to get involved in another European war."

Quinn considered, looking vigilant. "That would benefit the Germans, wouldn't it," he commented. Silence went around the room. Then Garret said: "Roosevelt has his hands tied. Blame it on the pacifist club."

"What club is that?" Professor Wainwright asked.

Garret smiled wryly. "Hollywood, sir. It's full of left-wingers. They use stardom to give them a hearing with their adoring fans. And like sheep, the fans follow. All it takes is a movie star or singer to endorse or oppose something. In this case most of them oppose war. They're holding rallies, telling everyone that Hitler really wants to get along with everybody. He's a misunderstood victim of the Great War. And the Nazis are saying that after Germany conquerors Europe, businesses will need to be rebuilt. There'll be lots of opportunity for American companies. They've been meeting with Henry Ford and other industrialists, telling them that business in the new Nazi Europe will be wonderful for America."

Paulette wondered about his cynicism, but Quinn chuckled as though he fully agreed. She felt perturbed. "Do you Americans really think that?"

Garret looked at her, his voice calm and telling her nothing of his own feelings. "Most do. Americans tend to look on the Nazis as a European problem. We're isolationists at heart. Places like Warsaw with bombed out streets littered with mutilated bodies seem a million miles away from life in middle America. Strange names like Tobruk, Cairo, and Tripoli mean very little to wheat farmers in Nebraska or the owner of Pop's drug store. The bobbysoxers hanging out after school are more interested in the latest Sinatra hit, and the word 'Nazi' has a strange sound to it, a totally foreign worry."

Fergus stood. "Being an old farm boy myself from the cornfields of Iowa, I can tell you Garret is right. Roosevelt will have a hard time convincing members of Congress to send the best of American tanks to the Egyptian desert."

"Well," Rhoda said, trying to please everyone, "maybe it won't come to an all-out battle in Egypt. Let's hope so."

"Hoping is just another form of whistling in the dark," Quinn said. Seeing Fergus shoot him a glance, he added quickly, "Sorry, Rhoda. I seem to be a doomsayer tonight." He set his empty glass down. "This isn't getting you two off to Athens on a very merry note, is it?"

Paulette was surprised when Garret glanced at his watch, set his glass down, and said something to Rhoda. She nodded and went into the bedroom, coming back with his coat and hat.

"Leaving already?" Fergus asked, walking with him toward the door.

"Afraid so. I've some work to do before meeting a client in the morning. I'll talk to you and Rhoda again before you leave on Wednesday."

Paulette was aware of Garret looking at her. She smiled. "Good night, Mr. Brandt."

He held her gaze for an extra moment. "Good night, Miss Harrington." He turned to Rhoda. "Thanks for having me over, Rhoda."

"It's pouring rain," she called from the window. "Fergus, don't you think you should give Garret a ride back to his hotel?"

"No need, Rhoda," Garret insisted, "but thanks just the same. I'll grab a cab. Good night, everyone."

Paulette watched him leave. Then at her elbow Quinn said, "I'm sure I saw him recently in Egypt. I wonder why he didn't want anyone to know?"

"He seemed quite certain you'd made a mistake," she said quietly. Her eyes met his dark ones. "Maybe you did?"

His grin said no. "He was right, though, about one thing."

"Oh? What was that?" She saw his thoughtfulness as he looked at the closed door.

"It wasn't at the British ambassador's, but the German embassy."

Rhoda walked up. "What are you two getting your heads together about, a conspiracy? You look awfully serious."

"I envy you for getting that flight Brandt arranged to Athens," Quinn sighed. "I'll be leaving again shortly for Cairo myself, but I haven't yet gotten a ride. The thought of another long voyage around the Cape is enough to make me consider staying here and going into another line of business."

Paulette turned, surprised. "You're leaving again so soon, Quinn?" She kept disappointment out her voice. She had hoped he would stay around London at least for a month or two before his next assignment. Especially with Rhoda leaving. Now she'd learned he was leaving at the same time as the Nickersons.

"Afraid so." He shook his dark head wearily. "I must be crazy doing this kind of work."

"Or dedicated," Paulette said with an encouraging smile. "Must you go by way of the Atlantic? With all the German U-boats?"

"No other choice, I'm afraid."

Rhoda looked apologetic, as if she were envisioning U-boats attacking Quinn's transport. "It's a shame you can't squeeze aboard and come with us. I'm sure the plane would be able to take you on to Cairo."

"What a help that would be. Osgood wants me covering the current situation at Tobruk."

Rhoda turned. "Fergus? Can something be arranged for Quinn to 'hobo' a ride with us on Wednesday?"

Fergus had been talking to the young English instructor. "What's that, darling?" He came up and Rhoda explained Quinn's difficulty in getting passage to Egypt.

"Usually Osgood arranges it," Quinn explained, "but he was out of luck this time."

"Going back so soon?"

"Osgood's orders. I'll be following up on the Rommel story."

"Darling, if he could get a ride with us it would save him weeks of dangerous travel," Rhoda told Fergus, her eyes suggesting he intervene.

Fergus looked at her. "I don't see why not. I'll need to get clearance from Garret first, of course. I'll see him tomorrow. Give me your hotel number, Quinn. If it can be arranged I'll ask him to give you a call."

"That would be terrific. I'm staying with a journalist friend in Kensington. Here's the number—on second thought, give me Brandt's number, will you? I'll call him myself. I don't want to take advantage of you two."

"I'll get the number," Rhoda said and walked to the telephone table.

Paulette stood from the sofa and went into Rhoda's bedroom for her jacket and shoes. Tomorrow was a work day and she still had her flat to straighten up before retiring. A few moments later Rhoda came in for Quinn's hat and coat and saw that Paulette was dressed to leave. She sighed. "I hate goodbyes."

"So do I. So let's don't say it."

"I'll write and send pictures. Fergus bought me a new camera. And try to come visit us, Paulette. I'll make room even if we must camp out at the dig." She smiled ruefully.

Paulette looked at her, nodding. "This summer, for sure."

They looked at each other, blinking back tears, then they hugged quickly. "Until this summer," Paulette said, her voice aching. "And take good care of yourself and—" she laughed through her tears but didn't say "the baby."

"I will. And you be careful, too. London may end up more at risk than Athens."

Paulette smiled and quickly left the room. Rhoda sat down on the edge of the bed and reached for a handkerchief to wipe her cheeks.

Quinn and Fergus were at the front door and turned as Paulette walked up. "I'll see you home, Paulette," Quinn offered, taking his hat and coat from her.

She nodded and held out her hand to Fergus. "Goodbye, Fergus. Enjoy Athens."

"We'll look forward to your visiting us," he said, patting her back as he opened the door. "Good night, Quinn. Give me a call once you talk to Garret."

"I will. Thanks, friend."

Paulette descended the inside steps to the front door of the apartment building and Quinn let her pass in front of him. It was raining as she stepped out onto the sidewalk, and he shoved on his hat and signaled for a taxi.

"How about something to eat?" he asked.

She guessed he was worried about her mood. "Thanks, Quinn, but I'm a little tired tonight. I want to go straight home and get some rest."

"Then what about dinner tomorrow night?"

She smiled. "I'd like that."

"Around seven?"

"That would be fine. Here's our ride."

Just as she stepped into the back of the black English taxi a blue sedan pulled to a stop across the street, honking its horn.

"That's Tony, the journalist I'm staying with." He looked apologetic. "Sorry, Paulette. Can you get home on your own?"

She laughed. "I do it every day. Go on, you're getting soaked. Enjoy dinner with your friend."

He grinned, stepping back with the rain falling from the brim of his hat. "I will. See you tomorrow night?" he asked again as if worried she might change her mind.

"Around seven with a raving appetite."

He raised his finger in a salute and dashed across the street to the blue sedan, avoiding puddles. A moment later the car drove away with a flash of headlights in the silvery rain.

"Where to, miss?"

Paulette gave her address and settled back into the seat, hearing the windshield wipers droning busily. She took one last glance out the side window up at Rhoda's apartment as the taxi left the curb. Warm lights glowed in the windows as though inviting family and friends in on this chilly damp night. This was the last time she would visit this place of many memories. It seemed that time had pushed her forward down a darkened street. What lay ahead?

4

Paulette started to prepare quietly for turning in for the night. In eight hours she would need to get up and dress for work at the magazine's office. She satisfied herself with a bowl of oatmeal for supper, indulged in a bubble bath, reread her favorite psalm, and settled into bed, drawing the sheet up over her shoulders. Her eyes soon adjusted to the darkness. Lights from the street cast a glow and revealed the profile of the bedpost, the tall bureau with a lamp, and her dressing gown hanging on a hook on the closet door. She could almost imagine, as she once did when a child at the orphanage, that the images were tall ghosts. Often her sleep was troubled by dreams of crashing dark Atlantic swells while she clung desperately to a small shallow raft being tossed upon the dark, glossy water. The headmistress, a kindly old woman who had given her life to care for London's "untouchables," had told the children stories about Jesus and heaven. After that she had thought of the images as angels sent to watch over her through the night. Her dreams then would be sweet and peaceful.

Paulette sighed. *Stop thinking and go to sleep.* She was staring at the window, going over in her mind all that she had heard tonight from Quinn. Strange, what he'd said to Garret about seeing him in Egypt when Garret insisted otherwise. And the other statement was odder still: "It wasn't at the British ambassador's, but the German embassy."

Garret Brandt's appearance was not unlike the handsome German soldiers she'd seen in Berlin before the war. It would be possible to mistake him for someone else Quinn had seen at a distance. Maybe she'd ask Quinn more about it tomorrow night at dinner.

The next morning Paulette had forgotten all about the incident as she rushed to get ready for work. She'd overslept after pushing off the alarm and now turned away from the mirror to search for her hat and bag. She was going to be late. She'd better splurge and get a taxi.

Paulette entered the magazine's building at twenty after nine to find the early morning rush for elevators now abating. She had the ride up to the fourth floor all to herself.

She walked quickly past the receptionist and down the long corridor until she reached her office. It contained her desk and several others, but it was comfortable, and gave her the uninterrupted silence she needed to concentrate on her writing and research. She enjoyed her window, which faced the London street, and offered plenty of light even on gray wintry days.

She edged around her desk, placed her coat, hat, and bag in her locker, grabbed her pad and pencil, and hurried into Mort's office three doors down.

Mort Collier was an energetic bachelor of medium height with a boxer's arms and barrel chest from strenuous workouts at the athletic club. At forty-five he was prematurely gray and kind-hearted beneath his rough exterior, working with the boys on the east end of London, sponsoring them in a city rugby team. He also kept two small dogs as house pets, and without fail scattered bread crumbs each morning for the pigeons in the park as he walked to work in rain, sleet, or pea-soup fog. Few knew this side of Mort Collier at *Horizon*, and he wished to keep it that way. "They'll never meet their deadlines otherwise," he had told her. This time, it was Paulette who was behind on her work.

He looked up and glanced at the clock on the wall as she entered, but he made no comment. Quietly she took a seat. Mort had already begun to detail work for the October issue to the small group gathered there: Charles Bingham, who was seated by the window with a serious face and thinning light-brown hair, and Smitty Bowles, a gum-chewing sort who constantly fiddled with his pencil when it wasn't behind his ear. Paulette stopped short as her gaze fell on a newcomer: a woman of perhaps thirty, a very sleek and attractive brunette wearing flawless makeup. Paulette thought at once of the beautiful American movie star Ava Gardner.

"Paulette? Meet Gloria Haskins," Mort said as though discussing the prospect of more rain. "She's our new foreign correspondent. Gloria, Paulette Harrington, my main feature writer."

Paulette smiled. "Welcome to *Horizon*, Gloria."

Gloria smiled back sweetly. "Thanks. I'm going to love working here." And her smile was enhanced as she turned back to her editor-in-chief.

"Gloria has the desk next to yours," Mort told Paulette. "She's had experience with the *New York Times* and comes to us highly recommended. I'm sending her to interview General de Gaulle about his views on the German invasion of France. She'll turn her interview notes over to you so that you can write the feature article for our next issue."

It was on the tip of Paulette's tongue to protest, but she caught herself in time. It would never do to begin showing jealousy among the tight-knit team of writers and editors at *Horizon*, but Paulette wondered why she had not been selected for the interview. It had been her idea, and she usually did her own research.

"All right," she said, "only—" she paused.

"Yes?" Mort asked a little impatiently, anxious to move on.

She merely shook her head as though the "only" were nothing, and looked at her pad of paper as if she were going to write something down to remember. She felt color warm her cheeks. She wondered if Gloria Haskins was as good a journalist as Mort believed. She'd be disappointed to think he'd hired her, bestowing the coveted interview in Paris, just because she was blessed to look like Ava Gardner.

Don't be catty. Mort is a professional. If the woman has worked for the New York Times, she must be capable. Yet the question lingered: *Why is Gloria Haskins, an American, working in London?*

Collier looked down on his desk at the mass of papers scattered in front of him, shifting them about thoughtfully. He went on giving instructions for the article. "There's a lot of controversy over the famous Maginot line and whether it will hold the Germans back as it did in the Great War. Again, our theme is about tanks and modern weaponry and the change in warfare tactics since 1917. We'll discuss the Panzer division threatening France and glean any possible insights about what could happen in the Egyptian desert if Rommel is sent against our troops. We'll conclude the article with the dim hope that Roosevelt will supply Britain with his newest Sherman tanks."

Paulette looked up. "Quinn O'Brien is back. He stopped by the Nickersons' flat last night. He has the same fears you do about General Wavell in Egypt."

"Yes, he called me this morning. He's offering to share any details he's garnered with you."

"I'll be seeing him tonight."

Mort closed the meeting abruptly, and they all began to disperse to their respective tasks. Paulette smiled at Gloria, trying to be friendly. "What brings you to work in London?"

"She expects a German land invasion, and she wants a front row seat," Smitty Bowles wisecracked as he hurried by, winking at Gloria. "Say—what about lunch?"

Gloria smiled. "Lunch with the boss today."

Smitty raised both brows and hurried on.

Gloria walked beside Paulette down to their adjacent desks. "I came to London for several reasons. I've a friend living here now who recommended me to Mr. Collier. Secondly, Smitty wasn't too far wrong. I do expect most of the action to be in London, rather than New York, and I want to cover it."

Paulette was thinking of what Rhoda had told her last night in the kitchen about the growing fear of a German invasion coming on the heels of the widespread bombing campaign. She shivered, and wondered if she were a coward at heart. She couldn't imagine herself deliberately seeking to come to London to cover an invasion if it did arrive. Gloria must be a stronger person than she had credited to her movie-star looks.

"Maybe you know my friend?" Gloria said. "He was at the Nickersons' apartment last night too, along with your friend, Quinn O'Brien. His name's Garret Brandt."

Paulette had reached her desk. "Yes. I've met him."

Gloria smiled. "Well, I'd better get to work. It'll be two weeks before I leave for Paris. Mort wants me to adjust to *Horizon*. Things are different here than in New York."

"Right," Charles Bingham said over his shoulder just before entering his work space. "Instead of coffee breaks, we get tea and biscuits."

Paulette smiled and Gloria laughed. "That suits me fine." Paulette went to her desk and drew up her chair, her smile fading. Two disappointments in less than an hour. On top of losing Rhoda, she'd lost the de Gaulle interview, and Garret Brandt's girlfriend had come to live in London. It looked as if she'd been unduly concerned about his earlier phone calls asking her to lunch or dinner. With a girlfriend with Gloria's looks, most likely all Garret had wanted was that interview with Gilbert Simington. She'd been right about him after all.

Paulette cast it all from her mind and dived into her load of work. There was nothing like writing and research to make her forget the things that depressed her. At least the Lord promised to never leave her. Through lonely nights and shattered dreams, His promise of comfort was sure.

But, if she did get the right opportunity, she would ask Mort why her idea on the de Gaulle interview had been given to someone else. It didn't seem quite fair. Let Gloria Haskins come up with her own ideas.

Paulette was still hard at work when Smitty poked his dark head through the door. "Hey—it's lunchtime. How's about walking with me and Charles to Joe's Ribs?"

She smiled but shook her head. "Not today, Smitty. I've got to catch up on things. I brought an apple and some crackers." She opened her drawer and reached for the polished red beauty.

Smitty grimaced. "Reminds me of a teacher I used to have in fifth grade. Was always after me about chewing gum in class."

Paulette smiled as he turned his head to look down the hall. "There goes our newest member. Probably lunch at a swank hotel. Nice quick climb to the top, huh?"

Paulette busied herself, refusing to say anything that might get back to either Gloria or Mort. She wasn't going to jump into a pool of gossip. Smitty left and she looked at her apple. She took a big juicy bite just as the telephone jangled. She gulped it down and picked up the receiver. "Paulette Harrington."

"Hi, beautiful."

She heard the busy sound of traffic in the background. "Where are you, Quinn?"

"Meeting Garret Brandt. Say—would you be terribly upset with me if I bowed out of our dinner date tonight?"

"No, of course not." She slowly set her apple down. "What's up?"

"Brandt. He thinks he can set me up on the Nickersons' flight all the way to Egypt. He wants to talk about it over dinner. Says there's this special place to eat that he likes. Potpies and all that British stuff. It's still new to him."

She smiled. "Don't worry about me, Quinn. Have your potpie with Mr. Brandt."

"Well, it's not quite the same as having a candlelight dinner with you."

"There's always another time, but you may not get another chance to arrange a flight with Fergus and Rhoda."

"Yeah, I was hoping you'd understand my dilemma. I should have known you would. What about lunch?"

She looked at her apple. "Not today, Quinn. I'm especially busy."

"But look, I'll probably be gone by tomorrow afternoon. I've got to see you again before I fly out. What about breakfast tomorrow morning? I'll meet you at seven in front your place."

"All right, tomorrow morning. And Quinn—" she hesitated, fingering the apple. "If I were you, I wouldn't say anything more to Mr. Brandt about seeing him in Egypt." She avoided mentioning the German embassy.

"I don't intend to, but why are you bringing it up?"

"No reason in particular, except I want you to get that flight. I sort of had the impression he didn't like it when you persisted on saying you'd seen him there."

"Did you? I didn't get that impression at all."

"I sure did."

"I'll let you know how matters go. Can I call you before you go to sleep tonight?"

"Lights are out at 10:30," she laughed. "Yes, of course you can call. I'll want to know what happened."

After he hung up, she munched her apple and went back to work. It was almost three o'clock before Gloria returned to work. *Must have been a nice lunch*, she thought.

∾∾∾

In her flat that night, Paulette generously waited until 11:15 to hear from Quinn before deciding he must be having a busy night on the town with Garret and wouldn't be calling. She yawned and turned the lamp out, thinking of research she'd need to do on the French story before falling into a deep sleep.

The next morning she got up early and was ready for Quinn at seven sharp. Strangely, however, he never showed, and finally, a little concerned, she quickly bagged a few tea biscuits and left for work. Later that morning while at her desk the telephone rang. Quinn's voice came loud and anxious from some busy public place. "Paulette?"

"What happened? How did your meeting with Garret go?"

"Too well! He hauled me all over London before dumping me off at my place some time after midnight. I don't remember a thing after meeting the pilot who was flying the plane this morning. I think I was drugged."

She sucked in her breath, and looked at the phone. "What? Drugged? But surely you're joking, Quinn."

"I don't know if I am or not," he complained. "I overslept this morning and missed the flight with the Nickersons. And that, after Brandt arranged everything so I could hitch a ride."

She shook her head, disbelieving. "If he arranged your flight, then what reason would he have for drugging you?"

"I don't know," he grumbled, "except my head feels as if something was put in my glass. I don't even remember how I got into my bed, but I didn't wake up until it was too late. The plane is probably over the Atlantic by now."

"Oh, Quinn," she sympathized, "I'm dreadfully sorry. Can you catch another flight soon? Maybe Garret could arrange—"

"Forget it," he said coolly. "When Osgood found out what happened he said he would try to see what he could do. In fact, he's been calling around all morning. I haven't but a few minutes before we'll need to run off to talk to someone he knows with an air transport business."

"I can't believe Garret wanted you to miss the flight. There just wouldn't be any logic to it, Quinn."

"Maybe. Maybe not. All that friendliness last night might have been a show."

"Why?" she persisted.

"That's what I intend to find out. I'm going to hunt up Fergus if I can and see what he might know about this. Anyway, I've got to go, Paulette. But I'm thinking Brandt was lying to me all along about arranging the flight. He was leading me along like a trout after a hooked worm. And I fell for it."

"Please stay out of trouble, Quinn. Just get the story Osgood wants and return safely to London. I still haven't gotten that dinner you promised me," she said with a smile in her voice.

"Blast it, Paulette, I'm sorry! I'd have much rather spent the night out with you. Next time, it's you and me on the town. Look, I've got to run—Osgood is hollering for me to hurry. Goodbye, beautiful! I'll call you from Egypt."

"Take care, Quinn!"

The line disconnected and she sat there a moment, pondering. He had overslept, that was all. What else could it be? As an investigative reporter, Quinn saw a conspiracy in nearly everything. And what reason would Garret Brandt have for sabotaging Quinn's flight? There was no deep, dark secret concerning Fergus and Rhoda's flight to Athens, and there seemed no reason for Garret to keep Quinn from flying with them and then on to Cairo. She remembered Rhoda being a little upset when suggesting to Quinn that he might accompany them, if he could gain assistance from Garret. Surely Rhoda's concern had merely been over her natural tendency to sometimes place others in uncomfortable situations they couldn't refuse. But hadn't Garret been the one to invite Quinn to talk about it at dinner? Evidently he hadn't been intimidated by the request.

She tried to dismiss her fancies.

Strange, though, that Quinn would even suspect anything as sinister as Brandt drugging him to miss the early morning flight.

5

It was Sunday afternoon and Paulette came home from church with her new blue dress covered with a coat, damp from drizzle. It had been over two weeks since the Nickersons and Quinn had left London and she assumed they had arrived safely. Garret Brandt had also left the city. Struggling against feelings of isolation, Paulette intended to spend the day curled up in a big comfy sweater and slacks on the sofa, reading before the fire. *I'm not alone*, she kept telling herself. *Not only is the Lord always near, but I'm as secure as I'll ever be. I don't need to cling to Rhoda.* Telling herself the issue was settled, she made herself a mug of hot chocolate and decided she was going to enjoy the rest of Sunday and ignore the drizzling rain pecking against the windowpane. *What is it about soft, gray, mizzling rain on leaves that makes one feel lonely? Stop it!* She settled on the tan sofa, curling her feet beneath her, and reached for the novel she'd been looking forward to reading for weeks.

The telephone jangled intrusively. She got up and crossed the small room to answer it. "Hello?"

"Hello," Garret Brandt said.

Her fingers automatically tightened around the receiver. When did you get back? she nearly inquired, but checked herself in time. It would never do to give him the impression that his presence mattered a great deal. Gloria had helpfully confirmed one day that he was away on business. Just exactly where, she didn't know as he hadn't told her. Paulette had found the news gratifying that he hadn't called Gloria since that night at Rhoda's.

Instead, she asked: "How did you get my number?"

"The same way I got hold of your address. From Rhoda, before she left."

She was sure of a concealed smile in his voice. She made no immediate response.

"Don't be unduly alarmed. I promise not to call you at three in the morning—unless I can't help myself," he said when the silence lingered. "Rhoda, bless her heart, has the gift of mercy. She can't bear seeing a poor bachelor spend Sunday afternoon alone in his apartment with nothing but love songs on the radio."

She smiled. "Yes, she does have that softhearted way about her." She couldn't resist. "Then Gloria is too busy this afternoon to see you?"

There came a slight pause. *I've surprised him*, she thought. He recovered easily. "I don't know if she's busy or not. I didn't call to find out." That was all, in that casual easy voice with no change in it. But he had suggested more than that, and Paulette read between the lines. He was saying he wanted her company, not Gloria's.

She said, before she could prevent herself, "I'm surprised you haven't called her. It was quite a change for her to give up her job in New York so she could move to London." To be near you, she could have added. He was now probably wondering how much Gloria had told her.

Well, now he knows you're not as indifferent to him as you've tried to make him think. If you'd been smart, you wouldn't have given that away so quickly. After all, if he'd called to invite her to dinner, why not simply accept and enjoy it? A dinner date didn't require that he first explain his entire life's history. She waited, expecting a cool dismissal, but it didn't come.

"Gloria's a good reporter," he explained. "As for coming to London, she has an aunt here who asked her to come and stay with her. Gloria's father was British, a colonel in the army during the last war."

Paulette felt both ridiculously happy and embarrassed at the same time. An aunt! Here in London. And a British father. So she had come because of her aunt, not because Garret had moved to England.

"Oh," she relented in a small voice. "She never mentioned her aunt."

"Didn't she? I'm sure she'll explain when you get to know her better. When can I see you?"

"You're quite persistent, " she said with a smile.

"It's not every day I meet someone who intrigues me. Since I saw you that first time at the lodge, I can't get you out of my mind."

"Really? Are you sure it isn't my uncle's Egyptian artifacts you can't get out of your mind?"

"I suspected you may have thought that. I can assure you, my fascination is with you and it is genuine. Have a heart, Paulette. How about dinner with a lonely American far from home?"

She laughed.

"When are you going to relent?"

She smiled. "The next time you ask."

"I'm asking now."

"Yes...well, thank you...I'd like that...shall I expect you at seven?"

"I'm downstairs using the public phone, with nothing more interesting to pass the time than looking out at the rain. Why not let me come up for a cup of real British tea? I promise to be on my best behavior."

Paulette looked at her baggy sweater and slacks with dismay. Not again. Not after Rhoda's.

"Give me fifteen minutes."

"I'm looking at my watch. All right, go."

She laughed again and hung up the phone. She glanced about, throwing her hands to her head. She began grabbing everything in sight that wasn't meant to be there and rushed into the bedroom with it. *It never fails*, she thought. She turned to the closet and brought out the new dress she had worn to church, and changed. She applied lipstick, brushed out her long honey-brown hair, and was just going into the kitchen to fill the teakettle when the doorbell rang insistently. She set the kettle down and went to the door, smoothing her dress and hair, reminding herself that the chime was rather like Garret Brandt's personality, insistent. In a way, she rather liked it. Especially on a cold, rainy Sunday afternoon when she was missing her friends and wishing for someone to talk to whose emotions wouldn't crumble into the same mound of dejection as her own. Garret was someone who radiated strength. As much as she was ashamed of herself for it, she wanted and responded to masculine support and leadership. That particularly annoying little secret about herself she hadn't shared with anyone, not even Rhoda.

She opened the door. She wasn't disappointed. He still had the same effect on her as he had when she'd first seen him at the lodge three weeks ago. He was emotionally unruffled, standing with a smile that wasn't the least embarrassed, his hands deep in the pockets of a navy blue raincoat. His warm, golden-brown hair was damp, and his vivid, gray-blue eyes held hers for a moment before drifting over her, his look saying nothing.

"Hello," he said.

"Hello," she breathed.

He stood there politely waiting, making no move, watching her.

"Come in," she said at last, looking away as she stepped back.

"Thank you."

He wiped his shoes carefully first. *Manners*, she thought, noticing everything, even as he was noticing everything about her and the flat. She closed the door behind him, noticing his height and strength. He turned to face her, and she randomly looked aside. He removed his raincoat. "Where shall I put it?"

"I'll put it here in the hall," she said of the cubbyhole meant as an entrance hall. She placed it carefully on a hanger, noting it was expensive, coming from a famous department store in New York. *Careful, Paulette. Don't let all your emotions out of the lockbox so quickly.*

She turned back toward the living room and hurried into the kitchenette. "I'll put the water on for tea."

He followed her in, then looked around at the neat yellow kitchen with frilly curtains and a small table for two by an equally small window. There was a clean linen tablecloth and a salt and pepper shaker in the design of kittens with big blue eyes. Paulette was embarrassed by his presence, but she was doing her best to hide it by getting him involved and talking incessantly. She opened a cupboard and took down a ceramic creamer, handing it to him. "Would you fill it with milk, please?"

"This where you keep it?" he asked casually.

"Yes, but be careful—the icebox handle is loose."

She took down cups and saucers and the sugar bowl, adding them to a large tray. He placed the creamer beside them, smiling. "Anything else I can do?"

She handed him the tray. "The sofa table is set up in the living room."

"What's wrong with the kitchen table?"

She hesitated. "It's unsteady. One of the legs is shorter than the others. And there's a fire in the living room."

"Cozy."

"I'll bring the tea as soon as the water boils."

She found a tin of sweet biscuits and arranged some on a pale blue glass platter with scalloped edging. She poured hot water in the teapot, and then she carried both into the living room and set them on the tray.

Garret had been looking out the window. She wondered if he'd expected a view of the Thames. She smiled when he turned. "My favorite alleyway," she jested. "It's especially nice when the garbage collectors rumble by on Monday mornings at five."

"Sounds just like Manhattan."

"Would you like a biscuit?" She handed him the platter.

"Is that what you call them? We call them cookies. Biscuits are big flaky things you get with a fried chicken dinner."

She laughed and poured the tea. "I suppose you Americans prefer to drink coffee." She knew they did. It made for small talk.

"Most of the time."

"I understand Rhoda and Fergus made it on time for the flight you arranged to Greece," she said casually, thinking that he didn't appear the culprit Quinn had angrily suggested over the phone.

"Yes, they arrived safely, thanks to our pilot."

"'Our' pilot?"

"I should say, the private pilots group," he said lightly.

"Poor Quinn."

He turned a quick, thoughtful look upon her, then was studying his teacup again. "He told you he missed the flight. I suppose he called you from the airport?"

"Yes, just before Peter Osgood—that's his boss at the *Times*—arranged for another flight to Cairo. He was very upset."

"I'll bet he was."

She sipped from her cup but watched him under her lashes. No explanation, no hint of guilt. "He said you had kept him up so late the night before that he overslept."

There was a ghost of a smile.

She wasn't getting very far. Maybe she ought to shock him. "He accused you of drugging him, that you didn't really intend to let him fly with the Nickersons."

His brows shot up. "Did he? Rather strange. Is he usually that paranoid?"

She hadn't expected that. She thought he might feel the need to deny it. She started to protest, but under his vibrant gaze that flickered with something between amusement and challenge, she stopped. On second thought, she leaned back against the soft divan with a relaxed glance.

"Paranoid? I hadn't thought of Quinn that way. Perhaps, sometimes, if not paranoid, at least suspicious. It's part of being an investigative reporter, especially for a hard-driving boss like Peter Osgood, who wants stories unearthed that will grab the front headlines. Sometimes I'm afraid Quinn and those with him find themselves coming up with news that will do just that."

The issue of Garret Brandt slipping something into one of Quinn's glasses now took on a foolish note and was neatly shelved, perhaps just the way he had intended.

"Tell me about your work," she said. "Were you successful at buying that classical vase for the company you work for?"

"Vase?"

"The one you talked about at the Nickersons' flat. Dr. Bristow arranged for you to meet the owner, in Athens I think you said."

"The owner changed his mind."

"That was unfortunate after going all the way to Athens."

"Owners often back out at the last minute, unable to part with their treasures."

"At least you were able to bring Fergus out to meet Bristow."

"Yes, there's that."

"And—Rhoda? She was feeling well?" *Does he know she is expecting?*

He smiled as if he knew what she was thinking. "She was doing better than Fergus. He's more nervous than she is about a baby on its way in a strange country. They're settled into a comfortable place. You're worried about her, aren't you?"

"Oh, dear. Am I that readable?"

"Your concern isn't anything to feel ashamed about, unless—" he stopped, as though he hadn't meant to say it aloud.

She set her cup down on the saucer. "Unless what?"

Once challenged he didn't back down or try to evade what he was thinking, but his eyes were unexpectedly curious, even sympathetic. "You trust in her a great deal, don't you?"

Paulette waited, trying to see behind his question. "I don't think 'trust' is the right word—"

"Depend?" His voice was quiet.

She felt the heat color her cheeks. Her mind was rushing back to their days in girls' school, then at the university. Rhoda seemed to have no trouble collecting friends, who soon congregated around her like bees gathering nectar at a flower. Paulette, on the other hand, although prettier than Rhoda, and some said more talented, sometimes came across in her conversation as too serious or intense. It had been Rhoda who always included her in gatherings and parties, Rhoda who defended her against gossip, Rhoda who bolstered her courage when sudden, unexplainable fears came crowding into her heart. They had roomed together until Rhoda married, had shopped together, had gone to the movies together. There had been dates with handsome young men, of course, because Paulette attracted many. But she hadn't found in any of them that certain "something" she was searching for. Could it be she was seeking security?

"She is all the family I have. We were so close when growing up and—" she stopped again, thinking she was beginning to gush like some sentimentalist. She glanced at him, wondering if he thought so.

He made no judgment on her emotions. Now he merely said, "She and Fergus appear to have a strong and contented marriage. I wouldn't think you need to worry about her."

Paulette, annoyed that she was revealing so much of herself, said swiftly: "I'm not worried. I'll miss both her and Fergus, is all."

"That's to be understood." His eyes were full of sympathy now and she was pleased that he seemed to care about her feelings. She wondered if he were trying to understand her because he was sincere, or because he wanted to make use of her weaknesses. *Now, what a strange thing to think when he's being so considerate.*

She was aware of her paradox; she was becoming more and more attracted to him, yet conscious of something about him that she could not understand, something which he did not wish to reveal. Paulette felt uneasy, yet the feeling in no way repelled her, but fascinated. She could see he was being careful with her emotions and offering strength, but in a very veiled way.

"And so the loss at sea denied you of any close family. I think you said your parents were aboard. Both of them?"

"Yes...both."

"No other family, beside Rhoda?"

"Well, there's an uncle—" she waited for a spark of interest at the mention of Gilbert Simington, but this time his look was smooth, and blank.

"But no other close, intimate relatives?"

"No," she admitted, leaning forward to poke at the log. Red sparks burst from it like tiny explosions. "I was raised in an orphanage until I was nine. I think I already mentioned Opal Harrington, Rhoda's aunt who worked there."

"And she arranged to bring you home, where you met Rhoda. But you haven't said how you ended up being sent to the orphanage. Who brought you there?"

She looked at him, rather surprised. "I don't know. I always assumed it was the authorities who took charge of the ship's few survivors. I was on the ship too..." She got up suddenly and leaned against the mantle.

His gaze sharpened with interest. He walked over to where she stood and the firelight cast him in a warm glow. "You were *on* the ship?"

She wondered about the emotional change in him. "Why, yes I was. I hardly remember it, of course. I remember clinging to something in the water—probably a piece of wood. A very fine gentleman rescued me." She turned back to look at the flames in the hearth. "I can only recall snatches of what happened, usually in my dreams."

"You don't know who he was?" Again, the level, unemotional voice.

"No, just a man—who placed me in a small boat with a few others." She sighed. "Sometimes I think he gave me his place on that boat. I owe him everything. He gave his life to save me. He...he went under the dark water after that. As far as you could see there was nothing except inky black swells rising and falling like mammoth mountains, avalanches that were ready to swallow you alive. I can still feel the fear in my dreams—" she stopped, turning away. She wished they could speak of something else.

"You dream about it," he said softly, "because of the trauma."

She turned and was brought out of the past by the sight of his face, with nothing except sympathy in those intriguing gray-blue eyes. He had a comforting strength that beckoned. She turned her back and walked to the divan, steeling herself against the foolish desire to pour out her fears. *Be careful*, she warned. She refilled their cups with the remaining tea. "It looks a bit strong now."

"I like it that way."

But he didn't abandon the conversation as she had intended. He said casually: "Have you ever tried to locate your parents' families?"

"It was my one big dream when I left girls' school. Rhoda's family tried to help, but there was no information to be had. According to the official passenger list there was no couple aboard by the name of Roger and Janet Weston. Strange, don't you think?"

He made no reply to that.

She sighed and sat down. "For several years I was absorbed by it. Then it seemed like I was becoming neurotic."

She smiled ruefully. "I finally set it aside and decided I'd better make a future for myself."

"What of your uncle? I suppose you've talked to him about it?"

"I managed to bring it up once or twice, but he says there are no more Simingtons alive." She paused for a moment, and then asked, "Have you tried to contact my uncle about seeing his collection?"

"No." He glanced at her, showing nothing. "But I have his address. Quinn gave it to me and suggested I call on a Thursday morning when he tends to be in a more congenial mood."

"Quinn gave it to you?"

"That surprises you. Why?"

"Just that I hadn't realized he knew Uncle Gilly."

That appeared to interest him more than the other things she had said. "Then it wasn't you who gave him the address?"

"No, I'd have no cause. Uncle Gilly doesn't like what he calls 'nosy' newspapermen." She smiled. "But Quinn was right about Thursday being a good day. That's when he's usually out for a walk in his garden. He has one of those fabulous places where the greenery is all cut meticulously into geometric designs."

There was a pause again. The log crackled, then fell apart into a bed of glowing red coals. Still, she made no offer to involve herself in trying to arrange a meeting, nor did Garret suggest it. He had been standing by the window and now gave her a measuring look.

"If you'll forgive my saying so, that cup of tea didn't do much to either warm or cheer you up. And I'm afraid my questions have stirred sad memories for you. It's stopped raining. Since we're a good five hours before dinner, why not let me take you around? It will do you good. And I need a change, too. There's still plenty of London I haven't seen yet." He walked up with that certain smile. "Until now, I haven't been able to find the kind of company to make it enjoyable."

He won, of course.

He didn't mention Gilbert Simington again that night, or any time soon afterward.

On their first dinner date he brought her to a place he said he liked on the Thames. It was cozy and quiet, and the food was very good. "I thought you said you didn't know much about London."

He let that slide by. She was enjoying his company more than she had intended to allow herself, yet she had grown thoughtful as they dined. He seemed to know it. He smiled. "What do you want to know?"

"How did you guess—?" and she laughed. "All right. Tell me more about yourself."

He sighed. "Women always ask that. Or, worse: 'What are you thinking?'"

"That's because we want to share in your mind and heart." No sooner had she said the words then she blushed, because it sounded as if she wanted to share in *his* mind and heart. That might be true, but it was too soon to acknowledge it. Thankfully, he appeared not to have noticed. He was going out of his way to put her at ease.

"You said you were an American," she went on. "But what part of the country? Your accent isn't, well, quite all-American, if you know what I mean."

"I think I do. Perhaps I've been studying German a little too much recently. I'm from Philadelphia—and that's very American."

He told her how he had grown up in the city, coming from a long line of archaeologists, historians, and railroad men.

"Archaeologists? From Philadelphia?" she asked.

After a slight hesitation, "Europe."

"Where in Europe? Germany?"

He looked at her evenly as if trying to make a decision. "Yes."

"I see." But she knew her voice sounded uncertain. She hoped it hadn't sounded like a conclusion, but the words stood there between them as though at a dead-end street awaiting a resolution.

Garret spoke suddenly, as if having decided. "My father was killed in the last war. My mother died a year or so later. In that, we have something in common. Except I do have family. I had a grandmother who arranged to have me sent from Germany to a rich boys' school in Philadelphia." He smiled ruefully. "I can tell you, I didn't get on well with my accent. After one too many fights in the dorm, I was dismissed. My 'Hun' nature just didn't adjust to the other boys with well-known political names."

"I'm sorry," she said, but she couldn't help being intensely interested and hoped he would go on.

"A cousin arranged for a private tutor in English. I worked slavishly on my accent and not only survived the next school I was sent to, but no one even guessed I'd come from Berlin. Later, I graduated from Yale, then worked in Washington D.C. for two years."

He tried to go on but she refused to rush. "What did you do there?"

"Oh, not much worth mentioning. I was a congressional assistant. I did research and updated the congressman's notes so that he would be ready for floor debates, things like that."

There was a strange reserve in Garret's manner, but whatever she had expected, this was far from it.

"That must have been interesting. I've always adored politics."

"Boring, actually. At least my part was. The congressman participated in all the debates." He smiled.

"But didn't you get credit for all background information and ready-made answers?"

"Never. Very unfair, wasn't it?"

"I should say. So you left."

"Exactly. For New York. My secondary major was antiquities. Because I enjoyed this subject so much, I gave it a good try and made favorable grades."

"And now you research and buy artifacts of antiquity for Kimball, Baylor, and Lammiter. I must say, you had to have more than favorable grades to get that position. You must enjoy traveling."

"Not really. It comes with the job. It's not something I'll want to do indefinitely."

He didn't say what he'd prefer long term. She assumed he would like to handle the business end of things in New York.

"There you have it," he continued easily. "My life story, unexciting and bland as oatmeal."

She laughed. She didn't think he really believed it about himself either.

He leaned a little closer to her and looked directly into her eyes. "I'm just an ordinary guy who wandered into a mountain lodge and was knocked out at first sight by a sultry British girl I can't stop thinking about."

If you blush, I'll never speak to you again, she warned herself. But it worked, even though she lost the upper hand in the conversation and didn't ask any more questions.

Garret Brandt didn't seem ordinary, and neither did he come across as just an "average guy from Philly." She also did not believe he'd been smitten by her at first sight.

Paulette saw him just about every evening for the next month, yawning her way through work in the mornings and switching from tea breaks to coffee.

"The girl has changed," Smitty Bowles commented to the others at *Horizon*.

"I'll say," Gloria added with a knowing little smile. "I haven't been asked to dinner in over a month from our mutual American friend. That's not like him. He usually has three or four favorites—one for each of his moods."

Paulette ignored the veiled barb and refused to inquire about his "favorites." She was certain Gloria, being a writer, could come up with a few overly-imaginative stories about Garret. But the suggestion, dropped none too subtly, remained in her mind to grow and fester.

"It's a good thing you have Mort to whiz you around London in the evenings," Charles Bingham wisecracked. "We wouldn't want you to be lonely, Gloria."

Gloria had smiled, unruffled by Charles' apparent jealousy, and went back to her desk to work.

Then the news that Garret was going away took Paulette by surprise. He called from the airport to tell her he was just about to board a flight for Malaga, Spain.

"This is terribly sudden, isn't it?" she asked, unable to hide her disappointment. They were to have attended her birthday celebration given by Gloria. Paulette had gone to extra trouble and expense to have her hair done at the beauty shop and to buy a dress that Garret had noticed in a department store window. Now he was at the airport ready to board a plane to Malaga!

"Darling Paulette, I'm sorry. This is one of those times when I've absolutely no choice. My life isn't my own. If I could, I'd be there. Especially on your birthday. Can you forgive me?"

His warm words won her over. "Yes, Garret, I believe you mean it. Oh, darling, do be careful. I worry about you when you travel—"

"Don't worry, Paulette. Look, I still want you to attend your birthday party at Gloria's. Will you do it?"

"I shall feel out of place alone, and—"

"On your birthday? Don't. I want to think of you with friends, having a good time. It will make things on my end seem a little easier if I know you're smiling. I'll be thinking of you..."

"All right, I'll go. And Garret?" she looked down at her wrist at the gold bracelet shimmering in the lamplight. "Your gift is beautiful," she said softly.

"I'll call you when I get back. If all goes well, six weeks."

Six weeks! "Goodbye..." it was on her tongue to say *I love you,* but she held back. Things were moving a little too quickly, and her heart and head were in a spin.

"Goodbye, darling."

It didn't dawn on her until later that night when she was in bed and about to fall asleep that Spain seemed a rather odd place to buy Greek or Egyptian antiquities. Perhaps some wealthy customer had contacted the New York company and wanted to buy something from a Spanish period. She wondered why he hadn't called her until he was already at the airport ready to board the plane. Was she being overly concerned, or should she be more curious about the man she was already deeply in love with?

6

It was six long weeks before she'd heard from him again, and she was still hopelessly enamored. At his suggestion, they had dinner at her favorite little café and then walked along the pier beneath the moonlight with the water shimmering like silver sails.

"The perfect place," he said, pausing, his hand steering her toward the railing.

She gazed out at the water for fear of betraying her feelings. She resisted asking the obvious, "Perfect for what?" It would have sounded like an invitation. He had kissed her before, several times, and each time her heart had been caught up in rhapsody.

"I always thought a woman should be proposed to in moonlight," he said.

Paulette was speechless. The proposal came as a total surprise, and so did the exquisite diamond cluster engagement ring he produced in a small silver box. She stood staring at its winking stones.

"You must know by now how I feel about you. I was struck the first moment I saw you at that lodge."

Her eyes lifted to his, and she knew her heart could not be hidden. At that moment she was certain of little else except the tenderness reflected in his gray-blue eyes.

He drew her toward him. "You wouldn't refuse me and break my heart, would you? What would I do without you? Now that I've found you, I can't let you go."

There was no need for words. She came to him in the silvery moonlight, convinced that he loved her as passionately as she loved him. Her heart sang as his lips met hers.

Paulette was happier than she had ever been in her life. She felt she knew him now, that he was no longer a somewhat mysterious stranger. She felt secure in his love, believing he understood her sometimes better than she understood herself. *I am loved*, she thought, basking in security. She was no longer alone. She had Garret, and he had her. "I am my beloved's, and my beloved is mine," she quoted to herself many times with delight as she prepared for the small engagement party to be held for them by Mort Collier. Paulette could hardly wait to write Rhoda and Fergus of the great and exciting change taking place in her life.

"When's the happy date to be?" Mort asked them at his flat, putting his strong arm around her shoulders in fatherly affection.

Paulette felt the heat in her cheeks, for no date was set. But Garrett, standing nearby said: "As soon as possible."

Everyone smiled at that, but again he surprised her by following through on his remark. After they left Mort's place and stopped for a midnight snack at their favorite café, Garret set out to convince her that a year's engagement was much too long to wait.

"We both know the war is going to get worse," he said quietly, calmly, placing his hand over hers at the table. "Life must be taken for what it's worth now. Tomorrow may be too late."

"Too late..." The very words sank into her heart like stones. Her fingers tightened around his. "I can't bear to think of that. We can't let the fast pace of world conflict rob us." But still, she held back, hearing a small voice in her conscience warning against haste, even though she loved and wanted him now.

But Garrett persisted. In other conversations he spoke of a coming onslaught of change that would shake all Europe, perhaps reaching even to North and South America. Few could remain passive, for there would be no place to hide. This generation would be forced into choosing sides. Paulette found herself trembling within. The danger, the uncertainty of life, had all helped to kindle the fiery passion that burned in their hearts and their kisses.

"We both know what we want," he said. "We love each other, so why delay?"

Held closely and protectively within his arms, her emotions agreed. *Yes, why wait? We love each other. Isn't that enough?* The old romantic song, "We Can Live on Love and Pale Moonlight," came to mind. "Just you and I, forever and a day, we'll build a dream house, we'll keep it that way..."

"Yes," she whispered. "I'm not afraid."

Was love and life and marriage left to chance? Deep down in her sensibilities she knew it wasn't. What's more, Garret was not the type to jump unwisely into a lifetime commitment. There must have been many women who had wanted him, she was sure of that. He seemed impossible for the wrong woman to catch. *He certainly isn't entering this solemn vow lightly,* she assured herself. *Why can't I just accept this for what it is? His love for me is true.*

Paulette wisely made an appointment with a minister at an Anglican church and explained her decision to marry Garret within two weeks. He counseled a longer engagement period and requested that Garret meet with him. "Is he a Christian?"

"Oh, yes, Pastor. He's a Lutheran."

"Would he be willing to meet with me?"

She blurted: "Of course."

He smiled. "Good, then. Have him call me, and we'll make an appointment as soon as we can."

Afterwards, Paulette worried about what Garret would say. Had she gone over his head? Perhaps she shouldn't have committed him like that. Maybe he preferred to meet with a Lutheran minister. She was relieved and a little surprised when he smiled and took her in his arms. "It's a good idea. You can give me his phone number."

Everything went smoothly. Compatibility must be tested in all sorts of situations and moods, the minister had said. But he was impressed with Garret, who seemed mature and ready and capable of taking on his masculine lead as God intended. And although the pastor advised them both to wait a little longer, he consented to marry them in a small chapel service with just a few friends attending. "I'm doing so because you've both convinced me you're sincere believers in Christ."

∾∾∾

Paulette planned a very romantic December wedding ceremony, and Garret allowed her to indulge every whim without balking over sentimental traditions as men sometimes do. Only one thing was missing: the presence of Rhoda and Fergus.

Paulette asked Garret to wear family cuff links to fulfill a tradition. They were gold, with an Egyptian inscription.

"Where did you get these?" The toneless command in his low voice startled her. The shutters were back, and his face was unrevealing. "Did your uncle give them to you?" he added more gently, as though he knew he'd sounded brusque.

"Well…yes. I thought you wouldn't mind wearing them since you were once interested in his collection." She looked at him anxiously. "But if you don't like them…"

"I like them," was all he would say and held them to his spotless white cuffs as if judging the effect.

Paulette wondered about his reaction, and then suddenly she caught herself and dimpled. She was being silly with her imaginings.

He smiled too. "You're analyzing me, darling Paulette." He caught her in his arms and kissed her, and the worry flew away.

He steered her toward the living room. "Now tell me more about all these plans you've made for the ceremony…"

They exchanged their vows on a Sunday afternoon three months after they'd met at the ski lodge, and when they left the chapel and parted from the smiling, waving guests, they were Mr. and Mrs. Garret Brandt.

≈≈≈

They spent a blissful ten days in Neuchâtel, Switzerland, where they had met, and, where outside of themselves little else mattered. The world, rushing madly to war, seemed to have paused. But if one took a closer look at Neuchâtel in the daylight hours, one could see tense faces and quickened steps. The city was sad and apprehensive, troubled by the gathering German divisions near their border with France.

They were sitting in an outdoor café after spending the afternoon sightseeing. Garret had left the table to make a telephone call. When minutes passed and he didn't return, Paulette casually glanced behind her into the restaurant to see if she could spot him. He was not there, and there was no one at the telephone booth at the corner of the foyer. She thought nothing of it in particular until she'd stood and left the little table to walk to the end of the square where there was a cart of flowers. Down the sidewalk facing the side street she saw him outside a flower shop. She smiled, reminding herself to act surprised when he brought her a corsage. A man came out, pausing in front of Garret. The incident took place so quickly she could never really be certain she had seen an exchange between them. The man, nondescript in a gray raincoat, went on his way, and Paulette watched Garret enter the flower shop.

She stood silent for another moment, then heard, "Does mademoiselle wish now to leave?"

She turned quickly, almost guiltily, and found the waiter's dark eyes fixed upon her. He glanced down the street, and then took his white cloth and swiftly swept it over an empty table.

"Yes, how much do I owe?" She walked back to her purse still on the empty chair at the table she'd just shared with Garrett, paid the bill, and left a tip. He bowed and murmured his pleasure, bidding her good day. Paulette placed the purse strap over her shoulder, picked up Garret's jacket that he had set on a chair, and walked to where he had parked their rented motorcar.

She was standing on the sidewalk, thinking, when some minutes later he walked up. She was surprised by the flicker of anger in his eyes.

"Why did you leave the table? I asked you to wait there for me." He unlocked the door and opened it for her.

"I didn't think it mattered so much. I saw that you'd left the phone booth, and since we were finished with lunch, thought I'd wait here."

He said nothing as he held the door for her and took his jacket. She knew him well enough now to recognize that when the muscle in his jaw flexed he was upset and was holding back a retort.

"Was it so important?" she asked lamely.

His gaze swerved to hers, sharply. He studied her face. "Was what important?" came the soft but even response.

"That I waited for you at the table."

He seemed to her to breathe a little easier. "No. It's all right. Get in, please." He was in quite a hurry, though trying not to appear to rush, and she felt the tension as he quickly turned the key in the ignition, backed up, and sped away. She glanced sideways to see him look in the rearview mirror.

After a few minutes of driving on the narrow streets, he relaxed and slowed down. They drove on in silence, and she could see he was taken with his own thoughts.

"I've upset you," she said.

He reached over across the seat and found her hand, squeezing it. "No. Nothing like that. You simply worried me."

She turned in the seat and looked at him, amazed. "Worried you?"

"I always worry when you're out of my sight," he said lightly. "I can't bear to be away from you for very long. Don't you know that?" he smiled and his eyes flickered. She knew he was trying to defuse the situation by teasing her.

"It was you who—" she stopped, not wishing to admit she'd seen him on the street. She'd been about to say, "It was you who worried me."

"Sorry if I seemed abrupt," he said.

She was silent for a moment or two. "You didn't say why I worried you." He couldn't have been upset just because she had left the table. "Switzerland seems a pretty safe place."

"Nazis are everywhere."

He braked quickly. His arm shot out in front of her, bracing her.

Stunned, she sat there, heart in her throat. Just ahead of them, oblivious to their vehicle, an old man in a rumpled jacket and a cap had pushed his wobbly, unpainted flower cart into the street.

"There are more pleasant things to talk about than war," he remarked as though uninterrupted. "And to do." He shifted smoothly and sped on. "What would you like to do this evening?" he murmured as he brought her palm to his lips.

She was picturing the flower cart. She glanced him over, then searched the floorboard—no corsage. He hadn't gone into that shop to buy flowers after all.

If I'm wise, she thought, *I'll not push the matter. He's keeping something from me deliberately.*

"Any suggestions?" he asked, pursuing the matter.

"No," she said in a small voice. "I'm rather tired tonight."

His head turned. She avoided his gaze and looked out the window.

Garret said nothing more until they got back to their hotel suite. She went into the bedroom and took rather a long time to remove her hat and gloves. She needed a few moments to lose her tension and to form her face into pleasant lines that wouldn't betray her thoughts. For the first time she understood how difficult it was for married couples to hide things from each other. *That's because we're not supposed to hide our thoughts from one another,* she told herself. She slipped off her high-heeled shoes and stood there in the shadows of the satin-draped bedroom. The joy had suddenly gone out of their honeymoon. The light from the sitting room cast itself on the wall and she felt his shadow looming. Turning quickly, almost guiltily, she saw him leaning there in the doorway. She couldn't see his expression because a shadow hid part of his face.

"You startled me," she breathed.

"What did you think I was going to do?"

"Nothing. Don't be silly." She turned her back, removing her necklace and fumbling. "I told you, I'm just a little tired, is all. I guess I'm jumpy."

He came up behind her and removed her fingers from the latch.

"You're all thumbs tonight." He unclasped it.

"It...it was mentioning the war, and the Germans."

His hand closed on her arm, and he turned her around to face him. "That won't work. Not when you love the journalistic work you do at *Horizon.*"

She looked up at him and saw his grave expression, but his eyes were unreadable.

"You saw me on the street."

She tensed slightly, wondering what her reaction should be. She couldn't lie, yet she didn't want him to know. Was she afraid of discovering something about him that might ruin their present happiness?

He must have been deeply troubled when she tensed, because he pulled her against him. "You're suspicious," and there was faint surprise in his tone.

"Who was it, Garret? And why did you go in the shop? Not to buy flowers, surely."

"Your only difficulty, darling, is that you don't know how to trust. What makes you think I didn't go there for a good reason?"

"Oh? Such as?" she challenged quietly.

"To buy you roses."

It hurt to think he would use that excuse to deceive her. "Then why didn't you?"

"I did, but I only ordered them."

There came a knock on the door. Garret's mouth turned. "That should be your flowers now." He went to answer.

Oh, no. What have I done? She bit her lip and sat down slowly on the edge of the bed, almost wishing he'd come back empty handed. He didn't. He entered the room with a fabulous bouquet of a dozen scarlet roses in his hands. "Your roses, Mrs. Brandt."

"Oh," came her feeble voice. "Oh, darling, I'm so sorry—" she jumped to her stocking feet and ran to him, throwing her arms around him. "I'm so ashamed," she said.

His arms enfolded her tightly. "You lack having had the dependable role of a father in your life. It seems to affect your ability to trust me."

She looked at him, surprised, wondering if that could be true.

"All you ever had was your uncle. And while Gilly might be a nice chap, I wouldn't call him a dependable father figure. He doesn't know life exists outside of his narrow cloister teeming with Egyptian artifacts. He left you to grow up alone in an orphanage. He could have contacted you and let you know you had an uncle. A proverbial 'rich uncle,' by the way, who could have made your early years a lot more secure, financially and emotionally."

"Are you a doctor of psychology?" she said with a grim smile, stepping away from him. "You may be right, at least about Gilly. But I had Aunt Opal."

"Yes, bless Opal Harrington. I'll wager she was a vinegary old dear, with an avid dislike for masculine mentoring. Am I right?"

She folded her arms and gave a small laugh. "Oh? Is that what you are? My masculine mentor?"

He held her gaze, then without a word laid the roses down on the table beside them and pulled her back into his arms.

Paulette was content once more, until the next morning when her doubts resurfaced.

≈≈≈

The bleak headlines of war in the Swiss newspapers interrupted their honeymoon and brought it to a swift end. Paulette had slept late that particular morning and was just awake and in her dressing gown, sipping tea, when Garret returned to the hotel room. He had several French newspapers with him and tossed them on a chair as he picked up the telephone and made a call.

He looked over at her as he waited for the connection. "We're leaving this morning, darling. Better get dressed."

Paulette picked up the papers and scanned the various headlines, her heart saddened by their dark news: *ITALIAN BUILDUP IN EGYPTIAN DESERT THREATENS BRITISH WITH SEIZURE OF SUEZ CANAL.*

Garret made his call, and when he returned a minute later found her still staring at the newspaper.

"We've a flight out to London on a Flamengo."

Paulette hurried to the adjoining dressing room. From her journalistic work at *Horizon*, she knew that a Flamengo was a government passenger plane. As it was unarmed, usually an armed escort was provided.

"How did you manage to get us seats?" she called into the bedroom where he was emptying drawers and tossing clothes on the bed.

"Luck," he said calmly.

With hairbrush in hand she looked around the door at him curiously. She knew better than that. Luck didn't exist, and certainly not on a government plane.

"Garret? How bad is it for British troops in Egypt, do you think?"

He didn't seem to have heard her question. Paulette paused, brush in midair. She stared at him. His back was toward her, and he didn't see her watching. He removed something from his pocket and, using a lighter, set the tiny flame to the edge. A faint smell of paper curling into ash came to her.

"Inferiority of numbers, inferiority of equipment, inferiority of methods," he said stiffly.

Paulette withdrew back behind the door, and stood feeling ill.

"Ready, darling?" he called a few minutes later.

"Yes," she said quietly, coming into the bedroom and adding a few final things to her suitcase. He closed the lid and snapped it shut. "Good. Let's go. I've called down for a taxi."

He walked to the door, but realizing she wasn't with him, he paused and turned to look back.

He gave her a pensive glance and appeared to read her troubled face.

"No need to be afraid, dear. I'll see that we get home to London safely."

She walked up to him and whispered huskily: "That man, in the gray raincoat—"

His face went smoothly blank. He set the luggage down. He studied her. "I thought we had that all settled." There was no anger in his voice, but it was too calm.

"Outside the flower shop," she continued haltingly. "Somehow I imagined that you knew him."

"Paulette," he said with mild exasperation. He took hold of her and his kiss silenced her. He held her close, as though wishing to blot everything from his own mind, as well as hers. "Never mind the man in the gray coat. I've never seen him before. You'll have to believe me." He kissed her once more, desperately, as if by sheer will he could make her believe.

It was easy to forget when she wanted to convince herself that her suspicions were bred of insecurity.

This is my beloved husband, she kept telling herself. *Nothing must be allowed to matter, to ever come between us.*

7

Paulette spent the week after their return from Neuchâtel searching for an apartment without locating anything suitable. Everything in the better section of London was beastly expensive and, constantly keeping tabs on her money, she had all but surrendered the idea of finding a roomier place to live.

"Guess we'll need to find some park bench," Garret teased her as she fretted about sky-high prices in the rental section of the *Times*.

She looked up at him from her paper but did not smile at his joke.

"Darling, it's very simple," he told her cheerfully. "Until we find just the place we like, we'll either stay here in the hotel or your flat. Which do you prefer? Your place or mine?"

She sighed and dropped the paper on the empty chair at their table in the hotel restaurant. She glanced toward the white-clad waiter. "After the price of my breakfast this morning? I'll take the flat. At least I have a kitchen, cracker box that it may be." She nibbled the sweet nut cake she had ordered. "And, I shan't need to tip the waiter for afternoon tea."

"I didn't know I married such a frugal young lady." Garret had ordered coffee and refilled his cup.

"Well," she protested mildly, "I've been working and saving ever since I graduated school. I can make a pot of tea for half what the hotel charges."

He laughed. "I thought it was a wife's prerogative to begin dipping into her husband's bank account."

"Is that an invitation, darling?"

His eyes were amused. "If I couldn't afford a luxury like you, I'd have delayed getting married. Seriously, Paulette, you don't need to worry. I'm able to take care of you, including afternoon tea at the Victorian Hotel." He smiled at her. "You can even order a second sweet cake if you like."

Nevertheless, for Paulette's peace of mind, the next morning they checked out of the hotel and made the move to her tiny flat in downtown London, which was one of a number of two-room accommodations making up the top floor of her building. It wasn't much, but Paulette still worried that her present landlord, Mr. Hoadley, might raise the rent.

Garret didn't appear concerned and assured her they would find the exact place they wanted. They just needed to be patient. He wanted a roomy apartment with space for an office where he could set up international telephone and telegraph connections to New York and Geneva.

"Why Geneva?" Paulette asked curiously.

"The company is making plans to open an office in Switzerland." He looked about, then dumped several huge suitcases and leather briefcases on the bedroom rug, immediately filling up the remainder of the limited floor space.

She groaned, pressing her palms to her temples help-lessly.

He stepped his way over the obstacle course of bags and boxes until he reached her, smiling. "Now, none of that. All things in their proper order and time. At least we have a window," he moved the curtain aside to display the alleyway of stone and gray buildings, "with an inspiring view," he added.

Paulette couldn't help laughing. He caught her into his arms and drew her head against his chest. He was looking out the window again. From the corner of her eye she could see a man in a raincoat passing by, glancing up at various apartment windows. Paulette looked at Garret as he drew her back from the window. The teasing glint had left his eyes, and she was looking into the face of a stranger.

～～～

Apartment hunting proved difficult. They searched all the right districts in London for the roomy apartment they wanted. The afternoon ended with little to show for the tiring excursion except Paulette's sore feet. The war brought a devastating scarcity of housing, and even apart-ments the size of the one they had now were going for triple the normal rent.

"The first one we looked at wasn't too disgusting," he said, "except for the cockroaches that scampered when you opened the kitchen cupboards." He smiled when she closed her eyes and shuddered.

"Looks like we'll need to be content for a while with little space," he continued. "The world is our oyster." His eyes were amused as he gave her a squeeze. "Think how comfy and cozy we're going to be through the long winter months."

She laughed. "What about your telegraph lines to New York and Geneva?"

"I'll have to go downtown, but it doesn't matter. With such a delectable roommate I'd be a fool to complain about a little thing like that."

∾∾∾

The month of January 1941 was hectic and exciting for Paulette. The British had just won a stunning victory in Egypt, defeating the Italians and driving them back to Libya. Besides news of the war, there had been a round of small parties and a get-togethers with her associates. Then she went back to *Horizon*, much to the relief of Mort Collier. The day after she returned, he came and rested his palms on the front of her desk, leaning forward, watching her evenly under heavy brows.

"Have you heard from Quinn?"

"No, not since before Garret and I were married. Why? Is anything wrong?"

"Maybe. I'm not sure."

She tensed. "But he arrived safely in Cairo last year?"

"Yes. He did. But not long ago he took a jeep and went out to visit the troops in the desert. That was before the Brits fought and defeated Grazini's troops at Sidi Brani. I just found out that he hasn't been heard from since."

"Oh, Mort, you don't think he's been captured?" she cried, jumping up from her chair. How could she let so much time go by without even a thought for Quinn?

"I wish I knew. The military there is looking into it, but so far there's nothing." He straightened, shoving his hands in his baggy trousers. "Look, I don't want to worry you. You know Quinn. He could just as easily have ditched the jeep deliberately and started off in any direction for a story."

Yes, that was like Quinn all right. No risk, no top story, as he often said.

"This puts us in a tough spot," Mort went on. "I've been counting on a story he promised me."

"Oh, did he? I didn't know."

"Little extra side money for Quinn," he said with a lop-sided smile. "Just don't let Osgood know about it."

"What story? Something about King Farouk?" she asked. "The one about his favoring the Germans?"

"Yeah," he said bitterly. "Nazi occupation instead of British protection. I want a firsthand story." He paused a moment and seemed to come to a decision. "And, since Garret is heading in that direction anyway, well, it just occurred to me that you might talk him into letting you go along. We need on-site information about the prisoners of war, too. If you get that story for us, Paulette, I'll see that you get promoted."

Paulette was thinking of what Mort had said about Garret and Cairo. How was it that she knew nothing about his going there? She hesitated, unwilling to tell her boss that she was in the dark about her husband's plans.

"Well? What do you say?" he urged.

She drew in a breath. "I'll—talk to him about it tonight. I'll let you know tomorrow."

For the rest of the day, concerns about Quinn, and Garret's undisclosed travel plans, interrupted her concentration. She was also concerned about what she had found in his jacket pocket that morning. At five o'clock she gave up. It was no use. She set aside her work, found her coat and hat, and turned out her desk lamp. She would go home a half hour early and make it up in the morning—oh, it was Friday night. Hoping a good meal would put him in the mood to talk, she decided to make something special for dinner. Yesterday's *Good Housekeeping* magazine had an interesting recipe on a new soufflé. She remembered that Garret had commented on an egg soufflé in Neuchâtel.

She walked briskly from the magazine's offices down the eight blocks to the apartment. Garret had told her to take a taxi, but she couldn't bring herself to spend that much money five days a week. Anyway, she needed to stop at Al's Market. She bought a dozen eggs, cheddar cheese, sweet green peppers (very expensive, because they were out of season), onions, black olives, imported Italian olive oil, and a still-warm loaf of French bread. She hurried the final block to the building, ran up the entrance steps, and entered the glassed-in lobby.

She fumbled for the key in her handbag as she climbed the stairs. Cairo. She frowned. Could Garret have intended to make a trip to Egypt without having told her? What was he waiting for? Her frown deepened as she thought of the many times he'd kept things from her. Too many times, she decided. Her heart became even heavier.

She entered the quiet flat and put the bag of groceries on the counter, then removed her coat and hat, and hung them up in the closet.

A few minutes later when she came back to the kitchenette, she was still frowning. She tied her frilly apron around her small waist and glanced at the kitchen clock. She had plenty of time to make the soufflé. She opened a drawer and took out the article she had previously cut from the magazine with its scrumptious photograph and the meticulous recipe. A few minutes later, with everything within reach, she set to work.

Cairo—why would he be going there? Another artifact? Naturally, what other reason would there be? And Quinn—

she prayed that he was safe, that he was merely up to his neck in a good story.

She remembered the brooding headlines she'd read last night before bed. War with Nazi Germany threatened to escalate, and that put Garret's travels in more danger, even though he was an American, and as such, was not at war with either Germany or Italy. His citizenship also afforded Paulette more safety in travel, should she decide to accept the assignment Mort had just offered her.

She knew Garret would be opposed to her doing a story on King Farouk and prisoners of war when she told him about Mort's generous offer. Her own mind on the matter was still undecided. She could hardly go against Garret's wishes, and yet if he were going to Cairo, what better opportunity could she have than to travel with him? It would mean a promotion and a raise. Perhaps those luxury apartments near the Strand weren't so impossible to attain as she had thought.

Thinking of Garret traveling to Cairo brought Egyptian artifacts to mind. Uncle Gilly had called *Horizon* at lunch and left a message to call him back Monday morning. She entertained a vague hope that he might ask her and Garret to dinner. She hadn't forgotten that Garret wanted to meet him and see his collection. Strange, how in all these months Garret had never brought it up again, or tried to use her to arrange it. Her conscience smote her. *You see?* it seemed to say. *He cares only about you. Don't you know that by now?*

Paulette timed dinner carefully. Because he didn't like to sit down to a meal as soon as he came home, she arranged things to be ready an hour after he walked through the door. Except he didn't arrive as usual. He was already an hour overdue when the soufflé was ready, perfect and cheesy and fluffy as a cloud. She tried to keep it warm, anxious that it would go flat. It proved a hopeless battle.

She picked up a framed photograph, recognizing the things that had first attracted her to Garret Brandt. She was lost in thought when she heard his usual quick footsteps coming up the stairs, then the key in the lock. She remembered then that she had left it unlocked after coming home from the market.

He came in, pulling off his tie. His jacket was slung over his shoulder, and he had a slight frown between his eyes. "Honey, always keep the door locked. I've mentioned it before."

Then he looked at her for a long moment as she stood in the entrance to the kitchenette. He appeared to be a mind reader, for he sighed and looked at his watch. "Guess I'm late again."

"Only two hours late." She folded her arms and looked at him without even a glimmer of a smile.

"One hour and thirty-five minutes, to be exact."

"It's seven forty-six and thirty-three seconds."

He smiled, set down the two briefcases he was carrying, and looked at her in that way of his. "I'm sorry. What can I do to help make it up to you?"

"You can't. It's too late." Tired, disappointed, and feeling sorry for herself she jerked off her apron and tossed it aside on the counter.

"Hey, wait a minute." He caught her in his arms. "Darling, it's not as bad as all that, is it?"

"Yes!"

"Honey, I'm genuinely sorry. I should have called." He drew her to him, holding her close and protectively, kissing the side of her face, rubbing her back soothingly. "You look tired again. You work too hard at *Horizon*, then you rush home to take care of me. I'm so accustomed to doing everything for myself that I've a bad habit of forgetting the effort you're putting in here. I must seem terribly thoughtless."

He glanced toward the stove. "I suppose I've ruined the omelette."

"It isn't an omelette, it's a soufflé. There's a big difference," she said sorrowfully.

"Of course there is," he soothed, sounding perfectly calm and reasonable, and looking very serious as she looked up at him, but she caught a flicker of amusement in his eyes that he was trying to conceal. "Nothing my love does is ever ordinary."

"What does that mean?" Was it another critical suggestion that she was too intense? That she was too careful about details that didn't matter?

"I simply mean that my girl is a perfectionist."

"And so are you, by the way."

"Yes, that rather leads us into some critical moments, doesn't it? Look, Paulette, I don't want to quarrel. If dinner isn't perfect, that's all right. I'll eat a cold flat omelette—"

"But that's just it! It wasn't a flat omelette when I made it so perfectly! You ruin everything I try so hard to do right—"

"Not everything. This is the first time I've been this late. I admit I should have called, but something important came up that couldn't wait. There wasn't a phone nearby. I said I was sorry."

Her anger collapsed as quickly as it had blown up. "Oh, Garret, I'm sorry too—I don't know what's come over me—"

He held her tightly. "It's all right, honey. You're tired, is all. And you're worried about something else. What is it?"

Whether that was really true, not even she fully understood, but agreeing with him was a way of apologizing for her fly-away emotions. "It's Quinn," she admitted. *And Cairo. And the matchbook and receipt I found this morning.* But she didn't say that. She couldn't, because she feared the answers, or the lack of them.

"Quinn?" his voice changed. "What about him?" He held her from him so he could see her face.

She explained what Mort had told her about his abandoned jeep and how the military authorities hadn't been able to track him down. "He could have been taken prisoner. Mort's worried sick, and so am I. Anything could have happened. Oh, Garret, what can be done, if anything?"

His hands freed her. "You know him better than I do. But my impression of O'Brien is that he's a show-off. He's probably blundered his way into some situation he can't talk his way out of. I'm sure Peter Osgood at the *Times* is contacting all the right authorities to try and track him down. In the meantime, there's little either you or Collier can do about it but wait. O'Brien will probably show up soon with a hot story under his belt."

"You don't like Quinn, do you?"

"Not particularly." He dropped his jacket and tie on the chair and was suddenly distant in his emotions. "Is there any tea?"

"Yes," she said dully, and turned toward the kitchen. He stopped her.

"I'll get it."

He was pouring himself a cup when she came in. She refused to look at the flat soufflé sitting on the stove.

"Quinn is all right when you get to know him," she said.

"Maybe. I don't intend to find out."

"Is that fair?"

"Maybe not. But again, where O'Brien is concerned I'm not worried about being fair."

"Garret! It was Quinn who first got me my job at *Horizon*. And he's been a good friend to me and Mort Collier for four years."

He looked at her evenly. "Maybe it's time to tell Collier you're leaving *Horizon*. You're obviously tired. Too much pressure working full-time on deadlines and adjusting to marriage."

"Don't be silly. I'm adjusting just fine. I've no intention of—"

He set his cup down. "You can tell Collier your husband has something to say about your schedule. And he's seriously considering asking his wife to resign."

"Well, don't *I* have anything to say about it?"

He straightened from the counter and headed for the bedroom. "Very little."

Her breath caught. What had come over him?

"Garret! Why—you're jealous of Quinn—even Mort."

He laughed as he disappeared into their room.

She stood there, trying to recover from the quick turn of events that left her surprised. She heard him moving about in the closet. "Call it what you like," he said.

He came out pulling on a navy-blue cardigan, and looking anything except the soothing, understanding husband he had been minutes ago over the ruined soufflé. His gray-blue eyes were cool and steady.

"You can't be serious," she said with a laugh, interlacing her fingers above her heart. "I don't care a bit about Mort or Quinn and you know it. Not in any way that should upset you." She went to him. "Oh, Garret." She wrapped her arms around him and squeezed. "There's only one man I want."

He responded to the warm invitation in her eyes and kissed her. "You have him."

"Do I?" she whispered gravely.

"Don't you know that by now?"

"Yes, I suppose I do." Her smile had vanished. Her eyes searched his.

"Suppose?" he shook his head in mock sadness. "What does it take to convince this woman?" He kissed her lips, her ear, her eyes.

It was now or never. "Garret," she breathed, moving away from him over to the fireplace. "There's something else Mort mentioned today." She sat down on the edge of the divan, watching him. "He wants to send me to Cairo." She watched the change slowly take place in his expression. "And I'm thinking I may like to go."

He studied her for a long moment. "Because of Quinn?"

"Well, no. That is, well, yes, because of Quinn, but not just because of him."

"Would you care to explain that?"

She tried, telling him what Mort Collier wanted her to do. As she did, she could sense she was losing the argument. So she tried even harder. She stood.

"I want that promotion Mort offered me today. I want to go to Cairo and interview Italian and German prisoners of war myself. I may even get an interview with King Farouk. It's a far cry from writing articles about this year's fashions."

His mouth tipped down. "I'll say it is. But I don't like the idea of you rubbing shoulders with Italian and German soldiers—or British, for that matter."

"Now, Garret, you're deliberately being impossible."

"Impossible." He considered. "Maybe. In my mind, I'm being sensible and calm about this. The answer is no, Paulette."

"But, Garret!"

"Look, Paulette, darling. You surrendered your independence when you became Mrs. Brandt."

"Of course I wouldn't think of going, not if you were dead set against it."

"You wouldn't? Good." He smiled. "Then it's settled. I'm dead set against it. Now, why don't you get your coat and we'll go out to eat."

"Oh, Garret!" she breathed, exasperated.

He walked over to her, taking her by the shoulders. "Germans," he said gravely, "will soon be swarming over the Egyptian desert from Tripoli to Tobruk. Even our obnoxious friend Quinn may have been taken prisoner as he wandered merrily through the desert. Do you think I'm crazy enough to risk you wandering about Egypt getting a story for Collier?"

"But it wouldn't be that way! I'd not be wandering about the desert at all. To interview the prisoners of war I'd need clearance, of course, and that means I'd likely have several British guards to escort me about." *And you'd be there.* But she didn't say that aloud.

"Honey, I would never deny you anything you really wanted to do that would make you happy. Cairo, however, is another matter. I love you too much to risk you to that kind of danger."

She melted. "Darling, how positively sweet of you. Sometimes you're an angel. And other times—well, we won't get into that."

His mouth turned. "No, let's not."

"I'll be quite safe, really I will. And what about Fergus?"

"What about Fergus?"

"Well, he let Rhoda go to Athens with him, and she's expecting a baby."

"That's different. He went with her. This is not the same. Fergus wanted that archaeological job with Dr. Bristow enough to risk anything to get it. I've already got what I want—" he held her close. "After months of very difficult endeavors. I had to chase you all around London to capture you."

She laughed. "You call three months long?"

"Miserably long."

"Everyone's saying we married too soon."

"Let them. We could have waited a year, but what would that have accomplished?"

Maybe we would have gotten to know each other better, she thought. She glanced at his jacket where it was still lying across the chair, then quickly away, lest he notice. She didn't care to remember what she had removed from the inside pocket of another of his jackets she'd brought to the cleaners that very morning on her way to work.

"Mort offered me a *promotion,*" she repeated, walking toward the window. "We could use the money, Garret." Her eyes brightened. She turned. "I was looking at an apartment on the Strand during lunch today. It has a huge sitting room and a view of the Thames. And there's a room for your office. It's expensive, but—well, if I was in a position to get a raise, we could afford it."

"We can afford it now, without your working. I'm serious, Paulette. I'd just as soon have you tell Collier you're resigning."

She watched him curiously. "And what am I to do all day? I can only make so many soufflés that go flat."

He laughed. "Anyway, I thought you didn't like Egypt. Even though Gilly swoons each time it's mentioned."

She turned quickly and looked at him. "How do you know that?" Had he seen her uncle then?

He smiled briefly, as if he knew what she was thinking. "You told me, remember?"

"Yes," she admitted, "I guess I did. I'd forgotten. But Garret, it isn't just the extra money. I do like my job, very much. I really don't want to leave, not yet anyway. Not with the war worsening. I want to do my part, if only in the field of journalism."

He watched her speculatively. "Being a patriot for one's country is all very commendable. I just don't think it's wise, though, to travel to Cairo right now."

She glanced at him. *Why not?* she wanted to say. *You're going there soon, aren't you?*

"New fighting in the region is ready to explode. Just look at the headlines."

Paulette hid a shiver. She pushed the frilly curtain aside and peered out onto the narrow street. Some pigeons were alighting on the bread crumbs that Mr. Hoadley was scattering. The sun was beginning to set, tinging the sky with an orange glow that was mixed with iron-gray.

"That doesn't mean Cairo will fall to the enemy anytime soon," she said. "I'll be perfectly safe with you nearby." There. It was out. She had carefully unleashed Mort's news. She sounded neither challenging nor suspicious.

Garret looked at her, his gaze sharpening. "What did you say?"

She let the curtain fall into place, and turned. "Well—you'd be with me, darling. What could happen?"

A brow arched. "I would, would I? And just how do I figure into this? Is Collier wacky enough to ask me to work for him as a journalist?"

She drew in a breath and plunged in. "Mort told me today that you are going to Cairo. Are you telling me he was mistaken?"

During those times when Paulette surprised Garret, or caught him unaware in pensive thought, he could appear—dare she say it?—dangerous. This was such a moment. *It is better this way*, she consoled herself. *The truth must come out.* She would explain everything now, including what she knew about Cairo and Berlin. Even what Quinn had said about seeing him at the German embassy. Their relationship was too important to have secrets between them.

8

Paulette often noted that when Garret was worried, irritated, or just plain angry, his gray-blue eyes became intensely hardened.

"Collier told you I was going to Egypt?" he asked, surprised and angry.

"He thought you were," she said casually. "I told him that of course you'd tell me right away if the company had plans to send you there." She saw a slight flicker in the depths of his eyes. He knew what she was trying to do.

"And just who provided him with this information?" he asked, expressionless.

"Mort didn't explain his source."

"Collier's going to explain what this is all about." He was emphatic as he walked over to the telephone.

"Garret—perhaps we shouldn't make so much of it. Mort hears so many bits of gossip."

"Maybe. I'd still like to know who is so interested in speculating on my itinerary that it becomes strategic information for Collier to plan your agenda at *Horizon*."

Strategic? She was nervous now that the incident might become a matter of contention. "But darling," she soothed, "the talk was wrong. Just gossip."

"That doesn't matter. What does matter is that someone finds my comings and goings of sufficient interest to keep tabs on them."

"But—but why should that be?"

"That's what I'm going to find out," he said grimly. "I intend to know why and who."

"You're not thinking it has anything to do with the war?" she asked in a low voice, frightened.

He gave her a speculative glance. "What makes you say that?"

She glanced down at the newspaper spread out on the table. She shrugged. "Oh—I don't know. The headlines, I suppose. So dark, and worrisome."

He didn't see her shiver, but seemed to sense it, because his arm drew her to his side. "Don't worry, sweetheart. Most likely it has to do with the antiquities I'm buying and selling," his voice was calm again, even a shade indifferent. "The competition is intense." He smiled. "But I'll get this straightened out."

She had no doubt. She wondered, though, if it really were the competition that was the main reason for his concern. She was irritated with herself now for not inquiring from Mort about who was behind the suggestion that Garret was going to Egypt.

He looked at her, aware of her tension. His gaze had softened and his hand touched her cheek gently, reassuringly. He picked up his empty cup and smiled. "Would you fill this, please?"

She took it, nodding, and went to the teapot. It was cold, so she took it to the kitchen. She half suspected he'd asked for tea just to get her away from the phone.

A few moments later as she moved about the kitchen she heard his voice. Garret's muffled questions were brief, and the long periods between told her that Mort must be giving thorough answers. She hoped so. She would hate to see trouble between her husband and her boss.

Five minutes later she returned to the sitting room carrying a steaming cup of tea. Garret was hanging up the receiver. At first glance, she couldn't tell how things had gone.

"Is everything cleared up?" she handed him the cup.

He looked thoughtful. "It's curious. Collier insisted it was your uncle who told him I was going to Egypt."

She was totally surprised. "Gilly? Why would he think that?" Suddenly, a thought crossed her mind. "That reminds me—" she looked thoughtfully toward the mail on the desk.

"Of what?" he asked, following her glance.

"Well—Gilly. He called me at work during lunch today, but I was out looking at the apartment on the Strand. He left me a message asking that I call him Monday."

He set his cup down untouched. "Did he? Rather odd, considering."

"Considering what?"

"Considering that he hasn't shown much interest in you and your new husband all the time we've been married."

It had disturbed her as well, but she shrugged it off. "You know that's just the way Gilly is. He's consumed with his collection."

"Collier doesn't know why Gilly thought I'd be going to Cairo on research. He mentioned it in passing to Collier when they met by chance at the doctor's office. It seems they both go to the same one."

"I didn't know that. I hope there's nothing wrong with Uncle Gilly. He's not that old, really. He was a very young man in the Great War."

"Yes. So, now we have it. Apparently," he suggested, "Collier claims his basis for sending you to cover Farouk was that he thought I was going there. Now he knows differently. So the matter is settled." He smiled becomingly. "Right, darling?"

"I suppose so," she agreed reluctantly.

"Suppose so? You're still wanting to go?"

She looked at him. "I suppose not, that is, not if you're not going."

"I told you I have no such plans."

She turned away, intertwining her fingers. "Garret— there's something else I should mention to you. Not that I believe it for a second, but it's important to get it out in the open." She turned swiftly, her eyes searching his. "I don't want any further misunderstandings between us."

He was serious once again. "Nor do I. What is it, Paulette? What's bothering you? Something Quinn might have said about Cairo?"

So he guessed. How long had he suspected? "Yes, I'm afraid it is. When Quinn mentioned seeing you with the British ambassador, you said he was mistaken."

"Why should that upset you?" he asked quietly.

Her heart sank. He was going to be evasive. "It didn't upset me. Not then." Her last words were so quiet she wondered if he'd even heard them.

He turned her about to face him. His expression defied analysis.

"Not then? But now."

"I don't know," she admitted her confusion. "After you left, Quinn said he'd been wrong."

"I'm surprised he'd ever admit being wrong about anything."

"He said it wasn't the British, but the German embassy where he saw you."

Garret stared at her.

Her eyes implored his. "If you were there, darling, I'm quite sure it doesn't mean a thing. Not even Quinn meant to insinuate...or suggest..."

His gaze was chilling. "Do go on, Paulette. Tell me what Quinn did not mean to suggest."

Dismayed by the unhappiness growing between them over a lack of trust, she kept silent. She should have known the subject would set him on edge, especially by bringing Quinn into it.

"Let me suggest it for you. Quinn didn't mean to imply he thought I was a secret Nazi."

Now that the unspeakable was out, stark and ugly, she couldn't bear it and turned away angrily. "That's not what I meant and you know it."

"And Quinn? That's not what he meant either?" She walked away, feeling pained by the brutal discussion. What had Quinn meant to suggest? Perhaps nothing, except that when Garret denied having been in Cairo it had made Quinn more thoughtful, even curious, until he had remembered where he'd really seen him. At the German embassy.

She turned. "Would he, in front of everyone, have mentioned seeing you if he had not thought so?"

"Shall I tell you what he meant to do?"

"How can you know?"

"I know," was his brief and chilling reply. "Why do you think he charged up to me the way he did? It was an attempt to throw me off guard, to force a recognition. It's an old tactic."

What old tactic? Why was it that things he said sometimes made no sense to her? She tried to remember just what Quinn had said and done on that night when he entered the Nickersons' flat. Yes, he'd strode straight up to Garrett. She recalled that Quinn had startled her by his abrupt action, but that was Quinn. Gregarious, friendly to strangers. It helped him get good stories as people loosened up.

"That's just the way he is," she explained.

"All right, Paulette, have it your way. I don't intend to spend the rest of the evening discussing your old boyfriend."

"That's very unfair, Garret. There's never been anything serious between me and Quinn. We're friends, colleagues. We share a common interest in writing."

"Forget it. We'll drop the subject. If you have any more questions, ask your colleagues."

It was one of the few times he had ever been abrupt with her, and it especially hurt because he was usually so gentle with her feelings.

He walked up to her. "You want to know if I was at the German embassy?"

"No—Garret, please don't say anything yet, because I wouldn't want you to deny it and then—"

"Find out that I wasn't being completely truthful? I didn't realize you believed I was in the habit of lying to you."

"Lying is a strong word. I didn't use it, you did." Her voice shook.

"Isn't that what you meant?"

"No, that's *not* what I meant."

"Why don't you come out and ask me? Are you afraid I'll fail the test?"

That was exactly what she feared, and now that he'd brought it into the open, she was ashamed. How could she have doubted him? Quinn…Quinn was wrong.

"Well?" Garret challenged calmly.

"Very well. You told Quinn that you'd never visited Egypt."

"No, I was more specific. I said I'd never visited Ambassador Hastings in Alexandria." He added quietly as if speaking to himself: "He never saw me at the German embassy, nor with the British ambassador…why did he push it?"

"Then you have been to Egypt," she stated, her voice losing its energy.

He looked at her, and a slight frown appeared. "Yes. I have friends in Cairo," he admitted.

"You misled him—"

"It's none of his business."

"Is it none of mine also?"

"If I thought that, I wouldn't be telling you now, would I?"

"You're only admitting it to me because you're cornered."

"My dear, you will never corner me."

She angrily walked to the window and stared at the walls of the dark buildings in the bleak, narrow alleyway. She was on the brink of runaway emotions, tempted to sway first one way, then the other. She must believe her husband. If not, how could their relationship grow? How could it last, with suspicion between them? Trust was an absolute necessity for spiritual, mental, even physical intimacy. Yet she was frustrated with him and angry. He was keeping things from her, but why? It couldn't just be her imagination.

So he had been to Egypt. He had friends in Cairo. Yet, he had told the truth. He had never visited Ambassador Hastings in Alexandria.

"Then Quinn was mistaken," she heard herself saying firmly. Her eyes followed him as he walked over to the chair, took off his sweater, and put his jacket on again. The sight jarred a memory. With a pang she remembered what she'd found in the pocket of the jacket she'd taken to the cleaners. "Unless—"

"Unless what?" he probed gently.

She turned, her face grave. "Unless he made a mistake, and the embassy he claims he saw you at wasn't in Alexandria or Cairo."

His gaze sharpened even as his voice remained quiet. "Meaning?"

She drew in a breath. "An embassy in Berlin," she managed.

The silence descended like a shroud. Paulette felt the blood drain from her face when he stared at her across the little room. For a timeless moment nothing moved except the flutter of her nervous heart. *I was a fool to let him know I found out*, she thought.

The clock ticked noisily as he stood there deep in thought, frowning to himself. The look of concern startled her, threw her off guard. She didn't know what to make of it. Then his gaze narrowed as he took her in. "How did you find out?" his voice was steady.

As Paulette faced him, she felt some of the same icy roadblock she had experienced the very first time she met him. Her heart sank. It was true about Berlin.

He walked up and looked at her as if wanting to see into her eyes to the bottom of her soul.

"How did you find out?" he repeated in a calm but determined voice.

"Because..." she didn't know quite how to suggest it, and so she began much earlier. "You went to Berlin not long before we were married, but you told me it was Spain."

He considered her. His brows lifted thoughtfully. "What makes you think so?"

"Are you saying you didn't?"

"No. Darling, I told you the truth. I did go to Spain. To Malaga."

"And Berlin also."

"Yes, Berlin also," he stated firmly.

She had come across the name of a Berlin hotel on a receipt in his jacket, along with a book of matches from a hotel in Cairo. Business, he had said when she inquired as to why he had left London. Urgent business in Spain, was the way he had put it, for the company he worked for in New York.

Garret took hold of her shoulder and turned her abruptly toward the light of the lamp so he could see her face.

"If I thought you—" he stopped, his lashes narrowing, his fingers tightening on her shoulders. "No. I can't conceive of you in that fashion."

In what fashion? Snooping? What did he suspect about her?

His fingers sent a shiver along her skin. "Who told you I went to Berlin?" he demanded in a soft voice, all the more devastating because there was no anger in it, no emotion at all except avid determination to know.

Something told her that if she showed fear now, he would never believe her. Why she should think this, she couldn't say, but somehow she knew she must not shrink in confusion and fear. *This is my husband*, she kept telling herself. *I love him. I don't care who he is, or what he's done, I love him.*

She met his gaze head on without flinching. "No one told me, least of all Quinn, if that's what concerns you. And I've said nothing to him about it, or anyone else. And...I don't intend to. Garret—I don't like you to hold me this way."

He immediately released her, as though he'd just realized what he was doing.

"I'm sorry." He reached out and ran his fingers softly against her face, and smiled a little. Her eyes wavered. The moment was painful.

"Paulette," he said with genuine anxiety. In a moment he'd brought her close against him, holding her tenderly as he kissed her hair. "I love you. Trust me," he whispered.

She held him tightly in return. "Oh, darling, I love you, too." She wanted to trust him, desperately. "I didn't mean to upset you. I didn't intend to ruin this evening."

"You haven't ruined anything, Paulette." He was emphatic, as though he were persuading himself as well as her.

She stared at him, desperate now to hold things together so their disparity didn't widen.

"Even if you went to Berlin," she whispered, "I don't care. There's no reason why you need to keep it from me. After all, you're not British. America isn't at war with Nazi Germany. And you once told me you had relatives there. Why shouldn't you visit while you can still get in as an American?"

He smiled faintly, as though he knew what she was trying to undo, but her attempt did little to heal the damage. "Did Gilly say anything about Berlin to you? That I have family living there?"

The mention of Gilly utterly bewildered her. "My uncle? No. Why should he? How would he know?"

He didn't choose to answer that. So she stumbled on, trying to make sense of it. "Gilly doesn't think about much else except his work, it's so demanding. He's busy writing his memoirs of the Great War in Egypt, including some archaeology he was involved in at Aleppo. I suspect he won't finish that huge old book for another twenty years. He's been working on it for at least eight."

He cupped her chin, continuing to study her face as she spoke, as if he too were trying to make sense of what she was saying, as though he wondered if she knew more than she was admitting.

"Then if it wasn't Gilly, who told you about Berlin?"

Now that the conflict was unearthed, she wasn't anxious to pursue it, yet she must, in order to get it behind them.

"I discovered it by accident."

"Discovered what?"

"A receipt," she said in a small voice.

"A receipt?" his head tilted.

"Yes. I took your jacket to the cleaners this morning. The one you'd left in Neuchâtel at the outdoor cafe."

She saw his mind working, remembering.

"Yes, go on."

"I checked the pockets first...and, well, I found a book of matches from a Cairo hotel and a receipt from a hotel in Berlin. There was a date on the receipt, of course. And your signature. You had written a number on the matchbook. I assume it's a phone number. And someone's name."

He came sharply alert, though his voice hadn't changed and he remained in complete control of himself.

"What name?"

"Ambassador Kruger."

A formidable reserve came down over his face. She had expected the revelation to fully upset him, and now, suddenly, his calmness surprised her. She could see nothing in his face except puzzlement.

"Impossible." His voice was quiet, thoughtful.

She didn't think he was speaking to her but himself. "What?"

His eyes came to hers. "I'd never put anything in writing. Do you still have them?"

Why wouldn't he put the name and telephone number—if it was that—into writing? "The matchbook and receipt?"

"Yes, darling. Where are they?"

Paulette was embarrassed to admit that she had them put away, as though her action said she thought they were important evidence. Evidence for what?

"I thought you might need them again, so I didn't want them to get misplaced. I—" she stopped making excuses for hiding them. "I'll go get them." Without another word she walked into their bedroom to her small bureau and opened the top drawer. Her fingers trembled.

Garret followed. He stood in the doorway with his back to the light and watched as she removed a red silk scarf and retrieved the book of matches and the hotel receipt. A feeling of betrayal weighed heavily on her shoulders. It was embarrassing to admit by her actions that she had questioned him. *But he had said Spain*, she thought in self-defense, *and now it looks as if he spent most of his time in Berlin. And what about Cairo?*

"Here they are," she said in a tone as light as she could manage.

He smiled. "Maybe I should take heart after all. You hid them, believing that in some way they incriminated me.

That must mean you're willing to keep this a matrimonial secret."

Paulette found the remark troubling. It sounded as if he were saying that he could count on her covering for him if necessary.

She watched his face as he turned the book of matches over and over again between his fingers, thoughtfully.

"The matchbook isn't mine."

Not his? But!

"Don't look defensive, darling," he said. "I'm not accusing you. There's no doubt you found these in my jacket pocket?"

"No. Absolutely." Her brows puckered. "They aren't yours?"

"No."

"Then how did they get there?"

He didn't answer. He leaned his shoulder in the doorway, staring at them, a deep frown on his face. "Did you find them in the inside flap, or the outer pocket?"

She took a moment to think, to make sure she got it right. "The outside, yes, I'm certain. There is no inside pocket."

"There is," he commented. And he opened one side of his jacket and showed her a pocket that would have gone unnoticed to most anyone who gave it a casual look. "I always have them special made this way. With all the traveling I do, it offers more security. All my jackets have a pocket like this one."

She had never noticed before. She went to another jacket in the closet and found it just as he said. She looked at him, wondering. Not his matchbook...

"It's your writing," she pondered. "I recognize it."

He looked at the matchbook again. "I admit it's close, but it's not mine. I don't make my K's connected to the r in 'Kruger.'"

She went to stand beside him and looked again at the handwriting.

"If this was mine, I'd have placed it in the inner pocket. Anyway, I'd never write someone's name on a matchbook cover or anywhere else. Not someone important."

She looked up at him, troubled. "Then how did it get in your jacket, and why?"

"Hmm...I wonder."

She read the thoughtful curiosity behind his words.

"There's a simple explanation," he said. "I must have picked up those matches by mistake at the hotel in Neuchâtel, or at a table in one of the cafés where we dined. Then I must have dropped them in my pocket without giving it much thought."

Was he deliberately understating the scenario?

"And the name of the ambassador," she protested, "and the telephone number?"

"I agree it's odd. But there's no reason why someone couldn't have known the German ambassador or intended to get in touch with him, most likely concerning problems about getting relatives out of Germany."

Even if she could accept that, there remained the hotel receipt. "The receipt is dated."

"Yes." He snapped a finger against it. "I stayed there a few months ago. I told you I had family in Berlin. At any rate, it doesn't matter. I'm sorry I made so much of it."

Didn't matter! What troubled her more than the book of matches and his earlier concerns was the fact that she didn't know as much about the real Garret Brandt as she thought she had. She had, so it seemed, married a stranger. He wasn't a man to lose control easily. His steadiness and yes, sometimes his overconfidence, were masculine traits that had drawn her to him. He'd been right when he said that Uncle Gilly had been a poor father figure. No, Garret didn't worry quickly. And yet, mentioning his visit to Berlin had at first surprised and distressed him.

Even though he was now shrugging off the whole thing as though it were of little consequence, she wasn't convinced. His quick appraising glance seemed to guess her feelings. He said gently, "Don't worry about it anymore. I didn't mean to barrage you with questions. I did go there. To see someone in my family who was ill. I didn't mention it because we weren't married then and I saw no need to involve you. I also told you the truth when I said I went to Spain."

"And Quinn?" she asked, bringing the subject back to where it began.

"If Quinn was in Germany," he said coldly, "maybe he's the one who needs to answer some questions. As for Egypt, I doubt if he was even there the night he claims to have seen me in Alexandria."

"Then why did he say so? What's to be gained by it?"

"I don't know. Perhaps he was trying to discover something."

"Discover what?" she persisted.

"Obviously, darling, something he didn't have the answer to, but believed I did. Since he's not in London, I can't ask him."

She believed Garret was wishing Quinn was indeed in London, and that he might deal with him.

"What did you mean by the term, 'old tactic'?"

He smiled suddenly. "Sweetheart, let's forget all this, shall we? The way things are going now, we may both be a bit overimaginative." He pulled her into his arms and kissed her briefly but firmly.

Although the kiss was distracting, she refused to become muddled. "If Quinn sensed a story connected with you, and was bluffing when he said he'd seen you at the German embassy, what did he possibly think he could uncover?"

"You're weaving a plot much too involved, Paulette. And I, for one, am getting hungry." He glanced at his watch.

But Quinn's bluff didn't work, she was thinking, *because Garret wasn't intimidated by his bold confrontation.* Yes, knowing Quinn as she did, it was like him to pull some gimmick to try to open a locked door.

She followed Garret as he walked into the sitting room, picked up his tie, and began to put it on again.

Another thought crossed her mind, an unpleasant one. What if Quinn had reason to think her husband was a Nazi sympathizer? Was that his story? No, because if he did think so, Quinn might despise Garret for it, but it wasn't a big enough story to garner a top spot in the *Times*. Garret was a private citizen, an American, someone working for a company buying antiques for museums and wealthy individuals. That was not what Quinn would consider a controversial story.

Ambassador Kruger. Where have I heard that name before? In the papers? The BBC? I don't remember. But it will come to me yet, probably when I least expect it. Kruger. She filed it in the back of her mind. She would think about it later. Much later.

We've survived our first serious conflict, she thought, *and we still love each other.* With a sigh of relief she watched him, happy that things seemed to have adjusted back to normal.

He appeared relaxed again. The entire conflict between them might never have happened. The explosion had settled. Surprisingly, there was very little rubble left. It didn't appear to matter to him that a question mark still remained over the matchbook and hotel receipt. She didn't think he had accidentally picked up the matches in Paris, but she must also leave room for the idea that it was possible.

Garret wasn't explaining everything to her, that much was clear. He was keeping a secret of sorts, but she would give him that right. Everyone, even husbands and wives, were entitled to some personal privacy, and as he said, it had taken place before their marriage.

She could see his thoughtfulness as he stood looking again at the matches, then gazing out the open window. Unless—was it possible that he really didn't know how the matchbook ended up in his jacket pocket? That was even more frightening, because it introduced a new entity. She shivered. Someone, a third person, had deliberately put it there.

Garret hadn't even looked her way, but as if reading her mind he said, "You must be cold," and closed the window. He surprised her by saying suddenly, "How would you like to move into that apartment on the Strand?"

Her worries sprouted wings and flew away.

"Oh, darling, that would be delightful!" Her conscience also sprouted to life. "But the area is so beastly expensive. I'd feel as if I'd nagged you into it. Like one of those miserable women who are rarely satisfied with anything their husbands provide."

He smiled. "You haven't nagged. Don't feel that way. I never intended we should stay here permanently. I'm getting claustrophobia."

She knew that wasn't the reason. He hadn't complained at all. He had made a joke out of their tiny two-room flat with its view of the alley.

"Anyway, I'm not as selfless in my suggestion as you may think," he said. "That particular apartment has the perfect room in back for an office."

"Telegraph wires and all?"

"And all."

"Well, if you put it that way." She smiled brightly and hugged him. "I'll call the landlord first thing tomorrow. Darling! You've made an awful mess with your tie again."

"Yes, I have, haven't I? I can't seem to get the ruddy thing right."

She was amused. Garret could handle almost anything, but he was an absolute case of all-thumbs when it came to his tie. She had watched his frustration every morning as he wrestled with it. She couldn't resist teasing: "I can't believe that a suave gentlemen such as yourself, who travels all over Europe and America, can't tie his own tie."

"Be a darling and fix it."

"It's really very simple," she taunted.

He placed his arms around her waist and drew her close, his eyes twinkling.

"You place this long piece of your tie here—like this. And this shorter end here, like so. You do this with it, then that, and presto! A perfect knot." She patted the silk tie into place against his chest, smiling as he watched her.

"I'll remember."

She laughed. "No, you won't. Face it, darling, I can do something easily that you can't. Isn't it maddening?"

"Very." But he didn't look maddened at all.

"What did you do before you had me to fix it? Did you go to Gloria?" It was the first time she'd mentioned Gloria Haskins in months.

"I wore a bow tie."

She laughed again. "Somehow I can't see you in a pretty bow tie."

To her surprise he lifted her off her feet and held her above him, laughing at her.

"Put me down."

He did, kissing her for a long moment.

"Are you sure you want to go out for dinner?" he murmured.

"After you've spent five minutes struggling with your tie?" she breathed.

He smiled and helped her into her coat. "Wear that little hat with the provocative feather."

She smiled and went into the bedroom to put it on, making certain her long hair was brushed back behind her ears and lying smoothly down her back the way he liked it. She also added the diamond earrings he'd bought her and a splash of perfume.

"All set," she told him, coming back into the living room. He hung up the telephone. She assumed he'd been calling a taxi.

He smiled and opened the door for her, making certain it was locked before following her down the stairs and into the glassed-in lobby.

9

Paulette held the telephone to her ear, hearing it ringing as she poured coffee into her cup. Garret had already left the flat before she'd awakened. She scarcely remembered his kiss on her bare shoulders before he'd covered her and left for an early Monday morning meeting with someone flying in from the New York office.

"Good morning, Uncle Gilly."

"Ah, Paulette dear."

"Garret and I got your message to give you a call." She included Garret's name to casually remind her uncle that she was now married, for his memory lagged sometimes where she was concerned. She had invited him to the wedding, but he'd missed attending due to a seasonal cold, or so he had said.

"I've been terribly remiss in my family duties concerning your marriage," he said, surprising her with his clarity.

It had never been Paulette's purpose to pressure her uncle into accepting either her or Garret, but she was relieved that he did remember and apparently had finally decided on meeting her husband. She felt a level of new anticipation, but warned herself against any false expectations. So she said, making a suitable excuse for his indifference, "We didn't want to impose on you, Uncle Gilly. I've explained to Garret how extremely busy you are with museum work."

"It's high time I've welcomed your husband into the family. I must say, I'm rather surprised he hasn't been in touch with me, considering."

She was caught off guard. There was a faint yet marked baiting quality to the tone of his voice that worried her. She managed casually, "Oh? Considering what, Uncle Gilly?"

"My dear, that's part of the reason I'm calling, but it will need a face-to-face meeting between you and me before I can sufficiently explain. Then, there's another matter, because I want you to have a certain lamp from the Jerablus digs near Baghdad as a belated wedding present."

Paulette didn't know what to make of his words.

"Since I'm planning on donating prized pieces of my collection to the Cairo museum, I think you should know what I'll be leaving you in my will, just in case."

Paulette hadn't expected an inheritance from Gilly, but it was his words "just in case" that caught her attention. Her fingers tightened around the phone. "Uncle, is something wrong?"

"Nothing is wrong. Nothing at all," but his voice denoted apprehension, convincing her otherwise. "Can you come here to the estate?"

"Yes, of course, I'll—we'll come. I'm meeting Garret for lunch. I'll explain your invitation to him then."

"No! First, I want to see you alone. This afternoon." His voice became composed. "Tomorrow is time enough to welcome Garret into the family." The tension remained in his voice even though she could tell he was trying to sound otherwise.

"Around eight o'clock this evening, then?"

"No, no, no! Four o'clock this afternoon. Tomorrow you may come at eight. I'm giving you a dinner party, my dear. A party, you understand? You and Garret are to be the guests of honor. I've invited Mort Collier as well. And a few old friends of mine from my days in Egypt. We're going to toast your marriage to Mr. Brandt." He chuckled again.

Gilly's behavior was not just odd, it was foreboding. In one breath he sounded tense, even—afraid? In the next, he chuckled nervously, reminding her of a schoolboy planning a prank.

"I realize my notice is rather short, but since all you need do is bring yourselves in your best finery, I don't see that there should be any trouble. May I count on your coming?"

"Yes. I—we would be delighted. Garret has been anxious to see your Egyptian collection since before we were married."

"Now he shall have his opportunity. The evening's outcome, I'm sure, will offer him more surprises than he could possibly imagine."

"He'll be so pleased," she repeated again, almost absently, wondering.

"Splendid. Dinner tomorrow, then. This afternoon, just you and me. And Paulette—it is *quite* important that you say nothing of this afternoon's meeting to Garret."

"I'd rather not keep secrets from my husband, Uncle."

"It's unfortunate that he doesn't feel the same way. I shall expect you at four o'clock, alone." He hung up.

Paulette was frowning as she slowly replaced the receiver.

The morning work at *Horizon* dragged by slowly. At last the twelve o'clock lunch break arrived. Paulette left the building and walked the block to the café where she and Garret often met for lunch. He was already waiting at a booth when she arrived. He smiled and stood to help her remove her coat. She slid into the booth, sitting across from him. "Did I keep you waiting long?" She took the menu he handed her.

"Only a little." He gave her a careful glance. "What is it? Pressure at work?" Reaching across the table he took her hand.

She laughed, trying to hide her uneasiness. "Am I that readable?" She set the menu down. "I called Gilly this morning."

The gray-blue eyes flickered slightly. "What's on his mind?"

"A dinner party in our honor tomorrow night. Even Mort's been invited. Isn't that surprising? He says he has a wedding present for us. A lamp."

Garret took the news thoughtfully, saying little at first. Paulette noticed that, although he stared at the lunch menu, it wasn't the choice of food that held him. His thoughts were on something far removed, because when the waitress asked if he wanted soup with the day's special, a hot roast beef sandwich, he said "Yes, that would be fine." Paulette knew he disliked soup. "Too messy to eat," he always said, "splashes on my tie."

"Have you decided?" the waitress asked.

Paulette smiled. "I'll take his soup."

The waitress noted the order, gathered their menus, and hurried away.

After a bit, Paulette said, "He's also invited some friends he knew when living in Egypt."

He looked at her quickly. "He told you that?"

"Yes. Since they don't know us, I can't see why they'd have any interest in toasting our marriage. Can you?"

"No. Sounds like a curious dinner party." He turned the subject abruptly. "What did he say about a lamp he wants you to have?"

"He said it was a very unique lamp discovered at an archaeological dig near Jerablus."

His gaze sharpened with interest, but his voice contradicted, sounding casual, even indifferent. "Jerablus? The digs out there have been off-limits to antique buyers for years. Did he say how he came across it?"

"No." She smiled. "I assume legally. I've no idea where Jerablus is, but I believe Aunt Opal once mentioned it when she talked about Egypt." She thought back to something her aunt had said: *Egypt—a horrid place, my child. Flies, flies, and more of the same. Heat. Dust. And the Egyptian men have little regard for women except to bear their children—all sons. If you went there alone they'd think you were coming to seek an affair with one of them.*

Garret was watching her closely. "I didn't know she knew anything about Gilly's past life in Egypt. You told me she hadn't been able to give you much information on your family."

"My parents, no. But I know they weren't from Egypt like Uncle Gilly. They lived here in London. Opal didn't say much about Gilly, either. Just that he had traveled through all that area during the Great War. Jerablus was somewhere between Baghdad and Aleppo—which doesn't tell me much. It's in the Egyptian desert, isn't it?"

"More like Arabia." He altered the conversation. "At one time there was a large Kurdish population living around Jerablus and Baghdad. But after the war the Allies decided they had the right to divide that territory. Believing they owed something to the Arabs who cooperated with Lawrence of Arabia, they ignored the rights of the Kurdish people and divided the land, creating several new Arab nations. That's when Saudi Arabia and Iraq were born. The Kurds got next to nothing except persecution from the Iraqis and the people of Turkey."

"I do remember something about the Kurds. That area was once called Kurdistan, wasn't it?"

His gaze complimented her knowledge. "I see you've done some homework. The digs near Jerablus and the area of Kut are very interesting. They think they've located the Tower of Babel near the Euphrates River."

"The tower mentioned in Genesis?"

"Yes. The first attempt at a 'global' religion and government. They've also located the city of Abram, Ur of the Chaldees. It had quite a civilization during Abram's time. Abram and Sarai may well have had a bathtub in their home."

She looked at him quickly. "You've been there? To Jerablus? And the Euphrates River?"

There was a short pause before his hand reached for the mug of coffee the waitress had poured him. "Once. A very long time ago," came the neutral tone. "I'd be curious to know how Gilly acquired that lamp. He gave you no hints at all?"

"Well, no, but he is donating a number of other pieces of his collection to the Cairo museum."

"He told you that this morning?"

"Yes. I would have expected him to sell them to individual clients represented by Kimball, Baylor, and Lammiter," she said with a smile.

She had expected him to smile as well, since he had suggested at the mountain lodge when they first met that his sole interest in Gilly was due to his work and interest in Egyptology. She was surprised by a momentary flicker of anger in his eyes. Yet she was sure that anger was not directed at either her or her light comment.

"He may have no choice except to donate to the museum," he said. Before she could ask why he thought so, the waitress brought their lunch, setting the soup in front of Paulette and the hot sandwich before Garret. "You've a telephone call, Mr. Brandt." She pointed behind the crowded counter to where a man in a white shirt held up the telephone receiver. "You can take it back there."

"I'm sorry," he said to Paulette. "Start without me, before your soup gets cold."

Paulette was still debating whether to tell him about meeting Gilly alone that afternoon when Garret returned some five minutes later.

She gave him a doubtful glance, adding oyster crackers to the chicken broth. He was looking at his roast beef sandwich as though trying to memorize its shape. She smiled. "Anything wrong with the sandwich?"

"Hmm? Oh. No."

"Who was the call from, darling?"

He looked at his watch. "It was Henley. The man who flew in from New York. I need to meet a plane at seven tonight. Someone important to the company is arriving from Switzerland. Henley wants to meet with him right away. He wants me there, too. I'm afraid I won't be home until late."

For the first time she didn't mind all that much. It would mean she wouldn't need to rush to get back from Uncle Gilly's before Garret arrived for dinner. She felt a little guilty and looked down at her soup.

She remembered that Garret was anxious to move into their new apartment on the Strand so he could set up the communications in his office. "Is the meeting about Kimball and 'friends' opening a new office in Geneva?"

"Yes. The man who'll be arriving tonight is somewhat of an expert."

She noticed that his mood had changed. "You look very sober," she said. "I thought the new office in Geneva was a cause for celebration. More clients and all that."

"Yes, sure it is." He smiled encouragingly at her, but even so, it seemed to Paulette that the deeper look in his eyes was one of concern.

The rest of the afternoon crept by slowly for Paulette, and she found it difficult to concentrate on the work piled on her desk. She had decided not to mention to Garret her four o'clock visit to Gilly, and her conscience smarted. It smacked too keenly of a clandestine meeting. The haunting question of whether or not she completely trusted her own husband was a depressing one that remained unanswered. She must find out what Gilly wanted to discuss with her alone, without the bold silhouette of Garret Brandt standing in the wing. She found his presence comforting and exciting. Evidently Gilly found it otherwise.

≈≈≈

Uncle Gilly lived alone in an oversized Georgian mansion outside London on a large secluded piece of wooded property, surrounding himself with his ancient Egyptian artifacts and an Egyptian butler who also served as his secretary. Opal once told her that Gilly had been wounded in the fighting at the Baghdad Railroad, constructed and paid for by Kaiser Wilhelm. It had taken years before Gilly was able to walk again. When he finally recuperated at a military hospital in Cairo, he came straight to London, bought the estate with a fortune left to him by his father, and shut himself into his private interests. The young sweetheart of his war years in Egypt had married his rival and also lived in London with their daughter. Opal had thought that Gilly had come to England with the singular motive of seeing her again, and even luring her away from her husband. But the young woman's Christian morals and dedication to her husband had kept her from committing such an adulterous deed.

"My opinion," Opal had told her, when Paulette was sixteen, "is that the young woman was much too good for him."

"Who was she, do you know her name?"

"No, dear. I never heard it."

Paulette arrived by taxi precisely at four o'clock. Black crows were cawing loudly in the tall fir trees that lined the curving driveway. She covered her ears and went up the walk to a wide entrance of brick steps and a thick oak door. She rang the chime.

How can he bear all those crows shrieking from early dawn until sunset? she thought. *Maybe it keeps him from thinking of the past.*

The door opened and Hamor the Egyptian, garbed as she remembered him, in a turban and long white tunic over tightly wound leggings, spread his hand and stepped aside, bowing her indoors.

"Hello, Hamor. I hope I haven't kept my uncle waiting."

Hamor bowed his head, a ghost of a smile on his wide lips. He silently shut the door, took her hat and coat, and after dispensing them in a closet, disappeared into another room, the sound of his sandals lost on the thick oriental carpet.

To Paulette, the dimly lit house met her with ominous silence. She attributed this to her own uneasy mood. *Hamor has the air of a respectable undertaker,* she thought, and looked around the large hall furnished with high dark chests and dim tapestries in expensive heirloom style. Quite an estate. Gilly's father must have left him a huge fortune when he passed on. Just what did she know about his father? Not a thing. Neither had Opal.

Hamor reappeared and silently beckoned her into the next room. She smoothed her hair and tried to find a smile as she went to greet her uncle.

Gilbert Simington wore a wine-colored silk smoking jacket with impeccable black trousers that were strictly Saville Row in cost and class. He'd been seated in a leather chair near one side of a giant fireplace, and stood to greet her as Hamor showed her in. A matching chair was drawn up opposite her uncle's, and a silver tea service sat on a tray next to it beside a plate of traditional English crumpets.

"Hello, Uncle," she hurried toward him, trying again for a warm, easy smile that would conceal her tension.

Gilly must have been quite a handsome man twenty years ago. His dark eyes and what had once been very black hair gave him an air of mystery and rakishness. He was tall and slim and carried an arrogance that might have made him insufferable had he been young again. Although in his mid-forties, he gave the impression of being much older. He wore a large silver ring on his right finger with a big blue sapphire that would have been gaudy in any other surrounding. But the room's furnishings and the cut of his clothes gave him an air that upheld his bearing.

"Paulette, dear girl." He played the affectionate uncle, lightly kissing her cheek. "Have a seat. The tea is about ready. Would you do the pleasure of serving? The rheumatism is acting up in my wrist, and Hamor is deserting us to spend the night with his cousin."

"Of course. It will be my pleasure." She sat down opposite him and picked up the teapot.

"I'll get right to the point," he continued after she'd handed him a cup of tea. "Your decision to marry Garret

Brandt was quite a shock to me. I knew members of his family in Egypt during the last war."

"Members of his family—in Egypt?" she nearly spilled her tea.

"They're no longer there. Most of them now live in Berlin. Devoted underlings of Adolf Hitler no doubt, even as they slavishly followed Kaiser Wilhelm in the first war. Please don't become upset! I'm in no way suggesting your husband follows the ideology of his relatives in Berlin. If I thought so, I'd never have hired him to represent my collection. And I certainly wouldn't have sent him to meet you and discuss my will last fall in Neuchâtel."

Paulette's breath caught audibly and her eyes were wide.

"I was afraid this would happen," he murmured with a sigh. "You're upset, poor girl. As well you should be. And as am I. Imagine my surprise when I went into the showroom last night and discovered that a valuable possession was missing."

Paulette emerged from her cocoon of shock, and setting her cup down stood abruptly, the heat of color in her cheeks. "Uncle! Are you daring to suggest that my husband—"

"No, no, no! Do sit down, Paulette. I'm not accusing Garret of the theft. I've made no judgment about him at all. But that doesn't mean you should remain in the dark about how and why you met him at the ski lodge. Do you wish to hear or don't you?"

She was shaking as she slowly sat down. "Are you saying you know Garret? That he was here in this house last night?"

"Yes," he stated unapologetically. "Yes to both questions."

She sat still and rigid, his words echoing in her mind like the noisy, cawing crows she had heard in the fir trees when she arrived.

"That can't be," she said.

"Then he's kept it from you. That doesn't surprise me, really. It wouldn't serve his purpose to inform you at this time. It would be a little embarrassing, wouldn't it? I'm sorry I must be the one to switch on the light. However, I think that in the end, you'll be satisfied that I've taken the time. You see, Paulette, as I mentioned a moment ago, it was I who first contacted Garret in Berlin. Yes, I know he's told you he works in New York. I'm in no way denying that. But it's equally true that he spends half his time in Berlin. I wrote him last year and requested he come to London to see my collection for himself. Make a report on its value, then meet with Kimball, Baylor, and Lammiter. He was also to meet you at the lodge to discuss your future, to learn your preferences in regard to the collection after I pass on. He informed you, didn't he, that I've made you heiress of everything?"

Paulette didn't move. Her heart slammed in her chest so hard she felt breathless.

He leaned forward and opened a silver cigarette box. "Care for a Turkish cigarette, dear? No?"

"You...sent him to the lodge to meet me?"

He took a long moment lighting the cigarette. The lighter, also silver, glimmered in the firelight from the hearth.

"Yes."

Paulette's mind whirled with a hundred questions. *It can't be true*, her heart kept crying out. The revelation was such a shock to her that she was still feeling all this was unreal. The extraordinary coincidence which had allowed them to meet and marry was not a coincidence after all.

Garret had already known she was an heiress, though she had not suspected such a fortune. He had not met her by chance as he had made her think. He'd already met her uncle and seen the famous collection when he'd pretended to need her introduction, which she'd denied him. No wonder he'd behaved strangely at lunch today. He hadn't wanted her to see Gilly at the dinner party tomorrow night, no doubt fearing she would discover his deception. He hadn't been concerned about the telephone call, or the man coming from Switzerland as she had thought, but about his own lies.

Heartsick, she hardly heard what Gilly was telling her. She stared at him blankly, but he must have taken it for rapt attention, for he went on.

"I knew you would be at the lodge with the Nickersons. I believed Garret Brandt would be the most qualified individual to explain the inestimable value of the collection to you, since he's one of the finest experts on Egyptology around. Naturally, I don't expect you to feel the same devotion to it as I. That is why I've more recently decided to turn over most of the items of antiquity to the Cairo museum. That will still leave you with a great fortune, dear Paulette. You'll soon be a millionairess."

Paulette was on the edge of her chair.

"Oh—there is one other matter. It concerns this house. I hope you won't be disappointed that I'm leaving it to the young daughter of an old friend of mine from Cairo." There was a faraway gleam in his eyes. He looked at her, stirring back to the present. "But I've not left you homeless. There is a certain house in Cairo that you may find *quite* interesting." A smile twitched his lip. "Its history will prove of interest to you."

Paulette could only concentrate on one thing. She was an heiress...and Garret had known since before their first meeting at the mountain lodge. That was all that mattered now—that he had known. She was remembering her first meeting with him and then how he had pursued her so intently thereafter. How after a short and deeply romantic courtship, he had insisted he was madly in love with her. He wanted to marry her. Now. There must be no delay. He loved her too much to wait.

And she had fallen for him, for all his devoted words, his fiery kisses. His promise to be true and faithful unto the bitterest death. He had married her without ever telling her that she was an heiress to a fortune, or that he had come from Berlin, or that members of his family were devotees to the Third Reich.

Her eyes came to her uncle's. He watched her sadly.

"Dear, I'm truly sorry. Perhaps I should have kept these facts to myself, but after the piece was missing from my collection last night—I'm afraid I rather panicked. I've no proof he took the royal black cat with the gold eyes, but where else could it have gone? There is no one else in the house except Hamor. And he's been with me for twenty years. At any rate, I didn't think it wise to keep the truth back from you. I only wish you had confided in me about your plans to marry Garret beforehand. Naturally, when I received the invitation I thought you knew everything. I had no idea he'd kept it from you. I found out just a few days ago that he'd been remiss in explaining these important issues to you. And then when the cat disappeared—" he sighed, set his cup down, and crushed the end of his cigarette out in the ashtray.

She sat staring into the pool of black tea in her cup, now lukewarm. Silence surrounded them. After a moment she heard the wood in the fireplace sizzling, turning to ash.

Ashes to ashes—

"He knew...I would be an heiress...all along," she heard her voice repeating, and marveled that it sounded so normal.

"He knew all along, yes. Perhaps he has his reasons for silence. I know I've wondered at his motives, and he has turned up lacking credibility. But enough of that. You are married to him now. From your heartbreak I can see you do love him. In light of that, perhaps I should give him the benefit of the doubt about the cat, as you must decide whether to confront him or lock the door on the past and go on together."

Paulette made no reply. Her emotions had mercifully taken on a numbness that left her somewhat dazed.

"It might be wise to say nothing to Garret about this for the foreseeable future," he suggested. "At least not until you've thought through the far-reaching consequences. The dinner party tomorrow night must go on. It's important he think I've welcomed the marriage."

Paulette sat quietly, unable to resist. Gilly stood and reached down a hand, his face grave. "Come along. I want to show you the lamp."

The lamp was now the last thing of any interest to her. Still, she allowed him to lead her from the drawing room into another section of the great house where the show-room was located.

Gilly was discussing the elaborate security system that was turned on twenty-four hours a day.

"As you can see, it's quite impossible for any outside thief to break in and steal. The only way into this chamber is by punching a code number into this lock system. Even then, I must use a key to unlock the door. And only I have the key. I keep it on my person every hour of every day."

The solid double door opened. She followed him into the showroom, barely noticing the cold of the large chamber. Gilly switched on an expertly arranged lighting system for the best possible effect. Ancient Egypt came to life. Paulette's troubled mind hardly noticed. In a silent daze she allowed him to lead her from one antiquity to another without actually paying attention to what he was saying.

The excitement that should have been hers at learning she was an heiress of a great family fortune was marred by the sickening disappointment that Garret had married her because of it.

And now?

Paulette blinked as a strange sensation of nausea and dizziness washed over her. Her uncle paused with her beside him in front of a large gold cobra, a royal emblem of the ancient pharaohs. He was running his palms over the coiled serpent as though he idolized it. "There are artifacts here that only a museum would be interested in owning and displaying," he said dreamily. "The burial coffin behind you will go to Cairo. So will my cobra."

She tried to focus on its diamond-shaped head glimmering beneath the light. The cobra's ruby eyes set in yellow-brown amber appeared to move and stare hypnotically at her. It was curled as though prepared to strike, and for a dizzy moment her imagination could see the head moving to and fro. The icy chamber came alive with sounds of mummies stirring in their coffins, hissing fabled curses. A shiver inched up her back. She spun around and met the long black almond-shaped eyes of the tall mummy case housing some Egyptian king or nobleman. Paulette heard the voice of her uncle calling her from the darkening distance. She saw his pale face swaying in and out of a gray mist, his eyes wide and his hands clutching at her as she fell.

10

Paulette was stirring to consciousness. Coming fully awake, she heard the clock in the outer hall announce the hour and with her eyes blinking open she counted the chimes. Nine. She was lying on a hard, cold floor, her head aching, her vision still blurred. She felt cold and began to shiver violently. It took several moments before she realized where she was. Her stomach was still nauseous as she attempted a low moan. "Uncle...?" but her voice was hardly audible.

She struggled to raise herself to an elbow, glancing around the room that was full of shadows except where the display lamps shone brightly on individual artifacts.

The golden cobra glimmered, and for a moment it seemed to Paulette that its eyes stared down at her with a fixed, unfriendly gaze. She stared back, her fingers going to her throat.

Don't be silly, she told herself. *It's just an image, it can't hurt you.*

She managed to get up from the floor, holding onto a table until she was certain the dizzy spell wasn't going to come rushing back. *I must be getting ill,* she thought. *Probably the seasonal flu.* She looked around again. Where was Gilly? He must have rushed to the telephone to call Garret. She'd better find Gilly and let him know she was all right.

Then she remembered the chimes on Gilly's heirloom grandfather clock—hadn't she heard nine? Could it possibly be nine o'clock? She lifted her arm and squinted at her wristwatch, but in the shadows she couldn't read the hands. She moved slowly across the showroom toward the light showering down above the cobra. Four minutes after nine! Impossible, but she had been unconscious since a little after four o'clock! Then—Gilly couldn't possibly be on the telephone. Where was he? How could he have left her lying on the floor all this time? Evidently he hadn't called Garret or a doctor.

She froze. Could he too be ill? She became aware of the sound of her heart in her eardrums astonishingly loud in the silent chamber. She cast an uncertain glance around her. A tingle walked up her spine. She listened.

The mansion was deathly silent, and outside the double-barred window not even a breath of night wind stirred the drooping branches of the willow tree. But she was not alone in the room. It wasn't just her imagination, nor suspicion. She sensed that someone was in here, someone in the shadows.

Paulette went rigid even as the blood surged in her temples. Her cold fingers tightened at her bodice as it seemed she had lost the ability to catch her breath. She must call out for Uncle Gilly—

"Uncle!" she managed hoarsely. But there was no answer. An Egyptian mummy stared at her with hard black eyes. She turned away. The cobra's head was upright, ready to strike. The doorway into the dimly lit hall stood wide open, but Gilly was not in sight.

Stay calm, Paulette. It's your imagination, pure and simple— and this mansion, and the silence, and these dreadful Egyptian pieces. There was no one else at the estate except herself and Uncle Gilly. She forced herself to turn and look behind her. There was nothing. She stood there, listening.

The scent of some Egyptian incense that Gilly liked to burn in the room for effect hung on the stillness with a sweetness that caused her stomach to churn. She loathed that smell. Her eyes searched the room again, this time with a discipline of purpose that bore into the shadows of the corners. She saw him, then. Slouched, with a crooked smile on his face, his head to one side.

He must be ill! Could she help? She moved toward him, a hand outstretched. "Uncle…"

No response. A broken teacup lay on the floor beside his polished black shoes, but no liquid had spilled. It seemed bizarre that he would have sat drinking a cup of tea after she had passed out. In fact, it made no sense at all. She searched his face, but there was nothing that suggested the presence of life.

She stepped back, hand at her throat, and turning away rushed blindly from the showroom into the hall toward the drawing room. Gilly was dead. And from the looks of him, he had been that way for hours. Whatever had taken place in that room had happened while she was lying unconscious on the floor. The idea was horrifying.

Between the showroom and the drawing room there was a square ballroom with eighteenth century paintings on the walls of what must have been members of the family who once owned the estate. The unsmiling faces seemed to watch her every move with the uncanny ability that ancient objects seem to possess. Paulette reached the archway that entered the drawing room. The silence was shattered by a familiar voice—

Garret stood at the desk with his back toward her, and he was saying in a calm, emotionless voice: "I want to know how he found out. The question is, did he notify Apollo? Yes, I'm certain. She'll need to be told—No. She thinks I'm at a business meeting. All right. Goodbye." He hung up.

Paulette's heart jerked painfully. Dazed, she stared at him, as if cemented to the floor. He turned and saw her. He looked as surprised as she was. They stared at each other. She was pale and terribly shaken, and her eyes portrayed her sense of shock and betrayal.

"Paulette!"

She whirled and ran blindly into the ballroom.

The next second he was beside her, and his hands were holding her arms so tightly she couldn't break away. "Paulette, wait—"

She cringed and turned her head away even as he held onto her as though by doing so he could wipe from her mind what she had overheard.

"It's not what you think."

"Gilly's dead," she breathed, looking at him suddenly, and with appalling realization. His gray-blue eyes read her suspicion and turned unexpectedly remote and hard.

"Dead? Where?"

Paulette did not speak, but her head turned in the direction of the showroom. He followed her gaze, then looked down at her, frowning. "How long have you been here?"

Then Garret hadn't known she was unconcious?

"Since four o'clock," she managed in a tight whisper as she tried to pull loose, but his fingers tightened.

"Did you touch him?" he asked evenly.

She shook her head no. Still gripping her arm so she couldn't flee, he walked quickly to the showroom, holding her behind him as he entered carefully, as though someone else beside a dead man might be waiting.

"Where?"

She pointed. "He...sat there and drank a cup of tea while I was unconscious on the floor..." and in a strange moment of near hysteria she giggled. Garret looked at her quickly, and intently. "Someone struck you?"

"No...I...I wasn't feeling well and must have fainted when I saw that *thing*."

He followed her glance to the cobra, then looked back at her. "Don't worry about that. Darling, are you all right?"

The very word "darling" had lost its warm intimacy. He had lied to her. How could she welcome his affection now?

"Yes, I'm fine. Are you disappointed?"

His gaze shot to hers. "What do you mean by that?"

"Just what I said. Isn't a husband who is in line for his wife's inheritance supposed to hope something will happen to her?"

His breath caught just perceptibly. She could see his eyes searching hers, then he said flatly: "So he told you he made you his heiress."

"Yes, he told me. And it so happens he told you— months ago."

He started to protest, then stopped. "I didn't marry you because you were to become an heiress. I would have felt the same if you were a penniless orphan."

"This is not the time to be discussing it. Don't you think we'd better call the police?"

"It so happens that nothing is as important to me as our relationship."

She turned her head away. "If you don't call the police, I will," and she turned to leave, but his hold tightened on her arm.

"Just a minute. Sit down. I want to look at him at first."

He watched her for a moment, as though he wanted to say something more, and he touched her hair gently. "Paulette—"

"Not now," she breathed, closing her eyes against his pleading gaze.

His jaw flexed. He dropped her arm and walked over to where the body of her uncle sat in the chair. She watched as he felt for a heartbeat, then looked down at the cup at his feet. "He's been dead for some time." He removed a hand-kerchief and carefully picked up a broken piece. He took a whiff. "Poison," he said. "I recognize the odor. It is used in Egypt."

"Poison?" her voice cracked. "You mean he deliber-ately—?"

"It appears that way." He looked around the room care-fully as though trying to decide whether anything had been taken. He stopped at the sight of an empty display pedestal. "The royal cat is missing. The black one with gold eyes. Did you see it earlier?"

She remembered what Gilly had said. Was Garret trying to establish an alibi that it was missing before Gilly's death? She couldn't bring herself to say anything.

He turned and looked at her, intently. If he noticed her frozen silence, he let it go, but he looked angry.

"Did you touch anything in here after you found him dead? The cup?"

She shook her head no. He walked to where she leaned with her back to the wall for support. "Come," he said gently. "I'll need to call the police."

In the drawing room Garret led her to the divan facing the fireplace. The fire was only glowing coals now, but some heat was still radiating.

"Darling, I can explain about what you overheard. Trust me, will you?"

She remained dully silent.

"I know what you think, but it isn't true. In time I will be able to explain everything."

Tears wet her eyes, but she steeled her emotions against him. *He's only saying that because he wants to use me to safeguard him against the questioning of the police.* "Please, Garret, I don't want to hear that now."

"Is it so much to ask for your trust? In the end, I'll prove you have every reason."

His tender words asking for her love and faith came dangerously close to melting her resolve, but she refused to meet his gaze and remained unresponsive as he touched her face as lightly as a moth's wing.

"I love you," he whispered. "Don't forget that, ever." He walked over to the telephone. She heard him dialing as she weakly lowered herself onto the divan and waited fearfully for the police to arrive.

Poison...but why would Gilly have taken his own life? There had been no hint. She couldn't believe he would do such a thing without first taking care of what meant more to him than anything else: his Egyptian collection. Not unless he was mentally ill, and he hadn't seemed that way at all.

How long had Garret been here? And why had he come? Had Gilly called him when she passed out? All this, and more, the police would surely wish to know.

A man arrived within minutes of Garret's call, and Paulette had the strange notion that he must have flown.

"This is my wife," he told him in a quiet voice, "Paulette."

Paulette wondered why Garret hadn't completed the introduction, and she found her hand in his. He was a tall, slim, quiet man who seemed quite ordinary, the kind of gentleman that she might have seen a dozen times and yet

not remember. His eyes, however, held that same character-
istic that Garret's possessed: they were cool and disconcertingly observant.

"I understand you passed out, Mrs. Brandt."

She was embarrassed to admit it and felt more comfortable in emphasizing that she thought she was coming
down with a change of season flu. She briefly told them
about what she recalled of the afternoon.

"And when I awoke it was nine o'clock. I remember dis-
tinctly because I heard the clock and counted the chimes."

"Five hours is a very long time to have fainted, Mrs.
Brandt."

She felt her face turning a warm pink, and was relieved
when Garret interrupted: "You say you had a cup of tea
with Gilly before going into the showroom?"

"Why...yes, but you don't think..."

"We should be able to find out quite easily. No one's
been here to carry the tea tray away, have they? You said
Hamor went out as soon as you arrived at four o'clock?"

"Yes, that's right." She was looking with confusion at the
table beside the leather chair she had sat in earlier. There
was no tray, no teapot, no cups!

The unobtrusive man was looking there as well, then at
Garret. "You didn't carry them to the kitchen?"

"Naturally not," Garret said. "Have a look for yourself.
Gilly must have washed them up before he reentered the
showroom with a second cup, the one containing the
poison."

"He wouldn't have done that," she found herself saying.
"He would never take his life without first making certain
his collection was disposed of the way he wished it to be."

They exchanged brief glances, and to her surprise, neither paid the slightest attention to her words.

The man left a few minutes later, and it was only then that Garret called another number. To her bewilderment, it proved to be the police that he called.

"Who was that man?" she asked uneasily, standing.

"Just a man who often works with the police. Sit back down, darling. I believe that unconscious spell of yours was from drugged tea."

"Drugged," she said indignantly. "I don't believe it for an instant. Gilly wouldn't have done such a beastly thing."

"No? The doctor will be here soon, and he'll be the first to tell you that you had a slight bout with poison. That's why you were nauseous and dizzy. I've never known you to be the fainting sort in the months we've been married. Why unexpectedly in the showroom?"

She could have told him why, that the dark news Uncle Gilly had given her had shattered her confidence and pained her heart, but now was not the moment to delve into their personal difficulties.

Policemen and a doctor arrived together and went into the showroom with Garret and shut the door, leaving her resting on the divan. Garret had brought her a freshly brewed cup of coffee before the police arrived, and she now sat sipping it while staring at the coals, but her emotions remained wounded and shivering. Only after what seemed a horrendously long time did they return and question Paulette.

One was seated on the chair adjacent to the divan, and the other was walking slowly about the drawing room, now and then taking notes. Garret sat himself on the end of the divan with his arm around her shoulders. Both police officers were in plain clothes, and their pleasant faces had a certain look of respectability.

The man sitting next to her spoke gently. "I'm sorry to trouble you, Mrs. Brandt. Your husband tells me you're not well. We'll make this as brief as we can." Paulette found Garret's nearness comforting, yet strangely intimidating. Did he really care? Or was he there to make certain she didn't say more than he wished? She felt incapable of either ignoring or opposing him.

"We thought you might be able to help us," the officer continued. "Your uncle had a secretary, an Egyptian named Hamor, is that correct?"

"Yes. He left to spend the evening with his cousin and his family."

"Did he make the pot of tea you and Mr. Simington drank before going into the showroom?"

"I'm afraid I don't know. It was already on the tray with the cups when I arrived."

"Well, that muddles things," Garret said. "Gilly could have dropped the drug into the pot beforehand."

"Why did you come to see your uncle this afternoon? The dinner party was to be held tomorrow night, wasn't it?"

She felt Garret looking at her, and knew that he too was curious about that. He wasn't the only one who kept secrets.

"He asked me to come and see him." She tried not to hesitate. "He had a lamp to give me for my wedding present."

"Where is that lamp, do you know?"

"No. We went to the showroom, but I became dizzy and fainted before he could show it to me."

"Did Mr. Simington appear unusually troubled about anything? Depressed? Worried, perhaps?"

Paulette sat very still, aware of Garret's hand on her shoulder caressing her, of his inquisitive gaze on her face, as interested as the officer in her words, her reaction to the questions.

"No. He seemed quite his usual self."

"What else did he discuss with you beside the lamp, anything?"

She stood and walked over to the fireplace, as if to warm herself. She kept her back toward them. "No," she said quietly. "Nothing."

"Nothing?" came the slightly doubtful voice.

"Nothing that convinced me he was about to take his life by poison." She turned, avoiding looking at Garret. The officer nodded gravely. "He did mention his will," she added calmly.

"His will," he repeated.

"Yes. He told me I would be his main heir."

Garret watched her, showing nothing unusual in his face.

"And this was the first time he'd told you this?"

"Yes." She purposely kept her gaze from shifting to Garret.

"What about the collection of Egyptian artifacts? Was he leaving them to you as well?"

She explained his plans, surprised that she sounded so calm about it.

"Did he mention to you that a royal cat was missing from the showroom?"

She held her hands behind her, out of sight, but her fingers convulsively tightened together. Her gaze averted to Garret. She would have expected him to show tension, but he was as composed as the officer and watched her sympathetically.

She shrugged. "He may have...we talked about so many things."

Garret's eyes flickered, and he looked at the officer. "It's my opinion he had Hamor ship the black cat somewhere."

"So you told us earlier," and the officer smiled faintly. "We'll be sure to ask his secretary and check the mail. There's one thing you haven't told us, Mr. Brandt. Did Mr. Simington telephone you that your wife was ill?"

Garret shoved his hands into his trouser pockets and walked over beside Paulette. "No. I had no idea she'd passed out. I would have gone to her at once. When she came into this room, it was a complete surprise."

"You didn't know she was here?"

"Absolutely not."

"Then just why did you come here, Mr. Brandt?"

"I told you. The timing of the dinner party for tomorrow night was not going to work for me. I was hoping I could have him arrange it on another day, after I'd returned from a business trip."

"For Kimball, Baylor, and—?"

Garret smiled. "Lammiter. Yes, I would not have been able to attend tomorrow evening, and I didn't want to disappoint Paulette."

She looked at him.

"I arrived just as it was beginning to rain and found the front door wide open. I thought that was unusual, and when there was no answer I entered and had a brief look around. There was no one here. At least that's what I thought. I made a telephone call to Paulette to see if she'd heard from him, but there was no answer. I then called an associate. It was then that Paulette came into this room, and you know the rest."

"And your associate can substantiate your call?"

Garret smiled. "Yes. Would you like the number, Tom?"

The officer wrote down the number from Garret's notebook, then stood. "Well, that about wraps it up for me, Bill," he said to his partner, "unless you have any more questions?"

The officer called Bill shook his head no. "No questions here, but I've quite a few for the Egyptian secretary."

"Then you're both free to go," he said to Paulette and Garret, and turned to the doctor who came in from the direction of the showroom. An ambulance had arrived out front, and two young men were carrying a stretcher.

"Mrs. Brandt may have been given a small dose of the drug," Garret quietly told the doctor.

Paulette didn't argue, but if Gilly had initially placed a small dosage of the drug in the teapot, wouldn't he have become unconscious also? She tried to remember back to when they'd been sitting in front of fire. Her uncle had asked her to pour, but had she seen him actually drink from his cup?

The room was cold. Garret took the woolen shawl from an ottoman and placed it around her, squeezing her shoulder comfortingly as he did. "It will soon be over and I'll take you home."

Despite his attentiveness, Paulette was not comforted, nor did she think he was authentic. He had behaved the perfect, concerned husband in front of the officers and the doctor, but was it real? The haunting thoughts of Garret's betrayal weighed like bricks in her heart. He had married her for her inheritance. And now Gilly was dead. Suicide, the doctor said. She had her doubts. There was one question that hadn't even been asked. And she had feared to bring it up, knowing how incriminating it would sound before the police. And no matter how she doubted Garret, there was no denying that she was in love with him. The question loomed larger and larger until it filled her heart with doubt and fear: Why had Garret kept from her the news that her uncle had made her heiress of his great Egyptian fortune?

11

To Paulette, it seemed hours before their taxi pulled to a stop in front of the Regent's Park apartment building. Garret carefully helped her out onto the sidewalk. He'd been silent on the ride home, as had she. He paid the driver, and then led her through the glass door. Once inside, he took her hand and held it tightly as they climbed the stairs to their front door. "All right, darling?" he asked. She nodded, trying to smile. He put his arm around her while he fished in his pocket for the key. She noted his somber thoughtfulness and realized he was as troubled as she, but that he was managing his emotions well. Just why had he been at Uncle Gilly's?

In another moment he opened the door and switched the light on.

Never before had the tiny two-room flat appeared so comfortable and secure to her. Her apartment might have been Buckingham Palace. The familiar yellow cotton towels and matching tea cozy, the plain icebox, the quite ordinary white tea and coffee porcelain cups, all became cherished items establishing her roots. "Home sweet home," she murmured.

"Which proves that mansions and great wealth bring neither security nor contentment," Garret said gravely.

Paulette glanced at him, hiding the flinch she felt in her soul. If only she could be certain he believed that. Had Garret's visit to the Swiss lodge been planned to work out as it had, with her becoming Mrs. Brandt?

"Straight to bed with you," he ordered pleasantly. "What will you have with the doctor's sedative?" He went to the icebox and searched for the bottle of milk. "A glass of hot milk or chicken soup?"

"Neither, thank you," she murmured, tired and exhausted. "All I want is a warm, soft bed."

"I must insist on the sedative," he apologized. "Tonight I'm the perfect nursemaid. Doctor's orders." Without further delay he picked her up and carried her into the bedroom and laid her on the bed, removing her shoes. He opened the closet and found her blue satin dressing gown. "You've just been through a very traumatic situation." He frowned. "I'm sorry I didn't find you sooner. I should have looked in Gilly's showroom."

"There was no way you could have known I was lying there all that time."

"No, but I should have looked instead of assuming the place was deserted."

She glanced at him. He seemed two men at times: one, mysterious; the other, disciplined, frowning in self-rebuke that he hadn't known to come to her aid.

"I've got to take precious care of you, darling. You mean too much to me."

Previously she would have found his words a thrilling promise of cherished endearment, bringing joy to her heart. Now, they were shadowed with suspicion.

She was under the covers losing her shivers by the time he brought in a tray holding a bowl of hot chicken soup. On the napkin beside the cup sat the foreboding white sleeping tablet, waiting. Discomfort tightened her chest. What if—? Absurd. How could she think such a thing of her husband?

The tension persisted. She claimed she couldn't swallow the pill. It was too large, she was still nauseous, the soup was much too hot. But he must have seen through her excuses, for his mood was reflected in the tightening of his jaw. Even so, he didn't make anything of her pretext. He left the bedroom, went into the bathroom, and returned with a glass of water.

"Take the sedative, Paulette," he insisted gently, but so firmly and with such a level gaze that she felt rebuked for her mistrust. She did so, meekly, avoiding his gaze, then lay back on the pillow and watched him silently. He sat down on the edge of the bed and without a word fed her the chicken soup. Their eyes met with each spoonful she swallowed.

After a moment, he remarked: "You've been watching me all evening as if you think I'm Bluebeard ready to eliminate his fourteenth bride."

"Don't be silly, Garret. Why should I think such things?"

"My question exactly." He set the bowl down. "Unless Gilly filled your mind with suspicions."

"Uncle Gilly is dead. It seems barbaric to blame him for misunderstandings between us."

He observed her. "I don't know what lies he told you, but tonight at the house, you were actually on the verge of thinking I placed poison in his tea."

Now that he had actually spoken the words, the grounds for believing anything so far-fetched seemed absurd. "You're exaggerating my response," she countered.

"I was upset—naturally I would be—about him. Surely you understand that?"

"Of course I understand. But it wasn't the loss of Gilly that made you withdraw from my touch in the taxi."

She tossed the cover aside and stood, snatching her dressing gown and tying the sash with a yank. The emotional conflict brought her to the brink of tears, but she steadied herself by gritting her teeth. "Very well. I *did* wonder about you, and still do. I wonder about your relationship with him, about why you married me."

He came around the foot of the bed and took her in his arms, holding her possessively. "You still wonder about that?" he asked softly. "Haven't I made it clear how I feel about you when you're in my arms?"

"Oh, Garret, there are so many unanswered questions. If you would explain them, I could be satisfied."

He smiled grimly. "I've told you several times I would answer all your doubts and questions, Paulette. But some things must wait. If you know I love you, can't you trust me with the things you don't understand?"

He cupped her chin and kissed her eyes, her lips. "Do you think I could ever hurt you? When I see fear and suspicion in the way you look at me, I wonder if you know me at all."

She was grieved by her own doubts. "Darling, I love you so much. I *do* trust you, but—" she bit her lip, her eyes searching his.

"But you think I married you for your inheritance," he said with a grim smile.

"No—I don't think that. But Gilly—" she stopped, seeing the restrained anger in his eyes.

Her marriage was worth too much to risk dark suspicions. There was a part of her that believed he might be right about everything, but she was still haunted by too many frustrating unknowns. Why had Gilly asked her to the estate before taking his life—if indeed he had taken his life? And why had he told her about Garret, causing her emotions to run riot while her doubts grew like weeds in rich, damp soil? And why was Garret keeping secrets while at the same time not allowing her the room to withdraw and keep her doubts to herself, but wanting to force them out into the glaring light for analysis?

"Could it be you were already untrusting before we married?"

His unlikely question startled her, making her the focal point.

"Untrusting? How do you mean?"

"You were full of doubt before you even met me at the lodge, doubts about yourself and about men in general. You grew up alone in an orphanage, denied the foundation you needed—parents who loved each other, a sense of trust and belonging. The father you needed was absent. That absence has affected your relationships. And now you're waiting for failure to occur in your husband. You just can't quite accept that he'll be steadfast and trustworthy."

He was right about her childhood deficiencies, and having no desire to become transparent, she wanted to sidestep this unveiling of her soul. She was having all her weaknesses strung out before him like beads on a string. It was true that while growing up she'd resented that her parents had brought her into the world and then vanished without cultivating so much as a trace of parental love and care upon her heart. They had departed, but she had stayed. The fact that they had no choice in the occasion of their death had done little to alleviate the insecurity of her childhood at the orphanage. Her childish mind had held them somehow to blame for leaving her clinging to a raft in the middle of the cold, black sea, later to grow up amid forty-seven other children with name tags, all of them suffering from various degrees of abandonment.

She dropped her forehead to his chest. "But that shouldn't affect our marriage. It's history."

"Is it? I wonder," he said quietly.

She looked up at him. "Well, there are things beside my own inclinations that cause me to have doubts, Garret. Although we've been married almost a year, you still remain somewhat mysterious."

He smiled. "All right then, let's assume I am very mysterious. You may fire away. What mysteries do I need to unmask?"

"First, just what were you doing at his house this afternoon?"

He lifted both brows. "Well, you heard what I told the police. It satisfied them. Why would you still have doubts?"

The shock of all that happened that night was setting in and she began to tremble, feeling cold.

"You're shivering," he said, holding her closely. "Don't you want to get back in bed?"

"No—just hold me. Hold me tight. Oh Garret—I'm afraid!"

"Darling," he said swiftly, kissing her temple and wrapping her tightly in his arms, "there's nothing to fear. Believe me, you're worrying about things that have no truth to them."

If only he were right. She clung to him.

"You doubt my explanation for going to see Gilly," he persisted calmly.

She glanced up at him. Although he radiated little except love and support, his face was unreadable in the dimness and she sensed his gaze was alert. Was it because he wanted her trust or because he wanted to find out how much she knew?

"Well, first, you'd left me with the impression that you haven't had the opportunity to meet Uncle Gilly, so I was very surprised to see you there. Not only that, but at lunch today you didn't mention that you'd be too busy to come to the dinner that I told you he was planning, yet you told the police you went there to ask him to delay it."

A slight pause followed. "You're right about that. But you'll remember that I received a call from Henley at the café. His call changed everything. I'd learned that it's necessary for me to go to Geneva. I knew the news would disappoint you, so I didn't care to mention it just then. You seemed happy about Gilly wanting to entertain us, so I hoped I'd be able to delay my trip until after the dinner party. But Geneva has turned out to be too important to reschedule. So I went to see Gilly to arrange another date for his dinner. If he agreed, I thought it might be better for him to call you and explain. As for Geneva, I was expecting to tell you tonight." He smiled. "Satisfied?"

Yes, thinking back that afternoon to the café she recalled that there had been a telephone call from the man working for the New York company. When Garret returned to the table, she'd noticed he was concerned about something.

Then, he was telling her the truth. "But—"

"You're still not satisfied."

"Darling, if Geneva is that important, why didn't you explain sooner?"

He appeared calm, even remotely distant, as though discussing some boring issue. "I just didn't want to trouble you with the details of my work."

She smiled ruefully. "Shouldn't a wife understand her husband's work?"

He planted another kiss on her lips. "Of course. But I didn't want to worry you, it's as simple as that. We both know there are risks."

"Why did you think I'd worry?"

"It was you, darling, who suggested that traveling throughout Europe is more dangerous now than it was just a few months ago. We know America isn't at war with Germany, but regardless, Hitler has no use for American citizens." Garret gestured to a newspaper that was opened to a foreboding headline about a German U-boat sinking a U.S. ship. "After this incident, I didn't want to worry you about my travel plans."

Paulette had read about the tragedy that morning. The ship had been carrying mostly American civilians from New York on its way to Ireland.

"But I still keep thinking you might have gone to my uncle's house for another reason, one that had little to do with postponing the dinner party."

The ensuing silence lengthened.

"And what might that reason be?" he asked quietly.

When she hesitated, he went on: "Let me see if I can guess. The promised inheritance—the Egyptian treasures? So we're back to that. Did he tell you I knew about his will before we met at the lodge?"

Her chest tightened, making her breathless. "Yes. He did. That was the reason he asked me to come and see him today."

"He wanted to warn you, I suppose. Did he suggest I had deceived you, kept the truth from you until after the marriage?"

"Garret, *please*—"

"That would make it easy for me to get my hands on the money. Right?"

"He didn't come right out and accuse you."

"He didn't need to. He knew you were a bright girl who could manipulate the information on your own once he dumped it in your lap. The conclusions you'd come to would naturally be determined by your worst fears."

Her sharp glance met his. She pulled away abruptly.

"Go on, please," he urged. "What else did he tell you?"

"He told me he'd contacted you months ago," her voice faltered, "before we ever met at the lodge."

His jaw flexed with restrained anger.

She felt pain in her heart, but knew she must go on. She turned toward him, waiting. The silence thickened. She felt a wall growing between them brick by brick.

He came up beside her, his face wiped clean of all expression except a thoughtful look, as though he was unexpectedly forced to decide something.

"So he told you he contacted me?"

"Yes," she admitted dully. "Because of your knowledge of Egyptology. He wanted your professional skills."

"He was lying. I contacted him."

"You contacted him?" she repeated, startled. "When?"

"I was working with the Cairo museum on the Nefertari collection. It was thought that Gilly had a certain piece that the museum wanted."

"But he told me that you knew of the inheritance."

A slight scowl formed. "Risking further misunderstanding, I will, nevertheless, tell you. Yes, I knew you were in line to inherit."

"But why did you never mention it to me? Why keep the inheritance a secret?"

"He asked me to say nothing to you until he explained it himself, and I honored his request. Perhaps I shouldn't have."

He gathered her into his arms, assuring her of his love, soothing her, holding her head against his shoulder and stroking her hair. "Paulette, darling, it played absolutely no part in my wanting to marry you. If you'd been the daughter of the lodge janitor, I'd still have fallen in love with you and asked you to marry me. I'm asking you to trust me about Gilly's will. Will you?"

"Oh, Garret, if you say so, then yes, how could I possibly think that you..." she couldn't go on and laid her cheek against his chest. "Yes...I trust you."

He turned her face toward his and kissed her gently and longingly.

The sedative was finally working, and she felt herself growing calm and hardly able to stay alert. She clung to him, feeling at last safe and secure as her eyelids grew heavy.

He laughed quietly. "It doesn't speak very well of our chemistry, darling, when you fall asleep while I'm kissing you."

"Mmm," she murmured sleepily, turning her head against his shoulder.

He lifted her and carried her to the bed. She was aware of a casual and gentle kiss as he laid her back on the pillow. "Good night, Mrs. Brandt."

"G'night," she murmured. "Good night, Prince Charming," she thought drowsily, and would have been embarrassed to know she had spoken the words aloud. She thought she saw him smiling as she fell asleep. At last, she was untroubled.

The sunshine poured in through the open bedroom window as Paulette awoke next morning, still groggy from the tablet but feeling better—until she remembered her uncle's death. She massaged her neck absently, glancing at the clock: 10:15!

Garret must have heard her stirring, because a few minutes later he came in with a tray containing coffee and a hearty breakfast of scrambled eggs, bacon, and toast.

She sat up, lightheaded, but well. "My! What have I done to deserve all this?" she said as he put an extra pillow behind her back and set the tray across her lap.

"I'm bribing you for your affections," he said lightly. He handed her a cup of coffee with cream.

"Mmm, just the way I like it."

"I washed the dishes and cleaned the kitchen floor. Doesn't that earn me a smile?"

She smiled warmly. "You're spoiling me."

He looked down at her. "You're looking more optimistic this morning. You should be feeling even better when I get back tonight. By the way, I called Mort."

"Oh?" she looked at him, wondering.

"He said to take the day off."

"He did? That's surprising." She sipped her coffee. "I'm behind on that write-up on King Farouk."

He showed interest. "What do you know about Farouk?"

"Not much at the present, except he loves to drive racing cars and throw gala parties in his palace on the Nile."

She expected him to smile, as many of the British did when hearing about the young Egyptian king and what were considered his reckless, immature antics. Instead, she wondered at his sudden somber look as he slipped into his jacket and reached for a navy blue tie.

"I don't believe Gilly died from drinking that pot of tea," he said quietly, surprising her over the unexpected change of subject. Almost at once, the sunny morning began to darken.

She raised her head, watching him, wondering. He was frowning to himself. "Oh? Why do you say that, darling? The doctor said I'd been drugged from the tea, which was the same tea Uncle Gilly drank."

"That's just it. He should have been out about the same time as you, yet you say you grew dizzy and fainted while he was showing you the display room. What I want to know is, did you actually see him drinking or finishing his tea?"

"Well, I do remember seeing him lifting his cup, even to his lips, between talking."

"Yes, I can see it now. He did all the talking, *reluctantly* informing you of my many transgressions and of your new status as his heiress while you sat having your tea in shock, too unsuspecting to notice that he appeared so occupied with talking and smoking that he was prevented from actually drinking the tea. And all the while he was keeping you distracted, waiting until you emptied your cup. He'd used just enough of the drug to put you to sleep. It wasn't his intention to harm you. He knew exactly what he was doing. Afterward he died by poison, poison which he administered to himself while you were unconscious."

"But, Garret, why did he want me unconscious? What was his motive?"

"I have some ideas about that, as well as why he decided to end his life. For one thing, he was a thief. Many of those Egyptian artifacts were not his property. The police are looking into it."

"Stolen! From where? Have they any idea?"

"Cairo."

"Is that what you were doing when you first contacted him? Tracking stolen artifacts?"

He frowned. "Something like that. After you became unconscious and were nicely out of the way, Gilly must have added the deadly strong concentration of poison to his teacup and returned to the showroom. He had enough time to humor himself in whatever Egyptian religious ritual he fancied before the poison began to work. He then sat down with his cup of tea and waited until the end came. Grisly, to be sure," he agreed, when she shuddered, "but absolutely fitting for the kind of person Gilly was."

She flinched, thinking of herself lying helpless on the floor, surrounded by mysterious Egyptian pieces with cold dead eyes. And Gilly—sitting slumped in the chair—slowly dying. She sighed. "You seem to know so much about him."

Again, he was expressionless. "I had a friend who knew him in Cairo during the Great War. He shared some of that knowledge with me."

She waited, thinking he would explain more, but he lapsed into silence.

"I still don't see why he would wish to kill himself," she mused a moment later. "Even if he was a thief, taking one's life is murder, and his action was so drastic. It makes no sense."

"It does, darling, if you understand Gilly. Vengeance," he said thoughtfully, "was as good a reason as any."

"Vengeance? Against whom?"

"Against me, is my guess."

She thought about that. "Certainly not just because of the disappearance of the royal cat?" She eyed him cautiously. "He seemed to think that you took it."

"Did he?" He looked half amused. "No one could manage to get past the elaborate alarm system he installed."

"He claimed that he'd shown you the collection earlier."

He laughed shortly. "Could anyone really think that Gilly, as fanatical as he was about that collection, would just walk out as casual as you please, and leave the door standing wide open? Right. And I dashed back in for a once in a lifetime opportunity and made off with a pharaoh's royal cat!"

She smiled, for it did sound unlikely. "But the cat *is* missing, Garret. I saw for myself that the pedestal is empty."

"He could have stashed it anywhere inside the mansion or even sent it out of the country. Casting the shadow of guilt upon me makes up his last little joke, fitting for the likes of Gilly."

She hadn't thought of Gilly as a sinister person before last night, and the idea was unsettling. Yet, she would no longer doubt her husband. Garret must be right. It all seemed so silly now to have doubted him. She owed Garret her loyalty even if it meant believing that Gilly had lied to her before taking his life.

"I've got to leave soon. I've a meeting with Henley that may last into the evening, but I'll try to get home early."

He was watching her, and she thought there was concern in his eyes.

She smiled for him. "I really am feeling much better," she said, thinking her health was the cause of his concern.

"Let's go out to dinner tonight. A quiet place, so we can talk." He looked at his watch, kissed her goodbye, and headed for the door. He paused.

"There is one thing I'm curious about."

"And what could that be?"

"You were suspicious of me at the mansion last night, and had ample opportunity to say something to the police officer. He asked if Gilly mentioned whether the royal cat was missing from the showroom. Why didn't you bring it up?"

She smiled slowly. He waited, watching her with cool interest.

"If I had mentioned the cat it may have led me to telling everything Gilly had falsely accused you of, including that he suspected you of stealing it, and that you knew months in advance about his decision to make me his heir. It would have gone badly for you, don't you think?"

"So even though you doubted me, you weren't yet ready to believe Gilly and turn me over to the executioners?" His vivid gray-blue eyes watched her.

"No," she admitted quietly, "I wasn't."

"I suppose you know that reveals much to me about your heart."

"I thought I'd revealed it long ago."

"And I promise to treat it with the utmost loving care."

∼∼∼

Strange, that when the sun was shining and she was far from the foreboding showroom with cobras and coffins, how last night's giants of doubt shrank into midgets. She could almost think that the night's happenings were nothing more than a nightmare. But Uncle Gilly was dead, evidence that all was not as well as the bright morning and the cooing pigeons outside the window led her to believe.

Her mind came back to Henley and the meeting that Garret was having with him. She briefly entertained the notion that the stranger she'd seen at Gilly's house before the police arrived had been Henley, though why she would think so was not clear even to herself. Perhaps he had been a member of the London police? She'd meant to ask Garret, but there'd been so much going on last night that she'd forgotten. What was their meeting about this morning? The sudden death of Gilbert Simington and the disposition of his collection of Egyptian artifacts? And what might it have to do with a trip to Geneva? Whatever it was, the meeting with Henley had evoked some matter of concern in Garret.

That evening he took her to a little seafood restaurant on Oxford Street that was within walking distance from their flat. At dinner they talked a great deal, and it seemed he was deliberately trying to direct the conversation away from Gilly's death. It was on the walk home that he told her the police were still working on the premise that Gilly had taken his own life.

"But let's not discuss that now," he said. As they strolled in the soft moonlight in downtown London, he put an arm around her shoulders and said unexpectedly: "Paulette, I need to talk to you about something."

She knew then that he had news that wouldn't make matters easier. She paused on the sidewalk and gave him a serious look. He lifted his brows, his face going deliberately blank under her scrutiny.

"Bad news?" she asked cautiously.

"I wouldn't say that." He smiled.

But her suspicions proved true. "Remember that trip to Geneva I told you about? The one for Henley? There's another business associate waiting for me in Geneva. I need to be at the airport first thing in the morning. I may be gone for several weeks."

"Oh, Garret!"

"I'll do my best to keep it from becoming an overly long trip. But it's an important one for the company. There's someone I need to meet who's interested in the Egyptian collection. Someone from Athens. Honey, I'm sorry," he said, reading her disappointed expression and putting his arms around her, ignoring indulgent onlookers. "If it wasn't necessary for me to go now, I'd try to get out of it, but Henley believes the meeting can't wait. You do understand?"

She sighed. "Yes, but why can't the interested customer come to London? Why Geneva?"

He hesitated. "With England at war, it's safer for all concerned to cross the border into neutral Switzerland."

Paulette found herself growing more curious about Henley. "The company of Kimball, Baylor, and Lammiter remains an illusive entity to me. Somehow Mr. Kimball, Mr. Baylor, and Mr. Lammiter don't sound like an international company that deals in Egyptian artifacts," she accused mildly. "Who are they?"

He smiled. "I've never met them."

"Never met—but then how do you—?" she wanted to say, "how do you work for them?"

"My business assignments all come from Henley."

"Henley? Only him?"

"There's another man. His name doesn't matter. He locates the museum pieces and contacts Henley, who in turn contacts me."

"Why is it always Henley you mention? Why not Baylor, Kimball, or Lammiter?"

He smiled, but his gray-blue eyes were remote as he looked at her. "Because there is no Kimball, Baylor, and Lammiter."

"They don't exist? You mean it's just a fictitious name, like Spring Mountain Farms?"

Garret laughed. "Something like that. Come." He took her elbow and walked her down the sidewalk.

"Then who really owns the company?"

He considered, as though his earlier explanation might have brought him down a path he hadn't quite meant to take, and he was wondering whether to go on or turn back. Watching his serious expression, she thought, *He's struggling between loyalties*, but she couldn't say just why she thought so.

"The company is part of a larger enterprise," he explained patiently. "It has associates all over the world. Henley is just one who is based in London. The other partner is based in Geneva."

"And the business associate is coming from Athens?"

"Yes."

"To buy a museum artifact?"

"To gather information on some of the pieces and offer information of his own. He's an expert."

"I see. Or, perhaps I don't. It's all rather vague, darling."

He smiled again. "Is it? I'm sorry. Let's displace the dismal subject with some happy news."

"Happy news? Is there any?" she asked with a wry smile of her own, looping her arm through his.

"Yes—how would you like to take a trip to see Rhoda and Fergus when I return? Purely vacation. You can meet Dr. Bristow."

She paused with a startled gasp and saw his grin. "Athens! Darling, you really *are* serious," she said, surprised.

"I'm very serious about going," he said. "Bristow's archaeology will be interesting, to say the least. I know you've wanted to interview him for a long time. I'll see you have your chance. I've a notion Mort will be delighted with the prospect."

"You know I'd love to interview Dr. Bristow." And, she would also get to see Rhoda.

"Then I'll see that you have your chance. When I get back from Geneva, I'll arrange a special flight. Dirk will be here in London by then. He's one of the private pilots I told you about."

"Yes, I remember."

"This time, nothing will be allowed to stop us. We'll have time to ourselves, as well as with Bristow, Fergus, and Rhoda."

She believed him. A vacation...with no difficult separations leading to misunderstandings and odd suspicions.

"Oh, you do know how to make me happy, darling."

"It's the least I can do for my one true love."

In the swirling tendrils of gray fog they kissed warmly. Paulette was sure their happiness would never end.

12

The damp March breeze blew through the open window in the tiny two-room flat in the top story of Regent's Park apartment building on Gloucester Place. The air was heavy with the smell of the city, and the breeze sent the cream lace curtains fluttering.

Outside the front door in the public hall, an uncertain creak robbed the early silence of its tranquility. A moment later an envelope addressed to Mrs. Paulette Brandt, posted from Cairo, Egypt, was quietly pushed beneath the bottom of the door.

The sound, though barely audible, awakened Paulette. She'd fallen asleep late last night reminding herself that she must rise early, for today's schedule was packed with important things to do. She would need to get her report done early this afternoon in order to leave in time to pick up a cake at the bakery—double chocolate fudge. Sleepily, her mind mused over yesterday's happenings.

She had gone in early then, too. Diving into work seemed to help displace some of the loneliness she was experiencing. She found it convenient to have a hurried lunch at the local café in the camaraderie of others from the magazine.

"Is Garret back yet?" Mort had asked, munching his fish and chips.

"He's still in Switzerland," she had said, trying to sound unperturbed.

"He's *still* there?" his loud voice sounded.

"Well, yes..." she said feebly, feeling as though she'd failed to do something to keep him contentedly at home.

"He left over a month ago, didn't he?" came the now low-voiced query. It was accompanied by a thoughtful gaze. The question reached to the core of her suspicions and fears.

"He's due home Saturday," she hastened.

"What sends a man to Geneva for weeks on end when he's only been married a short time?"

She wasn't able to explain it easily. Perhaps Mort knew it and hadn't expected an answer. He had never really liked Garret.

"Business," she said at last. "I thought I'd told you."

"Must be important. Kimball, Baylor, and Lammiter, isn't it?"

"That's a front name."

"I figured that. Do I smell a story?" he grinned maliciously.

"Are you suggesting that I spy on my own husband?" she said with an uncomfortable laugh.

"I could always send Billings."

"Don't you dare."

He laughed, showing he was merely joking.

This week was Mort's birthday, and she changed the subject by talking about the party she had planned and invited him and some others to her flat tomorrow evening for a small celebration after work.

"That's sweet of you, angel. Say—make it double chocolate fudge, will you?"

As the floorboard squeaked beneath someone's tread her eyes blinked open. She shivered as though the breeze had touched her bare shoulders. Yet the wind could not be responsible for the curious, underlying apprehension she couldn't shake off. She had felt it for weeks—ever since Garret left for his trip across Europe. She knew only that for some unexplainable reason, shadows hovered like cobwebs at the back of her mind.

She slowly raised herself to an elbow, listening. Had she heard someone at the front door? Garret would arrive home from his long business trip in Geneva tomorrow, Saturday afternoon. If only he had managed to come home a day earlier! She waited, her nerves taut, for the sound of his key in the lock.

As anxious as Paulette was to have him home, she hadn't forgotten their quarrel on the telephone a week ago. He had originally promised to return within three weeks, yet his absence was now dragging into its seventh. Days after she had hung up the telephone the little room had echoed with those last angry words she had hurled at him. That she had been right did little to cheer her lonely days and nights while she envisioned him enjoying an exciting schedule in Geneva. The fact that the early spring in London this year of 1941 was rainy-gray and bone-chilling hadn't done much to soothe her hurt feelings either. After all, he'd promised to take her to Athens. Naturally he had apologized for the delay and tried to assure her he was just as disappointed as she was. She must be reasonable now, he had said, she must understand that he had no choice except to stay in Geneva a couple more weeks.

He had been away almost two months. And what about the business trips to other parts of Europe? As it was, this last trip to Switzerland had afforded her even more solemn hours to concentrate on her disappointments. Well! She wasn't going to mope about a tiny flat with nothing to do but polish wedding gifts—most of which were the wrong color to match her few pieces of furniture—while her husband enjoyed hot chocolate, cheese fondue, and magnificent ski slopes. Paulette expected life to be a bit unfair, but not *this* unfair! The sound of his key in the lock was not heard. Instead, the wind rustled the shade on the window, then silence settled back into the tiny bedroom, convincing her she'd merely imagined hearing anything. It must have been the newspaper boy. She was usually so tired that she slept through it, but this morning there was much on her mind.

She pushed a wave of honey-brown hair from her eyes and squinted at the square ivory porcelain clock on the bedside stand with miniature pink rosebuds. What time was it?

The Victorian clock was just one of several ultra-feminine furnishings in her flat that Garret was stuck with due to the fact that they hadn't been able to move into the larger apartment on the Strand that they had anticipated leasing. The war had escalated, and London was overcrowded with military men and their wives.

She threw aside the covers and slipped into her dressing gown, stifling a yawn and a shiver in the nippy air. She went to close the window. As she looked below on Gloucester Place, she saw that traffic had begun to move and pedestrians were already out for tea or coffee at the corner bakery before going to work. There had been rain, too. The street was wet and the sky was thick with dense gray mist. Her guests tonight would most likely arrive with dripping raincoats and umbrellas to crowd the small hall. She had never liked putting down newspapers to catch the drips. It looked so messy, not to mention all those bleak headlines touting the rhetoric of the victorious Third Reich. Maybe she could use the funny papers. She found herself smiling wryly.

As she turned away from the window she looked at Garret's handsome photograph on her white dressing table. She almost wished he weren't so good looking. It greatly annoyed her to see women watching him in public, and that reminded her of Gloria Haskins. Even though she had recently nabbed Mort Collier, Gloria had been involved with Garret.

Paulette sighed and hurried to the kitchenette to start the coffee. Garret could be so thoughtful, so masculine, so protective of her and yet he remained strangely secretive—

She turned away from the gold-tone counter. Secretive? Not a proper word to dig back up now. *I'd better do some shopping this morning*, she thought firmly. *If he does come home tomorrow as planned, I don't want the icebox empty. Everyone will most likely devour everything in sight tonight.* The day was going to be crammed! If she could have known sooner about his arrival, she might have taken advantage of the sale at Crenshaw's market last week. She frowned. She was spending too much money lately, though Garret had told her to stop worrying.

With coffee cup in hand she hurried back to the bedroom to dress, glanced out the window again, and decided to take an umbrella. *I can be back here by two o'clock. That will give me several hours before everyone arrives.*

The tinkle of rain on the bedroom window drew Paulette's memories back to the morning's tight schedule. She was no longer smiling as she hurried to the kitchenette with her half-finished cup of coffee. New York, Spain, Paris, and now he had gone to Geneva. Garret had visited Uncle Gilly without her knowing. And Gilly had given him a tour of his artifacts. Had he shown Garret the wedding present that he had promised her? She remembered what Garret had told her about the lamp from the historic digs at Aleppo, not many miles from the Egyptian desert. Now that Gilly's death had been ruled a suicide, the Egyptian collection, along with the lamp, was under legal control until the myriads of details surrounding his will and the genuine ownership of certain pieces, including Nefertari, was decided. But she had been allowed to view the lamp just last week and "unusual" was indeed the correct word to describe it. The base of the lamp was blue marble, magnificently carved into the shape of a robed woman with a basket on her head, apparently carrying bread, or perhaps clusters of grapes or figs. Paulette believed that Garret's company would have clients worldwide that would pay generously for such a piece, not that she would ever sell it. Did Garret feel the same?

She had started worrying again. Almost desperately she tried to think of something else. She finished her coffee and cooked eggs and toast for breakfast. After rinsing the dishes to make them easier to wash later that afternoon, she left them in the sink and returned to her bedroom.

Even with several months of marriage, she still didn't feel she knew her husband. Paulette's married friends told her marital difficulties were "normal." Rhoda had once said that every marriage had its own peculiar difficulties that were added to the standard problems of adjustment that affected every couple.

"Suddenly two very independent people must cleave to one another and become one in God's purpose for their lives," Rhoda had said in her letter. "Believe me, the storms in the first year blow like hurricanes, threatening to pull the house of matrimony to the ground, but they're not unique. We all have them."

Perhaps, Paulette thought. It seemed to her, however, that her situation was more difficult than Rhoda's. Rhoda and Fergus had the good fortune of working together in the field of archaeology, whereas Garret was gone a great deal of the time, involved in things she knew almost nothing about.

She frowned. She stopped herself from pursuing troubled thoughts. Yes, all the doubt was behind her. Her more recent worries about their relationship were unnecessary, he had said. Paulette tried to console herself. *Everything is wonderful again, our future will be secure and happy, and all the strange fears, especially of the last two months, will fade like shadows chased away by the sunlight.* Garret had told her he wouldn't travel so much, that he wouldn't keep unnecessary secrets from her, that he loved her, and he had promised in his last letter that he would convince her. If the war didn't interfere—he would buy her a house and be home for dinner every night. She was the only woman he had ever wanted to marry, and now that he had her, he would never let her go.

I am the luckiest girl in all London, she thought as she brushed her shoulder-length honey-brown hair. Her large brown eyes, emphasized by dark eyelashes, smiled back at her in the mirror.

She finished getting ready quickly, then hurried to straighten the two small rooms. The less she left for tonight, the easier things would be when she got home. If there was anything that bothered her, it was returning after a busy day to find a cluttered apartment, or as Garret had called it, a "cracker box."

She finished straightening the sitting room for the gathering that evening and picked up the telephone to dial the grocery market to order the remainder of the things she would need, starting with cheese and crackers and nuts and smoked oysters. "Oh, and olives," she said. "Yes, the green ones stuffed with pimento. I want limes, too. And soda water. My landlord will be here to open the door." She hung up and looked down at her stocking feet with the toenails painted pink. Garret had bought her a darling pair of black party heels in Paris with ankle straps that would go perfectly with tonight's outfit. The dress was his favorite, black satin. She wished he could be there to see her in it. Anything else? Oh—she'd better call the landlord and ask for some furniture polish. Mr. Hoadley made up some kind of fragrant wax that did wonders to hide the scratch on her coffee table. She'd bought the table from the tenant who had left two years ago to move to Earl's Court. That's how she'd obtained most of her furnishings.

Oh, and I better order extra ice—oh, dear. No, I can't do that. The icebox is too small to hold it. Well, she'd ask them to drop the ice off in the evening around eight o'clock. By then what she had would be used up.

As she gave a last worried glance around the room, she hurried into the hall the size of a large closet. Near the front door, over the spindle-legged telephone table, she glanced in the mirror, put on her blue hat and tucked away a wave behind her ear. The gold earring glimmered, once more reminding her that Garret was lavish with his gifts. *We must start a budget*, she thought again. Maybe she'd wait until they returned from their trip to Athens! After all, she was the one who had so desperately wanted this vacation. And it would cost plenty. A whole delightful month with her husband in Greece, including visits to Dr. Bristow's station out at the digs in Corinth. She could hardly wait. She would get all the information and photos Mort needed for a feature article. Yes, everything was going wonderfully at last.

She pulled on the gloves that matched her navy blue wool suit, checked to make certain the seams of her stockings were straight, caught up her umbrella, and opened the door. The morning paper was in the outer corridor. She glanced at the worrisome headlines: *CHURCHILL DECLARES BRITAIN WILL CONTINUE TO STAND ALONE AGAINST NAZI GERMANY IF NECESSARY.*

Paulette laid the paper on the table. But England was getting assistance from America. President Franklin Roosevelt had shipped Churchill half a million rifles for the Home Guard. They were desperately needed. She had read how the civilian "troops" had been given a leaflet describing how to disarm a heavily armed German paratrooper using only an umbrella. She hoped America would soon enter the war, then remembered what Garret had said, "Roosevelt may have to wait until after the next election. He's getting stiff resistance from the American press by pacifist Hollywood actors and even heroes like Charles Lindbergh."

Turning back to leave the apartment, she noticed that an envelope had been slipped under her front door. The mailman usually didn't come until two o'clock. *It must be a note from Mr. Hoadley.* She cringed at the thought that he might be raising the rent now that more military personnel were moving into the area.

Paulette lifted the envelope and turned it over. Odd. It was from Rhoda, postmarked from Egypt. What on earth was she doing there? She hadn't mentioned a trip in her last letter.

Curious, she opened the envelope and removed a newspaper clipping and a brief message. She examined the clipping with stunned disbelief. The picture had been taken from one of the small, independent British newspapers in Egypt.

The ink was smudged a little from handling, but the photo was still clear enough to identify. The woman in the news photo appeared to be a thirtyish, attractive, sophisticated blonde. The caption beneath the photo called her Anna Kruger. Although Paulette had never seen her before, there was no doubt about her handsome escort in formal dinner finery. He was bringing her to what the newspaper called "yet another grand and gala dinner at the palace of the young, extravagant King Farouk." Garret Brandt had his arm around the waist of the woman who was looking at him with wide, vulnerable eyes, a Mona Lisa smile on her lips, and her hand resting on his arm in what Paulette felt was an intimate gesture.

Paulette, bound like a prisoner, stood in the tiny hall unable to move. She read the brief note: "If ever you plan to visit us, do it now. Especially with Garret in Cairo. Why is it that you didn't come with him, darling? Love, Rhoda."

Yes, Paulette wondered, shaken, *why didn't I?* The reason, while clear, did nothing to give her confidence. Because he would have insisted she stay here in London, that's why. Because he had said he would be "busy" on a crucial business venture in Geneva—but he wasn't in Geneva.

A picture is worth a thousand words as the saying went. Photos rarely lie. And this picture, sent to her by someone she trusted, and dated within the last four weeks, was proof that Garret was in Cairo. Once again, he had not told her the truth. As she looked at the woman beside him Paulette thought of the Cairo museum and the artifacts left to her in Gilly's will. Paulette was an heiress. Garret was committed to Egyptology. What else was there to say?

The telephone jangled, causing her to jump. She picked up the receiver on the third ring, her voice quiet and dull: "Hello?"

"Good morning, angel," Mort Collier said in a cheerful voice.

"Oh, Mort, it's you."

"Of course it's me. I'm supposed to meet you for breakfast this morning, remember?"

"Oh, Mort, I'm so sorry! It...it completely slipped my mind."

"Say, are you all right?"

"Yes. I'm fine. Mort—remember that feature you wanted so badly on those prisoners of war in Egypt?"

"Sure. I'm still sold on it. Could you be thinking of changing your mind?"

"As a matter of fact, yes. Yes, I am. I...I just got a wire from Garret. He's...he's on his way to Cairo."

"Really?"

"He wants me to join him. Can you arrange to get me there?"

"To Cairo? I sure can. Say, this is a rather fortunate turn of events. How soon can you be ready to go?"

"At once."

"We'll discuss it over breakfast. Want me to come by, or can you meet me at Piccadilly Circus?"

"I'm leaving now. Be there in twenty minutes." Paulette lowered the receiver. Looking in the mirror, she saw the face of a very grim and determined young woman.

PART TWO

Cairo, Egypt

13

The train clattered into the Cairo railway station and came to a puffing, shuddering halt. Paulette struggled with the heavy leather strap that lowered the window and leaned out.

In the station she saw that the red-capped British military police patrols were everywhere. The smell of coal-burning engine smoke was strong, coexisting with other smells of the city: jasmine, cooking spices, desert dust, and sewage.

Mort had told her that a Sergeant Tomlinson would be waiting to escort her to the military barracks where a colonel would hear her request for interviews with the German and Italian prisoners of war. She was to stay in the army's married quarters at the Citadel, where she'd been told there was a hospital, swimming pool, tennis courts, stables, and extensive parade grounds. She wanted to get Mort's story, but her primary objective was to find out what Garret was doing in Egypt.

Through the open window of her compartment Paulette saw a young officer standing on the train platform next to two red-capped MPs. The officer noticed her about the same time and shouted above the babble: "Mrs. Brandt?"

"Yes!"

He ran up to the compartment door as it opened, stepping up to the running board. "I'm Sergeant Tomlinson, ma'am. I'm to bring you to Bab-el-Hadid barracks. The colonel's orders."

"Thank you, Sergeant." She smiled her gratitude as he took her traveling bag and helped her down from the train compartment, though she could have easily descended by herself.

"This way, Mrs. Brandt. And do watch your step, if you please. This station is bedlam." He shook his head with military dismay. "Plenty of Ali Baba's forty thieves, too. I'd best get your other bags without delay."

"Yes, Sergeant, I have two. My name is on them."

"You wait right here, ma'am. I'll find them."

Paulette stood on the platform amid the noise of a departing train shrieking and whistling its way from the station. She glanced about at the crowds of British soldiers who were searching through piles of kit bags, boxes, and steamer trunks that were piling up high all around them. Within a few minutes Tomlinson had located her bags and was commandeering an Egyptian porter to carry them.

"It's not far from here to the barracks. Just across the *midan*."

A *midan*, she knew, was a large square or open space. As the sergeant led her out through the ticket barrier, Paulette glanced about her. So this was Cairo, full of noise, conflicting babble, and smells that did very little to impress her. In her view it was just a big, crowded, dirty city. She imagined that things had changed quite a bit since her Uncle Gilly had lived here as a young man. She could certainly believe the rumor that it was dangerously active with enemy agents and military deserters from all sides of the war. She was thankful to see so many British soldiers in uniform, most of them from Australia, New Zealand, and South Africa, but it was also clear that British occupation was deeply resented by the young Egyptians, some of whom had formed a strong political party to oust Britain from Egypt. Even now, she saw a group of Egyptian students demonstrating against Britain on a street corner.

"Who are they, Sergeant?"

"Don't pay them any mind, ma'am. This goes on all the time. Most likely they belong to the pro-Axis party. They shout 'Long live Rommel' in the streets. Rumor has it they're preparing a suite for Field Marshal Rommel at the Shepheards Hotel. Bah! Over our dead bodies, they will! We call the protesters the 'Sweet Melody Club.'"

"Is that a real place?"

"Yes. A notorious one. Where every evening's performance ends with the Egyptian national anthem, to which the Brits bellow taunting words. A riot always ensues. The Aussies usually end up cracking a few Egyptian heads." He grinned. "Lately the band's been protected behind barbed wire."

She raised her brows.

It was this nationalistic party that also posed a danger to the ruling Egyptian government under King Farouk, because they didn't think he was doing enough to resist Prime Minister Churchill's governing officials in Cairo, especially Sir Miles Lampson, who was governor-general. Yet it was said by many who knew the internal politics of Egypt that the young king was no true ally of Britain, but secretly favored Germany and Italy. He had refused to arrest the Italian nationals as the British prime minister wanted him to do, and Farouk even had them in his court giving him secret advice. On one of the many Anthony

Eden trips to Egypt, Churchill had instructed his man to inform the Egyptians of British security requirements. "It is intolerable that the Romanian legation should become a nest of Hun spies or that the Canal Zone should be infested by enemy agents," Churchill had warned. "I am relying on you to put a stop to all this ill-usage we are receiving at the hands of those we have saved."

The sergeant led her across the crowded concourse and the station forecourt in the direction of the barracks.

Once outside the railway station in the large open *midan,* the hustling throngs of Egyptian peddlers were trying to sell everything from flyswatters to guidebooks. The sun was hot in a hazy blue sky and the babble of voices and the smell of food being sold from "donkey carts" filled the air with a strange yet pleasant aroma of unusual spices. She noted the touches of British colonialism in some of the buildings and in the patches of red, yellow, and blue flowers amid sections of green grass near the cafés and hotels serving tea and cakes on the street.

"That's Bab-el-Hadid, Mrs. Brandt." Sergeant Tomlinson pointed across the *midan* toward what looked to Paulette like an ancient Crusader castle.

"Very interesting. From which Crusade?"

"Probably King Richard's, ma'am, though I couldn't vow to it." He pointed again. "Your husband will be meeting you there with the colonel."

Paulette didn't correct him. Garret would not be waiting for her because he didn't even know she was coming, but it was more trouble than it was worth to explain this now, for it would also mean telling him that Mort Collier may have deliberately "misled" the colonel into believing that Garret was expecting her. When Mort had arranged her trip, he had done so by creating the cover that she was expecting to meet her husband here while researching a feature on German prisoners.

Paulette shaded her eyes and stared ahead toward the Bab-el-Hadid barracks. The sandstone tower of ocher-colored stone reflected a burnished red-gold in the sunlight. She saw policemen ride past, mounted on well-groomed horses.

"They're the Cairo force," the sergeant explained, seeing her looking after them. "Our army's MPs don't use horses. They patrol on foot, in pairs."

She noted the British MPs with the now familiar red-topped peaked caps, feet slightly apart, hands clasped behind their backs, armed with revolvers.

They had walked to the barrack's gate where an armed sentry stood. The porter left Paulette's bags here, and she paid and tipped him for his service. Sergeant Tomlinson showed the sentry his pass and the sentry saluted, staring straight ahead.

"We'll need to get you photographed today, Mrs. Brandt. We have our own identity cards just for use here at Bab-el-Hadid."

"Yes, Sergeant, thank you." She followed him up the stone steps and along the balcony overlooking the parade ground. Here, she saw more MPs being inspected before leaving to patrol the streets of Cairo.

Sergeant Tomlinson stopped at the door of an office overlooking the *midan* and the railway station beyond it. The colonel's personal staff were busy at their desks as Paulette entered. Knowing she would need to deal with various ranks, she had studied British insignias before coming. She could now recognize privates, corporals, and a sergeant in charge of five radio room staff members, all in khakis.

"Get that photographer set up right away," Sergeant Tomlinson told one of the clerks. "Mrs. Brandt needs clearance."

"He's on his way, Sergeant."

"Has the colonel arrived yet?"

"Waiting in his office. He gave up duck hunting."

A smile passed between them, telling her the colonel must heartily approve of duck hunting. Sergeant Tomlinson led Paulette to a door. He straightened his jacket and shoulders, then rapped.

"Come in."

Tomlinson saluted. "Good morning, Colonel. Mrs. Brandt's arrived."

"Good. Send her in."

The sergeant stepped aside and Paulette entered a cramped room, full of papers, books, and a wireless army set.

A tall, slim man stood near a window facing the busy railway station. The door shut behind Tomlinson, and she and the colonel were alone.

"You," she said, surprised. "You were at my uncle's house in London." She stared at the quiet man who had been the first person Garret had called after Gilly's death.

He smiled almost sympathetically. "Yes, and I'm sorry we were not introduced properly at that time." He came forward, hand outstretched. "I'm Colonel Melvin Henley of British CID."

Garret's Mr. Henley is a colonel in the Central Intelligence Department! Paulette felt a little weak.

She must have looked it, for he motioned to a chair in front of his desk. "Won't you sit down, Mrs. Brandt?"

Colonel Henley removed his rimless glasses and massaged the thin bridge of his nose as he studied her with businesslike scrutiny. He had the intelligent but tired face of a dedicated man who slept too little, worked too hard, and missed regular meals. His quick, watchful gaze reminded her of Garret's, convincing her that he was an astute man who fully understood the situation of the world, and that he believed in an important cause far greater than himself and his local environment.

As Paulette looked back at him, she guessed that he was sizing her up, not according to appearance, but as to character and strength of purpose. This made her a little uneasy, because she believed she could stand to improve in both. It had taken all her courage to leave London and risk the flight to Egypt alone. Though she had prided herself on being of a stalwart journalistic mind when it came to thrusting herself into precarious situations for the sake of truth and a story, she had not enjoyed the tremendously long flight in the cold bomber now converted to private use. Mort had been able somehow to contact the group of American pilots who knew Garret, and to arrange for Garret's wife to be brought safely to Cairo, where Mort said he'd told them Garret waited for her.

All of this subterfuge had made her uncomfortable, but her own driving desire to know about her husband had all but silenced her conscience. *I'll get all this straightened out with the Lord later*, she thought, and buried the disquiet once more in the back of her mind.

She sat stiffly in the chair looking at Colonel Henley, her mind running in all directions.

"I don't understand," she said finally.

"No. I don't imagine you do. I can help to some degree."

"Is...my husband in the military? But that's quite impossible, isn't it?"

He smiled grimly. "Quite. Garret is *not* in the British military. He really is an American citizen. Shall we say he is...cooperating?"

She didn't want him to think she had come to Cairo just to check up on a wayward husband, so she told herself she must show determination to get Mort's story. The colonel had no jurisdiction in granting her an audience with King Farouk, but he could permit her a tour of the prisoner of war camp where Italian and German soldiers were under guard.

"I imagine you had a tiring journey, Mrs. Brandt. Can I offer you a cup of tea?" His expressionless face was offset by a fatherly glimmer of sympathy as he seemed to guess her confusion and weariness.

"I would like that, Colonel, thank you."

He poured them both a cup. "I apologize for the absence of cream. Sugar?"

"That will do."

"So you've come to us under the journalistic umbrella of *Horizon* magazine to tour a camp of enemy soldiers. Are you so interested in war, Mrs. Brandt?" The smile, it seemed to her, was not one at all, but a reaction to tone down his words.

"It appears that we have no choice in the matter of war, Colonel. Germany has forced it upon us, and we either surrender to tyranny or we resist."

"Garret deserves my hearty congratulations on his marriage. He met you through the Nickersons, didn't he? They're working with the archaeologist, Dr. Bristow?"

She believed he was watching her reactions alertly. "Yes." She had noted at once his use of first-name status for Garret. "You seem to know my husband quite well."

He smiled briskly, both brows lifting. "I've known Garret for several years. He saved my life once."

Her interest sharpened even more. "Oh? I'm extremely pleased to hear that, Colonel."

But he did not go on to explain. He didn't want to go into detail for reasons that might be obvious, considering he was in British Intelligence. "I'm also a museum enthusiast, as your husband can tell you. Egyptology has always intrigued me."

She smiled tiredly, hoping she looked calm.

His eyes were not unfriendly, only watchful. She almost felt herself on trial, as though she were being tested. This seemed strange to her, and she found herself watching the colonel, waiting.

He pushed two trays of papers aside and sat down on the corner of his busy desk. "Smoke, Mrs. Brandt?"

She shook her head no and watched as he painstakingly opened an Egyptian box, removed a cigarette, and precisely lit it with a match.

"Your husband will be surprised when he learns of your arrival," he said.

Her eyes shot to his. So he knew she wasn't expected. She searched for disapproval in his eyes, but saw only interest instead. "I'm confident he will be."

She found her cheeks turning warm as she tried to match his steady gaze. She hurried on. "My employer, Mort Collier, arranged this trip hoping for a feature story on the prisoners of war. I've been told the Cairo military has offered complete cooperation, and I must believe it's so, because I've been treated exceedingly well since your sergeant met me at the railway." This was her lame way of trying to win him over.

His thoughts might have been amused. "Good. You are a very *special* guest, Mrs. Brandt."

She looked at him curiously. She could almost believe it was the colonel who had arranged for her coming instead of the magazine. Naturally, it was pleasant to have the British military as a cooperating partner, but why should they be interested in her? Yet there was no denying that Colonel Henley was watching her with interest, cool impersonal interest that suggested he had something particular on his mind that benefited his own work. And just what reasons did Garret have for contacting a colonel in the CID while representing a New York company? Dare she suspect that Garret was involved in espionage also?

"Shall we be quite honest with one another, Mrs. Brandt? Whatever the reason you came here, I assume the prisoner of war story is merely a convenient cover. Am I right?"

Paulette remained silent.

"So I was right. I should explain," he said, "that I have an acquaintance with Mort Collier. When I was a younger man I briefly entertained a notion of entering the world of journalism. The Great War soon put me on a different track. I found I liked military life and remained in the army, but Mr. Collier and I have kept up a friendship through the years. We were students together at college. I'm pleased to see he stayed and graduated. *Horizon* is a good magazine. No frivolous stories, just good in-depth analysis of changing world affairs. I like that. I suppose you do as well, Mrs. Brandt, since you've chosen to stay there. No movie stars and Paris fashion, I see. Rather, you've chosen to come to Egypt to cover the war. That's commendable. I can see why Garret was attracted to you when you met. You do share much in common."

"You're very kind, Colonel. And you were also right about my husband not knowing I'm here, unless—" and she looked at him curiously, "you informed him."

"That is something you don't need to worry about." His smile faded, and she sensed his concern. This made her worry. His next comment startled her.

"For the present you and I are trudging the same course, Mrs. Brandt."

"The same course?"

"I assume you would prefer he didn't know. It so happens I am in agreement with that course of action. You're wondering why. It's because you could be of benefit to us, to Britain."

"Britain?" she asked, astounded.

"Yes. And to your husband. Before I can explain just what I mean by that, I must first be assured of your real purpose in coming to Cairo."

Of benefit to Garret as well? Where is he? "I think I explained my purposes, Colonel."

"It's your loyalty and the depth of your dedication, Mrs. Brandt, that interest me at present."

"I love my country, if that's what you mean, and my husband, naturally. What do you mean by my being useful?"

"That will depend on several issues and the future. You strike me as an imaginative young woman with the courage to pursue your plans regardless of danger. That could prove of benefit to us, should it be necessary. By 'us,' of course, I speak of America as well as Britain."

Paulette grew more tense by the moment, trying to make sense of his suggestion, and believing that she was beginning to understand made it worse.

She leaned forward. "Why did you mention my husband? How could I be of benefit to him? Colonel, is my husband not here in Cairo?"

Colonel Henley replaced his glasses carefully, watching her. "I was hoping you wouldn't ask that question yet. At present I would be risking a great deal by assuming too much of you. I must understand you first, Mrs. Brandt. Understand your reactions to several things."

Paulette was puzzled, struggling to understand where his strange questions were leading. He wanted something from her, that was clear, but what? And what did it have to do with Garret? Was she reading too much into his odd and intense manner? Perhaps it was just his way. She had heard once that CID men were odd.

"Are you saying my husband is not in Cairo? He must be here, since—" she stopped, thinking of the news clipping.

"I didn't say your husband was not in Cairo. Truthfully, Mrs. Brandt, why did you come here?"

Paulette sat very still, looking at him. Somehow she believed she could afford to be honest.

"You're right. I've a reason of my own for coming. A very *personal* reason. You'll recognize my husband in this picture, I'm sure." She opened her handbag, removed the folded newspaper clipping, and handed it to him.

He took it silently and brought it over to the window. She watched for his response, but there was none. After a very long minute he looked out the window toward the railway station, tapping the end of his glasses against his teeth.

"Where did you get this?"

"From Rhoda Nickerson."

He turned sharply. "Are you sure it was from Rhoda?"

"Yes. She sent it to me with a note, quite innocently, I think. She was merely surprised that he was in Cairo."

"I see." It was a thoughtful response instead of a polite remark. "Yes, I understand."

Paulette wished *she* understood. Have you seen this woman before? she wanted to ask, but caught herself. It seemed out of place to ask him. Any woman as attractive as Anna Kruger would be known in the social circles of Cairo and Alexandria. Suddenly she tensed. Kruger! Why had that name not dawned on her before now? Had she been dazed all this time? Kruger. The name on the matchbook. The matchbook with the number written on it. A telephone number? Of the German ambassador? An ambassador by the name of Kruger. Might the name and number written on the matchbook not have belonged to the ambassador at all, but Anna?

She saw Henley looking at her and suspected what her expression must reveal to him. She forced herself to calmness and leaned back in the hard chair, stilling her heart. "The photo disturbs you," he said sympathetically. "I wouldn't concern myself all that much, Mrs. Brandt, if I were you. I'm sure there is some reasonable explanation."

She wondered. "You know all about him."

"Perhaps more than you know about him," he agreed gently. "Look, it may be that I'm making a mistake with you. Time alone will tell. Somehow I think it's important to take the chance, partly because the times leave me little choice. Then again, I have a hunch you may not disappoint us. I would like to bring you to meet someone tomorrow. Would you be willing to go with me?"

He didn't say where, but she took that omission as deliberate. She decided she had little to lose in accepting, and perhaps much to gain.

"Yes. I'll oblige you, Colonel. I don't suppose you'd wish to tell me now what this is about?"

He smiled. "Tomorrow. I think several things will be cleared up then. In the meantime, please don't worry. Now, you're looking very tired and hungry." He straightened from the desk. "I'll have Sergeant Tomlinson see to your photograph and then bring you to your quarters at the Citadel."

Paulette stood. "Thank you. Am I allowed to leave the Citadel to do any sightseeing?"

He smiled. "Surely. But I will give you some fatherly advice. Be careful where you wander, as Cairo has its seamier side. If you need a guide, I can arrange for one of my staff to help you get about."

A guide would also mean the colonel would be well aware of her comings and goings, and at present she preferred it otherwise. She had business to attend to on her own. "Thank you, but I shall do well enough on my own, Colonel. I really did come to get that story for Mort. I'd like access to the prisoners of war."

"Do you speak German?" There was a hint of hopefulness in his voice that made her wonder.

"No," she admitted. "I was expecting a translator from your staff." She smiled.

He was thoughtful a moment, then nodded, more in understanding than a promise of cooperation. He smiled. "We'll see."

She persisted. "Mort told me there would be a translator."

"Did he?" was all he said, almost cheerfully. "Arrangements will be made with my staff. Naturally, all this will take a few days." He took her arm and led her toward the door. "Tomlinson will take good care of you. Garret would be very upset with us indeed if we didn't. If there's anything we can do to make you more comfortable, Mrs. Brandt, call Tomlinson."

Paulette thanked him again, but her mind was still on their strange discourse. She looked at him keenly. She said cautiously, "Is there anything I should do until I hear from you tomorrow?" Paulette wasn't sure what she expected him to say, but thought he might have some order when it came to Garret. She detected a deliberate look of detachment.

"Right now you must do nothing except go to your quarters. It's quite conceivable to anyone who may be interested in your agenda that Garret's wife would naturally be exhausted after such a trip to Cairo to meet her husband. Let's not do anything out of the ordinary. Shall we say that you are under my care until he arrives? That, too, would be assumed. Forget everything else we have been discussing. Keep alert, but be calm and natural. You're here to meet your husband. You're also here on business for *Horizon*. Let's keep it at that for the present."

Paulette did not understand. At least, she tried to convince herself that she did not.

As Sergeant Tomlinson entered the room and exchanged glances with the colonel, she knew she understood far less than she had come to grips with. Something important concerning Garret was in play. Amazingly enough, Colonel Henley wanted her to become involved.

14

The matchbook. Paulette's mind had considered the hotel name and address printed on it more times than she cared to count since her decision back in London to make the journey to Cairo. In the bright sunshine of early afternoon, with her security pass in hand, she left the Citadel, slightly surprised that Colonel Henley hadn't left a message with the sentry to halt her from leaving without an escort. Perhaps because she'd been overly tired yesterday she had mistaken Henley's attitude when he'd questioned and advised her. She blamed her own wariness about Garret on the feeling that she was under surveillance.

Paulette walked quickly to the railway station, which was already crowded with the day's rush, found a cab, and rode to the address in question.

When she arrived there, she felt her resolve tighten as she stood across the street and gazed at the hotel. Yes, there it was, looking as normal as any hotel on the streets of London. No mystery here, just a building, more a house than a hotel, with three narrow stories, each fronted with four windows, presumably each window a room, and facing a wrought-iron balcony, with a stairway at each end leading down to a courted garden. The front of the hotel had been restored to its onetime glory in the years of the ruling Victorian governor-general. The House of Cairo, the sign read, and its Arabic-style lettering in black brought back to her the questions first experienced when she had discovered the matchbook and the receipt from Berlin.

A donkey cart and driver in a white *galliyab* was parked in front of the entrance as if waiting for someone in particular. The front arch, like an arbor, led past a narrow but intricately carved door, and then past a flight of stately stone stairs that went up to the rooms above, and ended inside a cobbled yard with blooming flame trees. Paulette stood looking at the hotel, thinking how strange it was that the man she'd been married to for nearly a year now was so little known to her. She felt she was isolated from a secret life of his with only her suspicions to feed her imagination. She imagined his secret comings and goings and wondered, too, what he'd been trying to accomplish in Cairo for the so-called company of Kimball, Baylor, and Lammiter. Garret had friends in Cairo, he had told her. What kind of friends? Her heart pinched. Had one of those *friends* been the attractive woman in the newspaper photo?

Someone came bursting out the front door and interrupted her reverie. Paulette started with surprise. He was dark-haired, dark-eyed, with strong shoulders beneath a khaki short-sleeved shirt and trousers not so different from the hundreds of British soldiers in the BTE—the British Troops in Egypt—that she'd seen all morning. Quinn O'Brien stopped short when he saw her. His stern face broke into a quick smile as he recognized her. "Hey! I don't believe it. What luck." He raised a hand in a salute-style greeting and bounded across the street toward her.

"Paulette, you're the vision of an angel come to shed blessing on my day. For crying out loud, what are you doing here?"

"Quinn!" she cried. "I came to find you, of course!" She laughed in relief that he was apparently just fine. "We heard you were missing in the desert back in January."

"Ah, that. Sorry to cause any worry. A whiff of a story about an Italian general defecting to the Brits brought me to Tripoli, but it disappeared into thin air. You didn't come all this way looking for me!"

She grinned at him. "Actually, I'm here on assignment for Mort. Can you believe it?"

"No. How did you get that husband of yours to agree, or is he here with you, lucky devil?"

Seeing the friendly smile, yet inquisitive eyes, her emotions halted from rushing ahead with explanations. Not even Quinn was to know that she searched for Garret.

"Oh, Garret is so busy representing the company that I've time to do a little adventuring on my own. "

"So what's your feature on? The war or Farouk?"

"Perhaps both, if it can be managed." There was no certainty she could ever get into Abdin Palace to see the Egyptian king.

"Maybe we can get together on this," he suggested. "Though I won't be staying in Cairo long. I'm arranging a transfer to Athens. That's where the action is when it comes to emotional drama. Refugees by the zillion, starving old women and babies—all being bombed and strafed by the Luftwaffe. Sound worthy of Mort Collier? I'll say it is! He'd drool to get such photographs and story...say..." and he lowered his voice and leaned toward her. "How about a runaway countess from Bulgaria hiding as a peasant on that refugee trail over the mountains into Greece, fleeing toward freedom?"

He took her elbow and walked her slowly up the street. "Is there such a story?" she asked. "Which countess, do you know?"

"I'm working on it. I'll wire Mort and tell him we're both onto something red hot. What do you say, beautiful?"

"Not so fast." She smiled. "It sounds red hot all right, but, well..." and she glanced back at the hotel entrance. "Are you staying here?" she asked suddenly.

"No. Why?"

"You came from there, or was I mistaken?"

"I was there, but my venture turned into another dud. I was tipped off last night about a Bulgarian checking in straight from the refugee lines of Greece, but the lackey at the front desk has denied it until he's blue in the face." He gave her a measuring glance. "Are you saying you've a room here in the midst of a nest of Hun spies and yours truly didn't know it? I'm really slipping up!"

Hun spies here? She knew how it might sound if she explained that she'd come here with the hope of finding Garret. It might be best now to keep that to herself.

"No—I'm staying at the Citadel. Today I'm just having a look around Cairo."

"Not much to see here. I'll take you to the old bazaar in the north of town. You'll think you were back in the days of Ali Baba. So...hubby isn't in Cairo, huh? Where is he?"

They had come to a busy intersection and Quinn gestured to an unoccupied donkey-driven cart that was a taxi. Finding herself waylayed by friendly hands, she submitted and stepped into the back of the cart where there was a small wooden seat. Quinn climbed up beside her.

"Geneva," she said. "Garret's there on business." She saw no cause to explain that he had left Switzerland to have his photo taken with Anna Kruger in the *Cairo Gazette*. There would be time later to set the hazy facts straight if she chose to confide in Quinn. And she wanted to, desperately, for he had always had a friendly shoulder to cry on. But she was thoroughly aware that she was no longer free to unburden herself to another man. She was Mrs. Garret Brandt. Even so, Quinn could be a treasure of help and information, even if she didn't decide to turn to him for comfort.

"I may never forgive you for getting married while I was away doing my journalistic duty," Quinn said with a perturbed smile. "That wasn't very fair, was it?" But his eyes were friendly. "Mrs. Brandt," he said with cynical amusement that appeared to be directed at himself. "I'm not sure that suits you very well."

"Garret would disagree." She smiled.

Quinn took her left hand and looked at her wedding ring. He managed a grimace and a sigh of resignation. "Ah, well. It's not the first time I've batted out. Seriously, Paulette, you should let me contact Collier about Greece. It really is the place to be during the next few months. Not much happening in Egypt until Rommel comes charging across the desert into Cairo, or Mussolini's blasted planes bomb us again." He looked up at the sky with a scowl. "They nearly blew up the hotel I was staying at in Alexandria."

Paulette had read of the heavy bombing there and wondered what she would do if she heard the roar of airplanes headed towards Cairo. She held no grand illusions about her courage and prayed she wouldn't show herself to be a quavering coward.

"Then you think Rommel will defeat us and take Egypt?"

"Personally, I have little doubt. The Nazi war machine is unstoppable. But don't go around telling anyone I said that. I savor my head. The British at Gray Pillars have little forgiveness for 'propagandists.' That's what they call anyone who sees the light."

"Gray Pillars?"

"Oh—HQ," he explained. "That's the popular name for the building. If you lean forward and look, you can see it from here."

They were at Soleiman Pasha Square as he pointed down the street toward two separate buildings used by the military: Gray Pillars, and Semiramus Hotel area that was HQ for the BTE.

"I must say the British Army and Intelligence headquarters help me to feel more secure," she said.

"Don't get too secure," he advised. "The Germans' plan to occupy won't be easily thwarted."

"You keep saying that, Quinn. But Garret believes the Eighth Army in the western desert can hold Rommel off."

He shook his head and lit a cigarette. "Is that what he told you? When?"

She sighed and shrugged. "It's not just Garret who thinks so. Haven't we beat the Italians back toward the road to Libya?"

"Who told you that? Alexandria is close to being invaded by the Italian army! Really, Paulette, it's safer in Athens. Besides that, you can pay a quick visit to your old friends, the Nickersons. By now, Rhoda will be wishing badly for you to show up."

Rhoda's pregnancy would surely complicate things for her and Fergus all right. But knowing her cheerful nature, Paulette would bet that she was as optimistic as always about their future, no matter how dark the clouds appeared on the horizon.

"I'll think about it, Quinn," she told him. But she had no desire to venture forth across the Mediterranean toward Crete and Greece with German and Italian warships patrolling the waters. She wondered now how she could have told Rhoda that she would visit her in the summer with such certainty.

It's seeing the danger firsthand, she thought. *Suddenly danger and death attain their full stature.* She shuddered, and wondered if there were any Christian churches around Cairo where one could pray and hear words of hope and courage from the Scriptures. There must be, but if not, there would surely be chapels and chaplains serving the military. There ought to be a church at the Citadel. She decided she would look for it on Sunday. There was so much to pray about besides the war's outcome, including her marriage, Garret's whereabouts, and their future. *It is time to seek the Lord*, she thought. *Perhaps it's not too late.*

Quinn checked the time on his watch. "You look like you could use some tea. Are you in a hurry?"

"No, tea sounds lovely." She had questions to ask Quinn, and she suspected he had some of her. How many dare she answer?

She remembered something he'd said earlier outside the House of Cairo. "What did you mean back at the hotel when you said it was known for spies?"

"Cairo's a snake pit of conspiracy and betrayal." He shrugged. "I don't trust Abdul, is all. A friend of mine is sure he saw him at a Muslim Brotherhood meeting last week."

"Abdul? The man who runs the hotel?" she kept uneasiness out of her voice.

"Yes. He's as near to being a Nazi spy as we come to in Cairo."

"What's the Muslim Brotherhood? Is it a political organization?"

"That's what they call themselves. They're pro-Nazi sympathizers, misguided enough to believe Hitler will free them from the British and give Egypt sovereignty to run its own affairs. They're hoping Rommel will defeat us in the western desert. They stir up a lot of trouble and aren't above assassination of perceived enemies, usually Egyptians."

"If that's true," she protested, "why aren't they arrested?"

"Egypt is a sovereign state and technically neutral. They're civilians."

"But any order of the British military police here is law."

"Yes, but arresting them as Nazi and Italian spies would cause a riot."

"And there's no *proof* about Abdul?"

"Top enemy agents are just too clever to leave evidence lying about. Agents are like cockroaches in this town. They slip away into a thousand and one cracks as soon as you turn the lights on."

Paulette looked at him, hoping the devastating alarm she felt wasn't visible to his scrutiny. Abdul, the matchbook, the hotel, and now she had learned it was deemed by British Intelligence to be a den of Nazi agents!

Quinn paid the driver and brought her to the back of Ashraf's Garden, a tearoom on the Sharia Ibrahim Pasha, opposite the entrance to Ezbekiah Gardens. Inside, Ashraf's many silvery mirrors covered dark mahogany walls, and there were Egyptian urns of lush greenery and flowers. There were tables in rooms that opened out onto the garden, umbrellas shadowing tables where tea drinkers sat, while young Egyptian waiters in whitish-blue uniforms carried about huge pots of tea and plates of the typical sweet cakes indulged in by the British: fruitcake with marzipan, lemon curd tarts, slices of seedcake, maids of honor, rock cake, Swiss roll, and cream eclairs.

It was dim and cool inside, but Paulette preferred the airy garden surrounded by a high wall that separated the lush green from the noisy, dusty street. Ashraf's was crowded, and Quinn told her that it usually was at this hour of day. He then changed the mood of the conversation to the relaxed atmosphere of the quiet tearoom by passing on bits of information about British society that he thought might interest her, but Paulette, though wearing a fixed smile, was only halfheartedly listening.

He told her that Ashraf's was regarded as a private club for British civilians, especially the old-timers who had lived in Cairo for years, going back to before the Great War. Most of the soldiers went next door to the Tipperary Club. Only officers could go to the best hotels: Shepheards, the Continental, the Turf Club, the Trocadero Club, and the Gezira Club.

Paulette took a moment to look around her. There were staff officers and businessmen and many international women who had fled their countries from the war: French, Italian, Polish, Bulgarian, Copts, and Greeks along with the British. They all appeared to be wealthy, their hair was well groomed, their clothing stylish and expensive, and they all wore heavy jewelry, much of it no doubt smuggled out just before the invasion of the Italian and German armies.

Paulette didn't have tea and cake on her mind, or the pleasant garden with marigolds and jasmine. She was wondering how she could avoid a discussion about Garret, as she knew her companion was curious. She was again thinking of the House of Cairo. It could make sense now, why Quinn had said back in London at the Nickersons' that he had seen Garret at the German embassy. Ambassador Kruger had been scribbled on the matchbook. Dare she contact the German ambassador and inquire about her husband? If her husband was a German agent, the Nazis would likely consider her to be prying and a risk to Garret's cover.

Their tea arrived, and Paulette poured the hot amber liquid into glasses with silver-plated holders, mint leaves in each.

Quinn watched her over the lemon curd tart he cut into with his fork. "We're old friends, aren't we, Paulette?"

She looked up quickly from stirring her tea. "What?"

"I'm not blind. You're worried about something pretty serious. Is it your husband?"

Quinn had always been bold and a little pushy. He was so now, almost forcing her into a confession by offering his shoulder to cry on. She knew that to give in would not be wise. Instead, she managed a smile. "Am I so transparent?"

"I don't believe you were standing out front of the hotel sight-seeing." He lifted his glass of tea and drank, watching her. "Did you think Garret was there?"

There was sympathy in his dark eyes, yet she held back.

She decided to toss it back to him. "Why should I think that?"

"The House of Cairo isn't exactly a 'must see' on the tourists' circuit."

"You never really explained why you were there, either. Was the Bulgarian story just a ruse?"

He set his glass down. "Well, remember the friend I mentioned who tipped me off on Abdul? He happens to room there, or did. I thought he might have something more on Abdul's friends, so I went to see him again, thinking we could talk over breakfast."

"And did you?" she asked, silencing her alarm.

"He wasn't there. Abdul gave me some story about his packing up and leaving for London in a hurry." He frowned and slowly lit a cigarette.

"And you don't believe him?" she asked, her unease growing.

"No. He was to come with us to Greece. Something is fishy. If Tony just happened to uncover something he shouldn't have...well, you see how it is. Or might be."

Yes, she saw how it was.

He looked at her, still frowning. "What bothers me about all this is you, Paulette."

"Me? What could I possibly have to do with it?"

"I don't mean you personally. Look, I don't enjoy saying this, but I think I'd better come out with it. You think Garret had a room there, didn't you? Maybe he did. And maybe Tony knew it, too, and found out something about him and Abdul and the German embassy."

"Garret?" she said with believable indignation. "Don't be absurd, Quinn. What would he have to do with either your missing friend or Abdul?"

He shrugged. "I thought you might be able to tell me."

"How can I when there's absolutely nothing to say?" Her heart was thudding, but she calmly chose a slice of seedcake and forced herself to take a bite.

"If you're going to play it that way," he said, shrugging.

"There is no other way to play it. I'd advise you to go to the authorities at once. Your friend may have met with some kind of accident. If Abdul is cooperating with the Germans, and they thought your friend was snooping—"

He blew a smoke ring. "Leave all this, Paulette. Come with the news troop to Athens."

"I'm here in Cairo for a story, Quinn. I told you. Mort arranged with his friends in the military for me to do a feature on prisoners of war."

"Funny. Collier has friends at HQ? What does he share in common with straight aces?"

"I don't know why you say that. Mort was in the last war. He was stationed here."

"Was he? Who did he arrange for you to see, Major Bitterman?"

She hadn't heard of Bitterman. "No, Colonel Henley. A member of his staff is arranging my itinerary at the prisoner of war camp."

He whistled. "Nice itinerary, huh? Breakfast with Mussolini's top sergeant and lunch with Hitler's lieutenant. It's enough to make the weak-stomached ill."

"The colonel's arranged for me to stay in the married quarters at the Citadel. It's mostly empty now since the families were sent out of Egypt."

Quinn poured more tea. "Colonel Henley, you say. Yes, I've seen him around. A rather pleasant, mild-mannered man with graying hair."

Paulette didn't see Henley's temperament as benign. When it came to getting what he wanted, he was like iron.

"Why are you smiling?" she asked.

"I wouldn't have expected Collier and Henley to share much in common."

"They were both students of journalism before the last war. Knowing Mort, he'd naturally make good use of an old friendship to arrange for my stay."

Quinn nodded as he watched her. "I was surprised when I learned you married Brandt." He looked serious now, even troubled. "It was a little fast, wasn't it? Especially for you. You'd convinced me you wanted to take life slowly. That was the reason I didn't rush our relationship."

She picked up her cup and drank the now-lukewarm tea.

"All right. I'll keep quiet." He stubbed out his cigarette.

Paulette said quietly, looking at her tea, "I agree it was quick. If I surprised you, I also surprised myself." She set the cup down on the saucer with a rattle. When she looked up, Quinn shook his head.

"I won't ask how it's going. It's pretty obvious."

"Is it?" she said with mild dismay. "I didn't want it to be."

"Oh, come on. What's one to think when a wife comes halfway around the world looking in hotels for her husband? It's clear there's trouble."

"All's not lost," she said quickly, rejecting the image of her husband and the woman in the clipping that popped into her mind again. She had awakened last night seeing that incriminating picture come to life, with Garret's arm around her waist, and the beautiful Anna looking at him so expectantly, even fearfully as the photographer had snapped their photo. She couldn't tell Quinn that Garret had been here in Cairo during the last eight weeks, attending gala dinner parties at King Farouk's palace. She hastily changed the subject. "And you, Quinn? When are you leaving for Greece?"

"In a week, if I can arrange the papers. Listen, that little feature idea of Collier's isn't going to fly. Your readers won't be interested in some Italian soldier busting his uniform buttons in loyalty to Mussolini. Think about it, Paulette, and you'll see I'm right. If what you want is a saga that will rivet readers, then your feature story waits for you on the mountain roads from Bulgaria through Albania into Greece."

Paulette agreed that the story of women, children, and the elderly forced out of their villages by the Luftwaffe to flee for safety into the mountains of Greece was heartbreaking.

"There's always a chance the story will be cold and old by the time London and New York get it," he said, "but that's a chance I'm willing to take."

"A story like that—how can it ever be old and blasé?" Paulette protested with outrage. "Whole towns and villages uprooted and driven out by bombs to freeze to death on mountain roads?"

"That's the way I see it." He looked at her keenly. "That's why you ought to tell Henley to forget the status quo. Forget the prisoner of war story. Come with me to Greece, and your words will bleed when they're cut. A photographer is coming with me. The pictures and tales of horror and woe we send back home will have the pacifists howling for America to enter the war on the side of Britain!"

She was caught up in the fervor of his emotion. "But will they really care, Quinn? What if Americans say it's propaganda, warmongering? All the world is aflame, and who can put it out, and why should Americans be elected to save Europe? You heard what Garret said that night at Fergus and Rhoda's place. It's all so painful and so ugly that few care to learn more and become involved. We have our own lives to live, they say. We can carry only so many burdens before we're crushed beneath the load. If we fall, who will come to liberate America?"

"No one," Quinn said flatly. "It's my opinion the world would stand idly by and do very little. Maybe nothing."

She looked at him in dismay. "Is that all there is to life, to freedom in America? We must exist for more than the right to live indulgent lives. We must be zealous for more than self-gratification. If not, the cause for which America became a nation no longer lives."

"That sounds religious."

"Perhaps, I—maybe it is. You may not know it, but America's foundation as a nation was based upon Christian faith, morals, and the Bible. Take those away and the nation could come tumbling down."

His eyebrows shot up. "I'm not a religious person, Paulette. You're simply giving me the same argument as church people."

"Just a moment ago you sounded as though it was your argument as well."

He shook his head and pushed his cup away. "The only power I see, and believe in, is the power of government. Without an iron fist and a firm boot, the masses cannot be ruled. And without the rule of law, you have anarchy." He looked at her with a grave expression. "You might say that the State is a god. And the glory of the State is in its rulers."

She shook her head. "No, no, I don't see it that way, Quinn. I could never accept that. The State is subservient to the sovereign will of God. It's 'Thy kingdom come. Thy will be done in earth, as it is in heaven.' These are the words of Christ," she said. "We would all do well to pay heed. It is the iron jackboot of Nazism and all other 'isms' that threaten to turn the world into a dark and dreary evil empire. We must fight against putting the secular on the throne. An anti-Christian agenda threatens to deceive the masses into following false shepherds."

Quinn laughed, laughed loudly and long. "Good heavens, Paulette! I didn't know you could be an extremist on a soapbox! Well, you make a very pretty one. And if that witless husband of yours doesn't get back soon, he may find himself locked out in the dark. What do you say about that sizzling story just waiting for us in the mountains of Greece? Think of all that emotion you just unleashed being poured into Collier's feature. And you won't be the only woman on our team. We've got some nurses and humanitarian aid workers going along with us, and a doctor."

Paulette's energy had gone out of her. She was thinking about it, not knowing exactly what her answer would be, when Colonel Henley appeared, coming from the direction of one of the other tables in the shade of flowering trees. He paused beside them.

"Well, young lady, so you've had a good night's rest and are adjusting to Cairo." His uniform was neatly pressed and commanding, and he himself appeared fresh and alert, his light blue eyes gazing out steadily from behind his rimless glasses. He looked at Quinn, smiled politely, and put out a slim hand. "Quinn O'Brien, isn't it?"

Quinn looked surprised that the colonel knew him. He smiled. "I hope this doesn't mean my writing has gotten me tailed by security?"

The colonel was also smiling. "I doubt if Mrs. Brandt understands your little jest."

Quinn looked at Paulette. "Colonel Henley works with CID. Recently they've taken offense with journalists sending stories out of Egypt."

"Only stories that might enlighten the Nazis. Your name isn't on the blacklist, Mr. O'Brien. As matter of fact, you've come to us with high recommendation," Henley assured him. "We both have some of the same friends in high places."

Quinn laughed and stood. "That, at least, is encouraging to hear."

What mutual friends in high places? Paulette wondered.

Quinn said: "I've got another appointment, Paulette. Can you get back to the Citadel all right?"

"Yes, perfectly. Thanks for the tea, Quinn."

"What about dinner tonight?"

"I'm afraid I've first dibs on Mrs. Brandt's dinner hour," Henley said with a fatherly smile. "You may try tomorrow night, Mr. O'Brien."

"Maybe I've underestimated the CID," Quinn said jokingly.

"Let's hope not." The colonel turned back to Paulette. "May I sit down and join you, Mrs. Brandt?"

He pulled out a chair and sat himself, reaching for the teapot as Quinn saluted Paulette and left the garden by way of another gateway that led to the busy, dusty streets of Cairo.

Paulette looked after him, unsmiling, then became aware of Colonel Henley. She turned and met his sober gaze. Had he followed her here?

15

She let her question slip by without asking it.

"You went to the House of Cairo. I assume you thought your husband might be there."

He had trailed her, or had someone else do it. She mustn't underestimate him. "So, my slipping away from the Citadel this morning didn't come as a surprise to anyone after all."

He smiled. "We expected you might wish to do some sight-seeing. Even so, it's quite true, Mrs. Brandt, that you shouldn't wander off without an escort."

"Even with all the British MPs about? Besides, everyone seems quite friendly."

"Friendly faces are not always what they appear."

She looked at him, reading more into his suggestion than thieves on the Cairo streets.

"How long have you known Quinn O'Brien?" Henley asked.

"Three or four years."

"You're not certain?"

"He gave me my first job as a journalist. He introduced me to Mort."

"What did he discuss with you this afternoon?"

She didn't hesitate. "Enemy agents. He seems to think the House of Cairo has more than its share, including the proprietor, a man named Abdul."

"Did he mention your husband?"

She looked at him sharply. "My husband is an American, loyal to his country, and a friend of Britain—"

"Then he did mention Garret."

"As a matter of fact, he did. He asked me where he was, and I told him Geneva. Quinn thought that I had been looking for him at the House of Cairo."

"That's why you went there, isn't it?"

She avoided a direct answer. "Quinn asked me the same question. I told him I was sightseeing. I don't know for sure where my husband is. I told you yesterday why I came to Cairo, and I told Quinn also. I'm here on an assignment for *Horizon*. I have nothing more to say to either of you." She tossed her napkin down. "And now, Colonel, if you'll excuse me?" She pushed back her chair and stood.

Colonel Henley stood at the same time. He was laughing quietly. Paulette didn't think anything was amusing. "Please," he said softly, "do sit down again, Mrs. Brandt. I apologize for what must seem to you to be rude questions, especially in light of your concerns. Please," he said again, his eyes grave.

Paulette slowly sat down once more. "Colonel, if you have any information on my husband, good or bad, I should like to hear it."

"I promise to get right to the point."

A group of rowdy Egyptian demonstrators was heard down the street shouting in English: "British out! Rommel! Rommel!"

Paulette turned to the colonel and saw his alert expression. The angry voices shouted now in Arabic: *"Bissamah Allah, fi alard Hitler!"*

The colonel wore a twisted smile. Paulette could see his scorn. "They're marching in this direction." He stood. "We'd better leave."

The others in the garden were leaving also, except for the military personnel who remained, standing, looking toward the wall.

"What are they shouting?" she asked in a low voice. "Do you know?"

"'In heaven, Allah, on earth, Hitler.' It's a war chant of the radicals now that Rommel's Afrika Korps have arrived and scored victories. The Egyptians expect to see the Germans riding triumphantly into Cairo, so they are more bold with their insults. King Farouk's government is pro-German, and the people know it. Now that Rommel is getting closer to the city, protests are heating up. I'm surprised they dared to come here. They usually demonstrate in Abdin Square around the palace. That they've come so boldly in the middle of Cairo means they are confident. Come!" He took her arm just above the elbow in a firm grip and walked swiftly but calmly toward the tearoom.

A soldier came hurrying toward them who must have heard the loud voices and demonstration. It was Sergeant Tomlinson, looking from the garden wall and the angry voices of protest to the colonel with indecision.

Henley appeared to be perfectly calm. "We're quite all right, Tomlinson. Have you the motorcar?"

"Yes, sir, It's waiting in the alley."

"Then let's be on our way, Sergeant."

In the hot glaring light of the afternoon, Tomlinson silently opened the side passenger door and Paulette slid in, followed by the colonel. Tomlinson quickly got behind the wheel and drove away. Nothing was spoken throughout the mysterious ride until Paulette said, "May I ask where you're taking me, Colonel Henley?"

"I'm taking you on a house tour, Mrs. Brandt."

She looked at him expecting to see a smile, and saw instead, to her surprise, that his thin face was quite sober.

"I'm serious," he said. "I'm taking you to the house Gilbert Simington left you in his will."

Paulette suddenly remembered her uncle speaking of a house in Cairo. She had forgotten all about it in the aftermath that followed his death. She tried to focus on what Colonel Henley was saying.

"He bought this particular house six years ago. It has a checkered history, I'm afraid, one that's affected his life, and now yours."

Paulette had no reply to such startling news.

~~~

Central Cairo and the flowering Ezbekiah Gardens were mostly reserved for fine hotels, eateries, and shops, and were frequented by a mostly European clientele. The area reminded Paulette of an oasis that was distinct from its arid surroundings and Muslim culture. As Sergeant Tomlinson drove the motorcar in and out of foot traffic and military medic vehicles, she saw a small building overcrowded with British soldiers and a cross above the door. Colonel Henley followed her gaze as they drove by.

"That's a Christian center handing out tea and cakes to our soldiers. In the evenings they hold Bible studies. It is founded on the principles of Oswald Chambers' work here in the Great War. I recall that there were over sixty thousand soldiers in and around Egypt and the western desert. Chambers worked with the Young Men's Christian Association to provide studies during that era. I attended several myself. He was a great Christian. He and Mrs. Chambers lived right out at Zeitoun, at the base."

Paulette had heard of Oswald Chambers and his missionary work with Australian soldiers in the past world war until his unexpected death from illness. She had also heard that the YMCA, with which he worked, was still laboring in Cairo to bring wholesome activities to a second generation of fighting men being lured to the opium and prostitution dens in the infamous El Birkeh area in the city. In this moment of war and confusion, it encouraged her to know that there were men and women serving Jesus Christ and teaching His words to military men. Amidst certain darkness there were lamps of light burning brightly to show the pathway to the arms of God, where love and forgiveness waited through the mercies of Jesus Christ.

As she thought of Oswald Chambers, she decided to locate some of his writings on the Christian life and begin reading them during her devotions. She'd been neglecting her Anglican Prayer Book recently. She usually read one of the written prayers each morning and before bed. She envied men like Mr. Chambers who could speak to God as Father, pouring out their hearts before His throne. She had never felt comfortable doing so because she had never been certain of her eternal destiny. She believed it must come through the Anglican Church. She had a Bible, too, but rarely read anything more from it than a few psalms or certain passages from the Gospels. *Maybe I ought to start reading through the New Testament,* she thought.

16

Paulette was deep in thought as Sergeant Tomlinson drove from the western section of the city and edged into the narrow, crowded streets of Old Cairo. This was obviously not the British sector. Paulette put her thoughts away and began to look about her, wondering why Uncle Gilly had bought a house here, and what Colonel Henley meant when he'd told her the house had affected Gilly's life—and would affect hers as well. She experienced an uneasy moment as she remembered what Garret had said about her uncle: he was a vengeful man with suspect motives. Although she hadn't experienced ill-treatment from him in the past, she kept thinking about how he'd taken his life. What had prompted him to meticulously plan his own poisoning? A normal person would never do such a thing. Garret had seemed to think Gilly had hoped to render him harm.

And now this house.

Why had he left it to her? He knew she would never settle in Cairo. There must be some significance to what he had done, but she didn't have all the pieces to the puzzle.

Paulette turned toward Colonel Henley. "Did my uncle's lawyer, Mr. Jacobson, inform you of this house in Cairo being left to me?"

"Yes, this morning. I believe he is sending you complete details, along with the rest of the will."

She nodded, wondering. "Was there any mention of the London estate?"

"Actually, yes. But I hardly think I'm in a position to discuss it with you, Mrs. Brandt. This house, once known as the Blaine House, is another matter as it concerns your future...and Garret's."

"My uncle said something about leaving the London estate to someone else."

There was a sympathetic flicker in the pale blue eyes beneath his rimless glasses. "I'm afraid that's so. He willed it to the daughter of a woman he had once been in love with here in Egypt in the Great War. Her name was Beth Wescott. She later married an inspector in the Cairo police by the name of Julian Mortimer."

"I see." Paulette was disappointed, but not bitter. Uncle Gilly had every right to leave his possessions to whomever he wished. She wondered if Mrs. Beth Wescott Mortimer had been the young woman that Opal mentioned whom Gilly had loved and come to England years after the Great War to try to "lure" away from her husband. Paulette was thankful that if the gossip was true, Beth had refused his lurid trap.

As Sergeant Tomlinson slowed the motorcar, Paulette quickly surveyed the area. On either side of the street were closely spaced houses of stucco with wrought-iron lattice work. The residence that Colonel Henley had called Blaine House was located at the very end of the street, away from the other structures. The tall, blue-roofed house was flanked by rambling shrubs and stunted bushes and was set far back in its yard.

Sergeant Tomlinson drove up the shady, tree-lined driveway, stopping in front of a gravel path that led to the door. Paulette's mood grew more sober.

"No one is living here now?" she asked Colonel Henley.

"It's been vacant for some time."

They walked up the path, and Henley took out a key for the front lock.

Inside, the air was musty, and the rooms were dark from overgrown bushes at the back windows. Paulette felt a strange sensation, as though these rooms had been silent witnesses to fateful events in the past.

The house could be fixed up, but also needs the right furniture, she thought. Paulette looked up the staircase that led from the wide hall to a narrow landing around three sides of the stairwell. It looked as though the landing accessed two bedrooms separated by an office, and there appeared to be a large sewing room at the end of the hall. On the first floor she examined a drawing room and a smaller dining room that looked out on a garden at the back of the yard.

She walked to the bottom of the stairwell and stood there, gazing up into the dim silence. "Why did Uncle Gilly buy this house? And why did he leave it to me?" She turned slowly and found Colonel Henley watching her with alert thoughtfulness. Sergeant Tomlinson had passed through a large archway into the dining area and was opening windows, letting in fresh air and light. He then went to guard the front door, leaving her with Henley in the dining room.

"You'd better sit down."

She did so expectantly.

"What do you know about your parents?"

"Very little. They were on the *Valiant*. It was sunk by a U-boat in 1916."

"Did you ever ask for more information?"

"Yes, of course I did. It only led to dead ends. I believe they lived here in Egypt for a while before the last war, but they might as well have vanished into the desert," she said unhappily. "I haven't been able to find any record of their past lives. If I weren't proof of their existence, I'd think they were ghosts," and she smiled ruefully.

"They existed all right. Here in Egypt and elsewhere: Aleppo, Baghdad, India. They didn't go down with the *Valiant*, Mrs. Brandt."

Her eyes widened. "I was told they did."

"Individuals like your parents don't leave their footprints in stone. They live and die without trumpets or medals. Only the result of their work is left behind, and that is often classified."

She looked at him sharply. "Classified? My father was an agent?"

A flicker showed in his pale blue eyes. "No."

She relaxed. "Then what did you mean—"

"Your mother was," he said softly.

Her breath caught. She leaned forward. "My mother?" she whispered, unbelieving.

"I can't give you her name. It would undermine the individual whose right it is to choose whether to explain matters to you or conceal them."

She had no response. She stared at him in shock.

"I'm sorry, but I will tell you what I can. I think it will be enough for the present."

"Are you saying you *knew* my mother?"

"No. I only know about her. But I'm acquainted with someone who knew her. I'll let that person know of your desire to learn the truth. I can tell you she did her duty in the last war. You've every reason to take pride in your mother. I'm counting on you being very much like her."

Paulette didn't ask why. Her mind and heart were already too full. Her heart pounded with excitement. Her mother, an agent in the Great War.

"For Britain, of course?" she breathed.

He nodded, with a smile. "For Britain," he assured her.

Paulette's imagination took wings. "That's how she died?"

His smile vanished. "Yes."

She sat very still, awed by this news.

Henley paced slowly before a window where straggling rosebushes scratched against the pane in the breeze.

"I wish I had something honorable to say about Gilly, but I've only dark news about him." He turned and looked down at her soberly. "You'll need to hear it, since it affects both you and Garret."

She was fully alert, watching his every move. "Don't worry, Colonel. I can deal with whatever it is. Please go on."

He smiled grimly. "I'm gaining confidence in you."

She was proud of the compliment. For the first time in her life she had a starting point for who she was and what she was: a woman very much like her mother, who'd been committed to a cause worth dying for.

"The man you know as 'Uncle Gilly' is actually Gilbert Simonds, not Simington. He changed his last name because of a criminal record. He was in trouble with certain members of Garret's family, as well as with Garret himself." He paused to see if she was taking the news well. "He stole from them, in Berlin and here in Cairo."

Garret had mentioned that Gilly had stolen certain Egyptian artifacts, but she had thought he meant from the Cairo museum. "Garret said something about a disagreement that was the reason he visited Gilly in London. He never mentioned that it involved his family members."

"No. He had his reasons. You see, Mrs. Brandt, Garret was working with the Cairo museum on his great-aunt's collection of rare Egyptian pieces when he realized several were missing. A royal cat and some funerary pieces from King Tut's sarcophagus. As the genuine heir of his aunt's collection, he naturally wanted to trace their whereabouts and have them returned. He tracked down Gilbert Simonds and in the process discovered an even rarer piece belonging to the museum: Nefertari."

"What! The royal cat and other pieces in Gilly's collection *belong* to Garret?" She was astounded.

"Yes. It seems they first belonged to Garret's great-aunt, a woman with quite a reputation in the Great War here in Egypt. Her name was Helga Kruger."

Kruger! She stared at Henley. The name on the matchbook...the woman in the newspaper clipping...were they all related to Garret? Paulette didn't know whether to be relieved and happy, or even more worried about Garret and what he was involved in.

"Helga Kruger lived here in Cairo. She also had homes in Alexandria and Aleppo, to name a few. She was a wealthy woman who was not just loyal to England in the war, but was killed for her loyalties, and for Nefertari. She left everything she had to her son, who in turn, having no heir, left the better part of his mother's estate to his favorite nephew, Garret. You'll recognize these, I think?"

Paulette, trying to take all this in, looked on with surprise as he unlocked a box and removed a figurine that she immediately recognized as Nefertari. Next came the royal cat that Gilly had told her was stolen, and several other Egyptian objects. She looked at the cat. "That was in Gilly's collection in London. He accused Garret of stealing it."

"Yes. It belongs to your husband, and Nefertari belongs to the Cairo museum."

"How did they get here?" Paulette asked, wondering.

"Gilly sent them to the museum. We think he hoped it would make amends with Garret, but by then it was too late. Gilly had met him and knew that Garrett would not be satisfied until he was arrested. Although we have no proof, we think that was the reason he decided to take his life. He sensed there was no escape from his crimes. He then proceeded to get even with Garret by dragging you into the situation and planting doubts in your mind about your husband's loyalties."

Paulette was stunned. *I accused Garret of marrying me for the inheritance, when all the time he was the actual heir! If it wasn't so tragic, it might be amusing. But where is he now?*

"As it turns out, Gilly wasn't really your uncle. He took that role simply because he knew about your mother and must have decided having you as a niece in London lent him a certain respectability, though I understand he never had much to do with you."

Now she knew why.

"Simonds, however, *is* distantly related to you through his parents, so you see there is some truth to his claim of being a relative. We know a great deal about Gilly's deceased father, Sir Edgar Simonds. During the Great War, he was chief inspector of the Cairo police. Unfortunately, he was no better than his son, Gilly. This object—" and he held up Nefertari— "led to his death, the death of several others who wanted it, and even some who did not, including the woman who owned this house, Mrs. Sarah Blaine. I'm afraid Gilly was not merely a thief, but also a murderer."

Paulette's breath went out of her. Oh, no. Her hand went to her throat. "Sarah Blaine? Gilly murdered her?"

"No. He murdered a Turkish spy named Jemal Pasha."
He looked out the window. "Out there—in the rosebushes,
I believe. Of course, that is where Mrs. Blaine was discov-
ered as well. There is much more to that story than what
I'm telling you, but it will suffice for now. Are you all right,
Mrs. Brandt?"

Paulette wasn't sure. She cast a glance toward the windows where the branches still clawed, and she shuddered.

Henley looked sympathetic. He waited, gravely. He
must have decided she was all right, for he continued. "He
went to trial and was found guilty of Jemal's death, but he
received a reprieve from the death penalty. He served fifteen years and was released in 1932. He disappeared for
over a year, then in late 1933 he popped up again here in
Cairo. We traced his journey from Homberg, Germany. He
returned a very wealthy man."

"How? Where did he get the wealth?"

"No one knows. And if anyone in Germany knows, we
certainly don't have their cooperation. Gilly laid claim to
many Egyptian artifacts when he returned here, including
this Nefertari beauty—" and he turned it over in his hand
with thoughtful deliberation.

"He stole it?" she asked in a dull voice.

"He claimed he bought it from a dealer in Berlin."

"You don't think so?"

"We just don't know for certain. Garret insists Nefertari
was given to the museum in the name of Helga Kruger by
two nameless friends who worked with her in espionage.
The piece was in the museum until 1929, when it suddenly
and mysteriously disappeared without a trace. If it was
brought to Homberg, no one knows by whom. The authorities here in Egypt were stymied in their investigation by
one dead end after another. Interpol tried in Europe and
also failed. Garret, however, located it with Gilly while

searching for some artifacts belonging to Helga Kruger. The royal cat was stolen from Helga's house in Alexandria."

She was remembering things Garret had said that were at last starting to make sense. He'd been searching for and locating treasures that had not belonged to Gilly—nor to her, Gilly's supposed heiress—but to Garret's own family. So that was why he'd reacted as he did to the cuff links she'd given him to wear to their wedding ceremony. They had belonged to his family and Gilly had stolen them.

"Why would Gilly leave this house to me?" she wondered aloud incredulously. A house where at least two murders had been committed. The dark and gruesome thought made her shiver.

Henley took a long time lighting a cigarette. "We believe it was his way of getting back at Garret for unmasking him. He wanted to get even. He knew that if he could make you distrust him, and get you intrigued about matters Garret desperately wanted to keep from you, that it would bring him much unnecessary anxiety. I believe," he said dryly, "that Gilly succeeded."

Paulette felt ashamed that she could have been so deceptively manipulated, and by Gilly, who when young, had actually harmed someone in the garden...by the rosebushes...

"Who murdered Mrs. Blaine?" she asked uneasily.

Henley's face hardened as he appeared to be thinking of someone. "A German agent. The same man who murdered Helga Kruger."

She winced. A German agent. She looked around the dining room, through the arch, and toward the darkened stairway leading to the upper bedrooms. So much must have happened here during the previous war years. How strange that she should be standing here a generation later, finding herself involved, the story still working itself out.

She didn't understand everything, but perhaps she didn't need to. She had her own dilemma. Once again another death had taken place. Once again there was a war, an even greater, darker war, with a fiend at the head of a demonic regime called the Third Reich. Now she suspected there was a task for her, even as there had been for her mother, and Garret's great-aunt, Helga Kruger. Colonel Henley had spoken to her so strangely on her arrival at the barracks of Bab-el-Hadid. She believed he had something important for her to accomplish that would explain his reasons for bringing her here.

She walked to the window to stand beside him. She saw a large garden full of overgrown trees and rosebushes. It might have been a lovely retreat at one time, but now it reminded her of a forgotten cemetery. "What do you want of me?" she asked him quietly.

His face was serious. "Mrs. Brandt, there is someone else we must meet before we can discuss the matter." He looked at his watch. "He should be here by now—waiting in the garden. He came secretly, as he mustn't be seen with either of us. As you have guessed by now, Nazi agents thrive here in Cairo. If it's discovered that he has met with us, his life will be in danger."

She wondered about Henley's life, and her own.

"His name is Ambassador Kruger. Yes, he's related to your husband."

∽∽∽

Paulette walked to the kitchen door with Colonel Henley, which opened under an arbor and onto a flagstone path that led to the garden. Ahead, some overgrown rosebushes were in bloom, but the flowers were small and shriveled through years of neglect.

Henley stopped by a fountain now filled with weeds and clods of dirt. Paulette imagined that it had once contained clear, sparkling water and perhaps goldfish. Her eyes fell on an unusual Egyptian sundial. The afternoon shadow pointed to three o'clock.

The day was stifling hot with a light breeze that came and went but did not cool. The air smelled of spicy herbs and the woody scent of old trees and plants. A sudden gust of wind stirred the branches on some tall oleander bushes, so thick and overgrown they threatened to overtake the garden. The silence lengthened while Paulette stood waiting for just what she did not know. Then Henley stepped forward and someone came from behind the oleanders.

Ambassador Kruger didn't look anything like Garret or the woman she had seen in the clipping. He was gray and gaunt, his broad face a leathery brown, creased with lines, and his brilliant blue eyes might well have been made of the steel from a warrior's blade.

"I cannot stay long. Surveillance has been stepped up recently."

Henley looked troubled, but in control. "This is Garret's wife, Paulette. She may be the cover Garret can use."

Ambassador Kruger turned and studied her relentlessly, as though she were the rope that would lift them down a precipitous mountain ledge.

"You're sure she can be trusted?" he said to Henley, as though she were not there.

"She's Garret's wife," Henley said, as if that was enough. "Her parents were courageous British agents—it runs in her blood."

Paulette felt as though she were hearing all this in a dream. It was both fearful and encouraging to hear someone like Henley say this about her. She had a reputation to live up to. What if she failed? She mustn't think of it.

Kruger squinted, nodding, still looking at her as though she were oblivious.

"We'll talk here," Kruger said, motioning toward the shield of trees and blue shadows of the declining afternoon.

Colonel Henley gave her an encouraging smile, suggesting he knew she felt uneasy with the ambassador. *Do not let him intimidate you,* he seemed to say. *His life is on the line, and he needs to be cautious.*

Yes, who wouldn't be. She glanced around her, then nodded her assent. *The ambassador is related to Garret,* she reminded herself. *If Garret can trust him, then so can I.* She walked into the oleanders as the smell of earth and thyme overcame that of the disintegrating leaves.

Colonel Henley sat down on a dilapidated bench in front of the sundial and lit a cigarette, keeping watch. He looked casual enough, as if simply enjoying the warm afternoon.

Kruger stood in the shadows among mildly swaying branches and spoke to Paulette quickly but quietly. "What did Garret tell you about me?"

"He never mentioned you," she said in a hushed voice.

He looked satisfied. "He told me about the matchbook and the telephone number. Have you spoken of this to anyone else?"

"No. Garret told me not to mention it to anyone."

"And you haven't. Good. In the last war our family was divided in its loyalties, and we are once more divided over Herr Hitler. Did Garret tell you about his Aunt Helga's son, Paul?"

"Paul Kruger? No. I don't recall the name."

"No? Then he will. It will explain Garret's actions. Until then, you must trust."

"Where is he?" she whispered. "In Cairo or Geneva?"

"Greece. He went there to help his cousin, Anna Kruger. She is my daughter."

"His cousin," she whispered, "your daughter," and bit her lip to keep from smiling her relief that Garret's affectionate arm around her waist had not been motivated by unfaithfulness. He was in Greece helping his cousin Anna, the pretty blonde in the newspaper clipping.

"He never mentioned her?"

"No."

"He was very careful. Good. Anna's husband, Stephano, is a Greek. The two of them are in great danger from Nazi agents. Garret went to Athens to get them out safely and bring them to Cairo. He met with severe resistance. He is injured and in hiding. All three are hiding."

She sucked in her breath and must have turned a sickly white, because he grabbed her arm as if thinking she would lose her balance.

"I am sorry, Paulette. I thought Henley had prepared you for this."

"Injured? Oh—how badly? Will he be all right?"

"We don't know."

Don't know...

"We think it is serious."

Her breath left her in a gasp.

"Henley believes he will make it. Garret is strong. A fighter. He is somewhere in the mountains, but we have not heard from the agent who has the radio."

Paulette said with difficulty: "Was my husband shot?"

"Yes."

She fought to keep herself calm. "Are they all together? Garret, Anna, and Stephano?"

"We don't think so. We think your husband is alone. That is why it is so important for someone above suspicion to go there and contact him. If we can find Garret, we have a better chance to find Anna and Stephano."

The one meaning Paulette could find in Kruger's words was that he thought she was that person. She simply stared at him, certain her own panic was clearly written on her face. Did he somehow think that she had nerves of iron?

"Has Colonel Henley spoken to you yet about what he wishes you to do?" Kruger asked.

Paulette decided to risk a guess. "No. But I think both of you want me to go there. As Garret's wife, I might be the least suspicious person to show up in Greece."

"If I were the enemy, I would think it reasonable."

"You want me to go there," she repeated, "to bring Garret some message? Is that it?"

"That is our wish. And my concerns for Anna grow more urgent with each passing day. We *must* get them out. Unless Generals Papagos and Wilson can turn the Germans back, they are likely to enter Greece." His look of fear and agitation added years to his face.

"And the message for my husband?" she whispered, her throat feeling tight and dry.

"That, I do not know. One man knows the details, Henley."

"Was Anna's marriage to Stephano recent, and…unexpected?" She was curious about this, since it seemed dangerous for his daughter to marry a man that Paulette assumed was in the Greek underground. This would almost immediately put his daughter in the position of being an enemy of the Third Reich.

"Yes," Ambassador Kruger said briefly, and his mouth thinned. "Do not misunderstand me, Paulette. I willingly risk my life by working with the British, as does Stephano, but Anna—I fear for her. Until recently she was not involved. I have assured the Nazi Party she is loyal, but if she is caught they will not be satisfied until they interrogate her. If that happens, I hold no hope for her or myself."

"Yes," she felt stiff with emotion. "I understand, Ambassador Kruger." They would torture and kill her. Stephano too. And Garret...

Her thoughts kept rushing back to him. He had gone there to help his cousin and her husband trapped inside Greece with the Nazis already suspicious of Anna's loyalties. "You, too, must be in danger now," she said.

"Do not worry about me. I can handle myself. It is Anna."

She wiped her sweating palms on her skirt. "Yes."

"Colonel Henley will arrange your trip—if you decide to go."

Her decision seemed instinctive. Garret was wounded and in need of help. Of course she would go. She must find him. She must tell him how wrong she'd been about her suspicions. She must make him understand how much she loved and needed him, how sorry she was that she had failed to believe in him when he had asked for her trust—

Her emotions began to crack, and she bit her lip again. Ambassador Kruger laid a hand on her arm. "I'm sorry our introduction has been on such terms, Paulette. At another time it would have been an occasion for celebration. In spite of the brevity of our meeting, I am pleased with my nephew's choice of a bride."

She wanted to smile, but could not. She nodded.

"Any celebration must wait for only God knows when. There may be years of suffering ahead before the day dawns. Let us believe that the day will come."

Yes, she thought. *Let us believe.* She spoke slowly, "Ambassador, who do you think placed that matchbook from the House of Cairo in Garret's jacket in Switzerland?"

His bleak mood took precedence again. "Why Switzerland? Why not London?"

"I don't know," she shook her head, trying to understand. "Garret thought it may have happened in Neuchâtel."

"He may have said that to deliberately misinform you. He would not want you to become further involved in anything so dangerous. Now, naturally, things have changed... and you are very much involved."

"Is he then an agent?" she whispered.

He looked at her blankly and changed the subject. "You have friends in Delphi. The Nickersons, Henley tells me. That is good."

Yes, and Rhoda and Fergus must get safely out of Greece, too. And what of Dr. Bristow?

Colonel Henley stood from the bench, a sign that their time was up. The ambassador turned and faced the house. Its upper windows were watchful and dark.

"I must get back to the embassy before I am missed." His eyes softened for the first time. "I think you do the family name a great honor." He turned and walked quickly away through the trees, presumably to where some loyal soldier waited for him to whisk him back to the German embassy.

Henley's low voice awakened her. "I see he has informed you of our dilemma."

Paulette turned. She looked at him bleakly. Henley frowned and took hold of her arm. "Come. You need to sit down."

They went back toward the house. Paulette felt as though she was walking in her sleep. They didn't speak again until they were inside the dining room.

"What is it to be?" he asked. "Do I arrange your journey into Greece, or do you stay on at the Citadel and visit our German prisoners of war?"

"Colonel Henley," she said softly, "you didn't really think I'd stay safely in Cairo when my husband is in danger, did you?"

Colonel Henley took note of her solemn brown eyes, and a faint smile touched his face. "No, Mrs. Brandt. I did not."

Sergeant Tomlinson appeared. "No sign of anyone, Colonel. It's as dead as a dodo bird around here."

"Mrs. Brandt and I could both do with a cup of tea, Tomlinson. See what you can dig up in the kitchen."

"Yes, sir."

When Tomlinson had left them, Henley pulled out a chair at the table for Paulette, who sat gratefully.

"I'll try to answer any questions," he said kindly.

His understanding and sympathy weakened her. She struggled not to cry. *I must show courage*, she thought, aware of his keen gaze. She lifted her head a little higher.

"That's better," he said approvingly. "You'll do, Mrs. Brandt. You'll do very well."

She smiled tiredly. It helped that Henley thought so, but she thought again of Garret. "How bad is his injury?"

"I'm afraid it's serious."

She tried not to wince. She fought the rising fear and despair. Overwhelming guilt surged into her soul like the high tide. She relived the cruel things she had said to him, pummeling his character with her doubts, her suspicions, her fears. *I should have told him how much I loved him before he left*, she thought painfully. *Instead, I refused. I ignored the pain in his eyes.*

Henley wore no expression, but his light blue eyes watched her with a hint of pity.

Her head lowered. Her hand knotted into a damp fist. And there was no hospital near or safe enough to bring him to either in Delphi or Athens. *Dear God*, she prayed, but her pleas would not form into adequate words. How could she pour out her heart before God now, when she had never used her time to know Him when the sun shone on her garden? She had neglected the growth process and the opportunity to fellowship with His Spirit, His Word. Now double guilt stood up to mock her fears. She had not only failed her husband, but she had failed obligations to her Christian faith.

"Stay calm, my dear," Henley's solid, stable voice counseled. "We've heard from one of our men in Greece via the radio. He thinks he may know where Garret is hiding out in the mountains. He's been told a doctor is on his way to Delphi, a friend of the British. Once Garret is located, our man will do what he can. Naturally the best thing is getting him out of Greece and back here to Egypt. Garret's odds are favorable, but he needs time. And that is the one thing we do not have enough of. That is where your arrival comes in. It may buy us a little more, though we can't be certain of that, either." His lean face, though grave, was controlled. Then he looked at her sharply. "Mrs. Brandt, what do you know about the war facing us here in the Egyptian theater, as well as Greece?"

Feeling sick, she didn't trust herself to speak. She shook her head, indicating she was overwhelmed with the feelings churning in the pit of her stomach. Garret had been shot—how could he survive?

Quinn! She must talk to him...she had to turn to someone...

"Mrs. Brandt?" he repeated, drawing her eyes back to his. "You're aware that Greece is fighting for its very survival against Germany and Italy at this moment?"

"Yes," she managed. "We—we have troops there aiding the Greek army."

"Nearly sixty thousand fighting men, and seven squadrons of the RAF. Our air force in Greece is badly handicapped by the scarcity of landing ground and inadequate signal communications. And the RAF is overwhelmingly outnumbered by the enemy. Two of our squadrons fought on the Albanian front. The remaining five, supported by two Wellington squadrons from here in Egypt for night operations, have to meet all other needs. They are matched against a German air strength of over eight hundred operational aircraft."

She winced.

"You see our difficulty," he said softly. "You see what you are heading into?"

"My husband is there. Somewhere. And I don't care what it costs me, or how far I must go to find him—I'll go. No matter what. I'll go!"

He looked at her for a long moment, his eyes glinting, and they seemed to say: I was right about you.

He went on without a break in his stride: "Anna and Stephano are in hiding elsewhere, waiting to be contacted by one of our own. We hope to get them safely to Cairo."

She had forgotten about the ambassador's daughter and husband, so troubled was she over Garret.

"Then you know where Garret is located in the mountains?"

"No. He's on the move," was all he would say. "After you arrive, he'll make contact when it's safe for him to do so. Leave that to him."

"What if he becomes too ill? What if infection sets in—"

"One step at a time."

She nodded her understanding.

"The important thing is that you go to Greece. Once Quinn and his group get you there, you'll beg out of a tour into refugee country and go directly to the Nickersons and Dr. Bristow."

"Quinn?" She looked at him quickly. "You want me to go with him? How did you know about the story he wants to cover?"

"Quinn has helped us in the past. But until I give the word, not even he is to know the real reason you're going."

She nodded. "You'll be in touch with me then? In Delphi?"

"Somehow, by an ally."

"And the name of the ally?" she asked.

"He'll make himself known to you. That's his responsibility. Don't worry."

She wondered how Henley had known about Quinn's offer to bring her to the Bulgarian border, and about the Nickersons, but had given up becoming surprised over anything concerning the CID.

"Make it clear that while you came with the journalists to cover the fleeing refugees from Bulgaria, you are also there to visit the Nickersons. You're worried about them staying in Greece should the fighting turn in favor of the Germans. You are also expecting your husband, who is now in Athens on business for his company. You are waiting for him to clear up his work so he can join you at Bristow's compound at Delphi. That is all. Do nothing else. Just wait. Be natural. When Garret believes it's safe, he'll contact you."

"Suppose...suppose something happens and he doesn't contact me?"

He looked at her keenly. "Then we'll arrange for your escape."

Escape. She stared at him, alarmed. The war of course. The German push into Greece by way of Bulgaria, Yugoslavia, and Albania. She would pray that it wouldn't come to that finality. Her stomach fluttered.

"Let's not jump farther ahead than we need to, Mrs. Brandt. Your husband is alive, and we have God to thank for it. Unless something unexpected happens between now and when you arrive, you should be hearing from him."

Should. She tried to look capable and confident. She felt young and stupid. "Could you tell me how he was injured?"

His eyes met hers steadily. "The politics of Greece are involved and confusing for a novice to understand. Even Greek experts are often perplexed. Shall we say that not every Greek fighter is loyal to the present government of the king? There is a mood that hints of an ugly civil war among the Greeks fighting Germans and Italians. Many are Communists who could turn on their fellow Greek fighters."

She looked horrified. "Greek against Greek? Even in the face of German tyranny?"

"Sadly, yes. It is not impossible that one group of underground guerrilla fighters would turn on another group, even though they have a common enemy. Of course, this is rarely published in the newspapers of Britain or the United States. We are aiding the Greek underground, knowing that there are strong Communists among them."

"Does this complication have anything to do with the Greek named Stephano?"

"Yes. At one time Stephano was sympathetic to those secretly in favor of overthrowing the Greek monarchy. When he understood the diabolical mindset of the Communists, he backed out. But he knows too much. He also has too much sway over the thinking of young Greek students and intellectuals in Athens, and they couldn't afford to let him turn against them or unmask their leaders in the underground. They had plans to kidnap him and Anna and no doubt kill them."

"And this—Stephano—he's now on our side?"

"Yes. And he can give us important names. Anna was with her husband when the news came of a planned assault. There was little time. She notified her father. Ambassador Kruger protested the assault all the way to Berlin, insisting that his loyal daughter was there with Stephano. When he knew he'd been unsuccessful, he contacted Garret, a relative, whom he knew to be in Athens."

She looked surprised. "Then—Garret was already in Athens? Not Geneva?"

He seemed to pause. "Yes, we had asked him to leave Geneva some days before. Garret arranged for Stephano and Anna's escape into the mountains, where we hope to pick them up later by boat."

Her husband had rescued them. They were alive and in hiding. For a time they were safe. She felt exceedingly proud and became aware of Henley's understanding smile.

Sergeant Tomlinson appeared carrying two cups of tea. "They say, sir, tea leaves never go bad."

"That's wrong, Sergeant. They can lose both their freshness and strength. Let's hope they haven't been molding here since 1916."

Tomlinson whiffed the brew. "Smells aromatic to me, sir."

"We'll give it a try." Henley lifted his cup in salute to Paulette. "Godspeed," he said gravely.

Yes, she thought, her heart aching, longing, with tears beginning to moisten her eyes. She was seeing another face as she looked past Henley, past Tomlinson, another pair of eyes, disconcertingly gray-blue. *Yes, Godspeed—God be with you till we meet again, my darling.*

17

Paulette learned during the drive to the airfield in Alexandria that Quinn would be waiting and that he had been told of her rendezvous with Garret.

"Your association with Quinn and his crew should give you adequate cover upon your arrival at Delphi. I didn't mention Garret's injury, or Stephano," Henley said. "It's best to let Quinn think the meeting with your husband is your first priority—that you're still a romantic bride dreaming about starry skies on the warm beaches of Greece, so that a detour to Bristow's place will seem reasonable."

"Will I ever be able to explain to him what this is really about? What if Garret or I need him? You said you trusted Quinn," she looked at him. "Don't you?"

"About as much as I trust any newspaperman with an appetite for uncovering stories for the *London Times*. If the moment comes for further explanations, let Garret decide how much to share with him. Times may get rough, and he may need to include Quinn, but the longer this is kept in a very tight circle, the better I'll sleep."

It would be difficult to conceal her worries from Quinn, though. His journalistic instincts could detect the weakest scent of a story. If he got wind of the fact that a German ambassador's daughter was trapped and in danger in Greece, he would go for details like a hungry shark. He might, in fact, manifest the same journalistic interest in Garret's saga, if he learned he was wounded and in hiding.

Henley was placing an awful lot of confidence in her, she thought anxiously. He must be desperate...but then, so was she. Her feverish thoughts turned to God, and she found strength in putting her worries into prayerful words.

Henley had timed their arrival to the minute. Darkness would soon render them invisible to Luftwaffe reconnaissance aircraft. There had been air raids recently. In the twilight she could make out missing sections of buildings, the ugly scars left by Stuka dive bombers. The bombings had come as a shock to British civilians. After General Wavell's spectacular victory in driving the Italians out of Egypt at the end of 1940, the Germans reinforced the Italians, sending Field Marshal Erwin Rommel's Panzer divisions into the Egyptian desert. Enemy air raids on the area around Alexandria were increasing daily, and over six hundred people had been killed in just a three-month period. What did tomorrow hold?

He mentioned that the H.M.S. *Valiant* and the *Queen Elizabeth* had been sabotaged by German frogmen who had managed to get into the Alexandrian harbor to blow up the bottoms of the ships' hulls.

"They don't look damaged," she said.

"Purely deception. The navy is going through the motions of pretending they are still intact. They salute on the quarterdeck, raise the flags, and hold church services every Sunday. They don't want the Germans to know that they were successful, but both ships are resting on the bottom of the shallow harbor."

She turned anxiously to Colonel Henley. "There's Quinn, coming now. What is the message I'm supposed to give Garret?"

His expression didn't change as he watched Quinn walking toward the car from the harbor. "Tell him, 'the Oracle of Delphi.' That's it. No less, no more. He'll know the rest."

The Oracle of Delphi? She stared at him, somehow expecting more names, dates, and details. Delphi is where the Nickersons were working with Dr. Bristow. Would Garret contact her in Delphi?

As Quinn walked up, Henley got out from behind the wheel and Paulette opened the passenger door.

"Hello!" he called cheerily. "This is some trip the colonel's arranged for us, huh? The Blue Jobs are bringing us over in style," he said, speaking of the naval officers.

Henley smiled wryly. "You won't think much of the style if the Italian air force or Luftwaffe spot you between here and Delphi."

"Yeah, it is a long swim to Crete," Quinn said.

Paulette turned with actress-like cheer. "Well, goodbye, Colonel. Thank you for all your help. Mort will be so pleased when I return to London with that story for *Horizon*. Do come to see Garret and me when you get to London."

Henley smiled. "I'll do that, Mrs. Brandt. Goodbye, Quinn. See you when you get back."

Paulette turned just before boarding to offer the colonel one last smile. She wished he were going with her. She would miss his quiet confidence and strength, yet she was glad he would be coordinating the rescue effort from Cairo. She hoped deep in her heart to meet him again in happier circumstances.

~~~

Taking off, the British pilot flew toward the coast as the lights from the city of Alexandria receded into the distance. Off to her right, the last vestiges of dusk were fading in the west as the plane flew over the Mediterranean on its seven-hundred-mile journey. A glimmering twilight reflection off the sea met her gaze through the small, cold window. After two or three hours the moon appeared very close and bright. Quinn pointed out, above the loud roar of the plane's engines, that the moonlight would have exposed their craft to great danger were it not that the Luftwaffe had not as yet entered Greek airspace this far south. Flying past Crete, it was another hour and a half over the sea before she could see lights from a city that Quinn said was Athens in southern Greece. After another half hour, as they began their descent, she could see some hills silhouetted below in the moonlight, and what Quinn said was Mount Parnassus.

At last they landed in the small village of Arachova, somewhere near Delphi. It was quite late at night.

After coming carefully down an extended ladder, Paulette stood in the darkness of the April night in a large empty field where the wind stirred up dust and raced through olive trees. The soles of her shoes crunched verbena and released a sweet fragrance. Above, in the skies of Greece, the springtime stars were milky white, and Paulette thought it poetic that she could make out Hercules rising over the eastern horizon.

The pilot wasted no time arranging to get the airplane refueled by morning so that he could fly on to join a RAF squadron near the border of Albania, where the Greek army under General Papagos was being hard pressed by the German advance.

Paulette stood with Quinn in the field, his adrenaline running high on black coffee, talk, and the prospect of danger. They waited for the two men in Quinn's party who were to pick them up in a vehicle. Niko, he had told her, was a Greek student who knew the high hills near Macedonia with the confidence of a mountain goat. Their photographer would be a Canadian whom Quinn had worked with in Poland while covering the German invasion of Warsaw.

"That's them," he said when the distant sound of an engine grew louder in the stillness. Two beams of light came bouncing up over a hill. The headlamps rose and dipped as the vehicle progressed across the uneven field, its motor growing louder. Field animals darted away in fright and night birds shrilled and flew toward distant trees.

"It's a good thing the Jerries are still across the Alikamon River," he complained. "Any patrol within fifty miles of this place could hear their arrival."

The vehicle stopped some distance ahead with the motor rumbling. The headlamps flashed twice. Paulette started to walk forward, but Quinn caught her arm. "We'll just wait and make sure first."

She looked at him. "You must have experience with betrayals."

"In Greece, who knows? There's an old saying that if a Greek can't fight an enemy, he'll fight his neighbor."

"Not exactly flattering." She braced herself against the wind, which was whipping the hem of her long dark coat. She thought of Garret. Had someone betrayed him? She stood near a cluster of gnarled olive trees and watched Quinn approach the motorcar. She could hear talking in Greek. It seemed as though several minutes had passed before Quinn signaled to her. She hurried to join them.

"Niko says we'll need to stay in the local village tonight. The main road to Athens is blocked by a large caravan of Greek soldiers moving north toward Albania."

"Any hotels in the village?" she asked.

Quinn laughed. "For that you'll need to wait for Athens. Don't worry. He insists there's plenty of room at his sister's place. We'll sleep outdoors. Electra will put you up with her kids." He leaned in the window. "Where'd you get this tin can, Niko?" Quinn joked to the young man behind the wheel, dressed in an open-neck shirt and wearing a beat-up cap on his full head of black wavy hair. Niko spoke in Greek, waving his hands for emphasis, and his lively dark eyes settled on Paulette. For the briefest moment she wondered if she had ever seen him before. Then he smiled widely, showing white teeth, and said in good English: "Welcome to Greece, *kyria*. The birthplace of Western democracy."

"Thank you." The feeling melted away to nothing.

"But now it is in danger from Communism," the other man piped up from the passenger side of the front seat. "The name is Dabney," he spoke to Paulette. "Bill Dabney."

Paulette smiled at the sunburned face, heavy with freckles.

Quinn helped her into the car, saying, "What's this about Communism? Stalin's not invading Greece."

"Ol' Joe doesn't need to. There are so many Commies in the Greek underground you'll have a civil war even if the army defeats the Nazis. Greek against Greek." He turned toward Niko, who had a cigarette dangling from his lip as they started to leave, bouncing over the rough field and raising dust. "What about it, Niko? Is the Popular Liberation Army a front for the Commies or isn't it?"

Niko shrugged. "Who knows?"

"Many are afraid to say." Dabney turned toward the back, speaking over his shoulder. "Now there's a story for you, Quinn. What would you say if I told you that Ares, who runs the guerrilla group, is a Commie?"

Niko laughed. "You're out of your mind, Dabney. Ares is a hero to Greece. He's *my* hero!"

"Yeah? Well, I think you're crazy. I think the Americans and the Brits are crazy, too, for smuggling him arms and cash."

"That's pretty dangerous stuff you're throwing around," Quinn said. "Where'd you hear about it?"

"Here and there," Dabney remarked. "And that isn't all that's being said."

"What else are they saying?" Quinn was lighting a cigarette. He wound the window down a few inches in deference to Paulette. She was listening alertly, but knew nothing of the Popular Liberation Army or its leader.

"What about Ares?" Quinn repeated.

"He'll turn on his fellow resistance fighters once the Germans are beaten."

"You're crazy," Niko scoffed bitterly. He flicked a glance back toward Quinn. "Print that and you'll never get another Greek to trust you with the time of day."

"I wouldn't touch it," Quinn said. "C'mon, Bill, leaders like Ares are always targets for loose talk. You can hear gossip in the *tavernas* from a bunch of businessmen too afraid to fight the Germans themselves."

"Ares is a genius," Niko bragged. "No one can defeat him."

"Cowards?" Dabney said. "There are no cowards in the Greek army."

"That where you heard about Ares?" Quinn asked.

"He heard it from the Oracle of Delphi," Niko mocked, and turning to Dabney, laughed good naturedly. "And they say it is the Greeks who are suspicious! Say, Quinn, guess where I spotted Dabney yesterday? At the temple of the Oracle."

Dabney smiled wryly. "Funny man." He looked at Paulette. "We're boring her. My apologies, Mrs. Brandt."

Paulette smiled. "I'm not bored. Not all women are interested only in the temperatures at the fine Greek beaches. Some of us care about world affairs and patriotism, Mr. Dabney."

Niko laughed heartily. "She told you, eh? She is no— how do you say it in English?"

"Never mind," Dabney said, and turned his head to smile back at Paulette. "My second apology, ma'am. I wasn't underestimating you, though. Any woman who's come to do a feature on the slaughter of refugees in the mountains has got to have iron in her blood and—" he stopped abruptly.

Paulette laughed. "And water on the brain?"

"You can stop worrying, Bill. She isn't coming with us, after all," Quinn said. "Her husband decided to show up in Athens."

She had almost allowed her pride to overrule her wisdom. After her little speech, she must now pretend she had changed her mind on the story so that she could rendezvous with Garret for a few romantic days in Athens, romping along the white sandy beaches.

"Maybe it's best he did, Mrs. Brandt. That climb in the mountains is rough enough to get even Niko exhausted, and he usually keeps up with the goats and hares."

"Me? I never get tired," Niko boasted, grinning. "It is you English who must sit by the wayside and bemoan your lack of tea." He glanced at Paulette, his dark eyes bright in the moonlight. "You have English friends at Delphi, *kyria?*"

She wondered how he knew. "Yes. Fergus and Rhoda Nickerson. They're working with Dr. Bristow from the British School of Archaeology. Also, my husband is expected to join me there. He's here on business for a New York firm," she managed casually. "When he's finished, we'll take in a few days together in Athens. Afterward we'll both have a look at the refugee tragedy."

"You did not tell her about me, Quinn?" Niko pretended to sound perturbed.

Paulette turned a questioning glance on Quinn, who smiled wryly. "Niko wants you to know that he helps Bristow out at the digs during summer vacation."

Niko looked pleased by her surprise. His lean handsome face flashed a smile. "I, too, am a student of archaeology. You are surprised, yes, I can see. I went to the Berlin School in Athens until they closed and went back to Germany. Then," he said with a shrug, "I went to the British School."

Could Niko possibly be one of the friendly contacts that Henley had mentioned? Her heart beat faster. This was one of those times when an error could prove costly. Better to be too cautious than jump to conclusions.

"Then you've met the Nickersons?" she asked, keeping the excitement she felt out of her voice.

"I've met them," Niko said, leaning back against the seat. He offered no other explanation. Whether it was to bait her to ask more questions, or because of a genuine indifference, she was not to know, for he said: "I am driving out to the digs tomorrow. Dr. Bristow has asked for my help."

"You're in luck," Quinn told her cheerfully. "Niko can bring you out. You might even have a message waiting there from Garret."

"Your husband knows to find you there?"

"Yes. He arranged the trip that brought the Nickersons safely to Greece."

"Since you're working for Bristow," Quinn said, "you must have been here when Brandt and the Nickersons drove in from the airstrip."

Niko looked up through the rearview mirror.

Paulette wondered why Quinn brought it up. It seemed a small thing to point out. But Niko shook his head. "No, I was still at the British School."

She realized that Niko, by working at the digs, may have provided an opportunity she hadn't expected. It seemed almost too fortunate to be an accident, yet she couldn't be sure. Niko was not what she would have expected of someone secretly working with British Intelligence, but what did she really know about it? His youthful arrogance might just be a role.

"Maybe your husband will bring you to the mountains later, when Quinn and Dabney are getting pictures. You can hire me to drive you, yes, maybe?"

"Hey! Look out!" Dabney called.

Niko swerved in the darkness to avoid a large rut.

Quinn laughed shortly. "Trying to kill us, Niko?"

∾∾∾

In the headlight beams she could see that the village had narrow streets that were wide enough for only one vehicle. Quinn said that whole families lived in the flat-roofed houses in one or, at the most, three small rooms. His sister was coming through the front door to meet them even before Niko brought the car to a dusty stop. She wore the traditional country costume, a rather long-skirted dress with a kerchief over her head. She held an oil lamp, and three small children were pulling at her skirts. She ignored the men and stared evenly at Paulette, the British girl who had come for a newspaper story. A moment later her husband appeared, brushing past her. He was a big man with watchful dark eyes and an unsmiling face. Paulette caught a glimpse of a dagger in his belt just as the headlights went dark. Life here was extremely hard. It had been hard under the Greek king and government. Poverty was rampant. But it was harder still under the threat of German invasion. Already there was talk of an underground resistance movement should the Nazis be successful in turning back the Greek army.

"The Germans will not defeat Greek soldiers," Niko said a short time later as his brother-in-law brought out a jug of home-brewed wine called *retsina*. It smelled to Paulette like turpentine, and Quinn whispered that it tasted just as awful. "It's flavored with resin. Tastes antiseptic and makes the tongue revolt."

Paulette wondered why they would even bother to touch the stuff, but they did. All of them, including the host and Niko, who emptied their cups with a loud smack and held them out for more. Paulette glanced at the children, all seven of them on one mattress in the corner, four of them awake, watching her with large, round, dark eyes. They had been told by Niko's sister, Electra, that Paulette was going to sleep in their bed tonight. Paulette didn't think she would sleep at all, but how did one turn down such hospitality? Electra smiled at her, and stared at her clothes and shoes. Paulette thought of what she would end up giving her before she left the next morning. Giving was inevitable, even when she had brought only one bag with her on the airplane. She had been lucky to get that aboard, after all the equipment that had to be stashed before they left Alexandria.

Electra, alert to the fact that Paulette had refused the *retsina*, brought her a cup of goat's milk. Paulette smiled her thanks and sipped it.

"I think you would be wise to get some sleep," Bill Dabney was telling her quietly. "Dawn is almost here." He turned. "What time are you leaving in the morning, Niko?"

Niko leaned over to the bowl of olives on the table and grabbed a fistful, popping one into his mouth. They were the strong-flavored kind. Paulette thought them rather bitter, small, and hard, but they were a favorite staple in most Greek menus.

"Greeks are early risers," he was saying. "When the bird sings, we are already up and ready to battle the day. But you are a woman, *kyria*. An Englishwoman, at that. I have heard English and American women sleep very late. At least until eight o'clock. So," he concluded with what he must have felt was generosity, "I will be in the car at nine o'clock waiting for you."

Paulette covered a smile. He was crusty, all right. "I'll be ready, Niko. Thank you."

Electra waited shyly as Paulette stood from the chair at the table and moved toward the mattress on the floor in the corner. The men were on their feet and going toward the door. Paulette's head was heavy and her eyes smarted from all the tobacco smoke that ringed the room. The notion of stretching out and going to sleep sounded pleasant indeed. *Tomorrow*, she thought, comforted, *I'll see Rhoda. And just maybe Quinn is right; there could be a message waiting for me at Delphi from Garret.*

Paulette lay down on the rather lumpy mattress of covered straw, surrounded by sleeping children.

It was way past midnight. Outside, someone began playing what sounded like a harmonica. The tune was a Greek folk song that she found soothing. Her thoughts inevitably turned to Garret. Her heart ached with each sad yet hopeful beat. She was perhaps within a day of where he was held up, or even mere hours. How was he surviving? Did he know she loved him, that she was coming? *Please, God, help us. Help us all.*

18

True to his word, Niko was waiting in his motorcar early the next morning and greeted her with a grin as she came out carrying her one bag, absent of a certain outfit that Electra now held in her arms with shining eyes. She called out her gratitude in broken English, and Paulette waved and smiled. All seven children were gathered around their mother, looking at Paulette shyly. Several held up little hands, wiggling them in a goodbye.

"You've made them all very happy," Niko told her, coming to take her bag and opening the passenger door of the big dusty black car.

"I'm glad someone can be happy for a few days." She slid onto the leather seat, and he swung the heavy door shut.

He put her bag in the trunk, then got in behind the wheel, turning the key in the ignition. He backed out of the tight parking space with little regard for the rising dust blowing toward his sister's laundry. Paulette wound up her side window.

"The dust," he said, "is part of life. You'll get used to it."

She glanced at him, then around at the little village of Arachova with goats and chickens in the yards. "This is your home village, Niko?"

He smiled. "It is as the Americans put it, 'Home sweet home.'"

His English flowed more easily this morning, she noticed. His youthful Greek countenance that was full of good cheer and a ready grin was exchanged for a more thoughtful look. Had last night been real?

"Twenty-five years ago I was born right over there—" he pointed across the narrow street. There was a steep alleyway, and opposite, a coffeehouse with tables and chairs outdoors under an awning of sorts. There were other houses, too, all crammed together side by side, double- and triple-decker. There were roaming chickens, donkeys, and more olive trees. All this stood against a brilliant blue sky with mountains in the distance, their ocher-colored cliff faces standing guard like sentinels.

"Atop that house, in a room above those steep steps, is where I breathed my first—and Greece has never been the same since."

She smiled. "I can believe it. As for your country, I like it very much."

"Better than London?"

She turned her head quickly to see a twinkle of amusement in his lively dark eyes. He laughed.

"I just wish I were here under happier circumstances."

The twinkle in his eyes faded into shadow as he looked off toward the hills as if expecting to see enemy planes. "Yes. The Nazis. They outnumber us ten to one. Yet we will fight. We will beat them back across the border of Bulgaria."

She worried about Garret as he spoke of the German army. She wondered if he really believed that General

Papagos could defeat the German Wehrmacht and the Luft-waffe.

The village was perched on a precipitous hillside, and the houses were mostly built on tiers, appearing as steps, one behind the other. The whole village looked as if it were about to slide into the depths of the valley below. The thought of an earthquake sent chills of horror up her spine. The walls were white and the roofs were a rose red, and over every wall there were flowering plants and vines rich with grapes and great dollops of wool dyed the colors of amber and hyacinth and scarlet. Along the short main street there were places where rugs were for sale, hung out in the sunlight against the glaring white walls. The street was about eight feet wide and had few intersections.

The merciless sun beat down on the rocks and olive trees.

They drove along a high dirt road that skirted the side of Mount Parnassus. Below, to the left of a sheer rocky wall of cliffs, a gully descended to a valley with a river. The valley was thick with olive trees toward distant hills to the west.

Niko shifted gears and the vehicle chugged up an incline, around and down a serpentine hill. Paulette leaned back against the hot leather, thinking that she was wise to have worn a cotton sundress and hat.

She was wondering how to start asking Niko questions. She began casually: "Why did Quinn ask if you'd been at the digs when my husband arrived with the Nickersons? It seemed to me a strange question."

"Journalists always ask too many questions. Questions that sometimes make no sense to us."

She glanced at him. She tried again. "Then you've never met my husband, Garret Brandt?"

A glimmer showed in his brown eyes, and he was no longer the glib Niko, who from the moment he'd pulled up in the car last night had behaved carefree.

"I have met your husband, *kyria*. I have also met Stephano," he admitted in a low voice, though there was no one to overhear. "And...I consider Colonel Henley a friend."

His words were comforting to her. He could be trusted. Niko was her contact. He was, however, staring ahead on the winding road, saying nothing else. Was he waiting for some word of identification from her? Henley had not given her anything except the simple phrase about the Oracle of Delphi, but that was only to be spoken to Garret.

"Your husband came to Athens to help Stephano escape to Cairo," Niko said. "Colonel Henley, he explained this to you?"

Her relief and tension ran together. "Yes, he explained. My husband—"

"If he learns you are here, then we are sure he will contact you. He has not done so yet?"

"No. I thought you might have an idea where Garret is hiding."

He sighed. "I wish I knew, *kyria*."

"You know this area. Have you any suggestions?" she asked hopefully.

His eyes glinted thoughtfully as he looked toward Parnassus.

She noted that when Niko wasn't wearing his charming boyish grin that he looked older, even hardened. *It's from the danger of living so near to death*, she thought. *There are times when Garret and Quinn have that wary look, too.*

"I have searched. So far there is no sign of him." His mouth tightened. "But I will keep on searching until I find him, or until he finds you." His eyes shot to hers. He seemed to take note of the surprise she felt over his determination, because he looked away. "I am here to protect both of you. I do not want to frighten you, yet you must understand there are enemies among us, right here in Delphi. It is the reason your husband cannot show himself openly. He knows where Stephano is hiding. Therefore, Stephano's enemies also search for him. Those who want to find Stephano will not stop until they have located and killed him. And your husband, too, I am afraid. Until he contacts you, there is nothing we can do to help either of them escape."

Her heart beat faster. Henley had already told her these things, and she was able to remain outwardly calm. "You're with the Greek police, or the underground? Maybe," she apologized for her lack of understanding, "the underground and police are working together?"

He didn't answer. "Just say, I am a friend of the British and of Stephano. You see," he explained, "Stephano taught at the Berlin School of Archaeology where I was a student. I came to know him at a coffee shop in Athens. Everyone who was anyone in the intellectual strata met there to discuss ideas. It was somewhat of a club. A club of ideas, and Stephano had many. He was interesting because he was different."

She was curious. "You mean his politics?"

"He interpreted archaeology in light of politics. He saw little hope for the betterment of Greece through our monarchy. It was democracy and freedom that permitted the glory of classical Greece. He believed it was the answer for today's social problems."

"You speak as though he no longer believes it."

"He has changed." There was little to read from the sound of his voice.

"Stephano believed in ending the Greek monarchy?" she asked, surprised. "Treason?"

"Not treason," he said almost sharply. "Freedom."

She tried to understand how Stephano could be deemed an enemy to the Nazis as well as to members of some of the Greek fighters.

"You didn't have Dr. Bristow in mind, did you, when you spoke of enemies here in Delphi?"

"Dr. Bristow is also a friend of Stephano," he said half under his breath, looking off toward the mountains. "In fact, Dr. Bristow would come sometimes to the coffeehouse and listen to the discussions. He would never take sides, just listen. No, he would not involve himself in Greek matters that are none of his affair. His mind is consumed with discoveries at the digs. He eats and sleeps it. Nothing else matters to him." He appeared unexpectedly amused. "Sometimes I wonder if he even knows there is a war going on."

"I'm happy to hear that." She looked at him quickly. "That is, that he's not involved," she explained.

Niko's old grin was back. "You think so?"

"It makes for peace."

"Peace? Where a tyrant rules and the people submit, there is not true peace, there is compromise with injustice, *kyria.* Silence is not always golden, as the British saying tells us. Sometimes it is cowardly."

"You're not suggesting Dr. Bristow is cowardly?"

"No, no, you do not understand me. It is a Greek problem. We do not expect anything of Bristow."

"There are times when truth must not be compromised in the name of tolerance," she said a moment later, thoughtfully. "Still, Niko, you will agree one must choose his battles carefully. Else one simply becomes a rebel. A cause must be right and just. From your conversation last night with Quinn and Dabney, I assume there is more than the German invasion that divides the fighting spirit of the men of Greece."

His eyes flickered. "You mean the Canadian's talk of Communists running the guerrilla fighters?"

"Well...yes." She glanced at him, trying to get the pulse of his thoughts on the matter. "You didn't appear to agree with him that Communism was a threat."

He looked scornful. "Dabney meddles where he should not. It is mostly all talk. He would do well to stick to news gathering that concerns Canada."

Paulette was rather surprised by his anger. "What is your opinion of the leader they call Ares?"

He smiled, but his brown eyes were shuttered. "Do not worry about Ares, who he is, what he does. You have many worries already, *kyria*. The less you involve yourself in other matters, the better for you and your husband."

It was a polite but certain way of telling her she was out of bounds. Perhaps she was, but what if all this turned out to involve Stephano and Garret? Just who was Ares? Did it even matter?

"There it is," he said a few minutes later, interrupting her worrisome thoughts. "See those cliffs? They are called the Shining Ones. And that—those six remaining columns just below the cliffs—is what is left of the ancient temple of Apollo."

Delphi was still hidden behind the cliffs, but where the bluff connected to the mountain she could clearly see the ruins of the ancient temple, the stone glowing amber in the morning sun.

The reddish cliffs looked down on what she could not yet see, yet knew was there, Apollo's shrine. She imagined the thousands upon thousands of ancient Greeks who had come to Delphi to worship Apollo and to hear the mysteries of the Oracle of Delphi. In contrast she thought of Paul, apostle to the Gentiles, coming to preach the gospel of Jesus Christ to a world that was blind to His glory in spite of many miracles. How the message of Christ's death for mankind's sin and His bodily resurrection must have stunned the Greek mind.

She looked at Niko, noticing his thoughtful gaze. He was looking at Mount Parnassas, which was above the road. *He knows this area,* she thought. *He grew up here. Maybe he climbed some of these very rocks as boys do.*

Delphi was on the other side of the temple ruins. Niko followed the narrow road down through groves of olive trees and around a mount into the village. There was a small village called Crissa before Delphi, and at the bottom of the road the way forked toward a small picturesque fishing port called Itea, which hadn't changed much since the times of ancient Greece. Pilgrims from far and wide who had come to pay homage to Apollo would dock their ships at Itea, then walk the Grecian hills to the shrine. Many had to pay great amounts of money to hear an ambiguous or obscure voice from a priest or priestess who was hidden from view, as though their voice was the response of a god.

Paulette could just make out a few houses built near the sea as Niko drove past. The dusty dirt road continued to wind downward past more olive trees, then curved and came into Delphi.

"Welcome," he said, "or as they would greet you in ancient times: 'Charis.' There are a few hotels, but you want me to bring you to the archaeology huts, right?"

"Yes, is it much farther?"

"Only minutes. Your friends, the Nickersons, will be surprised, yes?"

Shocked might have been a better word.

Niko soon stopped the dusty car under the shade of a huge plantain tree, and Paulette got out to survey the scene. A young woman, very much pregnant and carrying a small shopping bag, was just ahead. Her face looked drawn and worried as she seemed to be in deep preoccupation with her private thoughts.

"Rhoda," she called. The woman turned and her eyes widened, coming toward her.

"Paulette! I don't believe it!"

Paulette hurried to meet her, throwing her arms around her. They both laughed when Paulette tried to avoid her extended womb.

Rhoda's naturally curly auburn hair had grown longer and was tied back with a yellow ribbon. Her few freckles across a pert pug nose had darkened in the summer sun. "This is totally marvelous. How on earth did you manage? And where is Garret?"

Paulette stepped away to look at her. Where is Garret? Was she serious? Then she didn't know.

"He's coming to join all of us, isn't he?" Rhoda continued.

Paulette, wondering, avoided an answer. "Look at you! Why, the baby must weigh eight pounds already. You're feeling well? And Fergus? I suppose he's working with Dr. Bristow today."

They finally stopped and looked at each other, then laughed. Rhoda motioned to a small hut. "We'll discuss everything inside over tea. It's too hot to be standing out here. Oh—Niko—hello," she said, just becoming aware of him. "Wendel and Fergus are at the digs. Someone came this morning to discuss the recent findings. Would you tell them Mrs. Brandt is here? And ask the newcomer to stay for supper."

A newcomer? Paulette hoped her pounding heart didn't show on her face. Could the man be the doctor Colonel Henley had told her had been sent? Niko, she noticed, was alert also, but his smile appeared as though he was merely his cheerful self.

"I will walk there and tell them. A visitor, you say? From where?"

Rhoda wrinkled her nose. "You know, the man didn't say. I don't think I even know his name." She shook her head in self-exasperation and turned to Paulette. "I'm becoming as absentminded as Aunt Opal used to be. Oh, well! They do say genius runs in the family. Come along, Paulette, you look exhausted. It's time for tea, the cure-all."

Paulette saw Niko walking away toward some olive trees that appeared to stretch to a rocky, distant incline. Then she followed Rhoda to the welcoming hut and the relief to be found with a trusted friend.

Paulette had so much to ask Rhoda, but now that they were alone, she wondered where to begin. She thought of the clipping of Garret and Anna from the Cairo newspaper. What else did Rhoda know? Then, again, Rhoda had also looked worried when walking along the road just now. What was troubling her? Was her careworn face part of the toll of her pregnancy, or was there something else? Perhaps she did know about Garret after all, and was behaving indifferently in front of Niko. It was possible Rhoda didn't know that he was cooperating with the CID. Whatever the cause, Paulette felt certain she would find out.

19

"And if it's a boy, we'll name him Delphi," Rhoda told her, pouring tea and passing the creamer. "The milk's been boiled," she assured her.

"Delphi? You wouldn't saddle the poor boy with *that* all his life, would you?" Paulette pleaded, amused.

Rhoda widened her eyes with offense. "And what's wrong with it?"

Paulette, tired and emotionally drained, giggled for no particular reason. "Imagine him in college as his girlfriend whispers, 'Delphi, I love you.'"

Rhoda rubbed her nose thoughtfully. "College...I can't imagine my sweet precious bundle as a man."

"That's what I mean."

"Yes, but during childhood we can call him 'Delfie.' It sounds so cute, don't you think?"

"Yes, if he were a kitten," Paulette said wryly, sipping her tea and leaning back in the chair. "Here, Delfie, come, Delfie, Delfie." She sighed. It felt marvelous to unwind for a few minutes, pretending there was nothing more crucial to occupy her thoughts than an exchange of mental impressions about masculine names. "Well, what does his father think about it?"

"I must admit he wasn't exactly enthused. This morning he said that one name like 'Fergus' in the family is enough."

"What about Ferdinand?" Paulette's eyes twinkled.

This time Rhoda winced. "Fergus is Irish. Why would we want an Italian name?"

"For that matter, why Greek?"

"Hmm, I see what you mean." Rhoda absently cut the sticky Greek dessert cake into several small pieces. "It's so rich you can't eat very much. Oh, well. Fergus and I might relent at the final moment and call him Charles or George. One can't go wrong with a good English name."

Paulette nodded and tried a slice of the cake. It was made of some sort of shredded cereal, probably wheat, sweet with honey, and deliciously crunchy with chopped almonds. It seemed to momentarily revive her strength.

"Yes," Rhoda said thoughtfully, licking her fingers. "Charles. Though not uncommon, it sounds so sophisticated. You know, the charmingly elegant sort of brute. He'll be positively dashing in college. 'Charles, darling, I love you.' Well? What do you think?"

"Better." Paulette went on philosophically, "But then, maybe he'll take after Fergus and enjoy digging around in the mud." She waited for Rhoda to look up at her.

She did, and seeing Paulette's teasing smile, Rhoda made a face at her. "Tell me about yourself. What brought you and Garret here? Not that we're not delighted to have you for company on the verge of the Nazi invasion. It does give my spirits a boost."

Paulette shuddered. Invasion? "I hope not."

"Things do look bad for us," Rhoda said, turning serious. She looked down at her enlarged abdomen and her brows knitted. "I told Fergus I'll be just fine. Now, even Dr. Bristow has asked me to go to Athens. It's a bit closer to Cairo if we need to be evacuated. Goodness knows I'd have a fit leaving before Fergus."

Paulette studied her while they chatted and came to the conclusion that Rhoda didn't know about Garret or Stephano. Rhoda was troubled about a German invasion, but unwilling to amplify her concerns, probably because she didn't want to worry Fergus. It was like her to put on a cheerful act even when she was hurting. Paulette noticed her pale complexion and tired-looking eyes.

Is she keeping something from Fergus?

That Rhoda appeared to be ignorant of Garret's condition was favorable; she already was burdened. Paulette, however, was a shade disappointed. Rhoda was the one person she believed she could fully trust with any secret, even a dark secret that was connected with espionage, but if Rhoda was uninvolved, Paulette ought not to entangle her.

There was Niko to discuss things with. He was apparently trusted by the CID. Then, again, she need not leave out Quinn. Not that he could be much help once he traveled north toward Bulgaria and crossed the river Struma into east Macedonia where refugees were fleeing from the German advance toward Greece.

"I suppose now that you've come, there will be even more reason for me to depart when you and Garret leave. I hope you don't plan to go for several weeks."

Paulette avoided a direct answer by simply shaking her head. She worried whether Garret would even be strong enough by then for rigorous travel.

"By then, Dr. Bristow thinks we'll all need to leave for Cairo. Poor Fergus is positively beastly on himself."

"Is he? Goodness, why should he be?" Paulette had finished her tea and set her cup down.

"You know how it is. He's convinced it was a dreadful mistake to bring me here, considering the turn of events in the war. He's wishing I'd gone to Cairo and waited there until we knew how things would go. Garret must be feeling the same way." She looked at her, faint puzzlement in her eyes. She leaned forward and lowered her voice. "Honestly, Paulette, I'm rather surprised he'd ask you to meet him here for a holiday. It's a strange hour to be planning another honeymoon with German planes threatening to bomb Athens."

Paulette was a bit perplexed. "I'm surprised you'd ask why I'd come after sending me the letter with the note and the newspaper clipping. I went first to Cairo, but Garret had already left for Athens. So, here I am."

"What newspaper clipping? Did I do something to make you think Garret was in Cairo?"

"The letter you sent from Cairo. You know, with the attractive blonde, Anna Kruger?"

Rhoda shook her head. "Kruger? The name sounds vaguely familiar."

"Her father is the German ambassador to Egypt."

"What's this all about?"

"The clipping you cut from the Cairo paper's society section and sent to me in London. You don't remember?"

Rhoda set her cup down, shaking her head. "Paulette, darling, we haven't been in Cairo. Garret arranged for us to fly directly to Athens, then Delphi. I didn't cut anything from a paper and send it to you."

Paulette stared at her, the truth slowly making inroads on her mind. She lifted her handbag from the floor beside her chair, snapped it open, and finding the envelope with the news clipping, handed it to Rhoda.

Looking at her with a frown, Rhoda took out the clipping.

Paulette saw the shocked look on Rhoda's face as she unfolded it. "Oh dear..." she murmured.

"Now read the note," Paulette urged quietly.

She removed it also from the envelope and spread it open on her knees. Then she looked up, her eyes wide, her lips parted. "This is not mine. I didn't send it to you. I've never seen this woman before, and if I *had* seen this photo in the paper, I assure you I'd never, never bring it to your attention."

"Yes, I wondered about it. I couldn't believe you'd do something like that, knowing it would hurt me. Even if it were true, which, thank God, it isn't. I've since learned that a picture is not always what it seems to be. Anna is Garret's German cousin. Her father is an ambassador in Cairo, and she's married to—" she stopped suddenly, and glanced over her shoulder toward the open window. Had she heard something?

"What is it?" Rhoda whispered.

"I thought I heard someone." Paulette stood and walked over to the window. The simple cotton curtains fluttered in the wind. Rhoda came up beside her and looked out. "Anyone there?"

"No, but I'm *sure* someone was a moment ago." Paulette hurried to the front door, opened it, and stepped outdoors into the sunshine. She looked up and down the yard, then toward the giant plantain tree where Niko's car was parked in the shade. There was no one in sight, just the morning breeze moving through the bushes and tree branches.

"It does get windy here," Rhoda said, joining her, and shading her eyes as she looked around. "You must have heard the wind. Let's go back inside."

Moments later, Paulette shut the door behind them and Rhoda walked over to where she'd been sitting and picked up the letter and clipping. "This isn't even my handwriting. Here, look." She opened a drawer and took out a sealed envelope. "I wrote this earlier to mail to a friend in London. Compare the two envelopes. My writing is much more flowing. See the way I make my R's and N's?"

Paulette carefully examined the writing, not because she doubted Rhoda, but because it gave her time to sort through her bewildered thoughts.

"But if I didn't write it, then who did?" Rhoda lifted her eyes to meet Paulette's. "And why?"

"I don't know," Paulette said in a low voice.

"I wonder," Rhoda mused. "Could that femme fatale—what was her name? Gloria something-or-other—have done this just to cause trouble?"

"Gloria Haskins," Paulette obliged. "No, I don't think so. She's away on assignment. Besides, she's been seeing Mort. Their relationship appears to be getting rather serious."

"Well, never underestimate women who have few scruples. Didn't she know Garret fairly well in New York?"

"Yes, but still..."

"All right, so she didn't send it. But someone did, and it wasn't me."

Paulette looked at her quickly. "I know that now, Rhoda," she soothed. She frowned, wondering, as she replaced the letter and clipping back into her handbag for safekeeping.

"It's all strange indeed," Rhoda said. "I don't like it, Paulette, not one bit. And that's what brought you here?"

"That was my original motivation for coming, so I took advantage of Mort's offer to do a feature on the prisoners of war in Cairo." She looked at her. "But other things have transpired since then."

"And how did you find out Anna Kruger is Garret's cousin?"

She needed to be careful. Henley had told her to remain silent. "I discovered the truth in Cairo. Garret has family there. In the past, he had a great-aunt, Helga Kruger, who was quite a woman, I'm told. Very wealthy, too. As it turns out, I married a man with a large inheritance. There's several houses in Egypt, one in Aleppo, another somewhere on the Mediterranean. And...I have some bad news. Gilly died."

"Oh, no!"

"But it turns out he wasn't truly my uncle."

"What!"

"Better sit down," Paulette said with a tired smile. "I've got quite another story to tell you about Gilbert Simonds, alias Gilbert Simington, from Cairo, Egypt."

∾∾∾

"Well," Rhoda said later, "I must say I'm baffled about Gilly. He was certainly an odd one. At least you've learned you have another relative, somewhere in or around Cairo. Perhaps you have an aunt or uncle to take the place of poor, misguided Gilly."

Later, as Paulette thought through the discussion about the letter, she realized that neither of them had come to a firm conclusion about who had sent it or what the motive had been. An hour later they were still sitting there with the teapot empty and the Greek sweet cake gone. The rising wind made weird little moaning sounds around the hut, and Paulette was deep in thought as Rhoda twisted a

strand of auburn hair around her finger, frowning to herself.

"Unless," she said, breaking the silence.

Paulette looked across the coffee table at her. "Unless?"

Rhoda drew in a breath, "Someone wanted to make sure
you left London and came to Cairo. That's the only reason I
can think why it would be sent to you. If it wasn't Gloria
Haskins, then that leaves something even more sinister:
someone *wanted* you in Egypt."

Paulette stirred, her stocking feet tucked under her.
Someone wanted her in Egypt. Why?

"We're back to square one," she said. She shook her
head. "Nothing much happened in Cairo."

"I wouldn't say that. Something did happen."

Paulette looked at her. "Such as?"

"You decided to come here, to Delphi. And you're here
to meet Garret."

Paulette's lashes narrowed. "Yes." She thought about
Colonel Henley. He had wanted her to come to Delphi. But
he would never resort to the low trick of sending a mis-
leading photo of Garret and Anna to lure her to Cairo to
work for him. And he wouldn't have written that letter and
signed Rhoda's name to it. He was too serious a man for
that kind of tactic. He'd been up front with her about the
possible dangers involved. Henley had played fair. Nor did
she think Ambassador Kruger would do such a thing. He
hadn't even known about her until Henley arranged the
meeting at the old Blaine House. Paulette could only think
that it had been sent by an enemy. Her own enemy, as
Rhoda suggested? Or Garret's? Could it be the same person
who put the matchbook with the phone number in Garret's
pocket?

"I don't like this," Rhoda said again, rising to her feet.
"Someone wanted you in Delphi badly enough to deceive

you. That sounds very risky to me. I think we should tell Fergus about this, even Dr. Bristow."

"No, Rhoda," she said quickly, jumping up from the chair. "I'd rather you didn't. The fewer involved in this, the better. Let's keep it between us until I can explain it to Garret."

"Well...all right, if that's what you want, but to me this is a rather foreboding circumstance. And I just plain don't like the idea that someone used my name to trap you into coming."

"It's not so bad, as long as I know it isn't true."

"I wouldn't say that." Rhoda frowned. "You still don't know why someone tried to deceive you into coming here at this time."

Rhoda could be right, she thought uncomfortably. The most obvious reason was that someone was planning to use her as bait to lure Garret from his hiding place, yet she couldn't explain this to Rhoda. But how could they have known weeks ago that Garret would be injured and hiding somewhere?

It might be that they hadn't, and planned to use her to trap him, if not here in Delphi, then in Athens where he had first gone to met Anna and Stephano.

Anger took over her fears. If someone thought she could be used as a way to reach and harm her husband, she would be doubly careful to see that they failed.

The sound of interrupting voices from another room turned both Paulette and Rhoda toward an open door that led into the bedroom. They entered, finding that Fergus' shortwave radio had been left on when he went to the digs.

"Fergus is able to pick up Greek, German, and Italian communications. The other night I wasn't feeling well and fell asleep on the divan. I woke up around midnight and decided I'd make myself a cup of hot cocoa." She laughed as she turned off the radio. "And there was Fergus bent over the shortwave set. He was writing down on a notepad the strengths and weaknesses of military positions as though transcribing for some general."

Paulette glanced at her.

"It was even in shorthand. Something I can't fathom. I told him he was carrying his hobby a little too far."

Paulette paused by the radio. The table it sat on had a drawer that was open a few inches where it looked as though someone had failed to close it, as though—what? Interrupted.

"That's Fergus and Dr. Bristow now," Rhoda said.

Paulette heard the rough motor of a jeep driving across the dirt road.

"Lunch won't be too difficult. I've already sliced up some vegetables," Rhoda said, returning to the living room.

Paulette lingered. "I'll be right there. Mind if I use your bath to wash up? My hands and face feel dusty."

"It's right there, darling, you can't miss it. The water only trickles out the pipe, though. You'll need patience. Oh—and there's perfumed soap on the top shelf. Fergus brought it from Athens for my birthday. Go ahead and open it." She went out toward the kitchen.

Paulette stood for a moment, her tension climbing. She bit her lip, then hearing the doors on the jeep, she quickly opened the drawer beneath the shortwave radio. She didn't see a notepad. She searched. It was at the bottom. She pulled it out, her breath coming faster. Her trembling fingers leafed through the pages.

She read the shorthand.

It was information on the German Twelfth Army—not on their positions near Aliakmon, but on the border between Bulgaria and East Macedonia.

Why was Fergus gathering sensitive information?

The jeep doors slammed shut and there were voices. Paulette put back the pad, shut the drawer, and started to dart away, then remembered. She stopped, left the drawer open a few inches as it had been, then rushed into the cubbyhole bathroom.

A minute later she caught her breath, started regathering her scattered wits, and began washing her face with cool water. She remembered Rhoda's perfumed soap and enjoyed the scented suds. *Lilacs*, she thought. Lilacs in the middle of Greece, with her husband lying somewhere in the mountains, injured and suffering as the Nazi army pushed relentlessly south toward Athens.

20

Paulette took a deep breath, and then walked through the door leading into the front room.

"Hello, Paulette," Fergus said with surprise in his voice. "I thought Niko had it wrong when he said you were here."

"I am never wrong," Niko spoke up cheerfully. He grinned at Rhoda, who came in with a pot of coffee in one hand and a wooden tray of cups in the other.

Fergus gave Paulette a perfunctory kiss on the cheek. "I'm glad you're here."

Paulette tried to read his troubled eyes to see if she could garner any firsthand knowledge about her husband.

"So Garret's planning to meet you here?" Fergus said.

"Looks like his business trip brought him to Greece at a very turbulent time," she said. "He'll join us as soon as he's finished up in Athens." She could see nothing in his expression to indicate he knew of Garret's actual circumstances. Then it seemed he hadn't been in touch Fergus either. This did little to relieve her fears. *What if he is so weak he can't contact his friends? What if...*

"This is Dr. Wendel Bristow," Fergus was saying. "I know his extraordinary work needs no introduction. Wendel, Paulette Brandt."

Dr. Bristow was all she had imagined. His skin was weathered by many outdoor hours, with lines creasing his forehead and crinkling the corners of his eyes that were brilliant blue against his tanned complexion. He must have had sandy-colored hair as a young man, for there were still blondish traces mixed with the gray. He was slender and of medium height, but his arms looked solid from hard labor. He was dressed in khakis with his shirt sleeves rolled up past his elbows. Paulette was aware that he watched her keenly. She had the uncanny feeling that she may have seen him somewhere before, and Dr. Bristow may have also thought so, for he seemed deeply interested in her.

"I've admired your work, Dr. Bristow," Paulette said, putting out her hand. "I've long wanted to interview you."

His smile was friendly. "You may have more opportunity than you need if we all become trapped in Delphi. So you are here waiting for your husband to come from Athens, is that it?"

"Yes," she said casually, "unless he had to go to Corinth, or even Salonika."

Fergus said, "If you know his hotel, I should be able to call him from here."

How was she going to get out of this?

"The phone isn't working," said Niko.

"It's the third time this month…very irritating, especially now," said Fergus. He looked at Rhoda, who was offering coffee to everyone. "That reminds me—this is Dr. Miklos, a physician who's just settled here in Delphi from Athens."

"I feel better already," Rhoda said with a laugh. "Coffee, Dr. Miklos?"

"Please, *kyria*. Thank you."

A doctor. Paulette tried to look calmer than her thoughts. This must be the physician that Colonel Henley had mentioned, the man who would help Garret once they knew his location. *Thank You, God*, she thought reverently. She no longer felt alone. Here was one known ally. That made two, with Niko.

Paulette's dismay receded as she felt that things were progressing in the right direction after all.

Again she noticed Dr. Bristow staring at her. Something seemed to be on his mind.

Paulette took over in the small kitchen. It reminded her of her tiny apartment in London. She thought of the happy times she'd spent with Garret when he'd helped her fix breakfast, bringing a wave of new longing and sadness. She resolved not to allow gloomy thoughts to overwhelm her. Soon now, Garret would contact her, and then Dr. Miklos would be able to treat him with whatever he needed. "Please, let it be soon, Lord," she prayed.

Lunch was served, and they all crowded around the small table, consciously trying not to bump elbows. The food was simple, but there was enough for everyone. Rhoda had made a lamb stew the day before and it was quite tasty with added vegetables and barley. Paulette was too tense to eat much. She'd already lost weight since leaving London for Egypt. She looked at Dr. Miklos. Did he know anything yet? She hoped his glance meant that he did, but his gaze remained on Niko as he answered his questions about why he'd left busy, crowded Athens for quiet Delphi and Itea. Walks in the countryside, he said, were worth far more to him than the money he made in Athens.

"My hobby is botany," he was saying. "There are rare wildflowers around the temple ruins. When I can take some time away from the medical needs of Delphi, I hope to collect and catalog them."

His voice was interrupted by Dr. Bristow, who turned his ear toward the news on the wireless. Fergus stood quickly and turned up the volume on the square wooden cabinet. She could feel the tension at the table as everyone fell silent.

The announcer's voice was saying "...a general southward movement of German forces is now in progress, aided in every way by the Bulgarians massing on the Macedonian frontier. General Papagos has suggested withdrawal of all troops in Macedonia to the Alakhmon line as the only sound military option. The king asks that all his subjects remain calm."

Paulette found herself gripping her fork too tightly. Rhoda was blinking rapidly, a nervous reaction she'd had since her school days. Fergus exchanged glances with Dr. Bristow.

"It does not sound good," Niko said.

"No." Dr. Miklos lifted his water glass and emptied it.

"What about the British army?" Rhoda asked her husband. "Surely between them and the Greek army they'll be able to hold back the Germans?"

"Yes, they're sixty thousand strong," Paulette heard her voice saying calmly.

Niko shot her a look.

"How do you know that?" Rhoda asked curiously.

Paulette hesitated. She couldn't admit that she'd heard it from Colonel Henley at the Blaine House in Cairo. "Oh, I think I heard someone mention it, probably in Egypt, when I was with Quinn."

"I'm certain our effort against this invasion will be vigorous," Dr. Bristow said.

Fergus switched off the wireless, and Rhoda stood. "Well, after the news, would anyone still care to have dessert and more coffee? I bought a date cake at the market this morning. How about you, Niko?"

"Nothing ruins my appetite, *kyria*," he said easily, but his expression was grim.

Paulette also stood, intending to help her. As she passed the window she stopped and looked out. She saw the wind rising, blowing dry dust in little swirls across the fields in the direction of the temple ruins. "The Oracle of Delphi," Henley had said. What would it mean to Garret?

"We have an excellent chance of holding the line against the Nazi advance," Dr. Bristow went on to say.

Where had she heard that before? The French. The Maginot line. Yet the Germans had broken through and pushed onward toward Paris.

Niko was the only one to eat a slice of cake. As Paulette went around the room refilling coffee cups, Fergus said, "Don't worry. When Garret hears the news report he'll contact you. It will serve us well to leave for Cairo. All of us."

"But we can't leave yet," Rhoda said. "What about Dr. Bristow's work, and yours?"

"I'm afraid Hitler won't suppress his ambitions for my work, Rhoda, nor for the birth of your child." Dr. Bristow turned to Paulette and smiled kindly. "Until your husband can get here, my dear, you may stay at my hut. There's an extra bedroom. Niko was using it last summer, but he won't mind relinquishing it, considering your dilemma." He looked at her for her acceptance, then across at Niko. "It's not all that far from Arachova. You can drive over each morning."

"Sure," Niko was scraping his dessert plate. "From the way things look now, our work will soon be cut short anyway."

Paulette returned her gratitude with a smile. "Thank you. That's one concern taken care of."

"There's no need for Niko to drive that narrow mountainous road to Arachova twice a day," Dr. Miklos spoke up. "You can stay at my house," he told him. "I've plenty of room, since I'm alone. It's just down the street near the Pilgrim Hotel."

Both Fergus and Dr. Bristow turned toward Niko. He said cheerfully, "Good, now we are all in walking distance of the digs. In return I can show you a place on Mount Parnassus where very unusual flowers grow."

∼∼∼

After lunch, the men walked back to the digs and Rhoda and Paulette spent the afternoon catching up with one another. They had always been close, and Paulette treasured this time to spend with her "sister." After dinner, everyone sat with coffee or tea and listened to the BBC. The news continued to be grim. They were all in agreement to turn in early.

Dr. Bristow's hut had three rooms and a small kitchen. There was a living room, where he ate and worked and burned his lamp until late at night, as well as a small bedroom, and an addition not much larger than a porch that became the "second" bedroom. The roof and walls appeared to have been nailed together by a novice. Still, it provided comfort and security, and Paulette was grateful for his consideration, as she would otherwise have had to sleep on the divan in Rhoda's living room. Paulette noticed a bookcase filled with volumes. *How typical of a scholar*, she thought, smiling to herself. *There may not be room for many items, but there is always space for one more book.*

"This is wonderful, Dr. Bristow. You were very kind to have me on such short notice."

"It is a bit primitive. I wish I could offer you more, Mrs. Brandt."

"Please, call me Paulette."

Dr. Bristow put down her bag, walked to the small window, moved the plaid curtain aside and peered out casually. She noticed he took time to scan the yard immediately around the thin-walled hut. Now why was he doing that?

She watched him. He smiled. "You must be tired. A young lady would most likely wish to freshen up. When you're ready, we can talk in the next room."

A little perplexed, she stood looking at the door as he closed it behind him. Then she quickly went for the jug of water standing under the table which held a basin.

From the living room a few minutes later came the sound of men's voices. Who could that be? Hurriedly she undid her hair, brushed it vigorously, and replaced the two small combs that held the sides up and away from her ears.

In the living room she found Dr. Bristow bent over a table, sorting through what looked to her at first glance like a photo album. The men's voices were from the wireless set. There was news in low, businesslike tones. Dr. Bristow looked up, saw her waiting, and straightened. "I've been gathering a few photographs from the old days. Do have a chair, and if you don't mind, I'll leave the wireless on in the background."

Paulette had the feeling that he was doing this to prevent anyone outside the hut from separating their lowered voices from the BBC and the incessant crackle of static. Her excitement grew. He must know something about Garret. She wondered who he might have expected to see out the window. Some local Greek, perhaps? The huts were not far from the main village streets.

Dr. Bristow sat down opposite her and crossed his long legs. His eyes were thoughtful and his face was serious to the point of activating her fears.

"What is it?" She bit her lip to keep from coming right out and asking about Garret. She could be wrong about Dr. Bristow being an ally. "Is it the war?" she found herself asking without emotion. "More bad news on the border with Bulgaria?" Her eyes went automatically to a large map pinned on the wall above the wireless, showing Greece, Albania, Yugoslavia, and Bulgaria.

"That, too. But let's start at the beginning, Paulette. I'm afraid I must shock you. I've learned just recently that I am your uncle. Great-uncle, to be precise. The younger brother of your grandfather, Brigadier George Bristow of India. George, bless his heart, was killed at Kut, near Baghdad, by the Turks in the Great War. I'm afraid you and I are the very last of the Bristows, my dear."

Paulette stared, speechless. He appeared to understand, and went on, keeping his voice low and calm. "Here is a photograph of your mother, Leah."

Paulette took the fading picture between trembling fingers. Overwhelmed, her eyes filled with tears. She blinked hard. The face of the young woman was quite attractive, similar to what had become known recently in stardom as a "sunny blonde" with an outdoor appeal and a healthy glow. She had on a tennis outfit and was standing in a court with another young woman who was even more attractive, with long flame colored hair and a charming smile.

"The girl beside Leah was your mother's cousin, Allison Wescott of Egypt. She married Colonel Bret Holden."

Paulette's throat was dry. She continued to look at her mother. *At last, I've found her,* she thought, with a cramp in her throat. *This is my mother.*

Paulette looked up quickly. "You're my uncle. Not Gilly—but you."

He smiled. "And very proud to have it so, my dear."

They smiled at one another for a moment, then Paulette shyly arose from her chair, walked to him, and kissed his roughened cheek. "I'm even more proud that I am related to the great Dr. Bristow!"

He blinked back a tear, raised her hand, and kissed it. "We've a lot of catching up to do. Let's hope the future is not ruined by the war. And now, my child, I've still much to tell you, and I'm certain you must have a hundred questions to ask me. First, more about Leah." He leaned forward in his chair, his fingers interlaced. "How much did Colonel Henley tell you about her?"

"He told me she'd been an agent. She was killed at Aleppo by a German agent."

"Yes," he said. "Rex Blaine."

Her breath paused. "Blaine? You mean—the owner of the Blaine House Gilbert Simonds left me?"

He nodded. "Gilly had a warped sense of humor, I'm afraid. The doctors who treated him in Cairo believed him...unsound. That would partly explain why he took his life. A sad and tragic situation. Let's go on to better things. Your mother was a brave and dedicated woman. She gave her life for Britain, as did Neil."

"Neil?"

"Neil Bristow, her brother. They both worked for the CID. Neil never married. He was on his way back to Alexandria from London, sailing on the same ship as Defense Secretary Kitchener in the last war with Germany. Their ship was torpedoed by a U-boat and sunk. So Neil lost his life not long after Leah was found near the huts of the Cairo Archaeological Club. By the way—the club was run by Garret's great-aunt, Helga Kruger. She owned the huts, as well as several houses in and around Cairo."

"Yes, Colonel Henley had mentioned Helga's many possessions. I received a surprise about Garret. Previously I had thought I was the heir."

"The one artifact that Gilly Simonds left you that does not fall under Kruger ownership is the lamp from Aleppo. It was actually discovered by Neil and Leah. So it is yours." He handed her another photograph of her mother standing beside a handsome young man with thick, sandy-brown hair and a ready smile. "That's Neil. I'm afraid I don't have a photograph of your father. Leah's marriage to Major Jeff Harrington was kept a secret, due to her position in British Intelligence. I don't believe even her closest relatives on the Wescott side knew she was married and had a small daughter named Paulette."

"Are you saying my name really is Harrington?"

"Yes. Opal was related to your father. When she took you in from the orphanage and adopted you, you were already relatives."

"Then—Rhoda is also related to me?"

"Exactly. She'll be surprised to learn the news."

"But why did Aunt Opal keep it all a secret?"

"I've no way of knowing, since she's deceased and I never met her. My instincts tell me that she may have been the sort of woman who was afraid to stir things up. She must have known about Leah being murdered, and was cautious of Gilly Simonds. He was a convicted murderer, and I think she was leery of him. It may have been easier for Opal to not contest his benign favoritism toward you. If he had wished to consider you a 'niece,' then she had just let him. And from what I understand from Colonel Henley, Gilly was indeed related to the Wescotts, who were related to your mother. So...Opal Harrington may also have entertained the idea that Gilly would leave you a great fortune if she kept quiet. She would have wanted that for you."

Paulette agreed to his assessment of Opal. "You haven't told me how you discovered my identity. I suppose it was Colonel Henley."

"Actually it was your husband. Colonel Henley learned part of the truth through him, then followed through using friends in the CID."

"Garret?" she asked, surprised. "He knew?"

"As Henley must have told you, Garret's been following this family trail for a long time. Beginning with his suspicions of Gilly and the stolen Egyptian artifacts belonging to Helga Kruger, he was finally able to trace you to your mother."

"Then it was Garret who informed you of my bloodline to your niece, Leah Bristow."

"Yes. He's been in touch with me since your marriage, promising to bring you to Athens to meet me. He thought it best to wait and allow me to tell you. And now we've gotten together at last, my dear Paulette, but sadly, under dangerous and pressing circumstances."

She hung on his last words, waiting. Did he know about Garret? He must, because he had brought Dr. Miklos here. *Colonel Henley would be proud of me for my patience*, she thought, her palms sweating.

Dr. Bristow—now Uncle Wendel Bristow—glanced toward the wireless, then leaned forward in his chair again. "Henley told you of Garret's condition?"

"Yes. Then you do know. Where is he?"

"If I knew that, I'd take Dr. Miklos there tonight."

Then Dr. Miklos was working with the British.

"We must move with extreme caution. Garret's life is in danger."

His words settled bitterly in her heart. "Because of Stephano?"

"He has crucial knowledge for British Intelligence. The less you know of it, the safer you'll be. Garret would wish it so, and I agree."

"You're working with CID?"

"I'm a bona fide archaeologist, my dear niece. Let's just say there isn't very much I wouldn't do for England. Especially now, in time of war. And Colonel Henley and Garret have become my very dear friends." He smiled. "And Garret is also my nephew-in-law."

"Uncle..." she felt almost shy saying the title, "suppose...he's fevered from infection. He could be unable to contact me. There must be something we can do to locate him!"

"There's a chance you are already under surveillance. Any anxious movement on the part of either of us could alert the enemy. There is need to keep our eyes and ears open for anything out of the ordinary. We've no choice except to wait. Garret, at present, happens to hold all the cards in his hand."

Wait—there was no other choice.

"Tomorrow," her uncle said, "I will show you the temple ruins. It will help get our minds off our dilemma, and I have another motive." He smiled. "I can spend time getting to know my new niece."

In spite of her fears for her husband's welfare, his kind words enabled Paulette to take his hand and warmly return his smile.

21

When Paulette awoke it was dawn, and her uncle was already up and moving about in the living room. Because they had made plans the evening before to walk to the ruins early, she rose at once and dressed in slacks and a blue woolen pullover. She moved over to the window to brush her hair in the still-cool morning air. The leaves of the plantain tree were beginning to show their bright green color as dawn progressed in the east. In the shadowed fields the breeze rippled pleasantly through spring grasses and early flowers. She thought of Dr. Miklos' interest in botany. Was this truly his hobby or had it just provided a cover for moving to Delphi?

Paulette meant to ask her uncle why he thought Dr. Miklos had invited Niko to stay with him at his house. She assumed it was because he knew Niko was an ally. Yet Niko had acted rather surprised by it all. She wondered where Dr. Miklos' house was located. She looked out the window, but could only see Fergus and Rhoda's little place. Their lights were still out.

When she came into the living room she could smell the welcoming aroma of fresh coffee. The light burned cheerily, and Uncle Wendel was dishing out cooked fruit and what looked like barley cereal.

She smiled. "Good morning, Uncle. Mmm, looks good."

"How did you sleep, my dear? Niko complains that the mattress is lumpy."

She laughed. "I'm surprised a student from a farming family in Arachova would complain. I found it quite comfortable, and I slept shamelessly well."

"Niko lives in Arachova now, but that's because he wanted to help me at the digs this spring. He's originally from Switzerland."

She set her coffee cup down so quickly that it nearly splashed. "Switzerland?"

"Didn't he tell you?" He sprinkled raw sugar on his cereal.

"Isn't he Greek? He looks it and speaks it so perfectly."

"Oh, he's Greek all right, but after his grandmother died he went to Geneva to attend the university."

Paulette was remembering that Niko had told her just the opposite. He'd been born and raised in Arachova and moved to Athens.

"He told me he attended the British Archaeology School in Athens."

"He did. That's where I met him, but he transferred from the Geneva school almost two years ago." He must have noticed her reaction because he stopped. "What did Niko tell you?"

She explained cautiously, because she didn't want to cast Niko in a bad light if she had merely misunderstood him. Now that she knew her uncle was an ally with Colonel Henley, it seemed reasonable to tell him that Niko claimed he was cooperating with Intelligence.

Her uncle seemed surprised.

"Niko? Working for Cairo Intelligence?"

"He knew about Garret's condition," she suggested in Niko's defense.

"So does the enemy."

She had thought of that, yet because she had needed a friend at the time she had relegated that possibility to the back of her mind. *How easy it is to allow one's self to be deceived by hearing what one wants to hear,* she thought. "Niko said he was sent here to protect Garret and aid us in getting back to Cairo."

"And did he say that you are to tell him at once when you hear from your husband?" There was a skeptical gleam in his eyes.

"Well, yes, that's what he wanted. But I wouldn't do that without first telling Garret about Niko. If anyone knows whether or not Niko is an ally, it would be Garret."

"Perhaps, but not even Garret knows who all the safe members of the underground are. No one does. It wouldn't be wise or safe for any of us. When did Niko tell you this?"

"When he drove me here from Arachova. Uncle, you don't think he's an enemy?"

"I don't know what to think." He scowled and pushed the bowl away. "I do know Dr. Miklos was sent here. He may know about Niko."

"Wouldn't he have warned you if he doubted him?"

"That's just it, my dear. Miklos wouldn't know." Paulette thought back to something Colonel Henley had told her. She looked at her uncle. "Colonel Henley assured me a physician was coming from Athens. 'One of our own' was the way he put it. I thought you knew him, that you'd arranged his coming here. Uncle, are you saying you don't *know* Dr. Miklos?"

For a moment he stared at her. "Good grief, what a dimwit I've been. I'd never met Miklos until yesterday."

She stood. "But—"

"You see," he said quietly, "my contact in Athens notified me the day before you arrived that the doctor couldn't make it, a sudden attack of appendicitis. Someone else was being sent. A physician named Miklos whom he trusted."

The words died on her lips. "And you think he may not be the *real* Dr. Miklos?"

"I've only his word for it. For all we know, Dr. Miklos may have been captured and replaced with the man we now have among us."

"How frightening!"

"In which case, he would either be working with Niko, or Niko himself is in danger. It makes me wonder why Miklos wanted him to take his spare bedroom."

Paulette's fingers tightened on the back of her chair. She watched her uncle move the curtains aside and look out across the field toward the little village.

She said quickly: "If Miklos were genuine, wouldn't he know if Niko was friend or foe?"

"It would seem so," her uncle said stiffly, "but in this kind of work, one never can be quite sure." He turned thoughtfully, as if unaware of her.

"There is more. Niko told me that when he was a student he knew Stephano and followed his political views. And in the car the night Quinn and I arrived, there was a discussion about a strong Communist influence in the Greek underground. There was a guerrilla fighter, a leader, whose name was Ares. Bill Dabney, a friend of Quinn's, called Ares a staunch Communist and an admirer of Stalin."

Her uncle's mouth tightened. "And Niko's response?"

"He laughed it off."

"A denial, a tactic consistent with members of the Communist *putsch*. The movement is called the Red Dawn. Ares is not a mere leader; he's the commander of the entire Popular Liberation Army in the Greek underground. He could be the number one traitor."

"And he's presently working with the Nazis?"

"Hand in hand," he said bitterly. "He is no friend to them, however. His ultimate goal is to also defeat the Nazis and make Greece a Communist nation, an ally of Russia."

Paulette thought she understood, but as Colonel Henley had told her, Greek politics was nearly impossible to understand. Like ancient Byzantium in the days of the Crusades, the Greek mind was shrewd, and intrigue filled their palaces. But it took little political savvy to understand the dangers of Communism and Nazism. As far as she was concerned, both ideologies could lock horns and destroy one another.

"I need to try to contact Henley," Dr. Bristow said. He swiftly left the kitchen and went to his bedroom. Paulette loitered at his door, watching.

"It's not certain that I'll be able to reach him, but first I'll need a few minutes to encrypt the message," he said.

She watched as he removed three planks in his closet wall, exposing a narrow compartment with a Morse code transmitter, and turned it on.

So that was it. Paulette turned and went back into the kitchen. Her coffee was lukewarm, and she hardly tasted it as she swallowed. She went to the window. Was Niko lying, or Dr. Miklos? Perhaps neither. Maybe it was Quinn. At the moment, anything seemed possible.

Bristow came out of his bedroom a few minutes later. His face told her to dampen her expectations.

"I couldn't get through. Reception is usually better after dark. I'll try again then. There is nothing more we can do right now, so why don't we continue with our plans to visit the temple ruins?"

Paulette's mind was no longer on classical Greek history, but she tried to oblige her uncle. It was difficult to concentrate on his discussion of the ancient shrine as they walked the dusty, narrow road.

22

The clear April morning was going to get warm. Paulette followed her uncle up a steep path full of loose stones. "Watch your step," he warned. "It's all too easy to lose your footing and slide. Soon after arriving from Athens I was laid up for weeks with a sprained ankle." He pointed across a narrow rush of water. "We cross here."

In a short time she was trudging up a tenuous tree-lined path with pine needles that were fragrant but slippery beneath the soles of her hiking shoes. *Uncle Wendel must be in excellent shape,* she thought with a smile, *he isn't breathing nearly as hard as I am.*

Walking higher up the mountain they emerged from the pine trees onto a large open space of glaring white rock. Fallen blocks of stone appeared to have been undisturbed for generations. She stopped and looked at some ruined walls. "And this?" she inquired.

He smiled. "In Greek history this is relatively modern, Paulette. It's the remains of a Roman marketplace from about the time of Christ. Ancient Greece, however, goes back much earlier. Come along, just ahead."

They branched left on the path and Dr. Bristow stopped, looking upward. Paulette stood beside him and looped her arm through his. Despite her worries, it was good to be here with her uncle, and she felt thankful to God for a sense of belonging. He smiled down at her, his light blue eyes crinkling at the corners, the strong sunshine making the silver in his hair glint.

"Well, there it is, directly ahead of us...do you see it? The shrine of the fabled Apollo, whom the ancient Greek world worshiped as the god of light and healing."

The god of light! She lifted her brows and looked at him. "So that's why they call the cliff faces here 'the Shining Ones.'"

"Yes, quite an awesome title. The ancient Greeks could make their gods of things in nature or even of things straight from their imaginations. In that, they were actually similar to people today who worship nature instead of worshiping the Creator who made nature and all things."

Paulette looked at him and smiled.

"Shall we go up?" he asked her. "The steps, as you can see, are quite steep. The ancient Greeks, for all their earthly wisdom—including being credited with the birth of democracy—did not know God. The Greek mind also created fabled deities that gave them pleasure: Zeus, Apollo, Artemis, and a host of others, all of them temperamental, petty, jealous, exhibiting untamed passions, and even more ambitious and selfish than fallen man. It was the human body that the Greeks attempted to perfect rather than human character. It was, therefore, only natural that their gods and demigods would exemplify men; they were only the inventions of men. Most men look in the mirror and wish themselves perfect; very few look into their hearts and strive for holiness. Like Adam in the Garden of Eden, man hides from a holy God, knowing that he himself is unholy. So you see, the Greek gods were born as a painless substitute for the holy God. They are splendid in the carnal ways man would be splendid, and possessing all the pathetic foibles of fallen man."

Paulette listened quietly, not wishing to interrupt his thoughtful words.

"This is the Sacred Way," he explained, as they walked slowly along. "We traverse the same stones the ancient Greeks did centuries ago."

The sun beat down upon her head. Paulette shaded her eyes and made out the gate of the temple precinct. It appeared to her to be immense, filled with broken walls, pillars, marble steps, pedestals, and altars.

When she reached the top of the ancient steps, there was a stone-paved promenade that serpentined its ascent between antiquated walls of both treasuries and shrines. They followed this promenade up through the building's ruins.

"This is the remains of Apollo's temple," he said.

The six colossal columns appeared a rosy hue standing against the light blue morning sky. Many of the great blocks of marble that paved the floor were cracked or broken, and some seemed to be protected and supported by retaining walls.

Paulette stepped around these stones and walked carefully to the edge of the floor. Here she stood between the columns and peered below, her breath taken away by the steep drop that sent a shivery tingle up her spine. She didn't like heights. Below the retaining wall she saw a sheer drop of many hundreds of feet down the cliffs of the mountainside. In the silence, sudden gusts crooned around the crags that to her sounded like a growing murmur of indistinct voices.

Then—another voice. Her uncle's. "I think this is a good place to read some verses from the book of Isaiah about false gods and the one true God. Listen, carefully, my dear."

To whom then will you liken God?
Or what likeness will you compare to Him?
"The workman molds an image, the goldsmith
overspreads it with gold...
Whoever is too impoverished...
Chooses a tree that will not rot; He seeks for himself a
skillful workman to prepare a carved image that will
not totter.
Have you not known?
Have you not heard?
Has it not been told you from the beginning?
Have you not understood from the foundations
of the earth?
It is He who sits above the circle of the earth,
And its inhabitants are like grasshoppers,
Who stretches out the heavens like a curtain,
And spreads them out like a tent to dwell in.
He brings the princes to nothing;
He makes the judges of the earth useless....
"To whom then will you liken Me?
Or to whom shall I be equal?" says the Holy One...
Have you not known?
Have you not heard?
The everlasting God, the LORD,
The Creator of the ends of the earth,
Neither faints nor is weary.
His understanding is unsearchable.
"I, the LORD, am the first;
And with the last I am He....
Present your case," says the LORD.

"Bring forth your strong reasons," says the King of
Jacob....
"That we may consider them,
And know the latter end of them;
Or declare to us the things to come.
Show to us the things that are to come hereafter,
that we may know that you are gods;....
Indeed you are nothing,
And your work is nothing;
He who chooses you is an abomination....
You are My witnesses," says the LORD,
"And My servant whom I have chosen,
That you may know and believe Me,
And understand that I am He.
Before me there was no God formed,
Nor shall there be after Me.
I, even I, am the LORD,
And beside Me there is no savior....
Thus says the Lord, the King of Israel,
And his Redeemer, the LORD of hosts:
'I am the First and I am the Last;
Beside Me there is no God....'
Fear not, for I have redeemed you;
I have called you by your name; you are Mine....
Look to Me, and be saved,
All you ends of the earth!
For I am God, and there is no other.
I have sworn to Myself;
The word has gone out of My mouth in righteousness,
And shall not return,
That to Me every knee shall bow,
Every tongue shall take an oath.
He shall say,
'Surely in the LORD I have righteousness and strength.

> To Him men shall come,
> And all shall be ashamed
> Who are incensed against Him.'"

Spellbound by the words from God Himself, Paulette surveyed the great mountains, the far valley, and the limitless sky that spoke greater volumes of the truth about God than any temple ruins to the mythical Apollo.

Her uncle put his Bible down and said, "So you see that idolatry and false teachers have been around almost as long as there has been true worship upon the earth. The book of Isaiah was written over 700 years before Christ, but did you notice all the statements by Almighty God in the Old Testament that are identical to what we now know about Christ? God said about Himself that beside Him there is no savior. He is the King of Israel, and to Him every knee shall bow. He is the First and the Last. But we know from the New Testament that *Christ* is the one and only savior, and that Christ is the true King of Israel, and the only one to whom every knee shall bow. These few statements alone should trouble any who teach that Christ is not truly the very eternal God of the Old Testament. And I was especially blessed to read in the first chapter of Revelation, verses 17 and 18, that God says, 'Do not be afraid, I am the First and the Last. I am He who lives, and was dead, and behold, I am alive forevermore. Amen.' The obvious question then is: When did the eternal Almighty God of the Old Testament, the First and the Last, die? There can be only one possible answer: He died when Jesus Christ died on the cross."

Paulette now blinked back tears as she looked at her uncle. "I thought I knew God," she said, "but now I want to be closer to Him, and to love and trust Him."

You are my God, she prayed silently, a thankful smile on her lips.

Some of the words he had just read came back to her: "Fear not, for I have redeemed you; I have called you by your name; you are Mine."

"Lord Jesus, my Savior," she prayed, "thank You for speaking to my heart through my uncle's reading of Your Word. You have known me, but though I have been Your child, I ask you to forgive me for being very far from You. I now want to submit to You, and want to know You as You truly are. Amen."

Above her head sections of the temple were joyous with the fluttering wings of dark-colored swallows. In the valley far below the olive branches swayed in dance and shimmered in the sunlight. The song of the birds became a choir. In the distance some sheep bells rung as a shepherd led them.

I, too, have a Good Shepherd.

It must have been minutes later when she became aware that her uncle had walked some feet away and was seated on a worn stone in silence. She left the edge of the temple floor where she'd been standing and walked over to him, a smile in her eyes and on her lips. She reached down and took one of his weathered hands, clasping it between her palms.

"Thank you, dear Uncle. God used you to free my burdened heart."

He looked at her with an understanding smile in his eyes and simply nodded his head. His purpose, she knew, in reading the Scripture to her had been accomplished.

"What chapters of Isaiah were you reading?" she asked.

"Selected verses from 40 through 45." He handed her his small Bible.

"I have mine at the hut, Uncle. I'll read those chapters again tonight."

"They are marvelous in that they are the very words of God about His love and goodness. His creation is so great it is unfathomable, and how much greater must be the Creator Himself? But we are especially blessed in that God has in these last days given us knowledge of Himself through His Son. 'He who has seen Me has seen the Father,' Jesus told His disciples in the upper room."

She sat down beside him and for a few undisturbed minutes they pondered the magnificent view and the One who made it all, and also provided for their eternal deliverance.

The wind stirred, rustling the olive trees and pulling at her sleeves. She looked at him, as if awakening.

"Uncle…what is the Oracle of Delphi?"

"Come along. I'll show you." He stood and pointed as they walked. "See that small Doric building over there?" It once held the gold that was paid by the travelers who came to hear the Oracle. It was here, also, where the priestess Sybil supposedly sat on the grim stone to predict the Trojan War."

She looked at a large stone, not knowing whether or not it was the one used in the false worship or whether it was just one of many.

She supposedly predicted the ancient Trojan war. Could there be a coded message for Garret in that fable? "Can you explain what the Oracle of Delphi means? Is it a book or some kind of writing?"

"No, though all false religions have their writings, just as the Greeks had theirs that were used in the temple worship of Apollo. However, the Oracle has several meanings, Paulette. First, it represented a person."

"A person!" This surprised her. She been imagining a book of sorts.

"Yes, usually a woman, a priestess of ancient Greece through whom one of their fabled gods was said to speak to a particular worshiper. Thus, pilgrims came from all over, landing by boat at Itea, or making the arduous journey by land over the treacherous mountain trails. They paid great sums of money to the Oracle for some divination that would tell their fortunes, their futures, or answer some personal problem on power, war, love—any number of questions. And, as is typical of false prophets, the utterances coming from her were usually ambiguous and obscure, or just plain wrong. God speaks to His own through His Word, not through fortune-tellers, astrologers, palm readers, and necromancers. All who listen to such are greatly deceived."

She had always sensed that those kinds of things were subject to great error.

"The Oracle of Delphi was also a shrine. People were told that 'hidden knowledge' and 'divine purpose' could be learned at the shrine. Thirdly, it could represent an 'answer' or a 'decision' given by the Oracle. So you can see the terminology itself is not distinct, which seems to assist those who are profiting from vague and ambiguous pronouncements."

"So," she said thoughtfully, "this supposed Oracle of Delphi could be three things. A priestess, a shrine, or the answer itself."

He smiled. "Something like that."

She laughed. "It's confusing."

"Evil deceptions usually are complicated and confusing. Evil hides, truth reveals. God is light. And His Word is a lamp for our feet and a light for our path. The Bible is true divine revelation."

"Yes...I'm just now remembering something I was forced to memorize in school."

The Oracles are dumm,
No voice or hideous humm
Run through the arched roof in words deceiving
Apollo from his shrine
Can no more divine....

"Ah, yes, Milton," he said. "*Paradise Lost.* That stanza is from 'The Nativity Hymn.'"

He looked at his watch. "Ten o'clock. We've been here longer than I'd thought." He looked down the hill in the direction of the village of Delphi. "You can stay and look around some more, if you like. I'm thinking I'd better find out if Niko and Dr. Miklos have shown up yet."

"I think I'll stay, Uncle. I'd like to look around the digs."

"They're not far. Take the steps from the temple to the amphitheater. You'll see a path leading uphill. It's about a quarter mile. It's a pleasant walk and a pleasant day for it. And as to Dr. Miklos' interest in wildflowers, you'll find some rare beauties in that direction. Just be careful to stay on the path and don't get too close to the cliff, my dear."

Paulette watched him walk down the path toward the village and huts. When he'd disappeared into the pine and olive trees, she sat down again on the worn stone to meditate on all that she had seen and heard. Her mind and her heart were very full.

23

The morning breeze ebbed as the sun grew hotter. Paulette looked up the hill behind the temple ruins. Archaeologists had discovered the statue called *The Charioteer* in the theater area where it was now on display in the museum below the temple shrine. She wanted to see the amphitheater and then visit the digs where Uncle Wendel was working. She left the temple floor with its six great pillars and took the steep steps upward, carefully avoiding broken stones.

She reached the top steps and stood looking at the ancient theater in the shape of a bowl, with semi-circular tiers of marble seats rising against a small hillock of rambling, overgrown holly bushes and tall sage-green cypress. All was quiet. The mood was eerie, almost expectant. She could imagine the voice of Aristotle giving a lecture, echoing as it bounced back from the surrounding mountains.

She wanted to take a few minutes to actually sit in the seats, so she went across to the other side and climbed most of the way up the tiers and sat down on the marble. Below her, the circular stage waited, empty. Far off in the surrounding distance the mountain crags looked on, undisturbed by the passing of thousands of years.

She got up and started to walk to the top edge when the silence was suddenly broken by footsteps. She stopped, uneasy. It couldn't be her uncle returning. She didn't want to be seen, though she couldn't have said just why she felt so. She stooped quickly behind the closest shrub, getting down as low as she could, and waited. Whoever was coming was confident, for the footsteps were hurried. A moment later a man entered and paused, his gaze circling the theater, looking up into the top rows.

Quinn?

In a moment of confusion she thought, *But he can't be here. He left with Bill Dabney for the Macedonia-Bulgaria border!*

She took a deep breath. *There's no reason to hide like this*, her mind repeated. *It's Quinn.* Still, she didn't move.

Had Uncle Wendel sent him here to find her? They might have met on the path back to the huts.

You're being foolish, she told herself. *Quinn is a friend. You've known him for years.* Why, there was even a time when their relationship had hovered on the edge, ready to tip into something deeper than friendship. And Colonel Henley had somewhat trusted him. What had he said in Cairo? "I trust him about as much as I trust any newspaperman with an appetite for uncovering stories."

Even so, she stayed put, hearing her heart pound in her ears. How terribly embarrassing it was going to be if Quinn decided to walk up the aisle and discover her on her hands and knees hiding behind a small shrub!

Then her attention was snagged by movement on the opposite side of the amphitheater. Other footsteps were coming along the rough path that led up from the plateau.

Quinn also heard it, for his head jerked in that direction. He, too, apparently did not want to be seen, for he turned quickly to take cover. As he did so he dropped something that bounced down the steps. He paused, stooped a moment to look for it, and then took cover behind a flowering pomegranate tree.

A moment or two later Niko came through the olive trees with the surefooted ease of a mountain goat. He climbed the path leading off toward the digs farther up Mount Parnassus. Dr. Miklos was not with him. *Maybe Miklos had returned to the huts*, Paulette thought hopefully, for she wanted to trust Niko. By now the physician might be meeting with her uncle.

Niko didn't look across to the theater, but glanced behind him, then hurried toward rambling holly bushes overspreading the stony track. There, he waited.

Did he think he was being followed, or was he expecting to follow someone who was soon to come along? Did he think Quinn would come that way? Or maybe he didn't even know Quinn was here. Paulette wondered, *Just who is following whom?*

She glanced uneasily from Niko to Quinn. Quinn stayed behind the pomegranate, motionless, and she knew suddenly as though by sixth sense that she didn't want to trust either man. Perhaps they hadn't followed each other, but were expecting *her*.

No one moved. There was no sound in the spring morning except the wind coming up, swishing through the tall trees.

Paulette stayed where she was. Oh no! Her foot was getting cramped, and she didn't dare change positions. She wasn't sure how much longer she could stay still.

Niko unexpectedly left the holly bushes and surged through the pines towards the higher levels where the path led above the Shining Ones and away into the upper reaches of Parnassus.

A moment later Quinn emerged and looked after him. She expected him to follow, but he turned suddenly and went down the steps from which he had come, back toward the shrine.

Paulette wondered why Quinn hadn't followed him. They had seemed to be friends and allies in the car at Arachova. He had even expected Niko to go with him on the trip to Macedonia until Niko decided he wanted to stay in order to work with her uncle at the digs.

Perhaps Quinn had been as surprised to see Niko walking by as she'd been to see Quinn. He may have come here looking for her, and hadn't wanted Niko to know he was back in Delphi, if he had left at all. Whatever his reason, the explanation would need to wait until she could talk with him later. There was a great deal more about Niko and his strange behavior than she had expected. And who had he thought might be trailing him? He'd been in a big hurry, too. She intended to find out why.

She finally felt safe enough to sit up and rub the cramp out of her foot. When she was sure they would not return, she got up and went by the spot where Quinn had stood when something flashed in the sunlight. She stooped and picked it up, feeling the heat on her palm. A cigarette lighter. She turned it over in her hand for a moment, reading his initials, then slipped it into her pocket.

It was late morning when she began the steep route that climbed between the temple ruins to the mountainside above. She came to a cliff where rocks had slid down a steep gully, perhaps from an earthquake. She knew Niko was a strong climber, and she quickened her pace for fear he would gain too much distance on her. Was he going to the digs? Most likely. Even Fergus might have gone there by now.

The path continued, circling behind a thicket of wild olive trees with ground that looked as though it had been rained upon by small rocks.

Paulette had expected to have reached the digs by now. When Uncle Wendel mentioned the spot, he had said it wasn't that far away. She had walked for forty minutes and seen nothing, including Niko. Could she have missed a turnoff? *But there hasn't been any turnoff,* she insisted to herself. The path was narrow and wound its way continually uphill. She worried now that the track Niko had taken might not have been the one her uncle had pointed out. There had been several tracks in the area, and it would be easy to miss it with so much on her mind. One thing she was certain about; Niko had come this way. At the moment this was all that concerned her. And if this way didn't bring them to the digs, where did it lead? Her avid determination gave her the strength to ignore the growing heat and trudge on. She wished she had brought a pack of provisions, but she hadn't expected to go on such a trek. A bottle of water and some fruit would do her well right now.

It was now high noon, and all around her was a dusty expanse of heated rock. At last the track brought her out on top of a cliff that had a view of the temple. Far below and to the right lay the temple area, its columns, porticoes, and Sacred Way looking small.

Immediately beneath her there was a cleft of a water spring, now dry, though there was a faint glimmer of yellow-green farther up the rock bed, telling her that there must be water somewhere nearby. She thought of Garret. Wherever he was, she hoped he had shelter, water, and food. A sudden movement caught her attention, and a second later a form emerged from the shaded area ahead of her. A man's silhouette came from beneath an overhanging cliff. He walked along the stony gully to a crag. Even from this distance and with his back toward her she recognized Niko in his flamboyant cap. At least she hadn't lost him.

A young man appeared, scrambling down from a boulder. He was dressed roughly in what looked like shepherd's clothes.

Niko stopped, and the man approached. They spoke, and then Niko followed him. They disappeared around some rocks.

Paulette breathlessly hurried after them. She was grateful for the breeze from the sea that cooled her damp blouse. She had long ago removed her pullover and tied the sleeves around her waist.

The rocky trail, slippery with loose gravel, was descending now past tiny blue flowers whose delicate cups turned to face the sun. Bees buzzed happily, their hind legs thick with golden pollen, adding a hum to the stark silence. She eased down, making sure her heels dug firmly into the ground. Some hawks circled at eye level, and the sun beat upon her back and head. She tried to imagine herself safely sitting at her desk at *Horizon*, getting ready to walk to lunch with her colleagues and worried about little more than paying her rent. That, of course, had been before she married Garret Brandt! And now, here she was inching her way down a precarious trail beside a cliff, wondering if her husband was burning up with fever and unable to contact her while his enemies searched to kill him. She *must* find him first, but where to look? And who could she trust beside God and her uncle? There were Rhoda and Fergus, of course, but what about Quinn? What about Niko?

She successfully conquered the hazards of the steep scramble down the craggy path of the cliff and was at last safely down in the rock bed and moving in the direction where she had seen Niko walking.

That this would lead her somewhere important she was almost certain, but would it be to Garret or to the camp of the enemy? What if he was rendezvousing with members of the *andartes*, the Greek guerrillas who were loyal, not to the king of Greece, but to Joseph Stalin? She realized with grim determination what a chance she was taking. Not even Uncle Wendel would know what direction she had gone as he'd expected her to go to the digs.

Whatever the outcome, she knew she was not alone. The great and mighty God, the One who Uncle Wendel had read to her about this morning from Isaiah, was near whether in life or in death. Death would usher her into His presence where she would no longer walk by faith, but see Him as He is.

Paulette continued on, not knowing how far she must go or what would await her. She had to find Garret. She needed to hold him again and tell him she loved him, that she wished she had never doubted him.

She rounded a gully, stepping her way between fallen rocks and tiny wildflowers of vivid yellows and blues.

Wildflowers. She stooped and with one palm resting against the boulder, looked intently at the flowers, thinking of Dr. Miklos.

What was it Niko had said to him yesterday? Something about a spot on Parnassus where unusual wildflowers flourished?

Yes, that was it, wildflowers. A rare spot on Parnassus. And these little beauties were unusual indeed. She had never seen anything like them before. Where the cliff side was damp in the shade, they grew there clinging to its surface.

She could be wrong about not trusting Niko. There could be a reason for the differences in his stories, as she had suggested to her uncle. Possibly, but her uncle had said too much was at risk. Niko was not to be trusted until Colonel Henley or Garret verified his identity.

And Dr. Miklos, she wondered again, her finger delicately touching one of the tiny blue flowers, *where is he now?* If Niko had promised to bring him to a rare spot, and Niko was in the immediate area, could the physician be here, too, perhaps farther ahead where there were even more wildflowers?

She stood and walked on, more cautiously now, for the gully was narrowing into an opening.

Paulette turned sideways and pushed herself between two boulders guarding both sides of the gully.

On the other side she stopped. She heard a sound like wind, or was it a waterfall? She could just make it out in the stillness. Ahead, the wall of the gorge was cracked and a small, slow stream came trickling through from somewhere above.

She looked up. There seemed to be a ledge, a path with greenery. She heard the pleasant tinkle of goat bells, and here by the water saw some goat tracks leading up to the path. There must be grass above, out of sight.

She followed the path for a short distance and when she looked up again she saw a shepherd's hut built without windows against the cliff. Huts were usually built by young Greek boys who cared for goats or sheep in remote places in the winter. They could also be used as a place to make and store cheese, or house sick or injured animals.

This hut was small, low to the ground, and constructed from various-sized rocks and stones with uneven cracks sealed with clay. The roof was made of dried scrub. From a distance, built into the cliff as it was, it appeared somewhat camouflaged as a part of the cliff, which was probably why she hadn't noticed it at once.

Surprisingly, it wasn't the hut that held her attention, but the rock face on the opposite side of the cliff. She could see a fissure gaping open wide enough for entry into a cave, perhaps used for protection of the goat herd in a storm. She almost ran to the area below the rock face where she could see gashes in the sandstone to widen the opening. Yes, the opening led into a cave. She stooped to the ground and picked up several burnt matches, perhaps used for a lantern. If only she had brought one, but naturally such a thing hadn't entered her mind. She'd had no idea that she would end up here. Was Niko inside? The shepherd? Or...

Her mouth felt dry. She loathed darkness, especially in tight, close places that gave her claustrophobia and a terrifying feeling of being trapped.

She looked up at the cliff top, then at the rocky walls. There was no movement above, nor any sound around her. Though her hand was shaking, she clamped her jaw with determination and reached into her slacks for the lighter she had picked up at the amphitheater. It wouldn't give much light, nor last very long, but how could she go back without knowing she had done her utmost? What if Garret were inside?

For a moment she paused. She closed her eyes and prayed for help and courage, then drawing in a slight breath, she slipped through the cleft of the rock and into the darkness.

24

As Paulette moved forward into the cool, close darkness of the cave, the only sounds she heard were from her own heart beating in her eardrums and her light footsteps. Niko could be anywhere, and until she knew she could trust him as a British ally she would be foolish to let him know she was here. But was he here? He could have been inside the shepherd's hut, or have gone through the broken section of rock to where the goats were led up to the grassy fields. In fact, she thought, pausing and listening intently, there might not be anything in this cave but strange creatures. She envisioned snakes, spiders, bats, and...? She fought back a rising tide of panic. *Calm down*, she lectured herself. She counted slowly to ten, all the while recalling the inspiring revelation of God's attributes that her uncle had read from Isaiah.

She moved forward again. If she were to see anything she must use the lighter. She flicked it, seeing flint sparks as a tiny yellow flame sprang up.

The precious flame probed the darkness, dispelling her blindness. "Among whom you shine as lights in a dark world." The paraphrased words of Paul from the book of

Philippians came to her mind. What was it Jesus had said? "I am the light of the world. He who follows Me shall not walk in darkness."

As her eyes adjusted, she was surprised that so small a flame could bring such clarity. She was in a passage which widened and sloped upwards toward the left. Yes, a flock of goats or sheep had been brought here because she could smell them, and there were droppings. She moved ahead, wondering how far it went. As it widened, she saw that some shepherd had brought in straw and scattered it, and there was even a watering trough. There was some sort of a barrier that could enclose perhaps eight or ten sheep. Probably a birthing place where the young were kept in bad weather.

To her glee she saw that the shepherd had several lanterns lined up, most containing oil. She immediately brought Quinn's lighter to one of the lamp wicks.

The recesses of the main cave appeared far larger than she wanted to explore even with a lantern. It looked to be a natural cavern with clefts and recesses that were shadowed in the light of her flame. There were stalactites strangely yet beautifully shaped. In other places fallen rock had accumulated for years, perhaps generations. Somewhere she could hear the faint drip of water. Yes, she could see how the Greek resistance movement against the Germans could hold out in the mountains for however long the war lasted. Fergus had said that the mountains were literally honeycombed with many such caves known only to shepherds and the peasants in the villages. The Nazis would have a hard time in Greece if they invaded. She was convinced now that Garret must be staying in some cave and was getting water and food from some friendly Greek shepherd. Her heart leaped. Why not *this* cave, *this* shepherd? Hadn't Niko come this way? It wasn't certain, but...

Perhaps she had first better find the shepherd and have a little talk with him. She turned to leave, but rebuked her nerves. She couldn't go until she had searched deeper ahead. For Garret's sake, she must have courage.

Once more Paulette cautiously moved forward, pretending she wasn't afraid and that her hands were not clammy.

She went cautiously along the tunnel, hesitated by a protruding slab, then followed a curving passage, until, as she rounded the first bend, she came to another opening, just wide enough for a man to pass.

Paulette slid through, lantern first. The lantern light was steady now. There was rubble here, too, as though there had once been a rock slide. Quite clearly in the dust at her feet were shoe prints. She raised the lantern but was unable to hold it steady. Her heart fluttered. A body lay crumpled behind the rubble, his shoes poking out. Was he dead? A little moan of horror escaped her lips. She wanted to turn and duck through the opening, running and screaming all the way back to Uncle Wendel, but she shut her eyes tightly and stood, clutching the lantern. *Garret doesn't wear shoes like that,* she kept repeating to herself, trying to bring sanity to her terror-stricken emotions. *It isn't him, it isn't, it couldn't be him...*

The silence thickened around her. She forced herself forward, forward around the debris until she could bring the lantern to see who it was. Somehow she wasn't surprised: It was Dr. Miklos, if indeed, he actually were the real doctor, and he was dead.

She backed away.

She bolted through the opening back into the tunnel where darkness loomed as impregnable walls to trap her inside the cave. Then she heard him. At first she thought she had imagined the distant voice calling her name. It halted her progress and sent her backing against the rock, which was cold to her touch.

"Paulette? Paulette? Where are you?"

She swallowed, her throat dry. The crazy pounding of her heart in her temples threatened to crowd out his voice. "Paulette...I know you are here."

Quinn. She closed her eyes, heartsick, then opened them quickly. The lantern light. Swiftly she extinguished it, then placed it on the cave floor while the darkness swallowed her. She inched along the cold wall, her sweating palms searching. She must get away from the trail of smoke. Quinn would smell it and find her.

"*Kyria*, do not listen to him! It is I, Niko! I am your friend. Follow my voice. I will protect you."

"He lies, Paulette. Trust me. Come this way before he gets to you!"

"Paulette," Niko called, "No!"

Her hands went tightly over her ears. Trust, the all-important word that echoed in the blindness of a deep darkness in which she could not see, could not know. She had not trusted Garret, and while there may have been reasons for doubts, there had never been any doubt of his love and faithfulness to her. It should have been enough to build a bridge to reach out to him until he could alleviate the reasons for her suspicions. Was it not somewhat the same in her relationship with God? There was enough blessing, faithfulness, and mercy to uphold her faith during seasons of trial when she walked through darkness, not knowing the way to escape her doubts and fears. God called to her to trust Him as He led her out of darkness.

As for Quinn and Niko, which man could she trust?

"Lord, I don't know whom to believe. Guide me."

"Paulette, you know me, we are friends. Would I turn against you now?" Quinn called.

"*Kyria*, he is an agent for Berlin. He killed Miklos. He killed Stephano. He wishes to use you as bait to trap your husband."

What? Stephano was dead? Was it true? But he was the important informant Garret and Henley were trying to protect and bring safely to Cairo. But if Niko was right about Miklos, why not Stephano? And what about Quinn being an enemy agent?

She saw a light moving in her direction, but whether it was from Quinn's flashlight or Niko's, she had no way of knowing.

Even as the thought came, she heard a sound from another direction. Then unexpectedly someone hurled themselves against the person carrying the flashlight. She heard the impact of bodies, and the light fell with a clink to the cave floor and rolled to a stop against a stone near her. There it sat gleaming like one bright golden unblinking eye. In the darkness she heard the two bodies struggling and the sound of heavy breathing, and then they were on their feet again. Someone was rammed against the cave wall and she winced, hearing the crack of bone. An overwhelming desire to flee compelled her to make a dive for the flashlight. Grasping it, she darted past them and ran for the cave entrance, leaving behind the sound of a vicious struggle between Niko and Quinn. Without any light, whoever won would be hindered from coming immediately after her. Perhaps she would have time to seek help.

The darkness began to lighten, and she knew she was nearing the cave entrance. She finally saw the bright shape of the fissure and slipped through it into the sunshine. The light stabbed painfully at her eyes. She covered them for a moment until her vision adjusted, then looked out toward the shepherd's hut. She ran to it, stopping breathlessly beside the entrance before stepping in and looking around.

It was empty. The shepherd must be with the goats. She turned to flee again when her eye caught sight of something on the floor near a bed of branches, twigs, and a goat skin blanket. She stopped, frozen.

Paulette moved toward the bed, stooped, and picked up a small strip of torn cloth. It looked to be part of a bandage...with dried blood on it.

Had Garret had been here? The possibility caused her spirit to soar, only to have it dampened by stark reality. If he were in the area he was in more danger than she. Either Quinn or Niko would survive the terrible struggle going on in the cave and come searching for her, perhaps also knowing that Garret was nearby and likely to appear if she screamed. And if Garret did come to her aid, he would be at a severe disadvantage in his wounded and weakened condition.

She jumped to her feet and whirled toward the door. The enemy must not find her. She had to prevent Garret from being drawn out into a struggle!

She bolted through the entrance and raced toward the hill where she had heard the goats. She made her way past the rocks where the trickle of water ran down into a man-made basin for the animals to drink. There were some stones gathered to make a sort of stairway through a gap and up a pathway that reached the hill. She struggled up the last steep section before making it to the top where she heard the musical goat bells ahead among some olive trees.

A dark form moved from the shade of trees. It was a Greek shepherd in leather breeches and a Greek cap, wearing a short inside-out lambswool vest and some sort of belt. Relief swept over her. He looked formidable enough to help her and Garret. Indeed, he may have already helped her husband. The man saw her and stopped.

"Please," she called, hoping beyond all hope that he could understand some English. Perhaps Garret had communicated with him—unless her husband could speak some Greek—nothing about Garret surprised her anymore. Paulette pointed back toward the gap in the rock. "Danger," she said and hurried toward him, unafraid. "Danger," she repeated, then stopped short.

She must be dreaming...it couldn't be. Was she recognizing her husband? But recognize him she did, with a short beard, somehow darkened, and an olive-toned complexion.

He came swiftly toward her and there was no mistaking the gray-blue of his eyes, even if he did carry a shepherd's staff in one hand. A cloak of sorts was thrown over his shoulder, conveniently hiding any sling or bandage.

As they approached each other Paulette remembered little else except that he dropped his staff and reached for her in silence. His actions spoke all the rest. His strong arm tightly held her against him and their precious embrace seemed that it couldn't end, as the world with all its troubles and dangers might just as well have vanished. As their lips met, nothing existed outside themselves and the warm breeze that seemed to sweep them away to the highest mountaintop with the world beneath their feet. There, they stood alone, united again at last, forever...

The sound of gravel rolling downhill from beneath someone's feet jarred her awake as the harsh reality of danger, murder, and betrayal once more tore them apart. Garret drew her away and motioned toward the trees. She scrambled upward to take refuge behind a gnarled trunk and low brush, expecting that he would follow, but when she looked back he was walking to meet the intruder. Her heart pulsated in her throat as she looked on, helpless to stop what was about to play out before her.

25

Garret had picked up his shepherd's staff and waited for the figure coming over the path. It was Niko. He looked bloodied and bruised, and he had a fierce expression on his face. He stopped, and the two men faced one another. Paulette held her breath. Niko rattled something off in Greek and threw up both hands in despair. He kicked at a stone and raised a tiny dust cloud.

Garret said something calmly, and when Niko dropped his head, her husband walked up to him and in a gesture that absolutely startled her, he threw an arm around his shoulders Greek style and then ruffled Niko's dark, curly hair. Garret continued to talk and Niko nodded, staring at the ground, listening.

Paulette suddenly relaxed. Thank God! Niko was not the enemy. Yet she remained where she was until Garret turned in her direction and gestured that it was safe to come down.

Niko was seated on a rock, head resting in both hands when she came up quietly. His knuckles were skinned and dried with blood and beginning to swell. *It must have been a dreadful fight*, she thought, miserably. Niko was no lightweight, and he was young and strong, yet from the grim look on Garret's face and from Niko's sullen mood, it seemed that they had lost...lost what? Quinn?

Her gaze swerved up to Garret's for an answer, for by now he would know from Niko all that had happened. Garret met her questioning look soberly. "Quinn got away—he's a Nazi sympathizer."

Paulette could hardly believe it. Even Colonel Henley had not suspected that, though his caution about letting Garret decide whether to include him had proven wise. Garret turned back to Niko and now spoke in English for her benefit.

"You're sure he's gone? He could be hiding, waiting."

"He fled when the shepherd boy came in, startling him. He would have killed me otherwise, but he wanted no more opponents in the darkness. You sent the boy inside with the goat just in time."

"I didn't send the boy," Garret said grimly. "I'd no idea either you or Paulette were in the cave. I've been up watching the eastern ridge." He pushed the cloak aside to show a small pair of military field glasses, probably given to him by Niko. It wasn't the field glasses that caught her attention, however, but the shoulder bandoleer laden with bullets and a very large pistol. No wonder, then, that he had stood his ground and appeared ready for anyone coming up the path.

"I saw both Quinn and Niko at the amphitheater this morning. Quinn returned to the temple ruins, or at least I thought he did, and then I followed Niko." She looked down at Niko. "He heard you coming up that rough path. We both did. I was hiding higher up behind a low shrub, and Quinn stepped behind a pomegranate tree. He dropped this." She brought out the cigarette lighter. "I thought that you were working for the enemy. I followed, thinking you knew where Garret was."

Niko nodded gravely. "I can explain everything, *kyria*."

"Niko works with the Athens police department," Garret told her. "I knew I could rely on him, as I had checked up on him months ago and informed Henley he was all right. Quinn," he said more gently, "neither Henley nor I were ever sure about. Henley trusted him more than I did. I went along with him because I wasn't sure about my feelings toward Quinn. I disliked him, mostly because I thought he was rather a wise guy. Also, he was too familiar with you."

She looked at him, surprised. Jealous? Garret? And over Quinn, of all people. It was almost amusing that her husband, who had most everything, could feel that way about another man.

"Darling," he said, "never mind all that just now. Are you all right?" He came to her, putting his arm around her shoulders and drawing her close. "By the way, just what do you mean by coming here like this? Do you realize what could have happened to you down in that cave if Niko hadn't been cautious about Quinn? And how did you get to Delphi! Why aren't you safely at home in our London cracker box, safe and warm, sipping hot chocolate?"

She was laughing and crying as she pretended to hammer on his chest. "You're a fine one to talk. You, who went to Switzerland and ended up in Greece with Nazis and Communists trying to kill you!"

He cocked a brow suspiciously. "How do you know all that? Who's been talking to you?"

"Henley, that's who. Your 'business' contact for Kimball, Baylor, and Lammiter. He is also Colonel Henley from Cairo Intelligence."

His eyes narrowed. "He told you?"

"He did. He sent me here to contact you."

For a moment his gray-blue eyes flashed with anger. "Henley? Henley sent my wife *here*, at this time? Why, that double crossing..."

"Now, Garret, darling, it was a matter of life and death—yours! Why wouldn't I come? He told me you were seriously injured and in hiding, with enemy agents searching for you."

"All true," he stated with calm sobriety. "But to send you when the Germans are on the verge of invading Greece."

"I don't care. I had to find you again. Oh, Garret, it is *you* that I've come so far to find! And now that I have, I must never let you go away again without things being right between us. Without your knowing how much I love you. What you mean to me. I didn't trust you, and I'm so ashamed. Can you ever forgive me?"

He was looking down at her with surprise in his eyes. When she had finished, his gaze turned tender and warm. He reached a finger to brush the tears from her cheeks.

"Paulette, did you risk coming all this way just to tell me you're *sorry*?"

"Why...yes. Yes, I did. And because you're injured..." she reached a hand to move the vest to gently touch where she thought the wound must be in his chest. Her fingers touched the bandoleer full of bullets and gun instead. "Oh, Garret!"

He laughed. "Poor darling Paulette, of course I forgive you. How were you to know? And yet I couldn't explain. I was under oath not to tell anyone about my work. Look," his hand closed over hers, holding it to his chest; "I'm getting better. I was shot and laid up for awhile, but the shepherd brought me here and cared for me during my first few weeks when it was rather touch and go. But when I dreamt of coming home to you, I had a very strong will to survive. After that the fever didn't stand a chance." He raised her chin and kissed her. "And now that you're here," he breathed against her temple, "I feel stronger already. We'll get out of this. We'll get back to London." He kissed her again. "I wish Henley hadn't let you come."

"But I am here, darling," she whispered. "And I won't leave Delphi without you."

"You won't need to worry about that. We're both leaving Delphi before the Germans arrive, if I can help it. But—well, there is something more to be done first." He scanned her, frowned, and breathed, "Blast Henley for this. The idea of sending my girl here. And at such a time!"

She searched her pockets for a handkerchief, found a crumpled one, and wiped her eyes.

"Come, honey," he said, suddenly gentle, "sit down."

As Niko went to bring the shepherd, she sat down on a rock and he dropped down beside her, his arm around her shoulders. "We'll get back to Cairo somehow," he said as if to himself, looking off toward Parnassus. "If we could get a boat, in good weather we could reach Crete in a matter of hours."

Paulette was now dazed with so many happenings and facts that she simply listened without taking it in.

I'm with him again, she thought. *He's safe. For the present we're all safe.*

There was so much to tell him, to ask about. She knew he had many questions as well. And Quinn, where was he? When would he show up again, or would he simply disappear until the time was ripe to accomplish what he'd been sent here for?

His arm gave her a confident squeeze against him, and he smiled and rubbed his beard. "Do you mind kissing a grizzly?"

"Not particularly. As long as you don't keep it. It's terribly scratchy, you know."

"Is it?" he leaned toward her.

Paulette laughed and leaned away. "How did you darken it? And what happened to your skin? You really do look like a very rugged Greek shepherd."

"The shepherd's bright idea. I was too sick to worry about it. I think he used shoe polish."

"Shoe polish!" She jumped to her feet and touched her face, then she looked at her fingers. "Why, I'm smeared with brown polish!"

He stood and pulled her to him. "You look marvelous to me, brown smudges and all." He kissed her again fervently. "Now, come back with me to the shepherd's camp, and we'll have some coffee and make plans."

≈≈≈

Niko and the young Greek shepherd boy, who was undoubtedly the real shepherd, were sitting by some rocks and bushes in a little flat area shielded by olive and cypress trees. Wildflowers sent off a sweet fragrance in the sunshine. Below them was a small stream where the goats were munching on brush and drinking water. The movements of their bells sent out peaceful notes that did wonders for Paulette's weary body and nerves. Her mind kept saying, *Garret is alive and getting stronger by the hour. We are together again. Oh, dear God, thank You.* She couldn't wait to tell Garret that she now know Dr. Wendel Bristow was her great-uncle. And there were so many things to discuss. She hardly knew where to begin.

But it looked as if this would not be the moment to have talks of that nature, for the Greek shepherd boy had made a fire and boiled coffee and Garrett was bringing out cups from a leather pouch.

There were also hunks of cheese in thick, moist slices, olives, hard-boiled eggs, a hard piece of sweet raisin cake, and some nuts. Paulette found it one of the most delicious lunches she'd ever had, especially after a grueling morning of mountain climbing, terror, and emotions ranging from despair to ecstasy. The coffee, though strong, was just the final treat to end it with.

She leaned back against the warm rock, growing drowsy from a full stomach after so much physical exhaustion. She was thinking that her feet were hot and tired, and she hoped her heel wasn't getting a blister. Now that she had sat down, she realized how achy she felt. In fact, there was hardly a place in her body that didn't hurt, including her head. A bee buzzed around the flowers growing close beside the rock she was using as a backrest. The sun glittered down. Her eyelids felt heavy and scratchy. She closed them to rest from the glare for just a moment or two...

～～～

The sun was dipping behind the mountain in the west where the expanse of sky was a rosy hue with shades of lavender. The evening winds were rising. She stirred and looked around. For a moment she thought she was alone and her fears rekindled. Then she saw Garret and Niko off together on their haunches, talking in low tones and making marks on the dusty ground. They were planning something. The shepherd boy was nowhere in sight. The goats were lying down, content with full stomachs and the approach of a stupendous Greek night when the galaxy would be milky white from a display of just a small fraction of the creative glory of God.

Paulette stretched and got up stiffly, brushing the dust from her slacks. She tried not to limp in front of Garret. He had enough to concern him without added worry about her. She must remember to heartily thank the shepherd boy for caring for her husband. Somehow she would try to do something for him. Money, yes, that could help. Maybe he could buy more goats, or if he merely looked after these for another owner, maybe he could start his own flock.

Garret saw that she was awake and walked over to her. He smiled warmly at her. "All right again?"

"Yes. You shouldn't have let me sleep."

"Why not? It's a long way back to Bristow's."

"Then we're going tonight?"

"We must."

She nodded her understanding. "You're up to it?"

"I'm doing well enough."

"How did Niko know you were here? Why didn't he tell me yesterday?"

"Niko didn't know until last night. Miklos tried to kill him at his house. Niko could taste something in the wine and, thankfully, didn't drink very much. He pretended to pass out and when Miklos left, Niko followed him straight to his meeting with Quinn. Later Niko followed them toward the hut, but the shepherd boy intercepted him near here and gave him my message. Niko went back for this—" he gestured lightly toward the bandoleer. "He has a friend working with the underground in Arachova. I never did see Quinn or Miklos last night. I left the hut a few days ago and hid up here disguised as a shepherd. Angelous got me some clothes from his relatives in the village. Then this morning Niko started back here and the boy met him and brought him straight to me. That's when you must have entered the cave. But the boy had seen Quinn in the area and warned us. So I sent Niko straight back to the cave."

"How do you think Quinn found out about the hut and cave?"

"From the man called Miklos. He isn't the physician Colonel Henley knew, but a Communist from Arachova. Angelous recognized him last night and warned me that Miklos knew about his hut. There are Communists scattered throughout the mountains. I might have been dead by now if "Miklos" had arrived while I was too ill to be moved from the hut. But he didn't come from Athens until yesterday.

"I had the shepherd boy keeping an eye on the digs, waiting for Niko to arrive. I could have contacted Bristow, of course, but since the shepherd was doing everything that could be done, I was hesitant to involve him in more danger. I wanted Niko here first—and a weapon."

"I thought Fergus might be helping you after I saw his radio receiver and the notes he was taking on the German buildup."

"He was. We arranged it back in London. Still, I wanted to keep him out of my troubles here in Delphi if I could, especially with Rhoda expecting a child, and matters not looking good for me."

"Who is Apollo?" she asked suddenly, remembering his telephone conversation at Gilly's house.

"Bristow," he admitted.

Paulette shook her head. It was all a little overwhelming. Uppermost in her mind, however, was her relief that Garret was alive and well. She wanted to do something for the shepherd who had cared for him.

She mentioned helping the boy financially.

He smiled. "You're a step ahead of me, but I was going to do just that. Walk with me down to the creek?"

She held out her hand and he clasped it, kissed it, and checked to see that her wedding ring was still snugly in place. He led her down a small slope to the clear blue water. The twilight was now fast seeping away. The trees stirred in the wind and the tall grass and flowers nodded their heads sleepily.

"Are you sure you can put up with me looking like this?" he asked.

She laughed and sank down to the grass. "You're really quite handsome with a short beard."

"How do you like my Greek cap?" He took it off and put it on straight.

"Very dashing, along with that bandoleer full of shiny bullets, too."

His eyes came to hers and flickered. "Do you think so?"

And I expect you're quite good at using the pistol as well, she thought, but she didn't say it.

"There are some things I need to tell you," he said quietly.

"Yes," she agreed soberly.

"When would you like to hear them? Now, or back in Cairo?"

She leaned back on her elbows and looked at him expectantly. "Now."

He smiled a little. "Sure you don't want to wait?"

She smiled, too. "Quite sure."

He plucked at several blades of grass and then looked off at the first evening star in the sapphire-blue sky. "I never intended to get involved in this kind of work. It all began a few years ago for me." His face was wiped clean of all expression except his light, thoughtful look, as though unexpectedly forced to decide something. Then: "All right,

Paulette. I expect you've guessed by now anyway. For a time I lived in Berlin, not New York, working with Paul Kruger, who was an uncle. He's dead now. Killed by the S.S."

She sat up. "Oh, Garret!"

"I was with him when it happened under the guise of a hit-and-run accident out in front of the American embassy. Except it wasn't accidental. Someone—an agent working with him, someone he trusted—betrayed him to German Intelligence. He was related to Ambassador Kruger in Cairo."

"Anna's father?"

"Then Henley also told you about her?"

"Yes." She was now ashamed to tell him what she had thought when she saw his picture with her in the Cairo paper, but it was time to be honest. "I need to tell you about the main reason I came to Cairo. Someone—I thought it was Rhoda, at least someone forged her name—sent me a clipping of you and Anna at King Farouk's dinner. I thought the worst," she said quietly, plucking at a blade of grass. "Especially after you'd told me you were in Switzerland."

He looked at her for a long disturbing moment. "You saw that miserable picture?" He looked angry. "If I'd known Henley was going to tell you about Anna and what I was up to here in Greece, I wouldn't have had to tell you I was going to Geneva."

"And you couldn't tell me?"

"No."

She said quietly, "All right. I accept that. I'm not making excuses for my behavior, but you can imagine what I thought when the clipping came in the mail."

"Of course," he said amenably. "Darling, I'm sorry you had to see it. It is just the sort of thing the enemy can take advantage of. And it turned out badly."

"Your arm was around her waist..."

"She is my cousin, and she'd just told me about her Greek husband, a man hunted by Greeks who are serving the Nazis."

"Stephano?"

"Good grief! Henley told you about him, too?"

"Did..." she hesitated. "Did Niko tell you he was dead?"

"Yes." He threw the crumpled blades of grass down with frustrated anger. "I blame myself."

"Darling, how can you? It wasn't your fault. You tried to protect both him and Anna."

"Anna is all right. We think we can get her out with us. If I hadn't gotten shot when I did, Stephano would be alive today."

She leaned over and laid her hand on his arm. "What more could you do? You were nearly killed yourself. And what of me? Do you think I could bear to lose you? Tell me about Paul Kruger."

"He was an agent. He'd been working with the British since the last war. More recently, he was cooperating with American Intelligence."

American Intelligence? Did that mean that her husband—?

"I was standing on the embassy steps when it happened. I was separated from Paul. It was only for a few moments, but that was all the time they needed to kill him. I may have been able to save him if I hadn't stopped and turned when a voice called out to me." He frowned.

"What are you thinking?"

"That I always felt I'd known that voice. Now I think I was right."

She felt an unhappy twinge. "Quinn?"

"Yes. Paul had gone on ahead of me and was crossing the street. I turned back toward him. I saw the car coming, bearing down at high speed just as he stepped off the curb to cross to the other side. It was raining and the headlights were blinding, shining on the water...I shouted. He turned. Then, he saw the car coming, but it was too late. An instant later, he'd been hit. The car disappeared around the corner." He lapsed into silence. Then, "If I'd just stayed with him while crossing that street—I could have pulled him back in time. And Stephano." His face hardened, thoughtfully. "I was deliberately delayed. I know that now—by Quinn."

She could tell by his voice that he was struggling to keep the pain from showing. "Did you go back to see who the voice belonged to?" She was trying to remember whether Quinn had ever mentioned going to Berlin on assignment.

"No. I went to Paul. I got to him first, in the street, before the Nazis could reach him. He was still alive, but dying. In his last moments he entrusted me with his assignment to help Henley."

"Henley!"

"Yes. That's how I met him."

"Did Paul Kruger and Colonel Henley know one another?"

"Only by name. Henley was trapped in Berlin, in hiding, trying to make it to the British embassy. The Nazis found out who he was and were after him. The S.S. were waiting for him to make a move from his hiding place."

"Why did they want him?"

"Henley knew the names of three other agents. Two of them, Americans. The Gestapo wanted those names. Paul Kruger was sent in to help him get out."

So that was the way it was. One agent trapped and in trouble; another agent sent in to get him out, similar to here in Greece with Stephano.

"Instead of Henley they managed to kill Paul. Before he died he asked me to take his place and get Henley out of Berlin."

"You were one of them?" she whispered.

"Not at that time. I was on a search of my own."

When she waited expectantly, he said, "I was working with the Cairo museum on the Egyptian collection of Queen Nefertari, tracking Gilly." He looked at her. "Did Henley tell you about Gilly?"

"Yes," she said sadly. "And about Blaine House that he left me."

"He left you that house?" He breathed furiously.

"As you once said, darling, he wanted to hurt you because he knew you'd discovered he was a thief. He knew he couldn't keep your Aunt Helga's collection because it belonged to you and Anna. He hated you for that. I was the one vulnerable person he could turn on. At first, leaving me the house seemed a blessing, but when Henley told me its dark history, it gave me the shudders. I want to sell it as soon as I can."

"Then you know about the Egyptian collection?"

She saw his watchful appraisal and guessed what he was thinking. "Yes. It was you all along who is the rightful heir. I confess to you that I was wrong, and I will never again have doubts about your motives for marrying me."

"A lot of the artifacts will be given to the museum where they belong. You don't mind?"

"No. I'd rather see them there. Honestly, Garret, I don't like Egyptian cobras and funeral pieces from mummies' coffins."

He laughed.

"So you did get Henley out of Berlin, obviously."

"As it turned out, I was successful. It was more good fortune than anything else. With the Brandt family right in Berlin in perfect standing with the Nazi regime, I had fair coverage for my role."

But none the less dangerous, she thought. *If he'd been caught*...she held him a little tighter.

"No one suspected me of being anything other than a very loyal Nazi."

"But they must have known you were Paul's nephew?"

"Certainly. But the Brandts and Krugers had parted over national loyalties one other time. My father was dedicated to Kaiser Wilhelm, but certain members of the Kruger family were known agents working with the British. Helga was one. Her son Paul was another, though he hadn't taken sides until she was killed for her service. They found her body stuffed in an Egyptian coffin in a houseboat on the Nile near ancient Thebes."

The thought horrified her. She shivered and he put an arm around her, drawing her close.

"And Henley?" she whispered. "How did you get him out of Berlin?"

"Someone, better left unidentified, was able to transport him into Switzerland. It was soon afterward that I returned to New York. Henley then contacted me."

The silence closed about them. "Then—there's no doubt. You are in what we call the Secret Service?"

"Not the Secret Service. That's something else entirely. But it's close enough." He smiled a little. "My job with good old Kimball, Baylor, and Lammiter looks perfectly genuine, but my trips abroad are, well, they have a double purpose. My recent business trips, and the ones I couldn't take you on, were part of my work with Henley."

Now his actions were making sense. Her eyes came swiftly to his. "On our honeymoon," she stated, "in Neuchâtel. Then, too?"

He didn't look pleased. "Yes. Mind you, I resented the intrusion. If a man can't be free even on his honeymoon... well, I was furious about it."

The man she had seen in front of the flower shop...the matchbook in his pocket...she sat up stiffly. "*That's* where I saw him. I *knew* I'd seen Niko somewhere before meeting him in the car at Arachova. Except his hair has grown longer and he acts and speaks Greek instead of French." She looked at him. "Niko was the waiter in the café that morning when you went to the flower shop. You stopped and talked to a man on the street. Niko was standing by our table."

He smiled wryly. "Yes. That was Niko, alias Francois. He was one of my contacts."

"But he really is Greek?"

"Yes, from Arachova."

She mentioned the doubts she'd had about Niko and how Dr. Bristow tried to contact Colonel Henley about it.

"Could Niko have put the matchbook in your jacket?"

"No, he would have no reason to do it. I'm thinking Quinn did."

"Why?"

"To intimidate me. To let me know someone knew who I was and knew about my relationship with Ambassador Kruger, my uncle. I admit it was unnerving to find out someone knew I was an agent."

Her brow wrinkled. "When would Quinn have had the opportunity?"

"Honey, he was right in London at the time. I wore that jacket the evening Quinn and I had dinner in London when he wanted me to arrange a flight with the Nickersons to Athens. He could have done it then."

She nodded. "Yes...and come to think of it, the way the 'K' was formed, I remember now—Quinn has that strange way of curling the letter." She then told him how she found the letter slipped under her door.

"Quinn must have contacted someone to have it delivered to the flat. We'll ask around when we get back. But I wouldn't let it disturb you any longer."

"But why? Why would he want to make me think you were seeing another woman?"

"Several reasons. First, it is simply a low but very effective tactic to put psychological pressure on an enemy. I also think he wanted to lure you to Egypt because he was romantically interested in you. He could even have actually captured you. He figured that once I knew he had you in his control—well, he could force me to tell him where Stephano was. Unfortunately for Stephano, they found him."

She looked at him amazed. "You think Quinn had plans to take me hostage?"

"If he had to. What did he tell you about why he came here?"

She explained, adding: "He wanted me to go with him and a Canadian photographer named Bill Dabney."

"I don't think he ever intended to cover that story. It was a ruse. There's no telling where Dabney is now. Quinn probably gave him some excuse as to why he had to stay in Delphi. Dabney probably went alone." He paused a moment and became lost in his thoughts. Then he picked up her left hand and touched her wedding ring again. "You know, Paulette, the greatest fear any of us have in this business is getting married. Knowing someone could find out where our wife is—" he stopped, becoming aware of her.

"Darling, you're trembling." He pulled her into his arms. "I shouldn't have gone into detail."

She was thinking about Quinn. How little she had really known or understood him.

"So that's why you were concerned in London about keeping the door locked. I remember seeing a man below our window, watching."

"Yes."

"And Quinn may have been the one I heard at Rhoda's soon after I arrived yesterday," she said.

He drew her to him, burying his face in her hair. "Don't be afraid. I won't let Quinn get near you."

She clung to him. "And to think I doubted you…"

His embrace tightened. "Well, you had reason to. But forget that now. It's over. And I've been thinking about this profession of mine as well. I can see it isn't harmonious with our marriage. I've decided to hand in my resignation to Henley." This was the last announcement she'd expected. She searched his face to see if he was serious. "You really mean that?"

He smiled tenderly. "I do," he said quietly.

She wrapped her arms around him. "Oh darling—I feel so guilty. I've been terrible, and you're being so sweet about it."

"Honey, I'm not doing this to make you feel guilty. It's something I've been contemplating since I realized I wanted to get serious with you—which was about three minutes after we met. I always told myself I'd need to change my work if I ever married. Our relationship is too important. I can't keep deceiving you about so many of my activities any longer." He cupped her chin. "And now that Henley has involved you, I'm not too anxious to let this go on."

"But what about the war?" she asked, troubled. "It's a terrible time to quit, isn't it? For both of us? When...when we both could do so much for America and England?"

"I'll go into something else. Something patriotic but safe and sane, and from nine to five. How would you like a stuffy professor who teaches Egyptology?"

She laughed, draping her arms around his neck. "Not patriotic enough. And I can't see you as a traditional nine to five type—especially a professor."

"It just goes to prove what a drastic effect a woman can have on a defenseless and unsuspecting man."

"Yes, you're very defenseless, darling. I noticed that the moment we met. As for Cambridge, I think that is one of several possibilities that would make me a very contented woman—someday. But you know very well you're not going to quit on Henley."

"No? I'll quit on the count of five if you've any idea about continuing to cooperate with him. I'll speak to him when we get back to Cairo," he said quietly, without any emotion.

She drew in a breath. "How can I ask you to give up what you obviously enjoy so much?"

"It's interesting you should say 'enjoy,' because I wouldn't have thought of my work as anything except duty and honor and love of country. Old-fashioned patriotism runs deep in certain quarters of America. You're right about it being hard to quit now with the war. The Germans make it very difficult."

She looked at him. Duty, honor, love of country. What telling words to choose when describing his work. She lapsed into sudden, meditative silence. Her gaze studied him anew with an entirely different thought coming to mind.

"Paulette, I'm very serious about this. I knew the adventure of marriage with you would mean a drastic change in my priorities."

This was one revelation about Garret she hadn't expected. The adventure of marriage. "I'll do what I need to," he said. "If we both give ourselves to each other, we'll make it just fine." He lifted her hand and kissed it, holding her gaze. "We've got to make it. Anything else is out of the question."

Her eyes spoke her agreement, her love. She caressed his face. "I love you."

He bent and kissed her gently. "Only thing is, Henley's not going to like my decision. He knows I'm considering it, and he's an eternal optimist. He's still hoping I'll change my mind. So you can see, changing careers isn't something I can arrange in just two or three weeks." His voice became detached. "It will take time for New York to train someone to take my place. Henley will have something to say about that. He's a stickler. Naturally he needs someone he can trust. But he understands. He's not married you see, and that's part of the reason why he isn't. Too much travel. And with the war on, travel is dangerous. Naturally, you won't speak of this to anyone."

"Of course I won't," she promised. "Not if you'd rather I didn't."

He watched her for such a long, meditative moment that she wondered if he had changed his mind.

"Niko is waiting. It's time we left."

"One thing more. Why would Quinn get rid of Miklos?"

"We'll need to ask Quinn that."

Paulette felt a little sick thinking about it.

Niko appeared above on the ridge. "Hey you two lovebirds. We go now, yes?"

"Yes," Garret said. "It's time."

The darkness would cover their return to Delphi. There were still so many questions stirring in her mind. Where was Anna? Did she know about Stephano's death? Besides their own departure from Greece, what else did Garret expect to accomplish? Somehow she believed there was something important that worried him. It would be a long hike back to the huts, shorter route or not.

26

The look of relief on Dr. Bristow's face did little to ease Paulette's conscience as he opened the hut door to her knock.

"Thank God you're all right! We were arranging a search party."

Rhoda walked toward her. "I had horrid thoughts of you falling and injuring yourself." She went no further when she saw Paulette's expression. Paulette came inside with Garret and Niko. Niko quickly locked the door and Dr. Bristow pulled the shades on the windows and switched on the wireless for background noise. Rhoda sank into a chair and looked from one face to the other as if trying to guess what was going on.

Garret left Paulette to speak with her uncle and Fergus, and Paulette turned to Rhoda. "I'm sorry I worried you. The day's events became, well, rather complicated."

Rhoda took in her soiled condition and Garret's change in appearance and raised her brows. "So I see. You're all right? Both of you?"

"We are now. Rhoda, have you seen Quinn at all in the last few hours?"

Rhoda picked up the tension circulating the room. "No. I haven't seen him since London. Didn't you tell me yesterday he'd gone for a story to Macedonia?"

"He's still in Delphi."

Paulette had tried to keep her voice relaxed the way Garret did, but she was not the cool and confident individual that her husband was. Her feelings were easily read by others, especially Rhoda.

"What's wrong?" Rhoda asked in a low voice, glancing toward Garret, who was talking in low tones to her husband. Dr. Bristow had quickly left the room and went to the back of the hut. Niko had slipped out the kitchen door. Paulette suspected he would be cautiously making a surprise call at Dr. Miklos' house. It didn't seem likely that Quinn would be there or anywhere near at hand until he had reinforcements to aid his bidding. She was sure that Niko had roughed him up quite a bit.

"What is it, Paulette? What about Quinn?" Rhoda repeated.

Paulette couldn't see how telling her about Quinn would jeopardize anything now. There would be no more meetings with him in friendly circumstances as though no one suspected he might be an enemy. Things were out in the open now, and he knew it.

She explained the bare facts of what had happened at the cave, and of Dr. Miklos' death. Rhoda, as expected, appeared stunned. "Quinn?" she spoke in a dry whisper.

"Yes, Quinn," Paulette repeated, as though she couldn't believe it herself, and sank into the opposite chair. Wearily she leaned her head back and looked down at her dusty shoes, thinking how swollen and sore her feet felt. Then, she became more amazed that she could think of anything as mundane as her feet when a man she'd known for years, and liked as a special friend, had turned out to be a Nazi who wanted to kill her husband.

Rhoda shook her head in shocked disbelief. She said after another moment, as though she couldn't bear to think about it either, "I'd better make some coffee and sandwiches. You and Garret must be hungry after such a long hike." She slid forward and pushed herself up from the chair. "Where's Niko?"

"He went outside, but he'll be hungry, too."

Paulette was watching Rhoda with a new worry. It was going to be difficult making a long trek with Rhoda so very pregnant. Paulette ran a hand across her damp forehead, pushing back her hair. It was impossible. Everything seemed that way. They were trapped. And if the Germans did arrive, the enemy would have everything they needed to come looking for Garret and the rest of them, with Quinn leading the way. She could imagine the treatment they would afford Niko as well. Quinn was not one who would likely forget the young Greek who had cracked his skull against the cave. And, of course, they would lose little time in interrogating her, and Rhoda, and Fergus, and Uncle Wendel—

No, she couldn't bear to think about Nazi storm troopers motorcycling throughout Delphi.

Uncle Wendel, bending over the radio, suddenly tensed. He held up a hand for quiet. Everyone stopped and turned expectantly. The announcer's voice froze the silence.

"Greece is now under German attack. Repeat. All Greece is now under enemy attack. German planes, tanks, and soldiers crossed the border from Bulgaria through Macedonia, and are pushing toward Salonika and Monastir toward Athens.

"Repeat. This is an alert. Greece is now under German attack…"

~~~

Fergus went to his hut, accompanied by Niko, to pack needful things for himself and Rhoda. Paulette had brought very little with her and already had her bag packed at Garret's order. So far, it disturbed her that neither her uncle nor Garret had mentioned they would be going with them. As soon as Niko and Fergus returned to Dr. Bristow's hut, Niko left for Itea to try and arrange a private boat to bring them to Crete. Paulette watched Garret and her uncle bend over a map spread on the table. They both believed the German thrust would spearhead on two fronts in a frenzied push for Athens. From Salonika in the north, to Larissa, Thermopylae, and Delphi to Athens. From Monastir, they would pass Delphi, and Patras to the Peloponnese. Paulette recalled from the newspaper reports in London of how the German *blitzkrieg* had stormed France and marched into a surrendered Paris. She tried not to think about thousands of German paratroopers landing all across Greece in another lightning strike.

Garret told her Greece would stand and not surrender easily. Even now, General Papagos was fighting along the Alikamon, east of Salonika.

He took her aside in the kitchen and stood with his arms around her. She tensed, suspecting something unpleasant was in the making. She looked up, searching his sober gaze. He smiled, and brought her head to his chest. "Worry won't do any good. It's a time to do what we must."

She could have told him it was impossible to not worry with the Luftwaffe on the horizon and paratroopers soon to drop from the sky. Feeling his shoulder holster digging into her did little to help matters either. Instead she said, "I'm worried about Rhoda."

"Niko will be back soon. A fishing boat might make it to Crete without trouble, and Fergus can take care of his wife. You look after yourself, will you?" He lifted her chin. "I love you very much, Paulette."

Tears filled her eyes and she held him tightly. "Garret..."

"Your uncle is going with you." He took her face between his hands. "There's something I must do before I can join you," he said very quietly and calmly.

She'd been terrified she would hear those very words. Her heart wrenched. "Anna?" she whispered.

"Yes. I've got to get her out before the Germans get here. If there's some mistake about Stephano being dead, only she can tell me the facts."

"But you don't know where she is," she pleaded.

"I do know where she is. She's in Athens."

"Athens? But—but that's in the opposite direction from Itea and the boat."

"There'll be other boats," he said, pushing a curl behind her ear. "We can cross from the Peloponnese to Crete. We'll join you there, or," he said just as easily, "in Cairo."

He made it sound so simple. He was doing it deliberately to soothe her fears, she knew that, but she also knew better. If he stayed behind he would risk his life. And yet— how could he leave his cousin Anna when Ambassador Kruger waited in Cairo, pacing the floor of the German embassy as she knew he must be doing, especially with the present news of invasion.

"There are still British troops here in Greece," he said. "Some sixty thousand of them. If I can't get a boat at Kalamata, then we'll join up with the army."

She shook her head miserably, clinging to him. "What if we can't hold the Germans back?"

"Knowing your gutsy prime minister, he'll arrange for another evacuation—Dunkirk style. I'll be on one of those boats with Anna."

"But I've just found you again," she choked. "Anything could happen."

"Yes." He held her tightly.

"I won't go without you," she gasped. "Not this time."

He gave her a gentle shake. "No. You need to go with Bristow, Rhoda, and Fergus."

"But..."

He silenced her with a tender kiss. The ground seemed to sway beneath her.

"I'll meet you in Cairo, darling."

"Where are you going now?" she said breathlessly. "Directly to Athens?"

"I'll stay here until later tonight. While Bristow's radio transmitter is working, I'll need to make contact with a number of friends across Greece while there's still time."

"Did Uncle Wendel ever hear from Colonel Henley?"

"Yes. Niko got a clean bill of health, as I knew he would."

"What if Quinn comes back when you're here alone?"

He smiled. "Then I'll be waiting for him."

"Garret!"

"Darling Paulette, don't look like that. I'm doing well. Better than I have for two weeks. Angelous the shepherd ought to hang his shingle out as a doctor. I don't know what he used to clean the bullet wound once he got it out— I was unconscious, but it worked. It's healing fine now. I made that trek without too much difficulty, even if we did need to stop and rest a dozen times. So put it out of your mind." He kissed her again lightly. "Do you have your bag packed?"

She didn't believe he was doing as well as he liked to appear. He was trying to make her feel good. She threw her arms around him again and didn't answer him as she cried. He held her, kissing her hair, murmuring words she would long remember.

When Niko returned from the short drive to the fishing village of Itea, he came with encouraging news. He'd found the owner of a fishing vessel willing to risk taking them to Crete.

Everyone was sober and silent as they left the hut. Fergus stored the meager bags into the trunk, and made extra room for the best of Dr. Bristow's books and stacks of research papers and portfolios. Fergus tried to lighten the mood by making a joke about his things being so heavy they would sink the boat, but no one smiled.

The goodbyes were brief and deliberately simple. Rhoda urged Paulette into the car to make her parting with Garret less traumatic. Fergus and Dr. Bristow gave last words to Garret.

Paulette turned in the seat and looked back over her shoulder at her husband. She sealed his image in her mind as though taking a last photograph. She was still looking out the rearview window when they were all seated, and Niko pulled away toward the road.

The wind tugged at Garret's jacket. Paulette lifted her hand in goodbye, though she didn't think he could see her now. Rhoda put an arm around her shoulders and Paulette fought back her tears.

∾∾∾

Itea was a little fishing village on the coast, the landing place for ancient Greeks who arrived from the Corinthian Gulf to pay homage to their idols.

The sea rippled with a pale sprinkling of diamond dust under the moon that was setting behind the mountains. Slinking silently across the bay came the fishing vessel with her prow curving and her sail unfurled.

"Niko, you're not coming with us?" Dr. Bristow asked him.

Niko smiled sadly. "No, *kyrie*. There is a battle to be fought, and I could not face myself, me a stalwart Greek, if I did not stay to help fight it. The *andartes* will head for the mountains where we will fight every last German until the day when we've driven them from our sacred soil."

Fergus stood with Rhoda, his arm around her. He turned her in the direction of the Shining Ones. "Just to the left of that cluster of trees is the old Pilgrims' Way. You can't see the temple columns even in daylight, since the curve of Crissa Bluff hides them, but that mountain there is Castalia. And just beyond, the cliffs where the temple sits. I'm sorry you were never able to walk up there. Someday we'll come back. The war can't last forever."

"The Oracle of Delphi," Rhoda said thoughtfully. "Even though Dr. Bristow has explained everything to me, I just can't help seeing a book in my mind when I think of an oracle."

Paulette turned quickly and stood looking at them. The Oracle of Delphi, the message Colonel Henley had entrusted to her to pass on to Garret! She'd forgotten to tell him. The drama of the day's events had pushed everything else out of her mind. The rugged Greek captain of the boat had come down to meet them, accompanied by two silent men who carried their bags and boxes of books and papers aboard. "Let us be going, *kyrie*," he told Dr. Bristow. "From Athens to Crete on a good day is twelve to fifteen hours. From Itea add two or three more. The Germans and Italians have ships prowling about."

Paulette stood unmoving as they began walking quickly to board the vessel. She turned to Niko. "I'm not going. Hurry, we must get back to the hut."

"You want your husband to do this to me, yes?" he slid a finger across his throat.

Fergus and Rhoda were aboard but Dr. Bristow was waiting ahead for her. She ran down the plank to him, holding his arms. "Uncle, please understand. I'm not going. I can't go. Don't wait for me. I'll see you in Cairo." She stood on her toes and kissed his roughened cheek. The determination in her eyes left him with no reply.

She heard the car engine start to crank over. Niko was trying to leave without her. She ran.

He was in such a hurry that he had flooded the engine. As it sputtered and died, Paulette grabbed the car door, flung it open, and jumped in, banging it shut. She glared at Niko, folding her arms. There was such vehemence in her gaze that he grinned suddenly.

"You win, *kyria*. But *you* must face your husband alone." He tapped a finger against his chest. "Me? I stay out of it."

He got the engine going again, and they drove back toward the village of Delphi and the huts.

Dr. Bristow scowled worriedly, but the car's lights were disappearing down the narrow little street. He quoted the first two verses of Psalm 20 quietly, "May the LORD answer you in the day of trouble; may the name of the God of Jacob defend you; may He send you help from the sanctuary and strengthen you."

∾∾∾

The car braked near the hut in a cloud of dust. "I must go to Arachova," Niko said. He read the time on his watch.

"Garret plans to leave at midnight. Tell him I will return before then."

"You're not coming in?"

He grinned. "I have already had enough trouble for one day. You must face your husband alone, *kyria*. I wish you good fortune."

Paulette glanced at him with a sudden smile and got out of the car. "Take care, Niko."

"Yes, always." He backed up and drove toward his home village a few short miles away. She assumed he wanted to either say goodbye to a girlfriend or he was worried about the future of his sister and her family. At the moment Paulette was content not to have a family to worry about. Imagine being trapped here with seven small children just as the German army was about to roll in with tanks and machine guns. They had raped and plundered villages in Bulgaria, and there was little to suggest they wouldn't be doing the same in the villages of Greece.

The yard was dark and sinister as she ran toward the hut. The wind rustled through the treetops, making eerie sounds that might have been considered harmonious on a night when all was at peace. She passed the hut where Fergus and Rhoda had lived. It stood dark and empty, soon to be taken over by German soldiers. She rushed on toward Dr. Bristow's hut. The door was open. Had Garret left it unlocked on purpose?

She entered, bolting it behind her as her skin crawled. "Garret?" she called. She threw aside her jacket and rushed toward the back bedrooms.

She stopped in the doorway of her uncle's room. Garret was bent over the radio set, and she heard various hums and whistles and static. He looked up. There was first a look of surprise, then love, then anger. He stood.

She walked toward him, her eyes pleading. "Darling, I can explain."

He pushed back the chair. "Where's Niko?"

"It's not his fault. I insisted."

"I'm sure you did, but I gave him orders."

"He's gone to Arachova. He'll be back before midnight." She moved toward him. "I had to come back. Colonel Henley would never have forgiven me if I'd left without giving you the message."

He came alert. "What message?"

"The message he sent me here to give you. It was the main reason he wanted me to come."

"Why didn't he send it by radio to Bristow?"

She shook her head. "I don't know."

He frowned thoughtfully. "This could be important, all right, if Henley feared it was too dangerous to burden your uncle with. That must mean it has something to do with Stephano."

"But Stephano is dead."

"Yes...and crucial information died with him. They didn't get him to talk, otherwise Quinn wouldn't have risked coming after me. He must still think I have what he wants."

"Names of top Communists in the *andartes*?"

His gaze sharpened. "Yes. Names the enemy wants to keep out of the hands of the CID."

"Stephano knew them?"

"He did. He stumbled onto them, actually. By the time he discovered he was in the midst of a bunch of Commies, he couldn't get out alive. He worried more about Anna. He knew they'd kill her if he tried to break away from the group. They needed him to work on the youth in the universities and help turn them all into a pack of devotees to Stalin. Common brotherhood and all that propaganda."

"When I was in Niko's car that night with Quinn and Dabney, it was Dabney who unmasked the Communist takeover in the *andartes*. Niko laughed him off. Now I know why. He suspected Quinn even then, didn't he?"

"We both did."

"And Niko didn't want Dabney to say too much and alert Quinn to the fact that many suspected that Greek generals were working for a Communist takeover of Greece after they defeated the Nazis."

"What name did Dabney mention? Do you remember?"

"Ares. That's not his real name though, is it? Ares is part of Greek mythology."

"Right. But Stephano knew his real name. And a number of others as well. Names of important individuals never suspected to be Communists. They're in the government, the church, the army, the academia. Those names are crucial. Especially now with the Germans invading Greece. America and Britain are supporting the *andartes* leaders with weapons and gold to fight the Nazis. We don't want that power given into the hands of the Greek underground and used to establish Communism." He pulled her to him. "What was Henley's message?"

"The Oracle of Delphi."

He looked at her for a long moment without moving. Then he turned and pondered, so deep in thought that she wondered if he'd forgotten she was there.

"He said you'd know what it meant. Do you?" she whispered.

"Exactly what did Henley say?"

"Just that, darling. The Oracle of Delphi."

"Nothing more?"

"No. Nothing."

He released her. "I wonder if it's possible..." he said to himself.

"It must have something to do with Stephano," she said.

He smiled a little. "Yes. I think so." He walked over to the radio. "It isn't working. No wonder Bristow couldn't get through tonight to Henley. It's a wonder he got through last night. The Oracle of Delphi," he said again.

"Henley expected you to know," she repeated.

"I think I do," he said evenly. "That poem by Milton."

She looked at him quickly. "Do you know it?"

"Stephano quoted it often."

Their eyes met and she saw his smile. *He does know*, she thought excitedly. She quoted slowly: "The Oracles are dumm, no voice or hideous humm, runs through the arched roof in words deceiving, Apollo from his shrine, can no more divine..."

The silence settled with heavy expectation as they looked at each other. "Apollo from his shrine can no more divine," Garret said. "But Stephano can. I can add to that something from Holy Scripture. 'He being dead yet speaketh.' That's from the true Oracle of God in the book of Hebrews. I think Stephano is giving us a message, darling. At the place of Apollo's oracle. We may just find the list of names I want to deliver to CID."

She took a breath. "Yes, how fitting. Of course! It's not Apollo's oracle now, but Stephano's. It was his way of leaving you a message."

"Yes, just in case something happened to him before I got here. He must have realized soon after leaving his hiding place that he was being followed. Probably by Quinn or one of those working with him. He must have climbed to the ruins and once there, seeing the shrine and remembering the poem he so often quoted, took advantage of the situation."

"But how did Henley know?"

For the first time he looked worried. "Anna must have risked sending a message to her father. But that would mean she knew Stephano had been caught. If she panicked—and came out of hiding, trying to get back to Cairo, anything could have happened to her by now. German agents would be watching every conceivable exit out of Greece."

"You think she's no longer in Athens?"

He frowned. "I don't know. They'd take her alive and force her to talk. I don't see how she could have held out against them. She wasn't strong, and she was deathly afraid of the Nazis."

Paulette was careful to not show her own alarm. She looked at him blankly. He didn't seem to notice, for he was deep in thought.

"But," he said, "Quinn was still looking for me this afternoon. That means they don't have the answer. But to get back to Henley, no, I don't think he has a clue about what Stephano meant by the oracle. But Stephano had a pretty good idea that I would. Anyway, it's worth a try. We've little to lose but time." He looked at his watch. "We can be up to the temple ruins and back before Niko comes with the car. Let's go." He paused, looked at her tenderly. "Are you up to it, darling?"

"I'm fine," she said, hiding her exhaustion. "What about you?"

He laughed, picked up his coat from the bed, and put it on. He steered her toward the door. "I never thought I'd be thankful to God for the Oracle of Delphi," he said wryly. "But Stephano may have just left us a very important message under the grim stone or thereabouts." He stopped by the small desk and retrieved a flashlight and a book of matches, stuffing them in his pockets. "We'll stay close to the trees, and out of sight, just in case Quinn hasn't had enough jaw smacking for one day," he told her.

They went out into the night that was black and windy and full of strange noises.

27

Paulette walked closely beside Garret up the steep path through the pines. Her eyes had adjusted to the dark and it was possible to see by starlight. Soon, they were at the gate to the temple area. Garret went ahead up the steps, taking her hand to guide her. At the top there was a wide smooth way through the buildings to the shrine itself.

In the starlight the huge columns stood stark against the night sky.

"This way," he said quietly against the whine of the wind.

Breathless, more from excitement and fright than the climb, she hurried behind him. He took her elbow and guided her across the Sacred Way. She could make out the little Doric building that once held the treasure Uncle Wendel had told her about this morning. This morning! Could it possibly have been just this morning? She had lived through so much that it seemed a month. Her heart beat with odd little jerks, and she had the desire to keep looking over her shoulder.

"There it is," Garret said. "The grim stone, as Stephano liked to call it."

The star-crowded sky was immense and deep. The silence crept up around them and seemed to watch their every move. The wind blew a dry twig across the broken stone floor and it caused her skin to crawl.

Garret turned on the flashlight and searched around Sybil's stone. Paulette's gaze flickered around her. She turned toward the columns and imagined the valley far below filled with olive trees, their tops moving in the wind. Merely thinking of the great drop made her dizzy. Soon there would be no more peaceful nights in Greece. There would be bombs, Luftwaffe attacks, tanks rumbling down the ancient streets, and combat with the Greek resistance. What would happen to Niko, and her other Greek friends? How many would survive the horrific onslaught? She walked to the edge of the floor and leaned against a column, looking off toward Delphi. She prayed for Niko and his sister, Electra, and her husband and children. She prayed for Greece and for the war's end. But down deep in her heart there was the grim certainty that the worst was yet to come before the dawn would break.

She heard Garret's slight exclamation. "I've found something," his quiet voice came to her on a gust.

She turned quickly, excitement giving hope. "Is it what you wanted, darling?"

"Yes. This is it. Bless you, my love, for risking so much to come so far. This list of names will help CID immensely during the upcoming struggle against the Germans."

Paulette gasped suddenly and a small cry caught in her throat. An arm like iron caught her around the waist, and she felt something hard and cold pressed below her ear.

"Sorry, beautiful," Quinn breathed sharply, excruciatingly tightening his hold. "All's fair in love and war, they say. All right, Brandt, you see what I'm holding in my arms?"

Paulette closed her eyes.

"I see," Garret said.

"You can put that paper packet back under the broken block of stone, just the way it was. Hurry up."

Paulette bit her lip. The wind whistled and moaned around the high columns. He held her so tightly she could hardly breathe.

"Anna is dead," Quinn said. "Just like Stephano. She wouldn't talk, either. Brave girl, after all. No, I wasn't the one who killed her. It was a Nazi agent. You can remove your jacket, nice and slowly. That's it...now that peasant vest. Good. Now the holster. Remember, one slip and she goes over the cliff." He moved her closer toward the edge.

Her heart raced. She hated heights and closed her eyes as she found her feet on the very edge of the rim, the wind whipping at her hair. She felt beads of perspiration breaking out on her forehead, and knew she was becoming lightheaded.

"All right," Garret said quietly. "Let her go now, Quinn."

"Not yet. Back away from the gun. That's it. Far enough to keep you from pulling any heroic stunts. Hands behind your head and turn your back toward me."

"Not until you release Paulette."

"For old time's sake, beautiful." He removed his arm and stepped away from her. Just as he did so she felt a wave of dizziness and sank to the ground. She screamed in fear of falling over the edge. Quinn jerked back toward her, giving Garret a chance to cross the space between them. Paulette's sweating palms reached for something to hold onto. *Lord Jesus!* She found the rough edge to the base of a pillar and clung to it, terrified and frozen. With all her heart she hoped she wouldn't faint and fall into the darkness below.

After a few moments she found the strength to pull herself away from the sheer drop. It was then that she heard both men engaged in a violent struggle. She managed to glance up, and in the starlight the two figures looked huge, their swaying bodies making frightening forms in the dimness. The first thing to impact her mind was that Garret couldn't survive such an encounter in his condition, but then she remembered that Quinn had been weakened in a brutal fight not too many hours previous. Garret had Quinn's wrist in one hand and seemed to be twisting his arm so that the weapon would drop from his grasp. Quinn struggled to resist but finally managed to flip the gun away with his fingers, and it bounced only a few yards away on the stone floor.

Paulette crawled as quickly as she could toward where she heard the gun land. Behind her the vicious fight went on. She heard a horrific thud, a strange gurgling sound, and then feet scraping against stone as though tripping. Paulette got her shaking hands on the gun, lifted it, and struggled to her feet. She turned and raised it just as someone went over the edge of the floor into the dark crags below. The sound of a dying yell faded and disappeared.

She froze with the gun raised. The other man was leaning against a column to hold himself up, and there was blood on his mouth and blood seeping through the front of his torn shirt where a bandage showed.

Paulette cried out in relief and horror. She dropped the gun and staggered toward Garret. They grasped each other at the same time and just held onto one another tightly.

Epilogue

The house, overlooking the Nile, had belonged to Garret's great-aunt, Helga Kruger. It was double-storied with some of the most beautifully carved hardwood furniture Paulette had ever seen. The garden was lush with palms, Bird of Paradise flowers, orchids, and flowering vines. It belonged to Garret now, along with most of Helga's assets, willed to him through Helga's son, Paul, who had never married. An Egyptian servant quietly brought in cool glasses of limeade for Dr. Bristow, Fergus, and Rhoda. Colonel Henley was out on the terrace, talking with Garret.

They had been in Cairo for two weeks now. The memory of that horrid night at the ruins of Apollo's temple had mercifully faded into the mist. Niko had found them as they limped down the trail to the huts, and obtained passage for them on another fishing boat cooperating with the Greek underground. With her loved ones safe and the list of Communist infiltrators turned over to Colonel Henley, Paulette felt at peace with herself and thankful to God. There was, unfortunately, the sad news about Anna that Garret had brought to Ambassador Kruger. Garret told her afterward that his uncle had taken the death of his daughter so hard that he intended to give up his position and renounce allegiance to Berlin.

Although the war had spread throughout Greece, and the British navy was risking their top ships to rescue stranded British soldiers on the beaches of the Peloponnese, there was a reprieve in her and Garret's life—for a time at least. They would stay in Cairo until Rhoda had her baby and Garret made a full recovery, and then they would decide whether to return to London or work for Colonel Henley in Egypt. Paulette even found time to write her article for *Horizon*.

The desert war had grown worse in their absence, with Field Marshal Erwin Rommel pushing his Panzer division against the British forces in the western desert and it was feared that he would capture the Suez Canal. Paulette was thankful for her new mansion and her deeper, more open relationship with her husband. She had already told Garret that she would abide by his decision—which he was in no hurry to make. He wanted time, he said, to simply be alone with her.

Paulette had told him she wouldn't mind staying in Egypt indefinitely, as Uncle Wendel was taking a position in the Cairo museum. Later, when it was safe, he intended to join Fergus at an archaeological effort near Aleppo. Rhoda was content just to be nearing the time when she could have their child in relative calm.

"I don't care if I budge for six months," she said lazily, her feet up on an ottoman and a cool glass of limeade in her hand. "This is heavenly, Paulette darling."

"You can stay as long as you want," she said cheerfully. "I'm going to love playing Auntie to either Charles, Sarah, or Delphi."

Rhoda made a face. "Don't ever mention Delphi to me again. Maybe we should call him Cairo." She looked at Fergus.

"What!" he gasped.

"Or, Cairene if it's a girl," Rhoda said.

"It's Sarah or Charles," Fergus said firmly. "What do you think, Uncle Wendel?"

Both Fergus and Rhoda had begun calling Dr. Bristow "uncle" just as Paulette did, and he enjoyed it. As they sat discussing names, Garret came up to Paulette, took her by the hand, and walked her toward the terrace. Colonel Henley, smiling sagely, toasted her with his glass and left them alone.

Garret's arm went around her as he pointed off to the Egyptian *faluccas*, the long narrow boats guided along by oarsmen in short white pants and turbans.

"How would you like a romantic ride on the Nile tonight under the Egyptian moon?" he asked, kissing her temple.

"Are there crocodiles?" she asked innocently.

"There might be." His vivid gray-blue eyes were warm with emotion. He leaned over and kissed her lips tenderly. "If there are, we'll be too preoccupied with one another to be concerned about them."

She smiled and turned toward him. She slipped into his arms smoothly, and their lips met. It had been a long, hard journey, but she knew that she was exactly where she belonged. She had come home at last.

Harvest House Publishers
For the Best in Inspirational Fiction

Other Books by
Linda Chaikin

A DAY TO REMEMBER
Monday's Child
Tuesday's Child
Wednesday's Child

Lori Wick

A PLACE CALLED HOME
A Place Called Home
A Song for Silas
The Long Road Home
A Gathering of Memories

THE CALIFORNIANS
Whatever Tomorrow Brings
As Time Goes By
Sean Donovan
Donovan's Daughter

KENSINGTON CHRONICLES
The Hawk and the Jewel
Wings of the Morning
Who Brings Forth the Wind
The Knight and the Dove

ROCKY MOUNTAIN MEMORIES
Where the Wild Rose Blooms
Whispers of Moonlight
To Know Her by Name
Promise Me Tomorrow

THE YELLOW ROSE TRILOGY
Every Little Thing About You
A Texas Sky
City Girl

CONTEMPORARY FICTION
Sophie's Heart
Beyond the Picket Fence
Pretense
The Princess

GIFT BOOKS
Reflections of a Thankful Heart

Melody Carlson
A Place to Come Home To
Everything I Long For
Looking for You All My Life
Someone to Belong To

Debra White Smith
Second Chances
The Awakening
A Shelter in the Storm